RAVENWOOD

ISBN-13: 978-1466438378
ISBN-10: 1466438371
BISAC: Fiction / Fantasy / Historical

For more information, or to leave a comment about this book, please visit us at:
http://www.lammaswood.com

PRINTED IN THE UNITED STATES
Third printing: October, 2014

To Laurie

You always knew there was magic in the commonplace.

Thank you for helping me see it.

Table of Contents

RAVENWOOD

NATHAN LOWELL

Durandus

CHAPTER 1
A WIDE SPOT IN THE ROAD

Somewhere up in the canopy, a jaybird greeted the dawn loudly and with the vigor usually reserved for mating and feeding. Tanyth sighed and turned over in her bedroll. The cushion of last year's pine needles provided a comfortable enough mattress and she didn't really want to crawl out, but brain betrayed body by insisting that time dripped through her fingers while nothing useful happened. She groaned and sat up, hips protesting and shoulders already flexing to try to stretch out the overnight stiffness. Cold morning air tickled down the neck of her shift and chilled the fabric while a second jaybird joined the first from somewhere down the draw. Together they filled the hollow with challenge and response. She rummaged down in the bedroll and pulled out her knit top, warmed and cozy from her overnight body heat. With a shrug and a wriggle the comfortable wool slid down over her head and around her torso. The cool air and movement reminded her that mornings required certain activities. She crawled out of the bedroll, gave the coals of her small fire a stir, and padded across the clearing to squat behind a bush.

"I'm gettin' too old for this," she muttered as her left knee creaked painfully.

Returning to the bedroll she lowered herself onto it, successfully battling the urge to crawl back into it as the dawn light stole silently between the trees and birds and bugs began a soft counterpoint to the song battle being waged high above her head. She added a few sticks to the fire and leaned down to puff life into the coals. In her head she said a prayer to the

1

All-Mother and watched as the grayed ashes took on golden life. The sticks caught, sending a thin tendril of smoke into the chilly late summer morning. She added a few more sticks and pulled the lid off her kettle in order to add enough water for a cup of tea. She gave her oatmeal a nudge and a stir and slid that closer to the small warmth as well. She'd set it to cooking in the dying coals of her fire the previous night and was looking forward to a warm breakfast of the rich grains flavored with some fresh apple.

While her breakfast warmed, she levered herself up from the ground once more and rummaged around in the bedroll, drawing out her pants and last clean small-clothes. She hurriedly slipped them on and buckled the solid belt around her, making sure her belt knife was clipped securely. The buckle locked in the last notch and she frowned a bit, trying to remember if it had been four weeks or five since she'd left Mabel Elderberry's tidy cottage. Time tended to blur for her on the road–each day much like the last, a seemingly endless cycle of rise, eat, pack, walk until the light began to fade, find a safe camp, bed down, and do it again the next day. An occasional, nerve-wracking encounter on the road and the periodic passage through hamlets and towns along the way punctuated the cycle only rarely. One last fishing expedition in the bottom of the bedroll produced a pair of well-worn boots and a clean pair of socks. Chilly toes welcomed the warmth and protection afforded by both.

She could hear the water boiling in the kettle and tossed a handful of aromatic leaves into the water before pulling the kettle back from the fire with a handy stick. While it steeped, she straightened out her bedroll and quickly rolled it up into a tight traveling package. She lashed it to the bottom of her pack and settled down to her traveler's breakfast, savoring the soothing spice tea as it warmed her belly while the comfortable bulk of the softened grain and apple filled it. In a matter of a few minutes she finished her breakfast, cleaned and stowed the cooking gear, and scuffed out the fire. She slipped a bulky tunic over her sweater, tucked her hair up into her wide-brimmed hat, and shouldered the pack with a not quite grunt.

"Shouldn't be feelin' heavier the longer I go." She grumbled to herself. Still, she smiled and forgave herself the grumble. She took up her walking staff and, after another scan of the clearing to make sure she'd left nothing, pushed through the screen of underbrush to find the short trail to the Kleesport Pike.

In a few days, she'd pass through Kleesport and she looked forward to a warm bath and a chance to resupply. She mentally weighed the few silvers left in her purse and nodded in satisfaction. The couple back in Maplesboro had been grateful for the poultices she'd done for their cow and given her a few coins in addition to a hot dinner of mutton and fresh bread. Another few weeks on the road should see her safely at Gertie Pinecrest's cottage before the Solstice.

Whether the woman would welcome her or not was a question that troubled her even as she went. Folks called Gertie the Hermit of Lammas Wood for a reason, but Tanyth been on the path for twenty winters and Gertie was the last of the old Witch Women. She kept the Old Knowledge of the plants and seeds. Tanyth desperately wanted that knowledge for herself. Tanyth didn't know if Mother Pinecrest would share it, and couldn't know until she went there and asked in person.

The low, easterly sun raked claws of light and shadow between the trees and across the packed surface of the Pike. Tanyth held back in the last cover of the forest and checked the Pike in both directions before exposing herself at the verge. It wasn't a dangerous area, as roads went, but prudence dictated caution and prudence was a teacher it paid not to ignore. The morning stillness hadn't yet broken and sounds traveled well in the quiet air. The two jaybirds back up the trail ended their squabble with matching squawks that receded as the birds took wing. The soft chipping of a sparrow in the weeds was punctuated by the periodic dee-dee-dee of a pine-dee in the copse behind her.

She heard nothing, saw nobody, and slipped through the weeds, parting them gently with her staff to walk between them without breaking the tender stalks. Her soft boots left no distinguishing marks on the low mosses beside the road and if a faint trail of darker grass marked her passage through the dewed undergrowth, that would be gone in an hour or two as the last heat of the late summer baked the moisture away.

Tanyth turned her face northward, and with the sun warming her right side as she strode through the bands of light, soon fell into the easy cadence of a ground eating stride. At fifty-three winters, if the spring in her step was not that of a younger woman, the ready economy of her movements and the long years of walking the paths of Korlay gave her a stamina and resilience to travel that few people could match, save perhaps the King's Own. Even they traveled on four hooves more often than two feet.

Thinking of the King's Own brought a familiar pang of regret and longing, dulled from much use and long habit. Her own, young Robert left home and hearth to enter service to the Realm as soon as he'd been able to convince the garrison commander at Fairport to take him. At fourteen winters, he lacked his full growth, but years of dealing with the physical and emotional challenges meted out by his father had matured and seasoned him ahead of his time. She could see his glowing face in her mind's eye as he spoke quietly but earnestly to her.

"It's for the best, Mother. When I'm gone, you won't need to protect me. You'll be safer." He'd smiled encouragingly, looking to her for reassurance, for acceptance of his choice.

She'd given a Mother's Blessing–catching a tear from her cheek and pressing her moistened finger to his brow, sealing it with a kiss.

She treasured the memory of his lanky frame turning at the gate to wave and smile, his face already alight from the excitement that the road ahead lured him with. There really hadn't been a golden light of morning that framed his glowing youth, she knew, but over time her mind insisted on adding the aura, burnishing her memory of the battered, haunted, child who left her ineffectual protection for the tender mercies of King and service.

He'd been wrong, of course. Infuriated by Robert's escape into service, no doubt aggravated by the loss of extra hands around the cottage, Roger Oakhurst turned his entire fury upon the only target remaining to him.

A squirrel scolded her as she passed, the sudden noise returning her to the road and the present.

Ahead, an ox cart emerged around the bend in the distance. Tanyth slowed her ground-chewing pace to regard the drover walking beside the animal as well as she could in the slanting light of morning. She paused and glanced behind herself to make sure the road was clear before walking to the side in preparation for moving out of the cart's way.

As they closed, the drover paid more and more attention. It wasn't that lone travelers were unheard of, but he eyed her uneasily and she kept the brim of the hat tilted forward as if looking at the road right in front of her feet, glancing up irregularly to judge their progress and to keep him from getting a good look at the trousered figure approaching. When they were a few yards apart, Tanyth stepped off the east side of the road and leaned on her staff to allow the ox-cart the full width of road. As the drover drew even with her, the sun was almost at her back and she stood firmly in a band of bright morning sun.

The drover, a strongly shouldered man of adult years, nodded politely as he passed and offered no more offense than a brisk, "Good morrow, traveler." The strong odors of working beast carried on the morning breeze and were matched by an undercurrent of healthy male.

Tanyth nodded and raised her hand to the brim of her hat without speaking. Dressed in baggy, men's clothing with her graying hair hidden under a floppy hat, she was as nondescript as any artifice might afford without drawing attention to herself by being unusual. If she were to speak, her clear alto would give up the illusion of "poor old man" and leave her revealed as "unattended woman." She sighed inwardly at the necessity but while most held elders in esteem, there were those too young or too callow to afford anyone the respect they desired for themselves. She wasn't too worried about the drover, but it never paid to take things for granted so far from town and witnesses.

The cart rumbled by and in the bed a pair of axes and a bow saw explained why he headed away from town with an empty cart so early in the day. No doubt, he'd return at dusk, his cart loaded with firewood. Tanyth realized that she must be closer to a village than she thought. She focused on the immediate tasks ahead and stepped back onto the smooth surface, turning northward once more.

After another mile or so, the smoky scent of village came on the breeze and she quickened her pace a bit, hoping some fresh water and perhaps a bit of cheese might be had for the price of a little casual labor, perhaps an hour on the butter churn should the village have a milch cow. As she turned a final bend, the small gathering of huts filling a clearing carved out of the forest beside the road gave her some pause. Each hut sported a small vegetable patch behind and a grassy verge provided rough grazing for a couple of goats. A gravel track led from the Pike up into the cluster of huts. She could hear children playing somewhere behind the village and a small flock of chickens scratched and clucked in the gravel of the path.

Her eyes tracked back and forth across the area looking for the reason this particular location had grown up. Usually hamlets grew on crossroads or river banks, traffic providing a rationale and travelers' coins pollinating prosperity until the hamlet grew to village and became more self-sufficient. The unprepossessing collection in front of her looked like little more than hovels, but she sniffed none of the sewery smell of mismanagement even while the rich aroma of ripening animal dung came to her clearly along with clean wood smoke and the laughing shrieks of children.

A lone yellow dog guarded the road's edge where the main path out of the hamlet joined the Kleesport Pike. The path was wide enough for a cart–indeed she noted an ox-pie and some fresh stripes in the hard-pan to tell her where the woodcutter had come from. A woman's voice shouted something unintelligible and strident from the direction of the laughing children and a pack of five came belting out from behind one of the huts, the oldest looking to be about ten winters and the rest ranging down in increments that were barely discernible. Their general looks were sufficiently different to suggest they weren't all siblings which meant more than one family with children.

Not a bandit camp, then. Tanyth relaxed marginally. There was still a lot that could go wrong but where there were children, there was less likelihood of violence. It wasn't a fool-proof test as her own life served to illustrate, but the probabilities of a peaceful encounter were greatly improved by the presence of young ones.

The small tribe skidded to a stop at the apparition of this stranger almost in their midst and the eldest of the group shouted, "Ma! Traveler's here!" He didn't sound alarmed but the low door of the hut they'd just run out from behind swung open almost immediately and a youngish woman bent head and shoulders to get out through the opening. She straightened with one hand to her brow and the other at the small of her back.

She regarded Tanyth for a moment before speaking. "Can we help you, traveler?" Tanyth recognized her bright soprano from the earlier shout.

Tanyth took off her hat and brushed a hand through her short gray hair. "Fresh water?" she asked preferring to take things one step at a time until she got a better lay of the land.

The eldest of the children perked up as she spoke and they all gaped a bit as their notions realigned with a new reality. "Ma, that's a woman!" The eldest said it with some surprise.

The woman blinked slowly and turned her attention to the boy for a moment regarding him with an arched eyebrow and a small grin. "Thank you for that report, Riley. Would you fetch a bucket of water from the well, please?"

Tanyth smiled a bit herself and spoke up. "I can get a bucket of water if you'll just show me where...?"

The younger woman shook her head slightly. "That's all right, traveler. This rapscallion and his vagabond band have been under foot all morning. Maybe if I give him a few more chores he'll decide bein' elsewhere is better." She graced the boy with another pointed look, and he hied himself off around the hut, looking back over his shoulder and gathering his cohort around him as he scampered.

"Would you sit a spell? We don't get many travelers who stop..." The woman smiled tentatively but there was still a hint of reserve, a mutual weighing that passed on the morning's wind.

"I don't want to be any trouble, mum." Tanyth hesitated. "I thought maybe I could get a freshening of my water-skin and maybe do a chore or two in return for some bread?"

"Naught but woman's work here, I'm afraid." The younger woman twisted her mouth in a wry smile. "You know the kind of work I mean?"

Tanyth snorted in reply. "Cookin', cleanin', and unpaid."

The younger woman nodded with a small laugh. "You know very well, then." She regarded Tanyth once more, her head cocked to one side. She shook herself suddenly. "Where are my manners?" She stepped forward and held out one smoothly tanned and callused hand. "Amber Mapleton."

Tanyth took the offered hand in her own. "Tanyth. Tanyth Fairport. Pleased to meet you." She answered the younger woman's smile with one of her own.

"Come inside, Mother Fairport. If you've the time to help, then you've time to tell me what's a foot in the world while I mend."

"Just Tanyth, Amber. I'm not that old yet."

The younger woman's glance took in the crow's feet and gray hair but she offered no comment except to quirk her mouth a little sideways and nod at the house.

Tanyth felt welcomed by that half smile and the two women ducked low, Tanyth slipping out of her pack before trying to pass under the lintel. Inside the hut sank down into the soil about two feet, and woven grass mats covered the floor. Tanyth admired the handiwork.

"We weave these mats and sell them in Kleesport." Amber made the announcement quietly but proudly as she saw the older woman admiring the flooring. "There's a slough filled with long grasses just up the hollow a piece." Amber nodded westerly, toward the forest side of the hamlet. "We gather it in the fall, weave it all winter, and sell it in the spring. It brings in a few extra silvers for the village."

"Have you been here long?" Tanyth perched on a vacant stool beside the hearth.

"This will be our fourth winter." Amber set about warming a teapot with some hot water, before throwing in a handful of tea. She topped it off with boiling water and set it aside to steep. She straightened from her task and cast an appraising eye across the walls and beams. "That first year was bad, but this year we're a lot readier for winter."

Their settling in was interrupted by the boy's return with the bucket of water as he carefully took the three steps down and placed the wooden pail on the corner of the hearth. He ducked his head politely in a half bow and offered a shy smile.

"Thank you, Riley. Go out and play with the others now and let us have a little peace."

"Won't last much longer," he said with a puckish grin. "Sandy's spreadin' the news." With that as his parting word, he scampered back out the way he came, just in time to pass another slender woman in homespun at the threshold.

"Amber? I heard we have guests?" The newcomer took advantage of the opened door to thrust her head into the hut and peer about.

"You may as well come in, Sadie." Amber hid a small smile by peering at the teapot.

The slightly-built blonde woman, not much more than a girl by Tanyth's reckoning, took the invitation at face value and hurried in, long familiarity evident in her sure movements around the small hut even as she eyed the newcomer curiously.

"Tanyth, this is Sadie Hawthorne. She lives next door. Sadie, Tanyth Fairport. She's just passing through."

The three women managed to pour a couple of mugs of tea before the next neighbor knocked on the door.

CHAPTER 2
WILLOW BARK TEA

Tanyth got back on the Pike as the sun passed zenith. Her delay over tea and talk lost her some time on the road but gained her a small loaf of fresh bread and a block of hard cheese along with the knowledge of why the village sat where it did. A path led into the woods to the west of the Pike. It ended at a deposit of fine clay back in the hillside beyond and provided the community's life blood. Most of the men worked to excavate the heavy mineral laced mud. One served as hunter, another as wood cutter, and a third drove the heavy lorry wagon back and forth to Kleesport. The women talked excitedly of plans to build their own kiln in the coming winter when the clay was frozen and the menfolk would otherwise be underfoot.

She smiled to herself as she tucked her hair up under her hat and made ready to go. She left some packets of dried basil with the women and measured out a few of her precious seeds to press upon them for planting in the spring. Rosemary and sage grew readily in the local soil and Sadie, who seemed to be the expert on growing things in the village, accepted them happily.

As she reached her stride and the ground began to roll away under her boots once more, she thought about how exciting it must be to be young, and to be working toward something that might be bigger than themselves. The hamlet was, as yet, unnamed but the women around the hearth planned for a larger community with a real name and even a school to teach letters and numbers to the anticipated horde of children. While Amber had used the excuse of "learning the news from outside," the women did little listening to happenings outside of their small circle and instead took pleasure in sharing their plans for the future with her. Tanyth smiled a gentle smile at their youthful enthusiasms and said a silent prayer to the All-Mother for their success.

The afternoon passed uneventfully except for the passage of one of the King's Own, a messenger on one of the rangy, long-legged horses they used for the service. Tanyth heard the horse and rider coming even over the sighing of the wind through the tree tops and stepped off the road to allow the rider to pass. She knew better than to expect a miracle but even so, she was faintly disappointed when the youth in the saddle was not her Robert. A young woman looking very serious and businesslike in her uniform wore the diagonal orange slash of the messenger corps. Tanyth waved a hand in greeting but the dispatch rider only nodded in acknowledgment without speaking as the horse trotted past leaving a musical jingling of tack and a swirl of light dust that rapidly dispersed in the afternoon breeze.

"Old fool! Your Robert is a grown man with wife and children of his own by now." She frowned and grumbled to herself but the thought of having grandchildren she didn't even know gave her a pang of melancholy. She huffed and stabbed the hard scrabble surface of the road with the iron heel of her staff for several steps in vexation.

The sun slid on its inevitable path while Tanyth paced her way northward. When it approached the tops of the trees on the west side of the road, she started watching for breaks in the trees on the east, keeping an eye open for game trails or paths. If there wasn't one, she'd have to find a safe camp off the road by herself, but she rarely had to resort to that level of bush whacking in order to find a safe hole. The Pike wasn't heavily traveled but it was traveled regularly and travelers had few choices along the way but to find camping spots off the road to spend the night. The hamlet she'd left behind might well do better to open an inn, she thought, rather than a brick kiln.

A pounding rumble reached her ears as the sun fell closer

to the treetops. She quickly chose the best of the options available to her and stepped easily onto the weeded verge, slipping into the underbrush at the edge of the encroaching forest. The trees were not so closely spaced that she couldn't slip between them and she took shelter beside a large black-berry thicket, hunkering down to lower her profile and peeking through the undergrowth to see what would pass.

In a matter of moments a large six-in-hand coach rattled into view and swooped past her traveling from Kleesport and heading for Varton, ninety miles to the south. She passed the carriage stations periodically along the road, but never stopped. The men who staffed the stations were not terribly well-mannered and were often bored with nothing better to do than tend the animals and await the arrival and subsequent departure of the coaches. Stopping there carried more risk than she thought prudent.

She waited until the sound of the carriage faded out in the distance to the south and kept to her place of conceal-ment even after it had gone. Before long a pair of the King's Own guards came riding by as well. The Guardsmen can-tered easily in the wake of the coach. They didn't seem to pay close attention to the road or the woods that surrounded it, but Tanyth lowered her head, hiding her face behind the wide brim of her hat. The King's Own were unlikely to assault her but that wouldn't stop them asking a lot of difficult ques-tions about why she might be hiding in the woods watching the coach and guard.

They passed without incident and Tanyth let out the breath she'd been holding. She spared a look around and noticed a game trail running behind the blackberry bramble and into the forest. A short way down the path she found a small clearing bounded by a thicket of juniper on one side and a huge boulder on the other. A soft splashing sound led her to a spring-fed creek on the far side of the boulder. A blackened smear on the rock showed where travelers had camped in the past. The site was a trifle exposed to the sky, but the bulk of the stone stood between the clearing and the road. Lit-tle would be visible through the trees in that direction. She smiled, dropped her pack and staff beside the rock, and went in search of tinder and wood for a fire.

Appropriately sized sticks littered the forest floor. She didn't have to stray far from her campsite in order to collect enough to heat water for tea and a bit of oatmeal for breakfast. She found herself looking forward to the bread and cheese from the village for her dinner. She even found a patch of wild onion to add a bit of flavor. In celebrating her good fortune, she dropped her normal guard and almost walked into one of the two men before she even knew they were there.

"Mother Fairport?" The taller one looked vaguely familiar. It took her a moment to recognize him as the ox cart drover from the morning. "You visited with Amber today? At the village?"

The two stepped back from her and held their hands out to their sides, palms forward to offer as little threat as possible. The smaller one she didn't recognize but then she'd only seen women and children during her visit. They both smiled and made no threatening movements. Tanyth kicked herself for leaving her staff where she could not reach it but crossed to the scorched rock to deposit her load of kindling before responding.

"And you are...?" She countered his question with her own.

"William Mapleton. I'm Amber's husband. I think I met you on the road this morning, didn't I?"

She nodded once. "You did." She turned to the smaller man. "And you?"

"I'm Sadie's man, mum. Thomas." He smiled and nodded his head.

"You two seem to be a bit off the path."

William's lips tightened. "In more ways than one, mum. We need your help back at the village."

"What kind of help?

Thomas piped up. "It's Sadie, mum. She's come down with a blindin' headache and I think she's a fever as well. Her skin's hot to the touch."

She looked back and forth between them. "Do you think I made her sick?"

The two men shook their heads and William answered. "Of course not, mum, but Amber said you have some knowl-

14

edge of herbs and such. She hoped you might be able to help. She sent me and Thomas here to try to catch you up and see if you'd come back to the village."

"Willow bark tea?" Tanyth asked.

The two men glanced at one other. "What about it?" Thomas asked.

"Did you give her some willow bark tea?"

They shook their heads in unison. "All-Mother preserve us." Tanyth muttered. She snatched up her pack and staff. "Let's go."

William took the pack from her. "It'll be faster if I carry the load, mum."

She didn't argue and he slung her pack over one shoulder like it weighed nothing at all.

Thomas led the way through the gathering dusk with Tanyth on his heels and William acting as rear guard. The Pike itself was just a lighter shadow in the dimness. The long road of the afternoon melted under their hurried strides and even Tanyth's conditioning showed the strain before they turned into the path leading to the hamlet sometime well after sundown but before moon rise.

The two men led the way to a hut where Sadie lay shivering under a pile of homespun blankets. "I'm sorry, mum."

Tanyth smiled gently. "Not to fret, dear. I'm here and I'll do what I can." Her nose told her a familiar story and she turned to Amber and one of the other wives from the afternoon. "Rebecca, isn't it?"

The woman nodded, pleased to be remembered by name. "How long has she been throwin' up?"

"Just a few times." Rebecca said. "She started this afternoon."

"And the runs?" Tanyth looked back and forth between them.

"Just started," Amber said. "Looks like the flux to me."

Tanyth nodded in agreement. "I think so, too." She turned to the two men hovering at the door. "You two, put the kids to bed, if they're not already. You've got work tomorrow and there's nothing you can do here. Thomas? Can you take a bedroll somewhere?"

He nodded and they beat a hasty retreat, leaving the women to their tasks.

Tanyth rummaged in her pack and pulled out a fold of canvas, holding it up with a smile of satisfaction. "This is the last of my stock, but perhaps we can get more in the morning." She handed the package to Amber. "Start some water boilin' in a pot. We'll make her some willow tea, and I'll show you two how to make it as well. There's naught we can do for the flux but try to make her comfortable until it burns through her. The tea will help and you should keep a stock handy."

The two younger women set to work on Sadie's hearth and Tanyth sat with Sadie, bathing her brow and offering soothing noises. She thought back to all the various times she'd helped people this way since that first night she fled Roger and took shelter at Agnes Dogwood's tiny cottage in the forest west of Fairport. Agnes was always taking in strays and Tanyth counted herself among them. She'd stayed in the cottage all winter, curled inward and hurting. With the spring, and with Agnes's gentle ministrations, she came to herself and began the long pilgrimage that brought her to tend the bedside of a stranger.

She shook herself back to the reality and Amber called to her from the hearth.

"How do we make this tea?"

Tanyth patted Sadie's shoulder reassuringly and crossed the small room to supervise adding the dried ground willow bark to the boiling water. When Amber took the pot off the heat, Tanyth pushed it back near the edge of the fire to keep the water just simmering.

"You'll want to get it a bit more than just steeped to get the full good out of it. Leave it for a few minutes at the simmer to get the most out of the bark. It needs to recover from being dried before it can give up the medicine."

The two women listened intently and then watched the liquid bubble gently in the pot. After a quarter hour, with the bitter aroma of the concoction beginning to swirl around the room, they took it off the fire. Tanyth had them pour the tea through a cheese cloth to strain out the solids.

"How much do we give her?" Rebecca looked at the murky

tea.

Tanyth gave a little shrug in answer. "Start with a cup. It's less than tasty so I've never been tempted to see how much of it I could drink myself. But when cramps are bad, even a bad cup of tea is worth it for the relief it brings."

The women shared knowing looks before decanting a mug of the tea and helping Sadie to sip it. After the first tentative slurp she took it readily enough and the exertion of half sitting and sipping the hot liquid tired her to the point that when she lay back in the bed, she fell into a quiet sleep.

"Was that the bark tea that put her to sleep?" Amber asked.

Tanyth shook her head. "I'd guess exhaustion. Fever takes a lot out of you and the flux just takes that much more." She eyed the sleeping woman. "If she can keep it down, it'll help with the pain, but we really don't want to give her enough to break the fever until it's ready to go on its own."

Rebecca looked at her sharply. "Why is that, mum?"

"Fever is the body burning out its poison. If it gets too high, it'll kill as fast as anything. Normally, it doesn't and gets just hot enough to cook the poison out of the blood without cooking the person from the inside out. But you want the fever to run its course so you know the poison is gone. The tea will reduce the fever a bit, but it's all to the good."

Amber caught herself in a yawn and Tanyth smiled.

"Let's take turns sitting. The night is more than half gone now, and she should sleep soundly for a few hours. If you two would like to get some sleep, I'll wake one of you in a bit to take a turn." She nodded at the pile of bedding going unused because the children were farmed out in other huts for the night.

Rebecca took the hint and burrowed into the bedding. Tanyth thought she didn't look all that much older than the children that probably slept there.

Amber asked, "Are you sure, mum?"

"Please, call me Tanyth? Or Tan? Mum makes me feel old." She smiled, hands pressing into the small of her back. "And right now I don't need anything makin' me feel any older than I am."

Amber smiled in return. "But will you be all right?"

Tanyth nodded and pulled her pack out of the corner where William had dropped it. She took out her bedroll and placed it as a pad on the floor beside the bed, using the pack itself as a cushion to lean against. "Much cozier than a fire in the open, my dear. I'll be fine. You get some sleep. Tomorrow will be full enough of mischief."

Amber crawled into the pile of covers beside Rebecca and the two of them soon snored delicately, leaving Tanyth to her thoughts and the night. The excitement of the evening, starting with finding two strangers in her camp, the dash back over the ground so recently covered in the light of day, and finding a simple case of the flux that these young people should have been able to handle without difficulty gave her pause.

Tanyth checked on Sadie who appeared to be sleeping comfortably and settled back on her makeshift seat, one she'd often used in the wild. She crossed her arms under her breasts and settled in for a bit of a rest herself, but her mind would not let go of the one real fact. Grown women, albeit young as they were, must have seen flux a hundred times before. Amber had even recognized it. It was the most common of ailments next to running nose and cough. They had to have known that Sadie was in no real danger, even if she were uncomfortable.

Why, then, had they sent the men after her? Her mind chased the question around like a kitten chasing its own tail, but like the kitten, she never caught up with any good answers. After an hour or so of sitting in the quiet, she heard Sadie's breathing lengthen and deepen. She reached up and placed the back of her hand against the sick woman's forehead. The fever hadn't broken, but the willow bark was working its magic. Tanyth gave a small prayer of thanks to the All-Mother before settling down for a short nap of her own. In the forest behind the hamlet she heard a solitary owl hoot out a single call before the night drew close around.

CHAPTER 3
A TEMPORARY DELAY

Small movements in the bed beside her woke Tanyth. Watery, predawn light gave her enough of a clue as to the hour to get her up and moving. She rose, stretching out sore muscles in neck and back with rolling motions. Sadie had thrown back the heavy blankets, leaving her shoulders and one arm exposed to the moist night air trapped in the hut. Tanyth pressed the back of her hand against the exposed skin of the young woman's arm and considered. Still fevered, but it was reduced.

She sighed and crossed to the hearth. She rummaged in the coals, adding some small sticks from the woodbox and fanning the flame to get a cheery fire going. Amber and Rebecca joined her.

"You didn't wake us!" Amber seemed at once contrite and distressed.

Tanyth smiled at the earnest face peering at her from under night-tossed hair. "Sleep will help keep you from picking up her flux and there was nothing to do but wait." She shrugged. "I had a pleasant nap right there myself, so no harm done, my dear."

Rebecca glanced at Sadie. "How is she doing?"

Tanyth followed the glance with one of her own and added another half-shrug. "Seems like the fever is down a bit, but unless I miss my guess, she's got another day before it burns through."

Amber nodded. "Thank you for comin' back, mum." Her voice was low, and Rebecca nodded her wide-eyed confirmation.

"I'm glad they found me." Tanyth looked back and forth between the two faces peering at her through the dim light. "But I don't understand somethin'."

The two glanced at each other before looking back at Tanyth. "What's that, mum?" Rebecca asked.

"How could you not know this was the flux? And why didn't you just give her the willow bark?"

Amber sighed. Rebecca looked a bit guilty.

Tanyth waited them out, poking the coals and pressing the pot of willow bark tea closer to the fire.

Finally Amber spoke. "I suspected it was the flux, but after Mother Alderton passed in the winter, we were scared that Sadie would follow her path. We knew you couldn't have gone that far so when she started throwin' up, William and Thomas volunteered to go after you." Amber looked stricken. "Thank you for coming back."

"But don't you know willow bark tea?" Tanyth softened the query with a gentle smile. "Surely you've seen flux and used the tea before."

Amber started to say something but stopped. Finally she managed to find the words. "We were afraid that it wasn't the flux. Mother Alderton was our healer and she always took care of us. None of us had time to learn before the All-Mother called her home."

A chilly finger scraped down Tanyth's spine. She noticed that a sharper light edged out the watery color of predawn. She heard doors opening and closing in the huts of the village over a rising tide of bird song. She sighed again. "Well, my dears, we've got mornin' upon us and I suspect hungry and scared people. We should get things moving. Then we can talk."

Amber and Rebecca nodded and shot smiles of thanks in her direction as they scampered out the door. Tanyth heard their voices reassuring their neighbors and directing the morning's activities. Sick or no, the men needed to get on with gathering the clay, the goats needed milking, and children needed to be fed and held. Tanyth knew there was some chance that the sickness would spread, but rested, healthy bodies had the best chance fighting off the poison. She set about filling a large pot with water and warming it on the growing fire. She opened the back door to let out the stale night air and was just beginning to think about breakfast for herself, when Sadie spoke to her.

"Thank you, mum. For coming back to save me."

Tanyth crossed to the cot and looked down at her charge. "I hardly saved you, child. You weren't in any real danger as near, as I can tell." She smiled down at Sadie. "You might have felt like you were crossin' over, but most people don't die from a simple case of the flux."

Sadie looked drawn and pinched about the eyes, very different from the smiling face she'd shown just the previous morning. "Mother Alderton did."

Tanyth gave a little side-to-side shake of her head. "Maybe she did. Maybe she didn't. Mighta been something that looked like flux but wasn't. Too hard to tell now." She focused on Sadie and gave her a little pat on the forearm where it rested on the covers. "But you are not Mother Alderton and you aren't going to die."

Sadie smiled weakly at the reassurance.

"So? How do you feel this morning? Need the pan?"

Sadie shook her head. "I feel empty just now, but my head hurts and I'm so weak."

"I'm warmin' the willow bark again. You'll need another cup or two before the day's out, I'm thinkin', but you'll be back on your feet tomorrow, I bet."

Sadie made a grimace. "Gah, that's horrible tasting stuff." She smiled. "But it does help. Thank you for makin' it."

"I'm glad I had some left. It wouldn't have been very much fun rummaging around in the dark looking for willow trees." She said it with a grin. "But it does taste pretty bad. A dollop of honey and a few mint leaves help a lot but we were in a hurry last night."

Sadie smiled. "Well, don't tell the kids but there's a bit of honey comb in that jar up there." She nodded to an earthen jar on the mantle. "If they knew it was there, they'd be after it all the time."

Tanyth looked surprised and reached for the jar. Inside

she found a honey comb that had leaked several ounces of the golden sweetener into the bottom of the container. She retrieved Sadie's mug, tossed the dregs from the previous night's concoction into the side of the fire and poured a careful measure of honey into the bottom of the cup before adding a generous amount of willow bark tea. She stirred it gently to dissolve the honey in the warmed liquid and could smell the rich aroma of summer flowers wafting up in the moist cloud above the cup. She handed it to Sadie who took a tentative sip, grimaced, and then did her best to drink the cup down without stopping.

"Gah, that's still horrible." She handed the cup back to Tanyth. "But thank you. It helps." She settled back into the bed and pulled the covers up around her shoulders with a small shiver. She mumbled something else that Tanyth couldn't hear, and passed the boundary between waking and sleep without a ripple.

Tanyth rolled up her bedroll and re-tied it to the bottom of her pack. The smell of the honey had stirred the need for her own breakfast and she pulled the bread and cheese from the side pocket of her pack. It was only slightly misshapen from having been confined in the small space over night and she quickly toasted the bread over the coals, melting a bit of the cheese into it and savoring the warmly mingled flavors of toast and cheese. By the time she'd finished her meager meal, one of the other women was at the door. Tanyth recognized the face but couldn't remember the name that went with it.

The young woman must have seen her trying to recall and smiled prettily. "I'm Megan, mum. Amber sent me to relieve you. She has tea ready at her cottage, if you'd like to join her."

Tanyth smiled warmly. "A cup of tea would go nicely right now." She picked up her wide hat and started for the door.

Megan stopped her with a quiet, "What do I do?"

Tanyth looked at her. She seemed distressed. "Do?"

Megan nodded. "Yes. What do I do for Sadie?"

Tanyth shook her head. "Nothing, my dear. Just sit with her and keep her company. She's had some bark tea and should sleep for a couple of hours if left undisturbed. Make yourself comfy and see if she needs anything when she wakes. If anything else happens, just call me."

Tanyth left the young woman standing in the middle of the hut and marveled again how women with children could seem so helpless in the face of common adversity.

She found Amber sitting outside in a sunny nook behind her cottage with a charming little teapot, a collection of delicate china cups, and the bulky form of her woodcutter husband looking vaguely uncomfortable with the delicate china clasped in his hand. He wore a sleeveless leather vest which left his arms free and showed his shoulders to good advantage as well.

Amber smiled a greeting and extended a hand to indicate the open stool beside their small table.

"How's she doing?" Amber didn't really appear worried about Sadie but offered the query as a conversational starter while she poured one of the blue flowered cups with a lovely tea of pale green. The scent of mint wafted moistly from the cup.

"Good morning, mum," William offered with a grave smile of his own.

She suddenly decided she liked William, not because of the shape of his shoulders or the attractive curl in his hair, but simply because of the warm smile in his eyes. She had to admit to herself that the rest didn't hurt. She smiled at him. "Good morning, William. Not out cutting today?"

He shifted uneasily and looked into his cup. "Oh, I reckon I'll be goin' out soon as I've finished my tea."

Tanyth turned to Amber. "She's better. Had some more tea and she's resting more or less comfortably at the moment." She took the offered seat and sipped the tea. A cutting board with cheese, bread, and fruit was in the center of the table and Amber pushed it just a bit toward the older woman as if in offering.

In a tree on the far side of the clearing a squirrel chattered a few times at some transgressor unseen from the sunny breakfast table. The morning breeze felt soft against Tanyth's cheek. She turned her face up to the sun, closed her eyes, and accepted the gift of warmth while she waited for the conversation to begin. By her reckoning they had a week before the Harvest Moon and the weather would start changing soon. . .

"So, you're probably wonderin'..." Amber began but her voice petered out.

"Yes," Tanyth replied without opening her eyes or turning back to look at them.

"Mother Alderton was our healer." Amber said. "The All-Mother called her home late last winter and we've been muddling along ever since. We're all pretty rugged. The outdoor work and all, I guess."

Tanyth noticed that William stared into his mug of tea without drinking it. In the light of morning he looked very young for all his broad shoulders and muscled arms. She looked carefully at Amber. "You never made willow bark tea?"

Amber looked startled. "Not from bits of bark!" She looked embarrassed by her outburst. "At home we'd pop around to the apothecary and pick up some willow bark tea whenever we needed it." She shrugged. "Mother Alderton made some for us when we needed it, and none of us have had the time what with the kids and the houses and all." Her voice petered out under the older woman's scrutiny.

"'At home'? What did you mean 'at home'? Where are you from?" Tanyth's voice was soft but insistent.

William spoke for the first time. "Kleesport, mum. We came out here as a group from Kleesport. There was something over two dozen of us to begin with. Some left. Some are still here." His face turned to look at what must be the graveyard. Tanyth made out some whitewashed stones set in the ground. "Mother Alderton said she came to keep an eye on us."

Tanyth's eyes swept back and forth between the two of them and then around the yards and tidy huts. The odd chicken scratched here and there and a pair of goats grazed on the weedy side hill. The garden plots seemed too small to support two dozen adults. "Why did she think you needed keepin' an eye on, then?"

"She thought we were too soft and citified to make it out here on our own." His voice was low, and he didn't look up from his tea cup.

Amber wouldn't meet her gaze either. "Were you?"

He gave a half shrug. "Some were. Mostly those left. A few were called home, like Mother Alderton. We're down to 18 adults now and the kids." He blew out a long breath. "Honestly, mum, I thought we'd have more of a going concern by now."

Amber added a morose, "We haven't even named the place yet. We can't seem to agree."

"So why do you stay at it? It's only a few days into Kleesport, isn't it?"

"Ten days on foot, mum. Two weeks by wagon." William sounded very dejected.

"It takes you two weeks to get a wagon load of clay into town? How many times a year can you do that?"

He gave another half shrug. "Only have the one wagon and team that can make the trip. Ole Bester and the cart is good for the woodcuttin' and all, but Frank Crane takes the cargo rig into Kleesport and back six times a year or so. We got one more load for this season. He was due back on Sickle Moon or thereabouts."

Amber added. "The new moon was just the other night so he's not too late. He'll be back."

William didn't look convinced to Tanyth, but she held her tongue. She sipped her cooling tea and thought about what they'd said. "You all came from town? None of you are farm folk? Nobody used to livin' on the land?"

William nodded. "Mother Alderton called us her poor little rich kids. My father owns a shipping line, but there's no room for me in it." His voice dripped bitterness onto the table.

Amber grimaced. "Daughters of goldsmiths don't get to play with gold. They're supposed to be pretty and snare good husbands."

"All of you are what? Runaways?"

"Not runaways, exactly. Just misfits, I guess you'd say. Most of us have families that we could go back to. Thomas doesn't. The knowing grins would be difficult to deal with, but it could be done."

"Your father would never accept me as his daughter, Will." Amber said this quietly without looking at him.

"Probably fair, because yours wouldn't accept me as a son, either." He gave her a grin that carried real humor and warmth. He turned to Tanyth. "Neither of our families thinks our choice of partner is suitable."

She smiled back. "I gathered." She looked back and forth between them. "So you all packed up and came out here to quarry clay?"

William snickered. "We thought of it as 'setting out to make our fortunes.'" He gave a sideways shrug. "Might work yet, if we don't all die or get disgusted and pack it in."

Amber sat up straighter on her stool. "Well, those that have packed it in are the singles and the impatient, for the most part. I know you and I aren't ready to give up yet, and neither are Sadie and Thomas or Megan and David."

"Clay's hard work and shipping it so far as a raw material is harder still, I wager." Tanyth offered the suggestion.

"We've got a factor in Kleesport who buys it. We give it to him wholesale and he brokers it out to those who need it for brickwork and whatnot." William shrugged. "We didn't run away, ya see? We still have connections there. Just scratchin' in the dirt like this is disheartenin' for some."

It was Tanyth's turn for a half shrug. "Anything worth havin' is worth workin' for." She paused. "Where's Mother Alderton's hut? Maybe there's stuff there I can show you how to use before I get on the road again."

Amber sighed. "Well, we were hoping you'd be able to spend a bit of time with us."

William looked at her with a hopeful gleam in his eye. "You'd be able to help us a lot, mum, if you could see your way to spend even a few days. We'd be able to send you on in the clay wagon when Frank takes it to Kleesport again. He'll be going back out again almost as soon as he gets back. A couple days rest for the horses and we'll load the barrels of clay for the ride into town. Save you walkin'."

"Walkin's no mind to me, William, and I'd be a day closer by now if I hadn't come back." She felt a little mean to be reminding them. "I need to be in Lammas Wood before the

Axe Moon."

William's eyes widened. "That's a long way to go. How were you planning to get there by then?"

"Passage from Kleesport to Northport on a ship. Should only take a couple of weeks by sea, but I need to be there before the days get too short."

Tanyth could see William running the numbers in his head. "Yes, but that's still not goin' to make it. It'll take longer than that to make it to Kleesport, mum."

"Well, not if I walked today, lad. It's just gone to the Harvest Moon and I can be in Kleesport in ten days. I'll be a few days late by taking the ship, assuming I can get passage, but the weather shouldn't be too bad and I'll be in Northport before the season gets too far advanced."

He nodded his agreement. "I can see that, mum. And every day you stay here is a day later."

Amber and William glanced at each other and Amber sighed. "Well, let me show you Mother Alderton's cottage, Tanyth. Anything you can do to help would be appreciated."

They all drained their cups and stood.

William gave his wife a hug and nodded politely to Tanyth. "I've gotta get Bester movin' or he'll think we're goin' soft." He walked off toward the barn.

Amber bustled about putting the cups and pot on a tray and Tanyth helped her take the precious china indoors.

"That's a lovely service, Amber. Was it a gift?"

Amber smiled. "From William when we moved out here. He said I should have something to remind me of the finer things."

"How thoughtful!"

"How pessimistic, but how right he was. There are days when the crud and the mud and the bugs all make me a little crazy."

Tanyth grinned. "I understand completely. Twenty winters I've been on the road. Some days, it's glorious. Others, it's somethin' considerably less."

Amber stashed the tea service solidly on the hearth and led Tanyth out the front door and around the edge of the hamlet to a small hut, no different from any of the others.

Tanyth noted that with some minor variations they might all have been stamped from the same mold. Simple post and beam construction with a rather pronounced peak to the roof. The roof was planked like the side of a boat and the walls were chinked logs, probably cleared from this very lot to make room for the hamlet. Like all the others, this one had a low door with steps down to a tidy room. A very businesslike hearth held pride of place on the east end and a matching door led out the far side of the hut, giving access on both sides of the building. Even though there were no windows, the doors on both sides gave day light during summer and the low buildings were protected from winter's cold by the earthwork.

As the two women entered the hut, a flock of children pelted by outside. Tanyth watched them run past the open door.

"One of those is yours?" She asked. "The ringleader? Riley was it?"

Amber smiled proudly. "Yes, Riley and his sister, Gillian. This will be his ninth winter. Gillian's seventh."

"You had them before you came out here?"

Amber nodded. "We're crazy but we're not that crazy." She smiled cheerfully. "William and I eloped almost ten winters ago. We tried to make it on our own in town." She shook her head and shrugged. "It was impossible. Everybody knew our families and that they didn't approve of us. The children came and we needed more for them than we could do for them in town."

"How did you happen on this place? It's a trifle out of the way."

Amber laughed. "That's a bit of an understatement, mum. It was a place that William knew from huntin' out here as a boy. About six winters ago, he came out and found it again. Then we set about recruitin' our friends and fellow castoffs to move out here to start a new town. It took a couple of winters but we finally managed it and here we are."

While Amber talked, Tanyth took in the hut and its contents. She stood near the foot of the steps and Amber crossed to open the far door to let out the chilly, stale air. A thin patina of dust coated the table and there was a pair of chairs along with what looked like an oil lamp, complete with glass chimney and reflector. Along one wall, a neat collection of shelves held bundles and bags, boxes and crocks. Tanyth turned her gaze upward and realized that more bundles of dried flowers and grasses hung in long hanks from the rafters.

Amber followed her gaze upward and gasped. "My goodness! What are all those?"

"It looks like a particularly well stocked supply of herbs and medicinal plants that has overstayed its time." Tanyth grimaced. "What a lot of work to go to waste."

"How do you know it's gone to waste, mum?"

"There may be a few things we can salvage here, but most things lose their strength if left too long." She waved a hand at the hanging materials. "This stuff all looks like it's been up there since last winter, or longer, and there's probably little that can be saved. The dust, if nothing else." She shrugged helplessly. "If there'd been anything that wasn't too far gone, we would have smelled it when we walked in. We didn't, so..." Her voice trailed off. "These all must be things that Mother Alderton gathered in the summer and fall of last year, never to be used."

Amber looked somberly at all the dried goods hanging from the rafters. "She died shortly after the Ice Moon. We just kept the cabin closed after that. There was no need to come in here."

Tanyth looked at Amber and then back at the rafters. "Pity. You might have gotten some use from this, if you'd known what you were doing with it." She said it wistfully and crossed to look at the containers along the wall. Each was labeled in a spidery handwriting of uncertain provenance but showed the contents and a date. Tanyth realized that Mother Alderton must have been very busy right up to her death.

"You say the flux took her?" Tanyth turned to look at Amber when she asked.

Amber shrugged helplessly. "We think it was the flux, but when your healer gets sick, how can you be sure?"

A cot stood in the corner and a porcelain lady's chamber pot was visible under it. The cot's rope bracing was exposed by a complete lack of mattress and it looked somehow indecent, exposing the china resting underneath.

Tanyth crossed back to the hearth and noted that it had been cleaned and swept some time ago. A fine layer of dust had built up on the fire scorched stones. The andirons and pot hanger were clean and free of rust. Small rodents had wandered through the dust at one point, leaving small turdlets in the trail. She ducked her head and looked up the chimney to see a well crafted fire shelf and throat beyond which was just black.

"The chimney is blocked?" She straightened and dusted her hands against her pants, looking to Amber for the answer.

"William put a cap on it last winter when we lost Mother Alderton. It kept the animals and weather out."

Tanyth stood on the hearth stone and looked around at the hut. "I'll need to stay for a day or two to get you settled with some simples." She looked at Amber. "May I use this cottage for now?"

Amber looked confused but as realization dawned, joy swept the listless frown away. "Of course, mum! Of course. As long as you want to stay."

Tanyth looked around the room once more. "Well, my dear, let's not get too carried away just yet. We'll see what we'll see, huh? And we'll want to talk about the terms before we get too far along."

"Terms, mum?"

"Come, come, my dear. You're a goldsmith's daughter. There are always terms." Tanyth smiled at Amber to take away any sting. "For now, we have a sick woman who'll need care, and I'll help you learn a few simple things like how to gather willow bark and make tea. We can probably find some other simples in the area." She cast her eyes up to the rafters. "I see cattail and burdock up there and some bundles of mint. I'm sure we'll find others as we go." She turned her gaze back on Amber. "In return you'll help get me a mattress for the cot, some wood for the hearth, and have the chimney opened so I can have a place that's not underfoot and littered with littles?"

The shrieking flock of children wheeled past the door in punctuation and the two women couldn't help but smile at each other.

"Agreed, and I may come join you!" Amber's mouth quirked in a rueful grin as she eyed the door.

"It's only for a few days, mind. Just until we get things settled here." Tanyth looked sternly at the younger woman, quashing the look of growing hope there.

"Of course, mum. Whatever you say."

Tanyth nodded slowly to herself, looking around the room once more. "In that case, we should go see how Sadie's doing and I can fetch my things back here."

Amber led the way out into the morning light and Tanyth felt something stirring in the wind that made the hairs on the back of her arms stand up.

"Foolish old woman," she muttered.

CHAPTER 4
SETTLING IN

Sadie slept comfortably, rousing briefly at Tanyth's touch but sinking back into a healing slumber almost immediately. Tanyth turned to Megan. "I'll be in Mother Alderton's hut if you need me, dear. She should be fine now although I suspect she'll need one more dose of tea before she's ready to get up and about."

Megan, a spare woman with luxurious chestnut hair and a constellation of freckles across her nose, nodded hesitantly and then her eyes widened as the import of what she'd heard sunk in.

Tanyth shouldered her pack and took up staff and hat. When she returned to Mother Alderton's, she found the ox and cart standing in the path and William coming down a ladder from the top of the chimney. He disappeared behind the roof line and emerged around the corner of the house, Amber and a chunk of oiled canvas in tow.

"The chimney should be clear, mum." He smiled. "If you have any problems with it, I'll be back around sunset and I'll look into it." He tossed the canvas into the back of the ox cart and with a quick kiss to his wife, led the lumbering beast off down the track and onto the Pike.

Tanyth eyed the position of the sun. "He'll not get in a full day's cutting today, I wager."

Amber shook her head with a smile. "No, he won't, but he'll get enough done today and there's always tomorrow." She eyed the sun's position herself. "If we're going to get some work done, though, we should be at it."

Tanyth nodded and entered the hut, ducking down to clear the lintel. She stood her staff beside the door and hung her pack from a handy peg, her hat going on the same peg. She was pleased to see that someone had put an armload of wood in the woodbox already.

Amber followed her into the hut. "We'll get you a tick for the bed, mum, and a bucket of water. I've already sent Riley for one. You feel free to send him on any errands like that you need." She smiled.

"We have two pressing bits of business, my dear." Tanyth pointed to the rafters covered with dried vegetation. "We need to clear that away before anybody thinks it's useful. A summer in the heat of this hut has robbed it of any goodness and the dust won't help any."

Amber looked up in dismay. "All of it is ruined?"

Tanyth relented a bit and shrugged. "Well, perhaps not all, but most of it is less than useful at this point. There may be some good in it, but at the moment, its most valuable function is as tinder."

The younger woman looked subdued. "And the other?"

"We need to show you some basics. Who else in the village would you like to have trained?"

"Who else?"

"Yes, it would be a waste to go through all this and then have something happen to you and leave the village without the knowledge again, don't you think?"

Amber looked startled by the thought but nodded in agreement. "Of course. That would make most sense. And we could check each other as well after you're gone to make sure we've remembered correctly."

Tanyth smiled. "Indeed you could, my dear. Excellent thinkin'."

Amber's gaze turned inward. "Sadie would be the most likely. She's the most knowledgeable of plants and growing things, but she's also rather sick."

Tanyth pursed her lips in contemplation. "She'll be movin' about by mornin', I'd guess. Who else might have the interest and potential to do a good job?"

A voice piped up from the doorway. "What about me,

mum?" Riley stood there with a bucket of water and an anxious look on his face.

Amber turned to her son in surprise. "You, Riley?"

He struggled through the door and down the steps with the heavy pail. "Why not me, ma? You said I'm quick to learn!" His child-voice fairly squeaked in excitement.

Amber seemed at a loss, so Tanyth turned to the boy. "This is serious work, young man. It will take a lot of time and a lot of effort to do well. You'll need to use what you'll learn responsibly. Do you think you can do that? If you don't, people could be hurt or die, and that would be a terrible thing to carry around with you."

Amber started to interrupt. "You can't be serious, mum."

Tanyth kept her gaze focused on the youngster as he settled his burden on the hearthstone before answering. "I don't wanna hurt nobody, mum, but seems to me if I start young, then I'll have more time to learn."

Tanyth nodded slowly. "Good thinkin', young man. Are you prepared for it to be borin' and messy?"

He looked startled. "Borin' and messy, mum?"

She shrugged, still watching his face carefully. "Most things in life are borin' and people–and their illnesses–are often messy."

Riley nodded in return. "Missus Hawthorne was kinda messy wif it runnin' out of both ends like that. Zat what cha mean?"

Tanyth's lips twitched slightly but she nodded. "That and sometimes worse."

He shrugged. "It's not that bad, I s'pose." He got a calculating smile on his face. "And I'm too little to be 'round too much yucky stuff anyway." He shot a sideways glance at his mother.

Amber snorted a laugh and hid her mouth behind her hand.

"Very well." Tanyth looked to Amber. "Is it all right with you, my dear? Might be handy to have a strong young lad like this to do some of the work for us. Crawlin' under logs and muckin' out vats and such."

Riley's eyes grew large but Amber saw the twinkle in

Tanyth's eye. "It's all right with me, mum, but shouldn't we have somebody not in our family? If something happens to us and we leave..." She left the thought unfinished.

Riley caught the question. "Where would we go, ma? This is our home now."

She turned to her son. "Yes, Riley, but if something happens to either of your grampas then we may find that we have to go back to Kleesport to live."

"What could happen?" Riley seemed genuinely puzzled.

"Oh, I don't think anything will happen!" Amber grinned. "I'm just thinking that if we need somebody besides me to learn this, then we'd be better off if the other person wasn't attached to me."

Riley nodded. "Well, Missus Hawthorne, she's the bestest grower we have. She'd be good."

"What about Megan?"

Amber shook her head with a glance at Riley. "Good with kids, and a decent cook, but not where I'd put my time."

Tanyth caught the look and stopped pressing. "Good enough, then. We'll get some things ready here while we wait for Sadie." She indicated the hanging material in the rafters. "Let's get all of this down and into the hearth and then we can see what we have."

In a matter of an hour, they cleared the rafters of dried material, and Tanyth stacked it in the corner behind the woodbox. "I'll burn it later tonight when it's a little cooler." She looked around once more, quite satisfied. "I'll go through the stuff on the shelf over there tonight, too, but that's going to be more delicate sorting than this lot." She waved dismissively at the dried goods and then paused. "What time is it getting to be?"

"Lunch time?" Riley's piping voice sounded hopeful.

The two women laughed. "Come along then, light of my life." Amber swept a hand toward the door with a nod to Riley. "I'll find you a bit of crust and some stale water to reward your efforts this morning."

He grinned happily. "Might we have a bit of cheese as well?"

"Only if it's moldy, my dear."

"Sounds yummy, ma." He raced out the door pelting for the Mapleton cottage and shouting for his sister that it was lunch time.

Amber watched him go with a fond expression and turned to Tanyth. "You're welcome to join us for lunch, mum. I promise it won't be crusts of bread and stale water."

Tanyth's stomach growled at that moment, the gurgling sound loud in the quiet hut. "Thank you. That would be lovely, if you're sure you have enough...?"

Amber smiled. "This is harvest season, mum, or near enough. It might be plain fare, but we've plenty for now." She lowered her eyes in embarrassment. "You're delaying your trip to help us. The least we can do is feed you."

Tanyth felt the warmth and a sharp pang inside. She'd been so long on the road, traveling from teacher to teacher, spending a season or so before moving on. It was to be expected. The women she visited seldom had family and were often glad for the company, but the connection was always the knowledge. Tanyth would share what she knew in exchange for whatever knowledge she could gain. More and more, of late, she found herself covering known ground and was anxious to meet Gertie Pinecrest in the far north at Lammas Wood. There were whispers in the night, quiet comments about the Witch Woman and what bits of the Old Knowledge she still carried. Tanyth hungered for that knowledge but this simple need, the small hamlet in need of a healer, the warmth and acceptance these young people gave her, plucked a chord in her that had been still for a very long time.

The thoughts flashed through her mind in a heartbeat, and she smiled at the young woman. "In that case, my dear, let me check on Sadie once more and I'll be honored to join you for lunch."

Amber beamed and the two of them set off for the center of the village, arm-in-arm. They separated at the Mapleton hut and Tanyth went to check on Sadie while Amber prepared luncheon.

Tanyth found Sadie and Megan chatting quietly. Sadie was smiling and had a bit better color but didn't seem too anxious to get up and move about.

Sadie beamed as Tanyth came in. "I heard you'll be staying with us for a few more days, mum."

Tanyth crossed to the cot and pressed a palm against the young woman's forehead before answering. "Yes, it seems that the All-Mother has a small task for me here." She shrugged and smiled. "We'll have to see how long, but at least a few more days." She looked down at the woman in the bed. "How are you feeling, my dear? Any better?"

Sadie nodded gently but stopped almost instantly. "Thank you, mum, I'm on the mend, although I still ache and I can't really seem to get warm."

Tanyth's take on the room was that it was already too warm and stuffy but she nodded to Sadie. "Another dose for you, then, and a long nap this afternoon to get you ready for a good night's sleep tonight."

Tanyth crossed to the hearth and looked in the pot of willow bark. It had been steeping all night and all day so far, so it was undoubtedly going to be exceptionally unpleasant. She nudged the pot closer to the fire to warm it up and stepped out the back door to pull a handful of mint leaves from the clump she'd seen earlier. Adding those to the pot filled the room with the fresh green scent of the mint and in a matter of a few minutes, the tea–willow bark and mint together–was warmed and ready. She fetched the cup and rinsed it carefully with hot water before pouring a healthy dose of the bitter tea into it. Sadie grimaced a bit at the flavor but took the cupful without complaint.

"Are you getting hungry, then, Sadie?" Tanyth asked.

Sadie's response was to turn just slightly green. "I don't think I could eat just yet, mum."

Tanyth smiled. "No, then you shouldn't. When you feel hungry again, that's the sign we're looking for. You'll be on the backside of it and ready to get up. In the meantime, sleep, child. Tomorrow will be here soon enough."

Sadie settled down in her cot, the warm tea having done its work at soothing even if the medicinal properties of the willow hadn't yet taken effect. "That's a good idea, mum. I think I will."

"We're going to take Megan away and let you sleep on your

own now. Will you be all right by yourself, do you think?"

Sadie nodded sleepily. "Yes, mum. That will be fine."

Tanyth nodded to Megan and the two of them left the hut. "You probably have your own work to attend to this afternoon, yeah?"

Megan nodded. "Indeed I do, mum. And thank you."

She smiled in return and gave the younger woman an encouraging nod. They separated, Megan heading to her hut, gathering her children as she went. Tanyth headed for the Mapleton's door and some food that her stomach assured her would be most welcome.

In spite of the fresh breakfast, she missed her morning oatmeal and lunch was a very attractive notion.

CHAPTER 5
AN UNEXPECTED INVITATION

After a light lunch of bread, cheese, and fresh tomatoes from the small patch behind the hut, Tanyth returned to Mother Alderton's to begin the long process of sorting through the jars, crocks, and packets on the shelves. It was a legacy of sorts that belonged to the village, and Tanyth felt drawn to discover what might be useful in the collection. Unlike the dusty, dried materials, which held little value beyond fireplace tinder, these jars and packages might still hold potency, depending on what she found and how it was made.

She spent a pleasant afternoon sorting through the collection and discovered blocks of bee's wax, small crocks of various salves and ointments, as well as a collection of dried and powdered materials. One crock on the floor held sweet olive oil. She also found a couple of bottles of neutral spirits as well as two well sealed bottles of lamp oil. Each jar, bottle, or packet was labeled neatly in a firm–if sometimes thin and spidery–hand. There was even a small alembic for distilling essential oils from various herbs. Tanyth concluded that Mother Alderton could have taught her a lot and she offered a prayer to the All-Mother in the late woman's name.

The shifting light from outside reminded her that the days grew shorter very quickly and that the current one was fading fast. She pulled her bedroll from its lashings under her pack and eyed the cot dubiously. The rope webbing didn't look that comfortable with just a thin bedroll to pad it and she was of half a mind to sleep outdoors when Riley came up to the door and hallooed.

"Mum? I've yer tick here. Ma had me'n the other kids fillin' it up with sweet grass all af'ernoon!"

She looked up to see the boy, surrounded by his pack, dragging a canvas ticking with odd bulges. She smiled at the flushed and sweaty faces. "Thank you, all!" She waved an arm to invite them in.

The small tribe of children–she counted five but it seemed like many more–wrestled the heavy canvas bag of sweet grass through the low doorway and onto the bed frame in the corner. Riley was the largest and eldest by what looked like a year. There were a pair of tow headed twins–a boy and a girl–next in line and then a couple of younger children who regarded her shyly through dark eyes. They were all nut brown and infused with the puppy-like energy of small and healthy children. They were also covered with grass litter and other assorted grimes. Tanyth smiled and remembered her own Robert, fondly this time–without her normal pang of regret.

Riley gave the corner of the straw-filled mattress one last tug into place and smiled up at her. "There you go, mum. Bestest tick in the village!"

"Thank you, Riley. I do appreciate the help you and your friends have given me." Tanyth beamed around at the flushed and sweat smeared faces smiling up at her.

Riley stepped into the silence. "all right, you lot! Out!" He waved his arms toward to the door as if shooing chickens and they all pelted for the open door way. In an instant they whooped and hollered outside, running off toward the barn.

Tanyth smiled to herself and spread her bedroll. She resisted the urge to lie down on it and try it out, half worried that, if she did, she wouldn't get up. The short night and stressful day had conspired to exhaust her. "Soon enough," she thought to herself. "Soon enough."

In the meantime she looked around for the pantry and what she'd been trying to figure out earlier struck her forcefully. There was no apparent pantry or root cellar. The hut itself was practically bereft of any kind of storage, other than what could be hung from the rafters or stacked on the shelving. Naturally anything useful would have been taken out, which raised an additional question about the table, chairs, and oil lamp. Surely those were valuable, but there they sat. She screwed up her mouth in consternation as she peered around the darkening hut. The sun drooped below the tree line in the west, robbing her of needed sunlight. Crossing to the hearth, she laid a pile of the dry and dusty vegetation down, with several small sticks on top. A flint and steel from her pack got the tinder smoldering and soon a small cheery fire shed light on the inside of the hut. Standing on the hearthstone, she spotted an iron ring set into the floor to one side. She crossed to it and pulled open the trap door revealing a hollow in the dirt under a simple door. It looked big enough to store several bushels of root crops. She dropped the door back on its hinge and stepped down the two steps to investigate further. It was noticeably cooler and the floor was lined with coarse river gravel to keep moisture from the bottom of the baskets, when there might be baskets in it. The whole thing was barely 2 yards square and a yard deep, but a clever arrangement of boards under a thin layer of tamped dirt kept it from being obvious when viewed from above. It was, of course, empty. Any food stuffs would have been salvaged first, but it gave Tanyth an idea of just how well thought out these little huts were.

She clambered up the steps and stood there looking at the empty larder, thinking ahead to winter. There was little enough room there to keep tubers from freezing and she wondered if there was enough food to see the village through. The equinox was only a few days away and the hours of daylight would soon be very short. She considered the food in her pack, and what she'd be eating if she were on the road. While walking the byways, she frequently found apples, pears, and berries this time of year. She wasn't above snaring a rabbit or two along the way and she was rather adept at fishing. While she could spend a few coppers to purchase tea and replenish her oatmeal supply at outposts along the road, the All-Mother provided much of what she needed.

She closed the back door of the hut, went to the front and climbed up the steps to the front of the hut. She stood there in the shadows as dusk crept across the vale. A group of men appeared from the narrow track back into the woods. Amber had pointed it out earlier as the path to the clay quarry. It was just wide enough to get the lorry wagon back there to load it. Judging from the looks of the men coming down the trail, clay was a dirty business. They all appeared to be in good spirits, laughing and chatting as they swung along. At the edge of the village they separated, heading for the various huts. Movement on the road caught the corner of her eye as William and the oxcart made a plodding return, the cart heaped with wood.

William's smile flashed white against his sun-stained face and Tanyth was a bit surprised by how quickly dusk had gathered.

"Is everythin' satisfactory, mum?" William called as the cart made its slow way up the path.

"Thank you, William. Very."

He knuckled his forehead in acknowledgment. "If you need anythin', just ask, mum. You're a guest of the village."

She nodded her thanks and the ox pulled the load of wood past and on toward the barn.

She waited and eventually heard the clatter of wood on wood as William dumped the load of firewood from the cart. In the forest surrounding the clearing, Tanyth heard the day birds settling. The soft noises of the wind through the branches died down as sunset progressed. She knew the night wind would begin soon and with it, night birds would begin to call. Standing there, with the sounds of wood and village all around, she found herself caressed by a gentle peace.

She stayed until the night chill began to work through her clothing before stepping back into the hut to pull her heavier, outer coat from the backpack. It wasn't much to look at, but it was mostly waterproof and stopped the wind from stealing her warmth. She checked the hearth once, to make sure the coals were well contained and added a smallish log to the andirons. She needed to check on Sadie and felt a trifle guilty for not having done so sooner.

When she arrived, Tanyth found Sadie up and about, sitting on a stool at the family table while Thomas turned a pair of grouse over the fire. "My goodness, you're not going to eat those, are you, my dear?" Tanyth asked.

Sadie smiled and shook her head. "No, mum. I'm having this nice bit of broth and some bread." She nodded to a heavy earthenware mug on the table along with some crumbs where a loaf might have been. "My poor body isn't ready for grouse yet."

"You're doing well enough to be up and about, then."

The younger woman shook her head. "Not really up yet. Enough to make it to the outhouse, and back. That's about all, mum, but I'm beginnin' to feel more like myself."

Tanyth pressed the back of her hand against Sadie's forehead and found it cool and dry. "Your fever has broken." She nodded to herself. "A good night's sleep and you'll be ready to begin working with us a bit tomorrow."

Sadie looked uneasy. "Do you think I could, mum? Mother Alderton always did for us and she was so smart and clever with her salves and ointments and all..." Her voice trailed off.

Tanyth smiled. "You rest easy on that score, Sadie. We won't deal with anything complicated. Just the simple things that you all should know anyway living way out here on your own like this. At least until you get another healer to join you."

"Do you think we could, mum? Find another healer, I mean?"

"I don't know why not. It's a lovely place and the cottage is very well built. It wouldn't surprise me if somebody didn't come along to fill it."

"Would you do it, mum?" Sadie looked up at her.

"Oh, merciful heavens, child, I'm no healer. I know my limits. I have some rough knowledge from workin' with the plants, but I'm just a poor herbalist."

Sadie looked crestfallen. "Oh." She sighed. "Well, it was worth askin'." She looked up once more. "Thank you, mum, for all you done for me. I knew I wasn't gonna pass on, but it was a might scary there for a time." Her eyes blinked rapidly a couple of times as if she were holding back tears. "Having you come back made a world of difference to all of us."

"You're welcome, my dear. I'm just glad I was able to help." She looked to where Thomas was still turning his grouse and smiled at him. "You take good care of her tonight, Thomas!"

"I will, mum, and thank you. Do I need to give her any more of this tea?" He nodded at the iron pot with the dregs of willow bark.

She shook her head. "No, and that should probably be thrown out and the pot cleaned before you try to cook with it again. It's a trifle bitter and you won't want that in the next pot of soup."

They all laughed and Tanyth headed for the door. "You sleep well tonight, and I'll show you how to scrape willow bark tomorrow."

She slipped out and closed the door behind her. The grouse had looked and smelled delicious, but two grouse were little enough to feed the family without her mooching from them. She sighed. Yes, food was going to be a problem. She needed to get supplied and soon.

Before she'd taken three steps toward Mother Alderton's hut, Riley came pelting out of dusk. "There you are, mum!" He sounded jubilant at having found her, if a bit breathless.

"I am, indeed, young sir." Tanyth smiled at him. "And now that I'm found...?"

There was an answering flash of white in the dim light as he smiled back. "Ma says you could come to dinner wif us, if'n you've a mind, mum."

"Would you like that, Riley?"

"Oh, yes, mum. It's a treat havin' company for dinner." He fairly wriggled with excitement.

"Well, then I accept. Lead on, young sir. Lead on."

He turned and walked toward the Mapleton hut, glancing over his shoulder now and again as if to see if she was keeping up. Inside the hut was an island of warmth and light in the gathering chill of evening. Amber and William looked up as Riley led her into the cottage and both smiled to see her.

"See, ma? I found her!" Riley's voice carried proud triumph as if there'd been some doubt.

"I see that, Riley. Now go wash your hands. Dinner's ready and I'm hungry." She smiled at her little one as he scurried out the back door to wash up.

William chuckled as he rose to greet Tanyth. "In one door and out the other, that one." He gave a little nod in her direction. "Thank you for comin', mum."

Tanyth nodded back. "Thank you for askin'. I was just wondering about my supplies. Perhaps you two can advise me."

He waved her into a seat as Riley belted back in from the back and took his seat beside a sleepy looking sister. Tanyth smiled at the little girl who grinned back with eyes down cast.

Amber brought earthenware bowls of a rich smelling stew of venison and root crops, liberally sprinkled with fresh cut chives. She sat bowls in front of each of them, and then unwrapped a loaf of fresh yeast bread. As she settled in her place she gave a little nod to William who spoke loudly and sincerely. "Thank you, All-Mother and All-Father for the bounty you've provided and the protections you've extended. We thank the Guardian of the North for protecting the land. We thank the Guardian of the East for the blessing of the air. We thank the Guardian of the South for the fire in our hearth and the Guardian of the West for clean water and the blessed rains that nourish our crops. Blessed be."

In the heart beat that followed, Amber and the children repeated, "Blessed be." Tanyth added her own belated, "Blessed be." It had been a long time since she'd heard a formal prayer and the rhythm of it soothed her.

The children quivered over their spoons but waited for Tanyth, as honored guest, to take the first morsel. She smiled and tasted her stew, releasing them from their bonds of etiquette to pounce on their suppers like the small, hungry animals they were. It was a rich broth, flavorful with meat and vegetables, and Tanyth found herself three spoons in before she knew it.

"Amber, this is wonderful stew!" Tanyth smiled to her hostess and accepted a thick slab of warm, crusty bread to go with it.

Amber beamed with pride. "Thank you, mum."

William grinned at his wife in some secret communion, and they shared a short laugh. Tanyth didn't ask and they didn't offer, but she suspected that a goldsmith's daughter didn't learn to cook at her mother's apron strings. Her mind filled in a lot of possibilities involving fires, iron pots, and meals gone awry.

They ate in a comfortable silence for a time, giving proper attention to the hot stew and warm bread, washing it down with fresh water. Tanyth had been on the road long enough that the settled meal tasted very good.

William broke the silence. "Supplies? How can we help, mum?" He turned his intense brown eyes on her.

She sat back on her stool, suddenly aware that she'd been shoveling the stew almost as fast as young Riley. "When I travel, I can only take what I can carry." She looked back and forth between them. "I normally restock my tea and some dried grains as I pass through the various villages along the way and the All-Mother provides nicely, especially this time of year, so I don't need to carry much." She nodded at the bowl in front of her. "Meat like this isn't something I see a lot of while traveling, nor yeast bread." She smiled at Amber. "It's wonderful and I thank you for supper."

"You're most welcome, mum. Thank you for taking time from your journey to help us."

Tanyth turned back to William. "I expected there to be a village somewhere along here–an established one–where I could buy a bit of tea and some oatmeal, perhaps some raisins or dried apple."

William's look turned inward as he thought. "Fox Run is about five days on toward Kleesport. You must have come through Mablesboro last week sometime."

"Such as it was, yes." Tanyth agreed. "Lovely little village and the innkeeper brews a fine ale." She smiled as she remembered the innkeeper's reticence about selling ale to a woman, but didn't mention it, or the episode with her staff on his instep when he got a mite too friendly. In the end a few coppers worth of ale had tasted fine with her meal of roasted pork and potatoes, and the innkeeper's lovely wife nodded approvingly as Tanyth donned her hat and pack and struck out once more. "There are lots of things to eat along the way, and streams full of fresh water and fat trout, if you know where to look."

"Sounds like you've got this down to an art, mum." William said.

"Well, I've been doing it for a long time. If I hadn't learned how to travel well by now, I'd still be back in Fairport." She smiled, her tone faintly self-mocking. "My first few years on the road were somewhat less successful than they might be now." She grinned at him. "Tender feet, sore shoulders, and peelin' skin were constant companions for quite a while."

Amber spoke up. "So, what is it you do, mum? If you don't mind me askin'...? I mean I know you travel and learn from herbalists, but how does that work exactly?"

Tanyth shrugged. "It's nothing set in stone, my dear. I started on the road with Mother Agnes Dogwood in Fairport. I spent a season with her and learned the basics. She knew of a woman who specialized in blackberry who lived in Shreeve. So, after a couple of letters back and forth, I arranged to spend a few months with her. She knew a woman further down the road who knew more than everything about burdock and cattail, and I wintered over with her. She was getting on and needed help through the colder months. In the spring I moved on to the next, then the next. It's been going on twenty winters now. Seems like I've always been on my way somewhere, all that time." She smiled at the two of them. "Now, I'm a tough old boot and heading up to the northland to meet with somebody that I've heard tales about but never thought to meet. Gertie Pinecrest is her name. She's a legend down south for what she knows about medicinal plants and their uses."

William shook his head. "Never heard of her."

"I suspect not. She's not well known outside of the small circle." Tanyth shrugged a shoulder. "No reason for you to know her. I thought she was a story myself for the longest time and then I met a woman who'd learned from her." Tanyth stopped herself from saying much more about that. Barbara Myerston had been a bit frightening in her abilities, vigorously competent and seemingly tapped into an unseen world that gave her amazing insights that she'd never talk about, even to Tanyth.

"So, she's expecting you, mum? This Mother Pinecrest?"

William asked.

Tanyth made a grimace. "No, actually. Mother Myerston sent me north with directions on how to find her. I need to ask in person if she'll take me as a student. Maybe she will and maybe she won't." Tanyth shrugged.

Amber's eyes got wide. "You mean you'll go all that way and not know if it's worthwhile? What if she won't take you as a student?"

"Well, the trip is always worthwhile. I get to meet so many charmin' people like you all along the way." She paused to beam at the small family, and saw that the girl had actually fallen asleep in her seat, head lolling back and mouth slightly open, while Riley stared wide-eyed, apparently enraptured by her story. "But I could get up there and have to turn around and come back, yes."

"Does she turn people away?" William asked with a small frown.

"I don't know. All I know is that she's supposed to be one of the keepers of the old lore, back from the earliest days when the world was filled with magic." She shrugged, embarrassed, and looked back and forth between the two adults. "That's what they say, anyway. I've studied with many of the very best herbalists in the land and they all hold Mother Pinecrest in the highest regard. So, I'm going to go try to find her, learn what I can, and then, maybe settle down somewhere and write up all I've learned about herbs and medicinals before I start to forget it myself."

"But if you get up there, and she turns you away with winter closing in, you'll be stuck up there." His voice carried a press of worry. "That's a harsh land. I've visited it more than once and it's no place to be when the snow starts piling up."

"It's not an ideal situation, but Mother Pinecrest is gettin' on. I'm afraid to wait too long for fear that she'll pass over before I've had a chance to meet her." She shook her head. "I have to get there and soon."

Amber's frown looked concerned and her eyes pleaded with her husband across the table. He gave a small nod in reply. He took a deep breath. "Mum? Would you consider wintering here with us?"

Tanyth cocked her head to one side. "Winter here?"

William nodded slowly with a glance at his wife who returned the nod. "Mother Alderton's cottage is available for you. None here would gainsay your staying, and you'd have a snug place to stay. We could surely use your knowledge here. Mother Alderton was called home before her time and before she could pass on much of what she knew."

"Before she realized she needed to, most like." Amber looked somber. "She was a dear lady and I miss her sorely."

"There are a couple of empty cottages, actually, mum. If you don't fancy staying in Mother Alderton's?" William didn't say it but the implication that she might not want to live in the house where the previous dear lady had died in her bed was clear in his face.

"It's a lovely little house." Tanyth assured him. "Marvelously built. Was that your doing, William?"

He colored, embarrassed by the praise, but nodded. "Yes, mum. I used to work in my da's ship yard when I was a boy. He wanted me to learn the business from the bottom up. I never got much beyond planking hulls before it became obvious that the business was going to go to my older brothers, Stephen and Richard. They were grooming me to be foreman, I think, but..." His voice trailed off. "It's not what I really wanted. Much as I like makin' the boats, runnin' the shipyard and dealing with the shippin' isn't somethin' I really wanted for myself."

"And they didn't like that we married in spite of them." Amber added.

"Well, you're worth any two shipyards, my heart." He smiled at her across the table. "And besides, we've these to consider." He nodded at the two kids. "They'll do better to make their own way than to wait on scraps from the high table." Returning to the subject in question, he looked up at the roof trees. "Anyway, I figured if it would keep the water out of the ships, then it would probably keep the water off our heads. I just planked the roofs as if they were hulls. It was a lot easier because I didn't need to bend the planks to make them fit. Just tight pegs with oakum and pitch in the seams.

Thomas and the others laughed at me at the time, but they appreciate not having to replace thatching every year."

"You built all theses houses at once? That must have taken quite a crew."

He nodded. "Yes, mum, well, it took almost all of one summer. We came out in the fall and felled the trees, clearing the land and pulling stumps. It's amazing what ten men and an ox can do when they've a mind. We camped rough and worked from sun up to sun down from Harvest Moon to nearly mid winter."

"How did you afford it?" Tanyth blurted the question before she realized it might not be the most polite one.

William just grinned. "One of the things about being a rich kid, mum. My father was happy to pay us off to get out of his hair, and we sell the clay to one of his companies. He makes a profit on it."

"Do you have to pay him back?" Tanyth was totally unfamiliar with how rich people lived so the idea drew her into areas that she might not have ventured in other circumstances.

Amber grinned. "We already have."

William nodded with a satisfied smile. "We're not beholden to anybody at the moment, mum. What we have is ours, so long as we hold it. Got the paperwork filed with the King's Commissioner in Kleesport and everythin'."

They ate quietly for a few moments before Amber spoke again. "Our parents, and I'm sure a lot of the people who came out here with us, Sadie and Thomas's folks, they thought we'd get out here and 'play house' for a while until we got sick or cold or tired of it and then head back to town with our tails between our legs beggin' for shelter." There was a tone of quiet bitterness to her voice. She didn't look up while she spoke.

"But you didn't." Tanyth was matter-of-fact in her statement.

Amber didn't look up. "Not yet anyway." She didn't sound very enthusiastic.

William looked at her across the table. "We're not going to." There was a bit of heat in his voice.

"Why would you, Amber?" Tanyth directed the question at the young woman and turned her head away from William.

She sighed and looked up. "It gets harder each year, mum. When Mother Alderton passed, I thought we were done for, but we muddled through. But when Sadie got sick and nobody knew what to do..."

Tanyth reached over to pat the younger woman's arm. "She'd have survived. It was just the flux." She said it softly and caught the younger woman's eyes in hers. "She's a strong girl and it wasn't like I did anything at all but make her a little more comfortable. She got better on her own."

Amber looked like she wanted to believe but she shook her head. "Your being here helped. Just being here."

"Perhaps, my dear. Perhaps. But that's a long way from giving up your dream. What made you say that?" She paused and when the younger woman didn't respond, pressed a bit more. "Not yet? Is somethin' else goin' on?"

Amber glanced at William before answering. "Frank hasn't come back with the wagon and team yet."

William clanked his spoon against his bowl a bit harder than he needed to.

Amber turned to him. "You can sit there and say 'Any day now,' William Mapleton, but what if something's happened to him or if he's run off with the money and the horses?"

Tanyth looked to him with a raised eyebrow.

"Well, if he's run off, then we'll have to try to rent a team for the rest of the season and then see where we are in the spring." William kept his voice low and reasonable sounding but there was a tightness in it. "If something's happened to him, then we'll have to deal with that, too." He sighed and turned to Tanyth. "He's never been this late on his return. A few days now and again. Once one of the horses threw a shoe. One time the factor was late settling up in Kleesport." He shrugged. "If something happened to the lorry wagon, then he might be delayed getting it repaired. One of the horses might have gone lame. Any number of things could be keeping him and he's only a bit more than a week over due."

Amber sighed and the anger seeped out of her. "You're right, husband. I know you're right, but I can't help worryin'." She turned to Tanyth. "He's bringin' back a load of grain and dried goods for our winter stockpile. If he doesn't get back, we don't have enough food to get through the winter."

William grimaced and shook his head. "Maybe, maybe not. We have a forest full of game that hasn't been over hunted and it'll be weeks yet before snow flies. Bester won't like it but he can make the trip to town if need be. We only need to get to Fernsvale to buy grain, and the potato and turnip crops are going to be very good this year." William considered before speaking further. "We're not going to starve. Not this winter. Last winter, it might have been different, but we've plenty and then some." He grinned. "It might get a bit boring by spring, but we'll be fed."

Tanyth dunked a crust of bread into her stew and savored it before responding. "Yet you're willin' to take on another mouth by invitin' me to winter over?"

William shrugged. "I see it as one more productive member of our community, mum. One who has the knowledge to keep the rest of us going and healthy."

Amber nodded. "I do, too. As William says, I'm being too hasty in this. He's right. Our food stocks right now are much higher than we had last winter, and we still have a few months to gather." She sighed and shrugged. "And Frank could be back tomorrow with the team."

Tanyth finished her stew, cleaning the inside of the bowl with the last bit of her bread before popping the savory into her mouth. "So, worst case, he's run off and taken your money with him?"

William shook his head. "No, our money is all safe in Kleesport. There's nothing to spend it on out here. He'll bring back a few coins but the majority of our funds stay in the bank in Kleesport. He's authorized to purchase goods for us, but almost all out money stays in the vault there. The accountants keep it straight and we don't get robbed out here."

"What if the accountants steal your golds?"

"Then the vault-keeper has to deal with the King's Own. They take it pretty personally. The King wants his tithe. He can't get it from stolen money. Besides, we're too small to worry about and we pay our accountant well to keep our affairs in order. The alternative is to keep the money here and we can't protect it here. As long as we're poor, nobody will bother us."

Tanyth eyed Amber and the look wasn't lost on William.

He sighed. "If we're attacked, everybody runs into the woods and hides. It's not much, but it's all we have unless we go back to town and cower behind the city walls."

Tanyth made a sideways nod, granting him the point. "At least you've thought that far ahead."

"We're right off the road, mum. Not that many dastardly people travel the Pike. There are too many chances to be spotted by one of the King's Own, and too much trouble brings them down from Kleesport or up from Easton. You were walking the Pike alone, mum. You know what it's like better'n us, I suspect."

Tanyth granted him that point as well. "Well, then. Let me sleep on it over night and I'll give you my decision in the morning. What are the terms?"

"Terms, mum?" William seemed surprised by the question.

"Terms, sir. Will you expect rent? How much support can I count on from the village? I haven't been here to contribute to the larders so how much will I be able to draw? That sort of thing?"

Amber spoke softly but it was evident that she meant every word. "Mum, Mother Alderton was a full member of our little family. She drew what she needed and gave back much more than she ever took. We can't put a price on that in terms of so many stones of barley, so many bushels of potatoes."

"But I'm not Mother Alderton, Amber. I'm just a little, old woman who's wandered too far from home."

Amber smiled. "You're a tough old boot with a lot of wear left on the sole, and I mean no disrespect in sayin' that, mum. If you'll stay and help us this winter, teach us what we need to know to keep going, and just do what you think you can, you can draw what you need from the stores and we'll gladly share whatever we have with you."

William looked shocked at his wife's plain speaking, but Tanyth's mouth twitched in an involuntary grin. "Very well, then. I think I know what I'm up against." Her face softened into a smile as she noted that both the children had fallen asleep in a huddled pile. "I think they have the right idea. Thank you for dinner, but now I need to go to Mother Alderton's cottage and sleep on it."

William and Amber both rose, but William was the first to speak. "Of course, mum."

"Thank you, sir, for a most interestin' and enlightenin' evenin'."

He grinned and knuckled his forehead. "Thank you, mum, for your kindness and consideration."

She turned to Amber and surprised the younger woman by giving her a close embrace. "Bless you, child."

Outside, night had fallen almost completely. Only a faint, ruddy glow showed over the tops of the trees to the west and the nearly full moon peeked through the treetops to the east. She crossed her arms against the chilly night air, heavier coat or not. She crossed the village with a few, rapid steps, the night sounds from the surrounding forest keeping her company. A woman's laugh from one of the huts behind her punctuated the sigh of wind in the tree tops.

She stopped at her door and turned to survey the tiny hamlet. "You could do worse, old woman." She murmured it to the night, but the words echoed inside her. "You could do worse." The cold struck though her then, and an owl called from the spruces. She slipped the latch and entered the hut, closing the door carefully behind her.

CHAPTER 6
DECISIONS

The short night followed by a long and stressful day put Tanyth in a mood to find her bedroll. A belly full of rich, warm food and the snug security of the cozy hut added to her body's demand for rest. She checked the fire and banked the few remaining coals against the back of the hearth, adding a smallish log to maintain the fire overnight. In her last moments of awareness, she rummaged in her pack for her meager supply of oatmeal and her tiny cooking pot, added some water from the bucket and settled it on the hearth where it could cook slowly while she slept. Her bedroll called her then and she sank into slumber even as her body sank into the luxurious sweet grass tick.

Her dreams that night were shapeless but haunted by the image of a great tree, its leaves flowing smoothly from lush green to a brilliant scarlet that faded to the glossy wet color of blood. They dripped from the branches to pool on the ground and soak into the soil. Those remaining on the tree turned a scabrous brown and cascaded faster and faster, piling up in a drift to protect the roots and no longer melting into the soil. The falling leaves revealed stark, forking branches, first in small glimpses and then in larger areas. Finally the tree stood exposed and, with it, a small bird perched near the bole, protected from the elements by the body of the tree itself. As the last of the leaves dropped from the tips of the branches, snow began to fall. It touched the branches, highlighting them in black and white against the gray winter sky even while it covered the ground, laying a blanket of glistening white over the leafy brown cloak at the base of the tree. The bird fluffed out its feathers and stood revealed as a small owl with bands of black and brown across its wings and rings of ruddy orange around brilliant onyx eyes. As the night wore on, so did the procession of seasons in her dream until the snow gave way to stripes of warming sun and gentle rains that washed the snowy blanket away to expose tender grass even as the bare, black branches grew fuzzy tips. The owl turned to face her in her dream and hooted a drawn out who-who-whooo. The last long whooo blended into a raucous cock-a-doodle-doo in her ears. It pulled her out of the dream and back to reality.

She lay there in her bedroll, momentarily disoriented by a roof over her head even as she lay warmly swathed in the bedroll she associated with an open sky. As memory returned, the image of black limbs against gray skies faded in her mind even as the sound of an owl's low call echoed in her ears. She sighed, blinked herself fully awake, and forced her body out of the warm cocoon of blankets. The fire demanded her attention as the chill, morning air scrubbed at her bed-warmed body. She found a few spikes of cattail to put on the coals and blew life back into the nearly dead fire, adding a few small sticks to fuel the blaze. She weighed the luxury of using the ceramic pot beneath the bed against the more practical notion of slipping on her boots and heading for the privy. Boots won and she scampered across the compound in the magical light of morning to deal with the much more mundane issue of bladder.

On her way back to the hut, the rooster's call from somewhere near the barn cut the still morning air once more. As the raucous sound echoed down the hollow, Tanyth heard the low call of an owl seeming to answer from the copse of spruces behind the village. The sound was almost identical to the who-who-whooo from her dream. It sent a shiver down her spine as the eeriness of the haunting sound echoed in her mind even as it faded in the pale dawn's growing light. "Very well, All-Mother. I got the message." She muttered it under her breath even as she grinned at herself for doing it.

She returned to the cottage and stoked up the fire to boil water for tea and to warm her oatmeal a bit faster. She stood, basking in the heat and listening to the sounds of the village coming awake. For the most part it was quiet, but the occasional clank of pot hook reached through the stout walls. She could practically feel the quickening of the world around her as the light of morning grew in intensity through the narrow outlines of her doors.

As she was finishing her breakfast, she heard the steady plodding of the ox and the crunch of solid wheels on the gravel of the track. She tossed back the last of her tea and scooped the last few grains of oat from the dish before rising and slipping out into the morning once more. The trees still hid the rising sun, but the morning had reached a fullness where the warming rays would arrive momentarily. William led the ox down the path toward the Pike and waved to her as she crossed to intercept him at the path.

"I accept." Tanyth said the two words quickly without any preamble of greeting.

William smiled. "I'm glad, mum. Amber will be pleased as well." He didn't stop walking and Tanyth fell into step beside him.

"Do you really think somethin' has happened to Frank and the team?" She asked. "Just between us?"

He blew out a sigh. "I can't help but worry that it has. He's never been this late, but so many simple things could have delayed him by ten days. Innocent things. Problems with a wheel. A horse with colic. Even a delay with the factor purchasin' the clay." He shook his head. "I hate to borrow trouble, mum, but we're gettin' to the point where it's more likely that somethin' unfortunate has happened." He returned her sideways glance with a shrug. "Short of sendin' somebody to find him, all we can do is wait it out."

"Thank you, William. I appreciate your honesty." She raised a hand in farewell and turned her steps back to the hut.

She pondered the implications of the overdue wagon, even as she focused on the immediate issues facing the morning. She'd used the last of her willow bark for Sadie and needed to go through her pack to inventory what she had left. She'd planned to get heavier winter clothing in Kleesport but that schedule was already delayed. She could be in Kleesport in ten days and the next village in three but it would be nearly a month round trip to the larger city on foot and the better part of a week to the village, assuming she could get what she needed there to begin with. She sighed and unceremoniously emptied her pack onto the smoothed surface of the bed roll and began sorting supplies from clothing and tools.

By the time the sun had fully cleared the treetops, she'd sorted out the meager pile and made a mental list of the things she'd need. Her boots would need re-oiling to keep them waterproof and supple, but the leather was still solid and the stitching sound enough for the coming season. She needed some warmer outer wear and a couple of sets of the longer pants to go under her normal walking around pairs. The pants themselves were baggy and styled after the many pocketed pants worn by tinkers to hold tools and bric-a-brac. A few evenings with some suitable fabric and she could line them against the wind and weather. Her lifestyle had kept her lean, almost bony, with hard muscles in narrow bands on her legs and belly. Adding another layer of fabric inside the pants would be no great difficulty. Age had still spread her hips–she grinned ruefully at that–and gravity had worked its inevitable course on her torso, but the bandeau she normally wrapped around her chest kept her cargo from shifting and helped disguise her while on the road by compressing her breasts against her rib cage. Considering the unpleasant chafing of the dangling alternatives, she found the binding to be more comfortable.

She checked her belt knife and pocketed a few items–a roll of bandage, a bit of aloe stalk, and a steel and flint. Small and lightweight, they could make a difference if need arose.

She took one last survey of her food stocks, she sucked air through her teeth, grabbed her staff and planted her hat on her head. The day was wasting and she needed to find some willow bark and fresh burdock, perhaps locate some stands of cattail and wild rose as well. The sun had burned the dew from the grass by the time she made her way across the compound toward Amber's hut. She met young Riley along the way. He fell into step with her.

"Ma sent me to see if'n you were all right, mum." He grinned up at her. "Are ya?"

"I am quite all right, Riley. Thank you for askin'. Do you know how Sadie is this mornin'? Is she ready to go gatherin'?"

He wriggled in what might have been a shrug, might have been a shake, and might have been just his excitement at the thought of gathering. "She seemed all right to me, mum, but you can ask her your own self. She's with ma."

Tanyth couldn't help but be amused by him and they strode along in silence.

At the hut, Riley opened the door and ushered her into the snug confines of Amber's cottage where she found a much improved Sadie and a rather flushed looking Amber tidying up the hearth and table while Riley's sister sat under the table apparently playing house with a bedraggled corn-husk doll.

The women looked up as Tanyth entered and both smiled a warm greeting. Amber spoke first. "Good morning, mum."

"Good morning, Amber. Hello, Sadie. Are you feeling better today?"

"Right as rain, mum. Thank you. Amber says you're going to take us gathering this morning?"

"If you're up to it. Gatherin' willow bark isn't very difficult nor does it require much skill more than bein' able to pick out the willows from the poplars and oaks." She smiled, aware as soon as she said it that the two city bred women may well not be able to tell an oak from a poplar, an ash from a hickory. She sighed inwardly and hoped she was wrong. "All we need is something to cut the willow with."

Sadie held up a small saw. "Will this do?"

"Perfect. We can save time by grabbing a limb rather than cutting the bits off out there and bringing them home." Tanyth was pleased by the young woman's initiative.

Amber finished her immediate tasks and looked around brightly. "I think we're ready, mum. Where are we goin'?"

Tanyth chewed her lip a moment in thought.

"Willows like wet feet. Is there a place where there's ground that's always damp?"

Sadie nodded. "Yes, mum, just up the path to the quarry. There's a patch that's always muddy. They had to put in logs to keep the path from turnin' into a muck hole."

"That sounds like a good place to start." Tanyth looked about at the smiling faces. "Shall we go?"

Amber dropped off her younger daughter to play with Megan's three while they were gathering and the four of them headed up the path toward the clay quarry. The rough road was easier going than forcing a path into the forest proper. Tanyth kept her eyes moving, looking for side paths and game trails. Deer would use this path if they could, she knew. Smaller game as well and it might be useful to have a brace of rabbits for her own stewpot.

As they walked through the woods, Tanyth explained what they were looking for. "Any kind of willow will do. Black willow, white, even weeping willows and catkins."

"Catkins?" Riley's voice squeaked. "Catkins are willows?"

Tanyth nodded and smiled down at the boy's upturned face. "Indeed they are. A kind of willow and the bark is as good as any other." Privately she thought it might be better because the small withes of catkin yielded a good amount of the pale inner bark and left a strong, straight, and pliable stick that was useful in a variety of ways.

They walked perhaps a quarter mile along the path before it dipped down to a swale. A bit of corduroy work on the track kept their feet from getting mucky and a stand of white willows grew on a hummock just south of the road. The pale hairs that gave the willow its name still coated the leaves and several strong trunks grew in a clump.

Tanyth pointed out a likely limb with the foot of her staff. "That branch that's growing into the grove? Prune it off close to the trunk and we'll take that. It'll make the stand healthier."

Sadie picked her way across the muddy ground but Riley bulled through the muck, apparently delighting in the squelchy sounds beneath his feet. Tanyth could feel Amber cringe at the damage he might be doing to his footwear but she soon relaxed as his enthusiastic enjoyment infected them all.

Before she applied her saw to the tree Sadie turned to Tanyth. "Do you wanna say a prayer first, mum? Invoke the spirits of the forests or somethin'?"

"We're doing the work of the All-Mother here, Sadie. I'm pretty sure she knows we're taking what we need and using what we take. Pruning that limb out of the inside of the stand will leave them better than when we found."

Sadie looked up at the trees around her. "Still, mum? If you wouldn't mind?" Sadie stood waiting and even Amber looked on expectantly.

Tanyth shrugged and turned to the north, raising her arms dramatically. She felt a little foolish but if Sadie wanted a prayer, she intended it to be a good one. "Guardian of the North, know we work to make the Earth we share more fruitful." She pivoted smoothly to her right to face the east. "Guardian of the East, the air will move more freely between the trunks as we remove this branch that blocks your passage." She pivoted to the south, not feeling so foolish any more. A growing warmth expanded in her belly. "Guardian of the South, by taking this branch we honor the spirit of the willow to harvest the healing medicines provided by the All-Mother in this growing thing." She turned to the west and finished the circuit. "Guardian of the West, may the healing power of water flow more easily through these trees as we remove this branch for our use." Tanyth faced the north once more and, lowering her arms, planted the foot of her staff on the ground. "So mote it be." As if in answer a raven cawed loudly from the top of a spruce on the ridge above, startling them all a little. She could see the black bird outlined against the sky as it perched somewhat precariously on the fir tree.

When she turned back, everyone stared at her. She had a hard time deciding who looked the most astonished. They all regarded her with round, staring eyes and a slack-jawed wonder. Riley recovered first.

"Whoosh, mum, when you does a prayer, you don't mess about, do ya."

His innocent exclamation broke the spell and the women laughed at his piping pronouncement. Tanyth's laughter joined the rest, all of them sounding just a bit brittle. Tanyth's body still vibrated from her effort and she felt a bit flushed and more winded than simply saying a few words might account for. The warmth in her belly flowed through her and a sense of well-being accompanied it.

On the hummock a few feet away, Sadie placed the blade of the saw against the edge of the tree and with a few swift strokes took the limb. It was only an inch or so at the base but long and spindly from working between the trunks of the other trees. With Riley's help, she extricated the awkward shape out of the copse and together they dragged it back to the road. The base of the branch was woody and dense but the length of the branch showed a good progression with many branchings and tips of first year growth that promised a fat layer of inner bark. Tanyth nodded and smiled. "Yes, this will do nicely."

"How many more do we need, mum?" Sadie was about to head back to the hummock.

"Just the one. It'll serve our purposes for teaching you how to do it and probably give enough bark for the village for the whole winter." Tanyth eyed it once more, measuring and gauging with her eye. "Yes, I think this will be more than enough." She looked back at the small grove and then cast a glance at the spruce where the raven still perched. "One more thing to do here and we can head back. Riley? Can you get a handful of that sticky mud?" She used her staff to point to a place in the ground where their feet had exposed a rather black looking slurry of mucky ground.

Riley looked at her as if she were mad and then looked at his mother for permission.

Amber nodded and shrugged.

With a very boyish grin and great enthusiasm he scooped up a double handful, digging his fingers into the soft, cold soil and holding up this clod of muck as if it were a golden prize.

Tanyth nodded approvingly. "Very good! Now plaster that on the cut on the tree, if you would? Make a nice covering for where we cut her."

He had trouble figuring out how to apply the mud at first but eventually went with a "slap it on and pat it down" approach. He had to stretch up to reach the cut and mucky water rolled back down his arm. He laughed as the chilly, messy liquid tickled his skin. Eventually he had it covered to his satisfaction and stepped back to admire his handiwork.

"Will that help, mum?" Amber asked.

Tanyth shrugged. "Some. Better than nothin'. It'll keep the tree from losing too much sap until the winter stops the roots and it should protect the exposed wood from vermin that might like to feed on it. I don't expect it will last through the first good storm, but in a few days, the tree itself will begin healing over. In the meantime, she has a little protection."

Sadie and Amber exchanged a glance as if to say, "We must remember this." Amber lifted the lightweight branch and handed it to Riley. He balanced it and was careful to carry it so that it didn't drag on the ground as his solid little legs began the short walk back to the village.

Amber smiled a mother's smile and the two younger women fell in behind the boy, leaving Tanyth to walk behind.

CHAPTER 7
SECOND THOUGHTS

After helping them scrape the bark from the willow limb, Tanyth showed them how to spread it on a clean cloth in a sheltered area to dry. She charged Riley with stirring and turning the long scraps of bark periodically. With the first task completed, Tanyth left them to return to her hut. The morning had not been without its share of surprises, but the odd feelings coursing through her during the prayer had taken her by surprise.

She sighed and continued on to her cottage for a cup of tea. She could have had a cup with Amber and Sadie, but decided she wanted to be alone for a time to think about what had happened in the woods. That something had happened was beyond her doubt, but what the something might have been was still open to interpretation. She hoped to examine it, in private, to see if she could make sense of her feelings.

Second thoughts about her decision to stay swirled in her mind. Twenty years of being on the road had trained her to solitude and the constant hubbub of being around people was beginning to tell on her already. They were very nice people, and the children were a delight that she'd almost forgotten, but she could only take them in small doses. She felt prickly and needed to find some quiet for a time. She worked hard to convince herself that it would be all right and that being around people–even as few people as there were in the village–would become commonplace, even enjoyable.

"In a pig's eye." She muttered to herself again. It was a long standing habit, this talking to herself, and not one she approved of.

She stomped around the corner of her hut, headed for the door when she saw the six horse team and lorry wagon making the turn into the hamlet from the Pike. An older man wearing a wide-brimmed hat and homespun shirt under a leather vest coaxed the team along and Tanyth shaded her eyes with her hand to get a better look as he drove the team up the path. The village erupted around her.

A pack of children seemed to spring up from the ground and the women folk in the hamlet all appeared to come out at once. Tanyth saw Amber and Sadie running down the lane toward the team, but they slowed their approach before they spooked the horses. Sadie beamed but Amber looked concerned even as the man who must be Frank raised a hand in salute.

Sadie stopped beside the track but Amber continued on to walk beside the lorry and speak with Frank. Tanyth couldn't make out the words but she saw Frank shake his head several times and point to the back of the wagon. Amber nodded in response and finally smiled. Frank never stopped the team but let it plod its way along the track to the barn. Women and children fell in alongside or followed along behind. Eventually the assembly disappeared behind the huts and Tanyth stood alone once more.

She turned to her hut and was startled by the large raven sitting on the ridgepole of the house, apparently staring down at her. It mantled its wings and cawed hoarsely at her once before turning and launching itself toward the wood behind her cabin.

Tanyth felt a thin shiver but waved a hand in the air as if to dispel smoke or a bothersome fly. "Don't be foolish, old woman. It's a raven." She was irked with herself for being startled, and entered the hut. She crossed to the hearth and prodded it roughly to life, fanning the coals with her hat, and tossing a few handfuls of dried catnip onto the embers, followed by a few sticks of dry wood. In moments, the fire crackled cheerfully. She filled her small kettle from the bucket and set it to warm by the fire and tried not to think about the raven.

She did step out of the hut once, just to get a bit of air, and felt silly being relieved that the large bird hadn't returned to the roof. She took a deep breath and let it out slowly. She shook her head at her own unease but her doubts about staying in the village returned. "Maybe you are going crazy, you old fool." She went back into the hut and made sure the door was closed firmly behind her.

She wanted her tea, and perhaps she'd finish the bit of hard cheese for lunch. She vowed to take her snares into the forest and see if the All-Mother would grant her a rabbit or two for the morrow. She felt crabby and hated the feeling but the sense of longing to be back on the road was almost palpable.

In the end, she brewed a pot of chamomile instead of her favored black tea and let the soothing aroma and gentle tea comfort her while she sat cross legged on her bedroll and nursed herself through a case of the crabbies. It was almost under control when she heard somebody approach the door then a soft knock. She thought about pretending she wasn't there, but realized that they'd probably just open the door and see her sitting on the bed anyway.

"Who is it?" She worked hard to keep her voice neutral and calm.

"Sadie, mum. I've brought you some fresh bread and cheese."

Regret for her uncharitable feelings washed over her as she realized that she was the one being unreasonable. "Come in, Sadie. It's open."

Sadie slipped the latch and walked down the two steps carrying a rough basket of split twigs even as Tanyth stood up from the cot. "Oh, I'm sorry, mum! Were you resting?" Sadie looked quite contrite.

Tanyth found a genuine smile somewhere and shook her head, holding up the cup of tea. "Just having a little tea and a think, my dear."

Sadie looked relieved and crossed to the table, placing her basket upon it. "I set an extra loaf to bake this mornin' before we left and there's a nice piece of cheese for you, mum." She smiled at Tanyth. "Thank you for your help this mornin'. It really is somethin' we should have done for ourselves. If we'd thought about it at all, we certainly could have."

"I'm glad I can help, Sadie." Tanyth was surprised to discover that she meant it. "And thank you for the bread and cheese. That was very thoughtful of you."

Sadie gave a little half curtsy, half bow. "It's the least we can do for you, mum." She glanced around the still almost empty hut. "I'll just leave you to your thinkin' now, mum. I need to get back to my own work." She scurried out the door and gave a little wave before closing it behind her, rattling it once to make sure it was firmly latched.

Tanyth stood there and shook her head in wonderment. She wasn't sure how she felt about the reverence they seemed to hold her in. On the other hand, she had to admit it wasn't much different from the feelings she had about all the women she'd studied with over the years. She was on her way to see the one above all, the one that all the others mentioned in reverential whispers. Just at the moment, she felt a bit like an impostor on the wrong side of reverence.

The smell of the fresh bread drew her to the table where she discovered a loaf of yeast bread and a small round of soft cheese in a damp cloth. Her mouth was instantly awash and she used her belt knife to slice off two fat slabs of bread, added a bit of the cheese and then toasted them over the coals using a stalk of dried rosemary from the cast-off pile until the cheese began to melt into the bread. She almost burned her mouth on it, but it tasted divine.

With her belly full and the chamomile working its soothing magic on her jangled nerves, she felt a bit less antisocial than she had before lunch. For the first time since arriving, she felt no urgent need to do something, other than clean the cheese from her belt knife and re-wrap the food. She left it on the table and contemplated refilling her tea cup, but decided that one more cup of chamomile would put her to sleep. Instead she found her snares and put her earlier plan into motion. Clapping her hat on her head and taking up her staff, she slipped out the back door of the hut and crossed the weedy open area to the woods beyond.

It felt good to be back in the forest. She noted several useful plants along the way including a drift of chamomile flowers that would more than replenish her meager stock and at least two different mints. She slipped into the forest, passing from the open clearing through the verge of understory and into the open forest beyond. Her practiced eye picked out a few likely stands of trees including several witch hazels and some chestnuts and walnuts. She gathered a pocket full of chestnuts to roast later and made mental notes about what she'd need for gathering. She pushed further into the forest and found several stands of blackberry and raspberry. In one spot a large trees had toppled, smashing an opening in the canopy in its fall and clearing the way for several wild rugosas. They appeared to be mature plants, at least several winters old, and were loaded with the fruiting hips that would be invaluable as winter wound into spring. She'd have to bring Riley out to help gather them up before the birds and animals got them. It would be a few more days, perhaps after the first frost of the season, before they'd be ready to harvest.

She wandered in a broad arc that took her back to the clay quarry road. One of the first skills Agnes Dogwood had taught her was how to keep track of where she was in the forest, and she had honed that skill for twenty years with each new teacher adding layers of nuance and knowledge to her memory. Even with the quick survey, she knew she could find the individual plants and trees that she'd mentally marked on her partial circuit of the hamlet. If the rest of the forest were as rich as the small slice she'd covered in her short tramp, there was no need to worry about food for the coming winter. Tanyth was relatively sure that she could feed at least half the village on what she'd be able to glean from the All-Mother's bounty around them.

Remembering the prayer of the morning and the unexpected response she planted her staff in the moist forest floor and whispered a quiet prayer of thanks to the All-Mother out of heartfelt gratitude for the gifts she'd found. She stood there in the peaceful afterglow, listening to the wind sighing through the branches and smelling the rich, loamy soil where her staff had dug into it. A waft of pine came down slope on the breeze and somewhere back in the forest a squirrel chittered. She took one last deep breath and let it out slowly before starting the short walk down the track to the village. As she stepped out into the open again, she remembered the rabbit snares in her pocket, but decided against placing them after all.

With a spring in her step, she continued on through the village to her hut. As she approached she met Thomas coming up the road from the direction of the Pike. He smiled shyly on seeing her and bobbed his head in a kind of self conscious bow. "Good afternoon, mum."

"Hello, Thomas. Lovely day isn't it?"

"Oh, yes, mum. Quite. Be fall for sure soon enough but right nice now."

"How's the hunting here?"

"Very good, mum. Lots of small game and several herds of deer that roam the hillsides on either side of the Pike, mum." He seemed almost embarrassed to be discussing hunting with her.

"I saw rabbit sign in the woods right here this afternoon." She pointed to the woods behind her hut in an attempt to draw the taciturn man out a bit on the subject of local game.

He nodded. "Oh, there's hare a plenty all over these hills, and the odd wild cat and coyote to keep them from takin' over, too. Do you fancy a bit of rabbit, mum?"

"I was going to set a snare or two this afternoon, but got distracted by the plant life."

"The woods around haven't been picked over here yet. Only Mother Alderton gathered much and even that was naught but what she used for her liniments, salves, and teas." As he spoke he rummaged around in the game bag over his shoulder and pulled out a field dressed hare. He held it out to her. "If'n you were gonna snare one, then you probably know what to do with that, mum. It's yours if you want it."

Tanyth was reticent about taking the food out of others' mouths but he pressed it on her.

"Please, mum. I've another pair for the family and some more fat grouse for the general larder. It's my pleasure."

She accepted the rabbit with a nod of thanks. "I'm much obliged, Thomas. Thank you."

He beamed and knuckled his brow. "My job, mum. It's why I'm here. I can bring you anythin' the woods will provide. You just let me know what and when you want it."

The hare was heavy in her hands and she nodded her thanks once more. "A fat rabbit like this once a week would be quite adequate to my needs, Thomas. Thank you." She paused for a moment before continuing. "You don't know where I can find some oats for oatmeal do you?"

He grinned. "There's grains up at the barn, mum. Draw what you need. There's usually plenty there. Oats, flour, millet, rice, dried beans." He smiled encouragingly. "You're one of us now, I figure. You help yourself to anything you find there, mum, and if you can't find somethin' you let me know."

His simple words warmed her in ways she hadn't antici-pated and the gift of the hare was unexpected. He knuckled his brow once more and nodded his farewell before continuing up into the village, leaving her standing there in the glow of the late afternoon sun.

CHAPTER 8
REALITIES AND REALIZATIONS

Tanyth was no stranger to rabbit anatomy and soon had the carcass skinned and jointed. She offered a prayer to the All-Mother in thanks for the meat and fur, then tossed the meat into her cooking pot, added water and some salt, and hung it on the pot hook over the fire to stew. With winter coming, the skin already showed the color change with flecks of white winter fur among the mottled brown. She rolled it for later curing and set it aside.

The day was drawing to a close before she heard the solid wheels of the ox cart crunching along the track outside. The sounds of the village were already becoming familiar to her and she began to feel more at home, more centered. She looked around the hut and tried to think clearly about what she'd need for the winter.

For twenty years, she'd lived in somebody else's home, or out of her backpack. She acquired and disposed of seasonal clothing as she went, trading heavy for light and light for heavy as she needed it. Small clothes and some bits and pieces stayed with her over the years. Other than clothes, her teapot, a single cook pot–now filled almost to the top with stewing rabbit–and her plate and cup, her pack contained only the herbs and seeds that constituted a stock in trade, a stash of tea and oatmeal, and little else. Everything in her life traveled on her back and that life was not geared for setting up housekeeping.

She started making a list in her head for things she'd need to get through the winter. A larger cooking pot was first on her list. The small one was all she had and as long as it was filled with rabbit, she'd be unable to cook her breakfast of oatmeal. A frying pan, something she had little use for on the road because of the weight and the nature of her diet, would become almost invaluable in preparing meals on the hearth. Her mouth fairly watered at the thought of baking some beans, an activity that would require another article of specialized equipment.

As she sat there, the spinning in her mind slowed. What she absolutely needed, she carried on her back. All thoughts of pots and pans, of foods and storage–all those were extraneous to what she needed. They might be convenient, of course, and even welcome additions to her life, but not anything that she needed. Her panicky response startled her as it passed and she realized what had happened. She closed her eyes and took deep, slow breaths to steady herself further. When she opened her eyes and saw the basket of bread and cheese on the table, she remembered that while the village was isolated–barely developed as a place at all–she was not alone. The people who lived in the huts around her had wintered here four times already and were cheerfully heading into a fifth. Her moment of doubt and fear subsided as the rabbit boiled over with a hiss, forcing her to focus on the here and now to adjust the pot hanger. She wanted the rabbit to simmer, not boil and that homely task centered her more.

"Foolishness, old woman." She berated herself for succumbing to self-doubt and anxiety even as she recognized the mood swing as a normal part of her life. She sighed aloud and set about getting her supplies in order to deal with it. "And you thought this was going to end sometime soon?" She chuckled to herself and shook her head.

Still, she thought another cooking pot would be nice.

With things arranged for her monthly reminder of mortality from the All-Mother, she found herself once more at loose ends and looking about her for something to do. She'd not had to deal with idleness in over twenty years. There was always something to do, something to learn, something to find or prepare or mend. She realized that part of her restiveness was the result of needing something to keep her hands busy.

She would need a gathering basket for foraging in the woods, and wondered where to get the materials to make one.

Thinking of the forest also reminded her that she had a pocketful of chestnuts. She dug them out and lined them up near the fire to roast, stabbing each one with the tip of her belt knife before putting it on the hearth. They'd make a nice accompaniment to the stewed rabbit. With her immediate needs addressed, she slipped out of the cottage and headed for the hut that Thomas and Sadie shared. She could tramp about in the woods herself until she found what she needed, but Thomas already knew the lay of the land.

She knocked on the door and heard Sadie call "Come in!"

She swung the door open and peered inside. Sadie was putting the final touches on dinner and Thomas was oiling his boots while the kids played a noisy game consisting largely of rolling around on the floor and crawling under the table and back out again. All activity ceased as she stuck her head through the low door.

"Mum!?" Sadie seemed flustered that Tanyth should be knocking on her door. "Is something the matter?"

Tanyth smiled and shook her head. "Not at all! I just wanted to ask your husband some questions about the area."

"Me, mum?" It was Thomas's turn to look startled.

She turned her smile on him. "Yes, you, Thomas. I'm looking for a stand of cattail, not too far away. Do you know of such a place? Someplace handy you can direct me to?"

He scratched his chin thoughtfully before replying. "Probably the nearest is up toward the quarry. About a half mile in, there's a bit of corduroy roadin' through a damp swale."

Tanyth nodded. "Yes, we were there earlier today."

Sadie added a quiet confirmation.

"Follow the swale north, up-hill about two hundred yards. There's a smallish pond there with a nice stand of cattails, mum." He hesitated. "Can I ask what you want them for?"

"Baskets. I need to make some baskets for gathering."

"There's enough there for that, mum. But there are plenty of baskets in the barn, if you need some." He started to rise. "I can fetch a couple for you if you like, mum."

"No, Thomas, but thank you. I just needed to know where

to get them." She smiled and gave a little wave before closing the door again. She looked up at the sky and decided she didn't really want to be wandering the woods at dusk. The sun wasn't quite below the treetops but it would be in a matter of minutes. She could hear the men returning from the quarry already and filed the information away. The barn was nearby and Tanyth turned her steps in that direction. She really wanted to see what kind of stockpiles were there and it appeared to be the center of the hamlet's effort, judging from the number of people who'd directed her there in the last couple of days.

The big doors hung on heavy iron hinges and stood wide as she approached. The building wasn't tall but it was much larger than she'd thought, its bulk masked by the huts and trees. The oxcart and lorry wagon stood tucked under a shed roof to one side and inside she could see box stalls with horses peeking out. She stepped into the open door and smelled the musky aromas of animal dung and sweet hay, along with an underlying tang of harness oil. The horses whickered softly and she could make out the pale shape of the ox in the stall closest to the door. She heard voices coming from inside and followed them back between the stalls to the far end of the barn. William and the older man she'd seen driving the lorry wagon were standing in a large store room at the back. There were barrels and baskets, tools, and piles of cloth. Cupboards with latched doors hung on the walls. The two men turned at the sound of her footsteps and William smiled.

"Good evening, mum."

"Hello, William." She smiled back and nodded to the new face. "I take it you're Frank?"

He nodded with a shy smile of his own. "Yes'm. Frank Crane. I saw you earlier by Mother Alderton's hut, didn't I, mum?"

"You did." Tanyth inclined her head in acknowledgment.

William spoke up. "Tanyth Fairport, this here is the man we were so concerned about. Seems the wagon gave him some trouble. Frank? Tanyth here will be wintering over with us in Mother Alderton's hut. She's the one that helped Sadie over the flux."

Frank nodded and smiled more warmly. "Welcome to the village, mum."

"Thank you."

"Is there something we can help you with, mum?" William waved a hand. "I think there's about anything you might need in here."

She turned to scan all the things and her eyes kept skittering over shapes in the dim light without actually snagging on them. "So I see. I just came to see what was here, but now that I'm here, I do have need of a second cooking pot and maybe an extra plate." She looked around at the wealth of goods stashed in the barn. "You've enough to open a small store in here!"

William beamed with pride. "Perhaps not a store just yet, but we have most things folks need and extras of stuff that wears out."

A thought struck her. "When I first arrived the other day, Amber said that you weave the grass mats and make extras to sell in town?"

He nodded. "We do."

"Well, I need to make some baskets for gathering nuts and such. Is there a workroom here somewhere?"

Frank chuckled a bit and William beamed more broadly. "This way, mum." He led the way through a side door and out to a fairly large workshop tucked up under another shed roof on the backside of the barn. It was a relatively spacious room, with shutters–closed against the elements at the moment–and workbenches arrayed along the inner wall. A large hearth took up one end of the room while a wide door hung on the far end. Tools hung from pegs on the wall, and racks of raw materials sat wherever there was room. The place looked big enough for several people to work without crowding.

"This must be cozy in winter." Tanyth looked around admiringly.

Frank nodded. "We get a lot done here."

William pointed out a bin tucked under the work bench. "There's grasses and reeds under here, mum, if you're thinking of weaving a basket." He pointed to a stack of empty wooden tubs beside the door. "There's some retting vats. Just get a bucket or two of water from the pump when you're ready." He looked around. "Is there a particular kind of basket you need for collecting?"

She shook her head. "Not really. Just something light enough to carry and bigger than my pockets for bringing things back."

He looked surprised. "How much are you talking about, mum?"

She gave a kind of shrug. "Well, I can only lug one full basket at a time, but something like a gleaner's bag would be best for collecting and then some baskets for storage." She looked between the two men. "You know what that is?"

"A gleaner's bag, mum?" William shrugged. "Of course. We have those already." He led her back to the storage room and pulled a sack from one of the shelves. He held it up for her. "Like this?" It was made of heavy canvas duck and had a broad strap attached across the mouth.

"That's it exactly. It's perfect." Tanyth nodded enthusiastically. "Might I use one?"

William held the back out to her. "Of course, mum. Anything in this room. Feel free to use anything you can find here. If you can't find it, ask one of us and maybe we have it tucked away."

She accepted the bag, looped the strap over her shoulder, and grinned. "Oh, this will make collecting so much easier. Thank you."

The two men looked pleased to be able to help and Frank pointed out a stack of peck and bushel baskets. "If you need storage baskets, those are available, mum. We'll be making more as soon as the snow starts flying and we can't get out, so don't be shy."

She just shook her head in wonder before asking William. "How do you do all this?"

He shrugged. "We just keep busy. Thomas keeps us supplied in meat and the gardens keep us in vegetables. Frank brings barrels of flour and dried beans and such when he comes back from Kleesport, so we don't have to spend every waking moment searching for food, like some do, mum." He waved a hand around the storage room. "That gives us time to make stuff we need, to hunt for stuff we can't buy, and generally lets us stockpile goods we'll need for later."

Tanyth stopped gaping at the stores and regarded William. "Are you the mastermind behind all this?"

Frank chuckled and William looked embarrassed. "No, mum." He jerked a thumb in Frank's direction. "Frank here was one of my father's warehouse managers. He's the one that keeps this all straightened out."

She inclined her head to him in a small bow. "My compliments to you, sir. I can't remember seeing anything like it in all my travels."

Frank smiled softly. "I spent a lot of time driving freight wagons, mum. Before I went to work for this rapscallion's da." He nodded at William. "When Will here asked me how to organize it, well, mum, we started plannin' and the next thing you know..." He held out his hands, arms to the side, "... it happened."

William smiled. "We couldn't have done this without Frank. And we need to figure out what to do about the lorry wagon. It was pretty nerve wracking not knowing where you were."

Frank grimaced and scratched his chin. "When that axle gave out, I was wondering how we'd deal with that myself. Luckily I wasn't far from Mossport and was able to get somebody to carry a message to the wainwright." He sighed. "It sure woulda been handy to have another person on the wagon so one of us coulda walked while the other guarded."

William nodded and then explained to Tanyth. "We've been having this conversation off and on for a year. If we send somebody with Frank, then we lose a pair of hands here. None of the kids are of an age yet where they'd be much use on the road and it's a long run in and back."

Frank shrugged. "Mostly, it's not a problem. I drive in. I drive back. Got loaders on both ends. But then something like this happens and I'm sittin' a-side the road waiting for somebody to come by. Can't leave the horses. Can't leave the cargo." He shrugged again, helplessly. "It worked out this time, but ever'body here worryin' wasn't helpful."

Tanyth nodded her understanding. "I can see where that'd

be. You've got–what? One more run in this season?"

The two men nodded. "Ya. Be going back out in a few days." Frank rubbed his lower back. "And I'm pretty glad we'll be holed up for a few months. That seat is getting' mighty tired of my backside."

They all laughed.

"Thank you for the bag, William. There's a grove of nut trees that'll be happy to share with me tomorrow, I think." Tanyth smiled and nodded to Frank. "Nice to meet you, Frank. Good luck with the seat."

She left the two men in the darkening store room, talking about the price of a barrel of flour against a barrel of clay, and wended her way through the gathering dusk with the gleaner's bag looped over her shoulder. As she approached her hut, the sound of hoof beats from out on the Pike signaled an approaching rider. As the rider got closer, she could hear the jingling of the messenger's bridle. One of the King's Own, bearing more dispatches, this time away from Kleesport. She wondered if it were the same young woman she'd seen only two days before but heading in the other direction.

The proximity to the main road gave her pause. The hamlet was rich although it looked like any other collection of hovels in countless other wide spots in the road along the way. Perhaps its obscurity was as good a protection as they'd need. What reivers or bandits would bother with a cluster of hovels? The thought bothered her, but perhaps she was borrowing trouble.

As she rounded the last corner on the way to her hut, a dark shape took wing from where it had been resting on the ridgepole of her roof. The large raven glided effortlessly into the forest and disappeared so suddenly and silently–without even a squawk–that she wondered for a moment if it had been real. Shrugging off the cold chill, she crossed the short distance to her door and ducked inside, closing and latching it carefully.

CHAPTER 9
STORM CLOUDS

The following dawn found Tanyth slipping out of her hut, bag over her shoulder, and staff in hand. She knew that taking one or more of the children might have been more effective. Small quick hands might be useful in finding nuts among the leaf litter, but she wanted to survey more as well. For that, the short legs and extra care would be more liability than asset so she set off alone before the sun peeped over the tree line in the east.

In a matter of minutes she was back at the chestnut stand and quickly scooped several handfuls of the ripened nuts into the sack. With the equinox just around the corner, it was perfect timing for the early nuts and she looked up at the spikey pods yet to open, judging that there might be a bumper crop as the fall wound on.

The chestnuts in the bottom of the bag gave it enough heft that it stopped flapping as she walked without being too burdensome to a woman used to carrying her life on her back. She continued due north, parallel to the Kleesport Pike, for a few hundred yards before turning westward to walk in the general direction of the clay quarry. She hoped her path would lead to the stand of cattails that Thomas had recommended. One thing she missed, and she'd need to check with Thomas on it, was a meadow. Many of the plants she knew best grew either in a meadow or on the verge of one where trees offered some protection but didn't block the sun completely.

Looking up at the arching forest canopy she could see sky in only a few places and the forest's shadows danced around her. The forest floor was relatively open with the tall, straight oaks offering few obstacles to passage. The mature trees stood well apart, having choked out competition at ground level decades before. The ground rose in elevation as she moved away from the Pike and she soon came to the small pond.

Trees grew nearly up to the edge on the easterly side and her eyes traced the ground's contour to the south. The rising sun had cleared the treetops and cast bright morning light on a brushy sward and a lush sweep of cattails on the far side of the pond. The green fronds swayed in the morning breezes. The darker spikes that gave the plant its name punctuated the stand here and there. From where she stood in the shadow of the forest, the brilliantly lit scene seemed like something from another world. She felt as if she looked out of the window of some vast cabin at a woodland garden just outside.

A soft splashing sound from the south told her where the pond's main outlet lay. The brilliant sun glinted off the water in places, but clearly illuminated the sandy bottom of the small pond. Streamlined shadows moved across the sand. It took her a moment to find the fish that made them, so perfectly did they blend in against the pale sand.

She made her way to the south around the end of the pond and worked over to the cattail patch. It took her several moments to recognize the low ground cover that grew with abandon in the dark moist soil on the south side of the pond. She was nearly walking on it when it came to her. Ground nut vines grew everywhere. She looked around in amazement at the spread of vines that extended from the west side of the pond, across much of the small hillside, and down into the moist swale to the south. She was fairly certain she'd find the corduroy road in that direction and the stand of willows where they'd harvested the bark just the previous morning. She felt like so much had happened in a very short time. She looked around, half expecting to see the raven perched in a tree nearby.

Cattails forgotten for the moment, she used the heel of her staff to dig a small hole in the damp soil and exposed a fibrous root with a string of hard tubers no bigger than the first joint in her thumb. "First year and fresh," she muttered.

She was able to pull the root up through the soft soil for several feet and found maybe two dozen of the small, round tubers. She straightened and surveyed the ground once more. She thought there were probably enough ground nuts in this one patch to feed the village for several days should it come to that. The only difficulty in harvesting them in winter would be getting down to them through snow and frozen ground. If things went badly over the winter this patch could be a life saver come spring. Without conscious thought she murmured a reverent, "Thank you, Mother," and stripped a few ground nuts from the root with practiced fingers, dropping them into her sack.

She turned her attention to the cattails once more, but with all the empty baskets in the storage room in the barn, she saw no reason to cut reeds and weave more. Casting her eye along the upper slope of the pond where the mid-morning sun painted the landscape in the lush green and gold of the last days of summer, she picked out several apple trees growing on the far verge. She picked her way through the drifts of ground nut vines to find a small copse of the wild apples growing in a tangle, their roots nicely watered by the pond. Some of the early summer fruit already rotted on the ground and the sweet fruit drew hornets and bees from miles around. She reached up, plucked one of the small red apples from a low hanging branch, and polished the smooth skin on the sleeve of her jersey. Unlike orchard grown varieties, the wild apple was small, barely two inches in diameter and graced with a red and gold skin that gleamed in the morning sun. Tanyth bit into it, taking a small nibble out of one side. It was hard, but her teeth worried a chunk off and the firm, juicy flesh exploded in her mouth. Not quite sweet, not exactly tart, the small fruit tasted slightly of both and crunched delightfully. She plucked several of them from that same branch, adding them to her gleaner's bag before heading south along the swale, heading for the path back to the village and feeling more at home with every step she took. The woods surrounding the hamlet appeared to hold a bounty waiting for harvest. She realized that some care would be required to keep from destroying the forest's ability to replenish itself each season, but she'd only seen one small slice of the woods. If this random section of forest was any indication, the surrounding hillsides must hold a king's ransom in wild foods.

She followed the swale to the quarry path and soon found herself swinging along the track toward the village, her bag not full as she might have expected but her mind raced with the possibilities that the surrounding landscape held. As she came around the last turn on the track, the small collection of huts was buzzing. Children and some of the women stood behind the huts and peeped around the corners at whatever was happening on the road side. Tanyth's belly turned to ice. She increased her pace to walk up behind the nearest hut where she found Megan with a small boy in hand.

"Megan?" Tanyth spoke softly, but the younger woman's attention was focused forward and she jumped.

"Oh, Mother, mum, you scared me." The younger woman flattened her back against the wall of the hut, pressing a hand to her chest.

"What's happening out there, Megan?"

"Riders, mum. They came from the Pike looking for water for their horses."

Tanyth leaned out to get a look at the entry track. Four men at arms stood in the track holding their mounts by the reins. Her eyes narrowed. "Not King's Own then?" She looked at Megan.

Megan shook her head. "Not as they've said."

"How long have they been here?"

Megan peeped around the corner again, staying low so she wouldn't block Tanyth's view. "About an hour, mum."

Amber stood in front of her hut and spoke to one of the riders–a thick set man dressed almost foppishly with plumed hat, lace cravat, and a red satin lining in his riding coat. Riley and Frank circulated with buckets of water, giving each horse a small drink before pulling the bucket away and going on to the next. The horses appeared to be well trained and obedient to the careful watering.

While the one man talked to Amber and her attention was focused on him, Tanyth didn't like the way the other three measured the hamlet with their eyes. One of them looked in her direction and she thought she could see his lips moving as he counted the buildings. She knew from experience that they couldn't see the barn from where they stood so the hamlet looked like nothing more than a half dozen huts in somewhat better condition than hovels, but still nothing to attract attention.

Tanyth knew that for some men, treasure was not measured as gold or silver. The attention that the leader paid to Amber made Tanyth uncomfortable.

"Has somebody sent to the quarry?" She asked Megan. "They should know about this."

"Yes, Sadie went up the trail about half an hour ago. They should be back any second now."

Tanyth glanced at the sun and calculated. She must have just missed Sadie on the path and the men should be on their way back down to the village even now. She leaned out to look once more. The horses seemed to be all watered but the men made no move to ride on.

"Take the children and head for the quarry. You should meet the men coming down. Where are the other women?"

"Charlotte and Becky should be in the barn. Beth is over there behind the hut." Megan pointed at a dark haired woman hiding behind the next hut.

The woman waved, her movements hidden from the road by intervening houses.

"Take Beth with you to help with the kids. Get as many of them as you can gather quickly but go now." Her voice was a low mutter against the late morning breeze and Megan motioned the other woman to follow them up to the trail toward the quarry. Tanyth watched the men at the front of the village as the women and children scampered up the trail. The men must have spotted them between the huts because Tanyth saw one of the riders turn his head in that direction and say something to his companion who also looked. Frank, with his bucket empty, stepped deliberately into the man's line of sight.

By then the conversation that Amber was having with the leader should have been breaking off. The man continued to stand there talking to her, tying up her attention and smiling in a way that he might have thought to be charming, but which Tanyth found to be somewhat less flattering than an open leer. With a glance behind her to make sure the small party was out of sight, she settled her hat and with a jaunty spring in her step, walked around the corner of the hut and directly toward Amber and the man talking to her.

At the sudden movement, two of the men-at-arms dropped hands to hilts but didn't draw when they saw it was just an old woman with a floppy hat. She marched over to Amber and stepped up beside her, claiming the man's attention with her eyes and interrupting whatever he was saying. Amber half turned and gave her a grateful glance.

Tanyth spoke clearly. "Good day, traveler."

His manner was brusque, as if not used to being interrupted, but offered a grudging nod. "Good day, mum." His eyes took in her gleaner's bag and the hat before turning back to Amber. "Many thanks for the water for our horses." He looked behind him to see that all of them had been watered before turning to leer at Amber again, "And for the most enjoyable conversation."

"You're welcome to the water, sir. Good luck in your travels." Amber was obviously hoping to dismiss the man by not giving him any more conversational ground.

He turned and vaulted to his saddle, smoothly taking rein and edging his horse around with his legs. He didn't seem terribly happy at being interrupted, but he signaled his men who followed him into the saddle. With a nod and wave to Amber, he led his small band back out onto the Pike and they rode off to the south.

As the sound of the horses' hooves faded into the distance, a half dozen men looking grimy and winded boiled around the huts from the direction of the quarry with Sadie pelting along behind. They all skidded to a halt when they saw no danger. Frank crossed to the leader of the quarry team and Amber reached over to take Tanyth's arm, leaning heavily on it but remaining upright. She turned her terrified eyes to the older woman.

Tanyth spoke quietly. "Let's go inside, Amber. Make some tea. You did fine, but the others are watching."

The younger woman took a short deep breath while her eyes flicked to the small knot of men standing with Frank.

"Of course." She turned and slipped into the hut, Tanyth on her heels, while Frank explained to the quarry workers what had transpired.

Inside Amber collapsed on a cushion while Tanyth filled the tea kettle and placed it on the fire to heat.

"My knees were shaking so bad, I didn't think I could stand up." Amber's voice was soft and quavery.

"Mine, too." Tanyth took off her hat and smiled at Amber.

Amber took a deep breath and blew it out, before scrubbing her face with her hands. "At least they're gone now."

Tanyth looked at her with a frown. "They'll be back."

Amber froze, looking sharply at Tanyth. "You sound sure."

The older woman nodded. "While the leader was keeping you busy, the other three were taking stock–counting the huts and taking note that you're protected by an old man and a boy too young to draw a bow."

"What can they want? They saw we have nothing worth taking."

Tanyth shook her head. "They saw women, apparently alone and poorly protected. What do you think they want?"

Amber blinked in astonishment. "That's preposterous."

Tanyth arched an eyebrow. "Where's William and when will Thomas be back?"

Amber blanched. "William is out cutting wood like always. Thomas usually comes home at sunset."

Tanyth eyed the position of the sun and sighed. "I hope that's soon enough."

CHAPTER 10
A WING AND A PRAYER

Frank knocked on the door. "How are you ladies doing in there?"

Tanyth opened to look up at him. "So far so good, but do you think they're gone?"

Frank shook his head. "I doubt it. They rode off making a lot of noise, but it died out awful fast. That one guy was counting houses and kept looking to see who else was around."

Tanyth sighed. "That's what I thought, too." She pointed to the men heading back to the quarry. "Why're they leaving?"

Frank scrubbed the back of his neck with one hand. "Because they don't believe there's any danger and William's not here to tell 'em to stop work for the day."

"What?" Tanyth was shocked.

Frank just shrugged.

Amber roused herself and climbed the short steps out the door. "Lemme try to talk to them." She scampered across the grass and shouted to get the men's attention. They stopped and waited for her to catch up.

They talked for a few moments but the burly foreman just shrugged and pointed at the sun with his thumb.

"They don't think there's a problem, do they." Tanyth said.

Amber waved her hands in the direction of the Pike and Tanyth could hear her voice, even if she couldn't make out the words.

"They didn't see it. So they don't know. First time we've

had this kind of problem here, so I don't know that I blame them."

She looked up at him. "You think they'll be back, don't you?"

He shrugged. "Yes, mum. I truly do."

"What do we do?"

Frank scrubbed the back of his neck again. "Well, the plan was for the women and children to take to the woods and hide. Ain't nothin' in the houses or barns worth losing a person over."

"How long d'ya think before they come back?"

Frank turned to look at the Pike and then glanced up at the sun. "I'd give 'em about an hour to let things calm down here and then they'll come back fast."

"Think they'll knock on the front door next time?"

Frank shook his head. "Depends on what they think is here."

Most of the quarrymen looked on in amusement as Amber continued her argument with Jakey. Jakey, for his part, merely stood his ground and shook his head, a truculent frown on his face.

"Do they know about the team do you think?"

Frank sighed. "If they don't, they'll find it soon as they look in the barn."

"What else is valuable here?"

"Food. Tools. Shelter." Frank ticked them off. "This would make a handy bandit camp."

"Rather exposed for a bandit camp, isn't it?"

"Depends on where they do their banditin'." Frank paused. "But prob'ly so."

Amber lost her argument with the quarry men, and Jakey waved his crew back up the trail to the quarry.

Frank spit neatly in the grass beside the house.

Amber returned, fury written on her face in scarlet hues. "They said we should all just calm down and stop seeing boggles under the beds." She turned to Frank. "Can you get the horses and take them up to the quarry? I'll round up whoever's left here and we'll all go up there, too. If they follow us up, then at least those lunk heads won't be able to argue about the threat."

Frank nodded and headed for the barn at a brisk walk.

Amber turned to Tanyth. "Can you help me gather everybody up, mum? You knock on the doors on that side? I'll get these. Have everybody meet up a the lane to the quarry and we'll scoot."

Tanyth nodded and started around. There weren't that many houses and in a matter of a few minutes the women and children were heading up the path following Frank and the horses. Tanyth and Amber stood at the end of the lane, watching the small party heading up into the woods, Amber counting them off as they went.

"That's all of them." She spoke quietly. "'Cept for Thomas and William."

Neither woman speculated on where the two men might be. Thomas was off in the forest somewhere tending his snares and hunting small game to augment the village larder. They both knew that William chopped wood somewhere in the forest just off the Pike where the men-at-arms might come across him. Neither of them wanted to think too much about that.

As the noise of the women and children receded into the forest, Amber turned to Tanyth. "Do you remember the other morning, mum? You said a prayer to the All-Mother?" She spoke softly, tentatively.

"Yes. I remember."

"Do you think you could say one now? Askin' for her protection here?"

Tanyth cocked her head to one side. "Do you really think it'll help?"

Amber sighed. "I don't know, mum, but it can't hurt."

The pleading in her eyes was more than Tanyth could bear. "I'm not a witch, my dear. I've no special powers, you know."

"That's as might be, mum. But there was something in the air the other morning. Maybe it was just a storm comin' but maybe there's somthin' out there listenin' and it heard you." She paused, a worried frown on her face. "I'm not too proud to ask for help right now."

Tanyth smiled. "Me, either." She nodded up the trail. "Go

up there a ways and give me some room to think."

Amber scampered a few yards up the track and took shelter on the verge, leaving Tanyth standing in the path where it emptied into the back of the village.

Tanyth planted the heel of her staff and leaned on it. She closed her eyes to focus on the area around her–the earth, the sky, the fire of the sun, and the water coursing in the hidden rivers in the ground. A sense of calm filled her and the strength of the earth itself seemed to flow up the length of her body, through the soles of her boots and along the path of her staff.

She opened her eyes and raised her arms as she had the day before, facing the north she started with the earth. "I call upon the Guardian of the North, Keeper of Earth, Bones of the World to guard this passage against those who wish us harm and ask that they do not pass." She turned to face out over the village, arms upraised and the heat of her belly pulsed in time with her heart. "I call upon the Guardian of the East, Keeper of the Air, Breath of the World to guard this passage against those who wish us harm and ask that they do not pass." She turned to face the woods to the south. "I call upon the Guardian of the South, Keeper of Fire, Life of the World to guard this passage against those who wish us harm and ask that they do not pass." With each repetition, while her voice was no stronger, it seemed to echo louder in the air around her. She turned to the west, looking up the path and repeated one last time. "I call upon the Guardian of the West, Keeper of Water, Blood of the World to guard this passage against those who would do us harm and ask that they do not pass." She competed the circle by facing north once more. "I ask in the name of the All-Mother. I ask in the name of the All-Father. Guard us from our enemies. They will not pass." She stabbed her staff into the ground and leaned on it as the emotions washed through her and left her weakened, all but panting in exertion.

"Very pretty, mum. Very pretty, indeed." The man's voice came from the direction of the village and the leader stepped around the corner of the nearest hut. He clapped his gloved hands in mocking applause. "But do you really think your earthy mumbo jumbo will have any sway over us?"

He held his hands out in a practiced gesture and the three bully boys followed him out into the clearing at the end of the path.

Tanyth whirled at the sound of his voice and stood there praying that Amber had the sense to run. The world around her took on an unnatural clarity and somewhere inside her, the anger welled up. "There is nothing for you here." She said it quietly but the words echoed in her and fairly crackled in the air around her.

"Ah, but there you're wrong, Mother, for there surely is a garden to be plowed and seeds to be planted." He leered with a suggestive roll of his hips and his men chuckled at his not so veiled threats.

"No." The word snapped in the air, a blow to the heart, a stone in the path.

The leader laughed easily and motioned one of the thugs forward while he crossed his arms on his chest and lounged against the logs of the hut, as if it were the wall of his favorite tavern. "Don't be foolish, mum. Surely, you don't think one small woman can stop even one of my men?"

The anger and pain of losing her son. The anger and pain of having her husband beat and humiliate her for years before she escaped and dedicated her life to the road. The anger and pain inflicted by all the men who'd accosted her, badgered her, assaulted her on the road. All that anger and pain rose in her in that one moment.

She focused on the approaching bravo and spit at him. "No."

He chuckled and, in what he might have thought was a subtle move, lunged for her, arms outstretched as if to sweep her up in a bear hug.

Tanyth stepped into the attack, pivoting her staff downward with the iron-bound heel grounded in the soil. The gnarled knot at the top speared the man in his chest with a meaty thump, his momentum doing the work and the force of his attack rebounding on him. He knocked himself backwards and landed flat on his back at her feet with a surprised grunt. His face turned red as he tried to pull air back into his bruised lungs.

"No." She said it quietly, but still it echoed in the air even over the downed man's wheezing grunts for breath.

The leader's face mottled in his rage. "You bitch!" He motioned his remaining two companions forward. "Take her. I want her alive. For now." His eyes fairly bulged in his head from his pent up anger and frustration. "Nobody makes a fool of me. Particularly not a feeble old lady with a stick!"

The two men drew swords and spread out to give each other room to swing. Their faces held murder and worse but Tanyth scowled at them. "No!" Once more, her voice carried to the forest and seemed to echo among the boles of the trees.

The two boyos glanced at each other and chuckled uneasily. They moved in smoothly and slowly, separating even more as they closed on the woman in their path.

"No." She hissed the word with every fiber of her being.

"Come on, mum." The one on her left spoke gently as if to a spooked horse. "You don't wanna hurt us, and we sure don't wanna hurt you. Why don't you just put down the stick and we'll all go talk to the boss nice and calm like, yeah?"

Tanyth glared. "No!" The word lashed out at the two men, even as they lunged forward together, clubbing at her with the flats of their swords. She dodged backwards and swung the foot of her staff in a short, vicious arc with a chopping upward motion.

The man on the left dodged the feint to his face, but the iron caught him where his fingers wrapped his sword's hilt. The blade flew from his hand as two of his fingers shattered and the reversing blow swung the knobbed end of the staff into his face, smashing his nose. He screamed in pain, and dropping to his knees beside the first man, cradled his injured hand to his chest while blood streamed down his face and onto his tunic. The sudden movements–and the sword spinning through the air–made the second attacker flinch backward, his attack halted by the unexpected response.

The leader growled at them. "For gods' sakes, Mort, it's one old woman! What are you–"

A sound like a humming bird snaked over Tanyth and a flash caught her eye even as the man's voice chopped off in mid-sentence at the sound of a heavy wooden thunk.

Tanyth spared a glance at the leader and saw him staring at the shaft of an arrow sunk into the wood of the hut less than a hand's breadth from his head. It still quivered from the force of its flight.

Behind her, Tanyth heard Thomas's quiet voice. "No."

The remaining attacker looked over Tanyth's shoulder and lowered his sword, arms outstretched in a gesture of surrender as he slowly backed away.

Tanyth glanced over her shoulder to see Thomas standing in the path, bow drawn to his ear, wicked edges of a hunting broadhead gleaming in the afternoon sun. She turned back to face the attackers. "No." She said it quietly this time but the word was final, inevitable as the rumble of thunder that follows lightning's flash.

The leader's face had drained of color as he realized how close to death he stood. He turned to glare at them. "Mort, Reg! Get up. Let's get out of here." He growled the words even as he backed around the corner of the hut, putting the heavy protection of the wood between the bowman and himself.

The two injured men scrambled backwards, eventually getting to their feet and backing away, the uninjured one nervously covering their retreat and obviously anxious to move out.

They disappeared around the corner of the hut. In a moment, the sounds of horses trotting away came from the direction of the Pike. Only when the echoes had died away into the distance, the quiet susurration of wind in the trees filling the air, did Tanyth relax her vigilant stance and ground her staff in the moist soil once more. She heard Thomas's light step and turned to thank him with a smile.

"Are you all right, mum? They didn't get to you did they?"

"I'm fine, Thomas. Thank you." In spite of her protestations to the contrary, her voice quavered a little and she had to lean on the staff more heavily than she might have preferred, just to hold herself up.

"D'ya think they'll be back, mum?"

She considered it for a moment. "I hope not, Thomas. I

hope they'll keep riding and look for some easier pickings." She looked at him. "And they'll have to heal a bit before they take on too much. Hard to swing a sword with broken fingers."

Thomas grinned and reached down into the weeds at the edge of the track. He pulled up the man's dropped sword. "Harder still when you don't have it, mum."

She smiled. "There's that as well."

They stood and listened for another moment. Deep in the forest the cawing of a raven echoed and Tanyth gave silent thanks to the All-Mother for her protection before heading for her hut. She felt the need for a cup of tea and perhaps a short sit down.

"Mum?" Thomas's voice stopped her.

She stopped and turned back to him, leaning heavily on the staff to keep herself upright.

"That was pretty fancy staff work, mum." He crossed to the hut and retrieved his arrow. "You bash people a lot on the road?" A smile made the question part jest, but dark eyes underscored his seriousness.

Tanyth sighed and looked at her feet. "Too often." She took a deep breath and looked him in the eye. "Too many men think a woman alone is helpless. Too many see it as their right to teach her the error of her ways. When I left my husband, I made a promise to myself that he'd be the last man to ever beat me." She felt weak and slightly sick.

Thomas didn't flinch from her gaze. "And was he, mum?"

She snorted a laugh and shook her head. "No, but he was the last one who got away with it." She grinned fiercely at him, pulled the staff up, and twirled it once before planting the iron-shod foot back in the sod. "I've carried this staff, or one like it, for twenty winters. I've learned a thing or two about usin' it along the way."

Thomas nodded slowly and Tanyth felt like he weighed her words in a way that betrayed his depth. He nodded respectfully and offered an honest smile. "In the King's Own, they taught us that no farmer with a stick was unarmed. They grow up with a hoe in their hands."

Tanyth offered a smile of her own. "And every woman in

Korlay grows up with a broom in hers." She cast an appraising look at her staff. "This one's just lacking the bristles."

Thomas snorted a laugh of his own at that, but he wasn't done. "Mum? Those boyos coulda killed you."

"They're not the first, Thomas."

He looked startled. "Others have tried to kill you, mum?"

She shrugged. "Some men don't take kindly to bein' told no." She sighed and regarded him levelly. "I've been wanderin' the byways for almost half my life, Thomas. I'm careful. I look where I'm goin'. I don't take risks." She took a deep breath before going on. "That only gets ya so far. After that, it comes down to who's got the strongest will and the fastest hands." She nodded to his bow. "Or the keenest eye."

Thomas's eyes wrinkled a bit at the corners as he smiled. "I'm glad you were with us today, mum. Thank you."

She ducked her head in response. "I'm glad I could help, Thomas."

Thomas knuckled his brow in salute and slotted the arrow back into his quiver. "I best go see how they're doing up the hill."

She gave a small wave and turned toward her hut. As she walked, the tension she'd carried in her torso began to ease and the knots in her belly began to uncoil. With that easing came a familiar sensation in her nethers and she grimaced with a bitter snicker as she picked up her pace. She clambered down the stairs into her cottage, latching the door behind her and pulling at the belt of her baggy trousers as she crossed to the cot where she'd earlier arranged her supplies. She slipped the strap of her gleaning bag off her shoulder and tossed it onto the bedroll so she could deal with the first rush of her monthly courses.

"Blood calls to blood, eh, Mother?" she muttered to herself.

Long practice saw the task dealt with readily and she was soon stirring up the coals left from her morning fire. It seemed an age since she slipped out to do some gathering in the early morning. There was still bread and cheese and she nibbled a bit of each as the water warmed over the coals. Outside she heard people beginning to move about as the families who'd sheltered at the quarry came back down to the village.

The strength leeched out of her legs and she took her small pot to the table to let it steep while she settled onto the rough chair. She folded her arms on the surface and lay her forehead across them, fighting the urge to sleep but losing as the aftermath of the fight washed out of her, leaving her drained and emptier than she could ever remember being.

The blackness washed over her for a moment and her eyes opened on an odd scene. Below her four men in matching livery rode hard down the packed surface of the Pike. She was looking down at them from above and periodically one or the other would look behind them as if to see what might be chasing them. Soon they were obliged to rein in their lathered mounts and let them walk. They sat stiffly in their saddles and if they spoke, she couldn't hear anything over the rushing of the wind in her ears. The one with red lining his coat seemed to be arguing but the three men shook their heads until he gave up. Wheeling his tired horse, he spurred his mount south. The three remaining rode slowly after him.

It was a most amusing view and she looked about her with interest, now that the men were riding out of sight. She raised her eyes to the horizon and saw the earth spinning below her and felt the wind lift her suddenly skyward. She cawed in delight.

Tanyth's eyes flew open, the cawing of a crow still echoing in her ears. Not a crow. A raven. She knew it as certainly as she sat at the table in her hut, but a sudden doubt battered at her mind. She threw herself out of the chair and clawed the door open to look outside at the normal looking afternoon beyond.

Amber approached and started to raise a hand in greeting, but something in Tanyth's face stopped her smile half-formed and the hand made it no higher than her waist, before falling back to her side and the younger woman increased her stride to cross the intervening space more quickly. At the door she crouched down to peer in. "Mum? What is it? Are you all right?"

Tanyth blinked herself back from the edge of madness and with a shuddering breath offered a smile in return. "Yes. Yes, my dear. Of course. I had an odd dream. It set me off for a moment, that's all." Tanyth didn't know what to say. She felt disoriented and groggy.

Amber nodded, offering a tentative smile before glancing nervously down at the road. "Now if William would just come home. I'd feel much better."

Tanyth looked in that direction as well but her mind was on the view from above. "He'll be along, my dear. They'd have no way of knowing that he was one of ours and he's probably off the road gathering wood."

The younger woman shrugged in half-hearted agreement. "It's one thing to know. but another to let go of the worryin'." She smiled at the older woman apologetically.

Tanyth nodded her head in sympathy

Amber sighed and straightened. "Well, I just wanted to thank you, mum. You let us know if there's anything you need, all right?"

Tanyth smiled up at the young woman. "Of course, my dear. Right now, I think I want a cup of tea."

Amber grinned and gave a little wave before turning back toward her own hut.

Tanyth left the door open for the light and returned to the teapot on the table to fortify herself with a hot cup of tea before she looked into finding something for lunch.

CHAPTER 11
FOUNDATIONS

The crunch of wheels on the road drew Tanyth from her hut just before sundown. She stepped out in time to see Amber fly down the path and launch herself into William's arms. The ox stopped when William did and seemed placidly unaware of the sobbing woman. William did his best to try to figure out what was going on, and Tanyth could see him looking about for clues as he tried to calm his wife enough to speak around the sobs.

Tanyth could hear her sobbing in the still quiet of the gathering dusk. "I was so afraid they'd killed you."

He responsed with a low rumble that she couldn't make out but it sounded soothing.

Frank came down the path from the barn and stopped at the bend, waiting for the homecoming to subside. He saw Tanyth standing in front of her hut and nodded once.

When William managed to untangle himself, he clucked to the ox and started his way toward the barn, holding Amber around the waist and looking curiously from her, to Frank, to Tanyth and back.

As they approached the top of the bend, Tanyth fell in and walked along behind.

William spoke to Frank. "Evening. Big doin's while I was out?"

Frank gave a kind of sideways bob to his head. "Bit of excitement around midday. Riders came and started to make trouble."

William looked at Amber. "And you thought they'd found

me on the road and killed me?"

Amber snuffled a little. "We didn't know. That was the worst part." She hugged him around the waist as they walked, almost knocking him down.

He raised his eyebrows at that. "So, you'd rather known that I was dead than just late?"

It caught them all funny, and helped to break the tension. She reached back and slugged him in the shoulder. "Don't you make fun of me, you beast." She hugged him again. "You know what I mean."

Frank stepped out of the path to walk alongside and the strange parade continued on to the barn.

William looked at Frank over the ox's back. "Anybody hurt?"

Thomas's voice came out of the gathering gloom. "None of us." He stepped out from behind one of the huts and fell in beside Tanyth at the rear.

"I can see I need to get this story in order. Let's get Bester here settled with a feedbag and see if I can find a cuppa tea and you can tell me from the beginning."

They walked about three more paces before not knowing got to him. He turned to Thomas. "Did you get into a scuffle with 'em?"

Thomas shook his head. "Mother Fairport did."

Tanyth started to object to the honorific, but the stricken glance that William shot over his shoulder stopped her.

"You?" William's eyes were round in surprise and Tanyth saw him measuring her anew with his eyes.

She gave a little shrug. "It was mostly by accident."

William stared hard, not knowing if he should believe her, or not. In the end he twitched his stick against the cart's tongue and picked up the pace. "Hup, there, Bester. We're almost home."

William refrained from asking any more questions. He backed the ox cart around to the wood shed and dumped the load into the growing pile there, ready for cutting and splitting for winter. The cart went under the shed roof, and Bester waited patiently while William released the harness and let him into the box stall at the front of the barn. With the ox fed and watered, William turned to the small audience gathered in the entry to the barn.

"So? What happened?"

Frank started. "Four riders came in just about midmornin'. Wanted water for their horses. The boss kept Amber busy by the house while the others tended to waterin' but they were countin' noses, and houses all the while."

"How long'd they stay?"

"Better part of an hour. Puttering and fetching. Long time for four horses, even allowin' for Riley and me havin' to fetch it from the pump." He paused. "About the time I figured something would break open, Mother Fairport here marches down from the quarry trail big, as you please, and plants herself next to Amber. The boss man wasn't too pleased with that so he rounded up his boyos and they headed on down the Pike."

William pursed his lips in thought for a moment. "Then what happened?"

Frank nodded at Amber and Tanyth. "We called the boys down from the quarry when it started looking dicey, but they got here just about the time the riders headed down the Pike. These two figgered they'd be back. I did, too, but Jakey figgered we were gettin' panicky over nothing. He wouldn't listen to me. Even Amber had a go, but he shrugged it off and went back up the hill."

William pursed his lips and looked at his wife. "They wouldn't listen to you?"

Amber shook her head. "No, I talked to Jakey and Karl both, but they just said there was nothin' they could do and day light was burnin'. They went back up to the quarry."

William pondered that. "Can't say as I blame 'em from what it mighta looked like at the time." He sighed. "Then what?"

Frank described how they'd rounded up the kids, women and horses and taken the whole lot up to the quarry.

William turned to Tanyth. "But you stayed behind, mum?"

Tanyth shrugged and rested her weight on her staff. "Amber and I were the last ones up the trail. We wanted to make sure we got everybody out before they came back. We almost made it, but they came back too fast and surprised us. Their leader started threatenin' and wouldn't leave us alone. One of 'em rushed me and he ran onto the end of my staff. It winded him pretty good. After that, the leader was pretty mad and he sent the other two bullyboys to round me up. They were almost on me when Thomas here convinced them they couldn't outrun a broadhead."

Amber looked up at William. "Is it over, d'ya think?"

William shrugged. "You seem to have done right by this group. I don't think they'll be back to trouble us."

Amber shook her head. "Ya, but are we safe?"

Tanyth spoke up from where she was standing in the back of the group. "No."

They turned to look at her.

"This bunch has gone, at least for now, but what about the next?"

William shook his head. "We've been here four–going on five–winters now and this is the first time we've had any problems at all."

Frank grimaced and turned to William. "If it hadn't been for her, it mighta been the last and we'd all be raven food."

William frowned but he listened. "What do we do about it?"

Thomas scuffed a foot on the packed ground. "We've too much invested to move lock, stock and barrel, but might make sense to build a cache up at the quarry. We'd have been fine if we'd just all run up to there, but the stores are all here."

Frank nodded. "The end of the track is a logical defense point and the quarry itself is just that much further along. Anybody moving up the track would have a hard time of it."

Thomas looked to Tanyth. "Do you have any ideas, mum? What can we do to make the village safer?"

She leaned on her staff and thought. "A bolt hole at the quarry is good, but that'd take time and it won't be long before winter's on us." She thought for a few moments. "Havin' a bell would be a start."

William frowned in consternation. "Where would we get a bell way out here, mum?"

"Just hang a piece of iron on a rope so you can bang it.

Sound would carry up to the quarry and you won't have to wait for a runner to go up and come back. Won't be pretty but it'd be loud enough."

Frank grinned "And having an alarm ringin' like that would give anybody thinkin' of trouble somethin' else to think about."

Amber grinned and nodded her agreement. "That'd be a help."

William gazed at Tanyth. "A start, mum? What else, d'ya think?"

"An inn. Someplace where travelers could stop and not look at the houses and get ideas."

William tilted his head quizzically. "An inn, mum? With food and rented rooms?"

Frank perked up a bit, too. "And beer?"

She smiled. "Well, perhaps a bit of beer." She paused before adding, "To those who can pay for it."

William looked troubled. "That's a lot of work, mum, running an inn."

"Start small. A common room, kitchen, hearth and rent out space by the fire for a few coppers a night," Tanyth said. "The Mother knows I've spent more'n enough nights on a floor like that myself over these last twenty winters."

William still didn't look convinced. "How's that help keep us safe, mum?"

She looked around their faces. "It gives the village some- thing other than bein' a collection of huts in a wide spot in the road. People react to that. And having a big solid buildin' where people can gather? And defend? That's different than having a bunch of small buildin's that newcomers can get the wrong idea about. Besides, once you have an inn, then people might wanna come live here and work in it. It'll be somethin' that'd tide you over until spring, too, when you can't quarry."

Amber nodded her agreement but added an obstacle of her own. "That's well and good, mum, but who's gonna run this establishment?"

Nobody answered directly but they all looked at her.

"What?" Amber looked around in alarm. "You're not thinking that I can run an inn."

Nobody answered.

"Are you?"

Tanyth nodded. "I think you'd make the perfect innkeeper, Amber."

"That's crazy. What do I know about running an inn?" Amber shook her head in exasperation and turned. "I've hungry kids to feed. You are all welcome to come along but this is foolish." She turned and stalked out of the barn.

William looked at Tanyth with an "I told you so" look but Frank was eying the older woman wth a gleam in his eye. "What else, do you think, mum?"

She thought for only a heartbeat. "You better name this place before somebody names it for you."

William looked startled but Frank nodded. "I've been sayin' that for the last two winters." He turned to look at the younger man. "Why haven't we picked a name, William?"

William frowned. "I don't like the names people picked out for us." He said it in a low grumble. "Come on! Let's go get some supper." He followed Amber's path out of the workroom without looking to see if anybody was following him.

Tanyth watched him go with some amount of amusement before falling in behind. She turned to Thomas who walked beside her. "What names have they offered?"

Thomas smirked. "Clayton was one, but that's not the favorite."

"What's the favorite?"

Frank spoke from behind. "Mapleton."

She looked over her shoulder. "Mapleton? Named after him?"

Frank chuckled. "Yes'm. He hates the idea, but most folks like it. He just won't stand fer it."

Tanyth looked at Thomas. "Do they really like it because it's the right name? Or are they just twittin' him about having a town named for him?"

Thomas shrugged. "Dunno. But it's been a running argument here for the last two winters."

They trouped along in William's wake and took advantage of Amber's hospitality by lounging about her hearth and feasting on fresh tomatoes, hot bread, and strong cheese. William seemed lost in thought but Amber had already apparently forgotten the conversation about being the innkeeper even as she proved her skill at hospitality by feeding them all, along with her own kids and a couple of the other children. Sadie provided the bread and their mood was festive in spite the darkness that had swept across them during the day. Or perhaps because of it.

As the meal wound down, the extra children trundled off and the rest curled into snug beds and were soon asleep. The conversation lagged for a bit before Sadie, bird bright and looking for an answer, moved on to the next subject. "What's this about an inn, then?"

She looked back and forth between William and Tanyth, waiting for an explanation, but it was Frank who spoke up. "We were talkin' about ways to cut down the risk of unpleasantness like today. Mother Fairport here says she thinks we oughta have an inn."

Sadie looked at Tanyth with a wide eyed smile. "That's a wonderful idea, mum. Why do you think that'll keep us safe?"

Tanyth shrugged. "Harder to ignore an inn, but also if the place has an inn, then it's harder to figure nobody'll notice if you get up to mischief." She indicated the houses around with a nod of her head. "This village is like any other of a hundred others in wide spots all up and down the road. Easy to think nobody'll notice if there's trouble, and you'd probably be right."

Sadie turned to William and Amber. "You don't like the idea, Amber?"

"They want me to be the innkeeper." Amber sounded aghast by the idea.

Sadie shrugged, unfazed. "Sounds about right. You do all the greetin' in the door yard now. Might as well have an inn to go with it. What do you think of this, William?"

He shrugged. "I think she's got the right of it. We'll be safer if we're bigger and having an inn would at least make us look bigger."

Sadie looked at Thomas and Frank. "What about you

two?"

Thomas shrugged. "I think it's a good idea."

"I think so, too," Frank said. "Mother Fairport thinks it might get more people to come live here and it'll give us a bit of income that's not dependent on clay."

"So what's the problem?" Sadie looked pointedly at William.

He didn't look up from the bowl in front of him. "It'll take time and money we don't have."

Frank spoke up. "It might if you're thinking about something like one of the inns in Kleesport, Will, but you've seen the inn at Mossport, and I know you've traveled enough to have slept on taproom floors yourself."

William gave a grudging nod. "True. And we could probably build something better than that poor excuse for an inn in Mossport, but where do we get the materials and labor?"

Frank shook his head. "That's the least of our problem. We've got enough good timber right here to build another building as big as the barn without clearing more than we'd need for next spring's garden as it is."

William sighed. "We really need a smith out here if we're gonna do this."

Thomas cast a disgusted look at him. "Now you're just finding rocks in the sand. We don't need a smith. We need a barrel of nails and some hinges for another door or two."

"If we could make them it would be better," William insisted.

Frank snorted. "Better, but not needed. And we'll have Jakey's crew layin' about until spring in another few weeks. We only have one more trip this season and then we won't quarry any more until spring. There's still plenty of time to settle a frame and put up a roof. Once that's in place we can work on it even after snow flies, if need be, but I bet we'd have it done before the Solstice."

"What about the kiln? We were gonna build a kiln this winter so we could start firing our own bricks." William looked around the table, the challenge on his face.

Amber cleared her throat delicately and all eyes turned to her. "I've been thinking about that."

William cocked his head. "Really?"

She nodded. "It was an interesting idea, but you've seen the brickworks outside Kleesport."

William shrugged. "Yes. Of course. That's what gave me the idea."

She looked at him with one arched eyebrow. "And do you want to live beside that?"

Frank shifted his weight uncomfortably and even Thomas looked anyplace but at Amber and William.

Finally, William sighed and answered, "No."

She shrugged. "So, we don't build a kiln. We keep shipping the clay to Kleesport. It's a steady work and gets us a bit of coin to spend with the merchants there for what we can't make ourselves, but this inn?" She shrugged. "Might make more sense for where we are."

They looked at each other for a long moment, before William grinned. "And you'd be the innkeeper?"

She sighed and her shoulders slumped. "If that's what it takes." She hesitated. "But what do we call it?"

Sadie shrugged. "We can just name it after the village. That's what everybody else does."

Frank twisted his mouth into a wry grin. "So, what do we name the town?"

They all turned to Tanyth. She looked startled. "What? You want me to name it?"

Frank grinned. "You're doing pretty well so far."

They were all smiling at her, encouraging her. She took a deep breath, and closed her eyes to think. The only sounds were the crackling of the fire and the faint sigh of wind through the eaves. "Ravenwood." The word was out of her mouth before she thought.

Frank pounced on the name. "Ravenwood! I like it."

She looked at them with something akin to shock. "I'm sorry. It was just the first thing that came to mind."

William nodded and a considering look covered Amber's face. Sadie clapped her hands together in delight and sprang to her feet. "It's perfect. We'll name the town Ravenwood and then the inn can be Ravenwood Inn!" She fairly bounced on her toes in excitement.

William watched her with some amusement. "Well, I guess

we now live in Ravenwood." He looked at Tanyth. "At least it's not Mapleton."

Amber laughed. "That really bothered you, didn't it?"

He nodded, a rueful grimace on his face.

Frank chuckled but offered Tanyth a sympathetic explanation. "When you've grown up in the shadow of his father, the name carries extra freight."

Thomas groaned at the pun and tossed a bit of bread at the older man.

The nearly full moon painted an oblong of silver on the floor through the open doorway and William eyed the glow. He heaved himself up off the floor and handed his wife up as well. "Let's go figure out where we'll build your inn."

They all clambered out of the house. William with Amber on his arm led the procession which soon picked up a few more adults, a handful of interested children, and at least two drowsy chickens. They spent an hour in pleasant contemplation by the light of the moon and discovered that they had more than enough room for a relatively large structure that would neither block the track to the barn nor require them to demolish any of the houses.

Tanyth observed the proceedings from the front of her hut and watched the sky for ravens.

CHAPTER 12
A CHEEKY BIRD

Tanyth found morning long before the sun did. She woke suddenly, her heart in her throat, sure that somebody was in the hut with her. Her hand slipped to the hilt of her belt knife where it rested inside her bedroll. Habits formed from sleeping wild hadn't been broken by sleeping under a roof for a few nights. Her eyes raked the shadows. There wasn't anyone there. The faint glow from the banked coals in the fireplace gave sufficient light for her to make out every corner of the hut well enough to know nobody hid in the shadows. She took two deep breaths and tried to convince herself that it was too early to rise, but failed to calm the pounding in her chest.

After a few moments of lying with her eyes closed and her pulse racing, she gave up and crawled out of her bedroll. Her stockings offered her feet some protection from the cold floor until she stepped on the hearthstone, which still carried a little warmth from the banked fire. She plucked a pair of smaller pieces from the woodbox and proceeded to stoke up a fresh blaze. While it worked up some heat, she returned to her bedroll and dug out her outer clothing, slipping on her warm tunic but leaving her pants off until she had enough warm water for tea and to clean herself a bit. She sighed as she realized that she really needed to take time to wash out some small clothes, at least. She returned to the hearth and added another stick to the growing blaze there, pushing the tea kettle closer and considering her dwindling stock of tea and oatmeal. The routine of fire and warmth soothed her jangled nerves and she slipped into the simple routine of morning.

After dealing with the mundane matters of hygiene and breakfast, she slipped out into the dawn. The sky was still nearly dark–only the translucent scale of morning to brighten the east and wash the dimmest of the stars out of half the sky. The morning air had the cleanest bite of the day and she took several lungs full, letting each one out slowly before taking the next. It wasn't cold enough to see her breath, but she could tell the day was not far off.

She stood there, listening. She wasn't sure what she was listening for, or perhaps listening to. The trees in the surrounding forest whispered among themselves in the last of the night's breeze. The breeze faded and they hushed as if they'd been talking about her. She smiled at the idea, as if she were important enough for the very trees to talk about.

The humorous thought gave rise to an idea that was more serious. Twice in two days she'd prayed to the guardians and the All-Mother for protections and boons–first giving thanks for the willow bark but later asking for help in what might have been a dire time. Something in her made her walk to the clearing behind her hut and thank each of the guardians in turn for their assistance in her time of trial. She closed her circle with a simple thank you to the All-Mother and the All-Father. She felt better once she'd finished. She stood there for a few minutes savoring the quiet calm and taking strength from the fertile earth beneath her feet.

She stood there long enough that she heard Thomas slip out of his hut and head off up the track toward the quarry, no doubt heading out for a day's hunting. She heard Frank and William chatting softly as they met on the path to the barn, each heading up to care for the animals entrusted to them. In spite of the chaos and danger of the day before, she felt at peace. She'd been on the road long enough to know that nobody was really safe with the wild things loose in the world, but a little judicious planning and attention to detail could help.

She sauntered around to the front of the hut and crossed the dewy grass to examine the scratchings on the ground and the sticks they'd placed to mark the corners of the new inn. As the morning sun clawed through the trees, she smiled at the placements and squinted her eyes a bit to try to envision the building. If they were right in their estimates, the building might well appear–at least in frame–within a relatively few weeks. Frank and William had both agreed that foundation, framing, and roof were entirely feasible before the snow closed in for the winter.

She paced off the length and smiled when she came to where Amber had drawn the outlines of her new kitchen by scraping the dirt with a branch in the near dark. It wobbled a bit but it was a good sized area. It would provide them with plenty of room to start with and offered space behind for growth. Tanyth smiled. Amber may have been opposed to being the innkeeper at first, but as she warmed to the idea, her natural talents proved the obviousness of the solution.

She heard the jingling of harness and the pounding of hooves coming along the Pike from the south. The sun was barely into the trees, still throwing ribbons of light between the trunks and lighting the sky with a morning display. A messenger wearing the uniform of the King's Own pounded along and sped past the village without looking in. Tanyth had watched the pattern of messengers on the Pike long enough to know that in a day or so, another of the King's Own would come riding the other direction.

She admired the layout of what would become the new inn for a few more moments and then walked back to her hut and the chores that awaited. Her mind caught up the logistical problem of how and where to resupply her dwindling store of tea and oatmeal. While there was tea in the village, it wasn't the same, and oatmeal was all but unheard of among them. There was also the problem of winter clothing. She'd planned on shifting her wardrobe when she got to Kleesport, swapping her lighter sweaters and jacket for something a bit more sub-stantial for the coming winter in the northlands. With time on her hands and some suitable fabrics, she could certainly fashion her own. She made a mental note to ask Amber about it. She'd know how to make the arrangements.

William and Bester came down the track from the barn,

heading out for their day's labor. He smiled to see her standing in the morning light and raised a hand in greeting. When he got nearer he spoke, his voice carrying over the crunching of the oxcart's wheels. "G'mornin', mum. You're up early."

She smiled. "Good morning, yourself, William. I couldn't sleep so got up and had my breakfast." She fell in beside him. "How are you? Now that you've had a night to sleep on it, what do you think of this?" She swept a hand to indicate the scratchings on the ground.

He gave a slow nod. "I'm fine, mum. And I think this is really a very good idea." His eyes swept the area as he walked along. "Amber does, too, now that she's had a chance to think about it." A glowing smile spread across his face. "She'll be wonderful as the innkeeper."

Tanyth nodded. "I think so, too."

They were almost at the Pike and Tanyth stepped off onto the verge to let Bester and the cart pass out onto the packed road. "Have a good day, William. Blessed be." She raised her hand in a wave.

William smiled. "Thank you, mum. You, too. Try not to have any more excitement today, please?"

She laughed in response. "I'll do my best."

William steered Bester northward and was soon lost to view.

Tanyth turned to retrace her steps. The chilly morning was giving way to the sun's warmth but she thought another cup of tea would taste good. A flash of movement drew her attention and she looked up to see the raven settling onto the ridgepole of her roof once more. The bird fluffed its feathers and then sleeked them back, seeming to ignore her presence below. It rolled its head as if settling skull to spine and then shifted its head from left to right as if showing off the heavy bill in profile, first on one side and then on the other. Tanyth realized, with a bit of a shock, that it was actually looking at her, first one eye, then the other. The liquid gold of the bird's eye seemed to almost glow against the black feathers and some trick of the morning had a bolt of sunlight shining almost horizontally through the trees and reflecting off the glossy blackness.

Tanyth's immediate sense of surprise subsided and she spoke to the bird without really thinking about it. "Well, aren't you a cheeky thing."

The raven gave a soft caw as if answering.

Tanyth tried to decide if her odd dream from the previous day had been real and contemplated the idea that she'd been actually looking through the eyes of a raven–perhaps this raven–as it soared above the Pike, wings easily out-pacing hooves. The whole idea was fantastic, yet there seemed no other explanation. She could have been dreaming it, wishful thinking driving the images in her exhausted brain into patterns of desire–and after all, isn't that what dreams are?

"But why a raven?" She murmured.

The bird opened its bill and gave a series of short cackling sounds, not exactly a bird laugh, but certainly not the full throated caw one expected to hear.

She chuckled, at herself as much as the antics of the bird, and resumed her steps toward the house. When she got closer, the bird flicked its tail, leaving a squirt of white droppings streaked across the roof as it jumped into the air and flapped heavily southward across the open land of the village and disappeared into the forest beyond.

Tanyth's lips quirked into a sideways grin. "Cheeky thing!"

From the forest, near where the bird had disappeared, she heard a raven's croaking caw.

She stopped with her hand on the latch and looked over her shoulder, momentarily overcome by the memories of veiled comments from some of her teachers. Comments about the birds of the air and the fish in the stream. Comments that hinted that magic had been loose in the world before and that it might be returning–or perhaps had never left.

She shook herself to try to toss off the incongruous ideas but they'd just swirled in her mind–leaves lifted by a zephyr, stirred around and redeposited in new patterns but not blown away. She sighed in exasperation at her own silliness and wondered if perhaps the change that was beginning to sweep her body was giving her odd things to think about to distract her from the deeper changes.

The raven cawed again as Tanyth slipped into the hut.

Shaking her head, she poked up the fire and re-filled her kettle from the bucket. It would be a few minutes before the water was hot enough for tea and the early waking caught up with her suddenly. The comfort of her bedroll called her and she stretched out on top of it to rest her eyes while the water came to a boil. Sleep drew her downward as soon as she stretched out and she was barely aware of hearing the raven call a third time as the black waves of sleep swept over her.

A man lay flat on the ground behind the bole of a heavy oak. He faced away from her, head up and peering over the root at something in the clearing beyond. She was surprised to see he wore the same clothing as one of the boyos they'd run off the day before. Lying on the ground and facing away, she couldn't see his face but her view shifted, swinging left and right in a pattern that looked familiar but which she couldn't quite place. Her attention was drawn upwards along the man's line of sight. She could see him peering into a clearing with a collection of huts and with a pang of alarm she recognized them, even from the unusual angle.

She cawed once more in alarm. The man rolled his head around to look at her. She recognized the face as the man who'd been knocked down and winded during the scuffle. He picked up a small twig and threw it at her. It fell short and bounced off several small branches. Still, take no chances, and with a final caw, she spread her wings and dropped off the limb to glide between the loosely spaced trees, putting distance between her and the watching man.

Tanyth woke with a pounding in her chest.

CHAPTER 13
SKUNK IN THE WOODPILE

"A dream. Just a dream. You're a paranoid old woman."

Tanyth kept telling herself that, but it didn't do anything for the pounding in her head.

She made herself not tear the door open. She fought the urge to hare across the intervening space and confront the man–if he were actually there. She stirred her tea and took a sip, burning her tongue on the near boiling liquid. She set the cup down on the table and drew a deep breath. She didn't dare close her eyes to concentrate, but she squinted them and blew the breath out.

"Focus, old fool. Focus."

First, was the village in danger again? She needed to find out if the bravos had come back to worry them. The day was still young and she knew Frank was about.

Second, were these dreams? Visions sent by the All-Mother to help guide and protect her? Or was she just going mad?

As she sat there at the small table in the half light of early morning, she wasn't sure which of the two things alarmed her more–that they might be being watched by people who wished them harm, or that she may be going mad. Age did strange things to people sometimes and she'd seen plenty of examples over the many winters she sought out all the old herbalists and healers she could find. She sighed, considering that the price of wisdom sometimes appeared to be too dear.

With her fear controlled, if not conquered, she needed action. She sipped the cooling tea, unwilling to waste the precious leaves by walking off with the cup half full. She stood from the table and slipped into her warm tunic. Her hat went on her head and she took staff in hand.

She slipped the latch on the back door of her hut and slipped out, closing it carefully behind her. She wondered if there was somebody watching on that side of the village as well, but she forced herself not to look at the tree line. With one step after another, focusing on the ground and not her steps, she sauntered as naturally as possible around the outside perimeter of huts until she was able to make a bee line for the barn. She found Frank rolling a barrow of muck out of the barn and onto the pile.

He smiled to see her. "Morning, mum. You're up early."

"Too early, and I think we may have a problem."

He parked the barrow and dusted his hands together, looking at her intently. "What kind of problem, mum?"

"I think one of the men that was here yesterday has come back. I thought I saw somebody peeking out of the trees opposite my cottage."

He looked startled. "Are you certain, mum?"

She shook her head. "No, actually, I'm not." She smiled apologetically. "It might have merely been a trick of the light."

"Was it just the one?"

She shrugged. "I only saw the one, but who knows if the others were there as well and I just didn't see them."

He pursed his lips in thought and then fetched the hay fork from its hook by the stalls. "Let's go see if you saw what you saw, shall we, mum?"

Together they slipped out of the barn and worked their way down the tree line on the south side of the village's clearing. Tanyth hadn't been on this side before and spotted several patches of yarrow and wild carrot growing in the understory where the forest tried to reclaim the clearing.

They walked quietly, keeping eyes and ears open. Tanyth heard nothing but the normal sounds of the forest. The *tzeep, tzeep* of a sparrow in the undergrowth sounded loud in her ears and even the soft passage of wind through the treetops above carried clearly. She kept glancing northward, looking for the angle, the view she'd seen in her dream trying to match the reality against her memory even as it slipped sideways in her mind each time she tried to recapture it.

Frank offered no comment as they walked further and further, just kept his eyes sweeping the trees and undergrowth to their right.

Tanyth was about to give up on the vision when the scene snapped into focus. She stopped in her tracks, her head twisted to the left and the angle on her hut matched the angle from her dream. Her breath caught in her throat. Frank fetched up his step and looked to her in concern.

"Did you see something, mum?"

Tanyth turned her head and looked straight into the woods in the opposite direction. Just behind the verge of undergrowth a large oak lifted a canopy of leaves to the sky. "Here."

Frank peered into the brush and poked the hay fork ahead. Nothing stirred so he stepped into the cover of the forest. Tanyth followed and was relieved to find nobody there. She stepped carefully around Frank and walked further into the woods, glancing back periodically, looking for the tree where the raven had perched. She was still not sure if what she'd seen was a vision, a dream, or something else and the uncertainty scraped her nerves raw. There were several likely candidates for perches but she was unable to pick out one that she could point to and say with certainty.

"What are you looking for, mum?" Frank's voice was low but drew her back to the reality.

She turned to see him with the fork planted in the ground and looking alternately at her and then around at the surrounding woods, unsure what he should be looking for but obviously alarmed at her actions.

"Sorry." Her reply was likewise hushed. "I was just looking to see if I could see anybody. I must have been mistaken."

Frank nodded. "Well, mum, there's nobody here now for certain."

She sighed and made one last turn around. "Maybe I was wrong." Her eyes went to the base of the oak and the large roots behind which the man in her vision had been lying.

Frank's eyes followed her gaze and he stepped closer to the tree to peer downward. He looked up at her, eyes wide in surprise. "He's gone now, but there was somebody here right enough." He pointed with the tines of the fork and she stepped closer to see what he was looking at.

In the small depression behind the tree, small clumps of forest grasses were crushed and a seedling had been bent over and nearly broken off near the ground. Her mind overlaid the image of the man rolling over and tossing the small twig at the raven and her eyes went to a sparse and broken hemlock with a single solid branch about five feet above the ground.

"We need to let the others know." Frank's voice carried anger and urgency.

Tanyth nodded absently, lost inside her mind, somewhere between madness and horror.

"Mum?" Frank was looking at her, half turned toward the village but unwilling to leave her standing there alone.

She shook her head and smiled, if a bit tentatively. "Yes, of course, Frank. Thank you for coming with me."

"Thank you, mum, for being so watchful."

She shrugged and shook her head again, walking ahead of Frank and stepping out into the open light of morning.

They walked briskly away from the woods but Tanyth stopped in the track that led to the Pike.

Frank halted beside her in surprise. "Mum? We need to let the others know."

"Let them know what, Frank?" Her voice wasn't challenging but curious. "That we're being watched from the woods, certainly, but what do we do about it?" She looked around her. "What can they want?"

Frank grimaced. "Just to make trouble, I suspect."

She shook her head. "There has to be something more to it. They can make trouble any where. They know we have nothing worth their time here, so why are they still here?"

Frank shrugged. "Well, there's still the women, mum?" He blushed when he realized what he was suggesting and to whom.

She caught the embarrassed look on his face and it tickled her more than it might have in other circumstances. "That's possible, but I suspect they want something more than a fast tumble."

"You have a reason for sayin' that, mum?" Frank asked.

"They rode off. Now they're back. Yesterday the idea of a little strike-and-go on some defenseless women might have appealed in a kind of spur of the moment idea." She pursed her lips and leaned on her staff. "That moment passed when they rode away."

Frank rested the butt of the fork on the ground and cocked his head quizzically. "There's some truth to that, mum." His brow furrowed as he thought. "But what could they want?"

"We have food, water, houses."

"But they got a good enough look yesterday to know we ain't rich here."

"Except they know there's something up that trail and they didn't get to see that yesterday." She nodded at the track that led up to the clay quarry.

"That's true enough, mum, but if they've had a man watching the village, they must have had a chance to scout up there."

"Or they will soon. Jakey and the others went up just after sun up and our friend must have seen or heard them go."

"So, we can assume they'll know who, how many, and what's going on here. That's more'n they knew riding in yesterday. But why'd they come back for a second look, mum?"

Tanyth shrugged in reply. "I don't know, Frank. That's what bothers me." She eyed him for a moment. "How soon before you take the next load to town?"

He blinked at the sudden change in subject. "Jakey and the boys say they'll be done in another couple of days. The wagon can only carry so many barrels of the clay safely and they're filling the last one tomorrow or the next day. I'll be taking the lorry wagon up there today so we can begin stacking them."

"First things first. Is there an old wheel rim or barrel hoop we can hang up as an alarm bell?"

He nodded. "I suspect there's at least one up in the store room." He motioned with his head and they started up the track. Three chickens scurried out of their path, clucking angrily at being disturbed in their scratching.

Frank went around the side of the barn and under the

shed roof where the ox cart usually rested. He rummaged in the weeds growing up along the foundation and pulled a half buried metal barrel hoop out of the ground. He held it up in boyish triumph. "I knew it." The rim was hardly new but it appeared sound except for a break in its smooth curve. A small chunk of metal was missing from the ring.

He lugged it out and set it beside the front of the barn while he rummaged in the tack room and brought back a long strip of leather. He held it up for Tanyth to see. "Busted reins. Be good to hang this on though."

He fashioned a quick loop and held the rig up by the leather strap. "Whack it, mum!"

She looked around for something to hit it with for a moment then felt foolish for overlooking the staff that was already in her hand. She hit it once with the gnarled knot at the top. The resulting gong didn't seem quite as sharp as she'd have hoped.

Frank screwed up his mouth in a grimace. "Didn't sound much like an alarm bell, did it, mum?"

She shook her head ruefully. "Nope. I was hoping for something with a bit more clang to it."

He nodded at the barn door. "There's a couple iron pokers standin' just inside the door there, mum. Try one of them."

She stepped into the barn, and selected one of the indicated fire irons. She leaned her staff against the barn door and gripped the poker in both hands.

Frank grinned at her and held the leather up higher to give her a good target.

She drew back and gave it a good whack. The resulting discordant clang echoed up her arms and across the valley. She grinned and saw the answering grin break across Frank's face as well.

He laughed in delight. "All we need to do is hang this someplace handy." He lowered it to the ground and let it lean against his leg. "Where do you think?"

She grimaced in thought. "Not in the front of the village."

He frowned in concentration and turned his gaze to the line of trees behind the huts. "Someplace behind the line of houses but maybe not as far as the quarry track?"

She nodded in reply. "Is there enough of an overhang to hang it off the eaves there on the backside of the last hut?" She pointed to where she meant.

He nodded. "Yup. We'll wanna ask Megan and Harry first, but that looks like a good place." He took the ring over to the barn and leaned it against the building. "Harry's up at the quarry now, but I'll see him in a bit when I take the wagon up."

Tanyth put the poker beside the ring and retrieved her staff from its resting place. "I'll talk to Megan, too." She looked up at him. "And thank you, Frank. I appreciate your going with me to look in the woods."

He smiled. "You call on me anytime, mum." He shook his head in amusement. "Funny things happen around you, but it ain't been half dull here since you arrived."

She laughed. "Thank you, I think."

He tipped his head in a shortened bow and turned for the barn. "Well, I need to harness up a couple of these critters and get that lorry up the track, mum, but hollar if you need anything."

"I will, Frank. I will." She watched him amble into the barn and move among the shadows, speaking softly to the horses and moving deliberately around them. She surprised herself by noticing how nicely he filled out his jacket. She snorted softly and turned her feet toward her hut. "Fool woman. Got no time for that silliness."

Still, it bothered her. What did they want with the village? Simple harassment didn't put food in the pot and even bully boys needed to eat. Her thoughts chased themselves around in her head but caught up to no conclusions. Part of it seemed logical to her. She cursed the darn foolishness that young men got themselves into all the time. The fact that they'd come back, and that she couldn't figure out why, bothered her almost as much as the raven visions.

The memories from the two episodes exploded in her. She'd been distracted enough to overlook the implications but the reality of it crashed over her again between one step and the next. She had to grab her staff and stop to keep from losing her balance. She leaned heavily on it, not quite gasping for breath.

She'd been able to dismiss the dream of the raven's flying. Just a dream, of course, she didn't really see the men through a raven's eye. But what of the morning? How could she have known about the spy in the wood if not for the raven? "Madness." She hissed the word. "Madness." Suddenly conscious that she stood in the middle of the track, she drew herself up, gathering her strength and straightening her tunic. A cup of chamomile tea would set her right. She was sure of it. With her resolve held firmly like a shield, she resumed her sedate stroll to the hut. As she entered she studiously ignored the streak of white bird droppings on the roof.

CHAPTER 14
AFTER MADNESS, LAUNDRY

The chamomile tea helped sooth her nerves as did focusing on washing out her meager supply of clothing. She spread the wet clothes on the grass outside her back door and let her mind idle on the idea that she might be going mad.

"You're not going mad." She said it to herself but had difficulty accepting it in the face of her experiences.

She poured a bit more hot water over the chamomile and pulled a chair up to the hearth. The exertion of laundry had warmed her body, but she still felt cold inside. The warmth of the fire, and the growing warmth of the day, slowly unwound her and she sipped her tea in contemplation. Whatever was happening, it was not madness. She'd had a vision that seemed real. "Twice!" she reminded herself. The first could have been a dream. The second might have been as well except that she'd taken Frank and investigated only to find that the man–or somebody–had actually been there. "Not madness." She said the words distinctly aloud as if to convince herself.

She breathed easier. "Not madness." She repeated it softly and stared into the fire. "Not madness."

The sound of feet outside her door and the whisperings of children interrupted her revery. A timid knock sounded followed by a polite silence.

She smiled and crossed to open the door. Riley stood there with several of his small chums. In their arms they carried her clothing. "Riley? What's all this?"

"Sorry to disturb you, mum, but we found these blowin' away."

She looked out and realized that what had been a calm morning had turned into a breezy afternoon. She laughed and held out her hands. "Thank you so much for rounding these up."

The children all stepped up and placed the articles of clothing into her hands, as if jewels to the queen. She had to bite back her laughter at their solemnity. When all the clothing had been delivered–what little of it there actually was–she bowed to the assembly. "Thank you very kindly. I'll take pains to make sure it doesn't happen again."

Riley stepped forward and held out a small coil of rope. "Ma sent this over, mum. She says you should ask any time you need help."

"Thank you, Riley, and thank your mother for me. This'll help a great deal."

"You're welcome, mum." He stood expectantly.

"Is there something else, Riley?"

"Yes, mum, we was wonderin' if we could help you gather herbs and stuff."

His entourage stood like good little soldiers and looked hopeful, if a bit awe struck.

Her eyes went to the tree line and she considered. It wouldn't do to take the children into the forest, but perhaps there was something they could do. "Yes, Riley. I think you can. There are some very valuable materials right here in the village that should be harvested and set to drying before the frosts come and destroy them." She looked from small face to small dirty face and smiled. "Would you like to help me?"

They all nodded happily.

"Excellent. Then one moment while I put away my clothes and I'll be right out and we can begin."

She stepped down into the hut and tossed the clothing onto the cot. She pulled out the gleaner's bag and dumped the collection of nuts and fruit onto the hearthstone. She pricked several of the chestnuts with her belt knife and slid them into the hot ash for later. She slapped her hat on her head, picked up her staff and stepped back out into the early afternoon sun.

"What'll we pick, mum?" A little girl with wavy blonde hair was looking up at her with wide green eyes.

"Mints, I think." She leaned down to get at the little girl's level. "And who are you?"

"I'm Sandy, mum!" She announced it proudly. "I'm Megan and Harry's offshoot!"

Tanyth smiled at the gap-toothed grin looking up. "Well, Sandy, let's go find some mint. Do you know what mint is?"

Tanyth headed off to the back of the hut where she'd already noticed that Mother Alderton had some very healthy stands of peppermint and cat mint.

Sandy fell in beside her on one side and Riley, not to be outdone, took the other. The three of them led the parade of small people around the corner and into the taller plants. "I do, mum. Mint is a weed!"

"A weed?"

"Yes, mum! Momma says that every time she finds the mint has jumped the fence and gotten into the garden! 'Get this weed out of my vegetable patch!'" Sandy smiled up winningly. "She usually uses a bad word that I'm not allowed to say."

Tanyth controlled her grin with an effort. "Well, mints are very robust plants. They spread easily and grow very fast."

"Is that a good thing, mum?" Riley asked.

"Yes, Riley. Unless you're trying to grow vegetables and the mint keeps getting in the way."

He nodded sagely. "Yes, mum, I can see that."

Tanyth stopped in a weedy looking patch that was so rich in mint varieties that the aroma nearly overwhelmed her. "Well, here we are!"

The children looked disappointed, and Riley spoke up. "I thought we were gonna go collectin', mum!"

"We are." She smiled at them. "And you're all going to be very helpful, I know."

Sandy tugged on her pants leg. "But we di'n't go anywheres, mum. Just behind your house."

Tanyth nodded. "Yes. That's because I need to collect all this before the winter kills it. Almost all of these plants are different kinds of mints. They have different smells, and different flowers, and different shapes, but they all have two things in common."

The children all looked up at her expectantly.

She reached down and pulled a couple of leaves from a nearby plant, crushing them between her fingers before holding her hand out to the children, one at a time. "Smell. What do you smell?"

"Smells green." Sandy looked up at her after almost rubbing her nose in the crushed leaves.

Tanyth nodded happily. "Yes, it does. That's a very good description. That green smell is the smell of mint. All these plants have that same smell. Not exactly the same, mind you, but enough to tell it's a mint."

When all the children had sniffed her hand, she smiled. "And the other thing is that they all have square stems!"

The children's eyes all grew large and they started looking at the plants around them. Tanyth crouched, trimmed a stalk of gray catmint off at the base with her knife, and stood up again showing them all the four cornered cross section of the stem.

"Any plant that has a square stem and smells green like that is a mint. They smell good, make nice tea, and sometimes people even make mint jelly!"

Sandy announced clearly. "I like jelly. It's very good on bread."

Tanyth laughed. "Yes, young miss, it is indeed."

Riley looked about him. "How much of this do we have to collect?"

Tanyth could see him measuring and calculating how long the mint collecting might go on and he wasn't happy with the answer. "All of this needs to be harvested before frost kills it." She watched his face drop before taking pity on him. "But we'll only gather a few stalks to set to dry today. We can get more tomorrow." That announcement cheered them greatly.

She took off her gleaners bag and handed it to Sandy. "If you'd hold that for me, Sandy?"

She nodded solemnly.

"Just hold the top open so everybody can put their stalks

of mint into it." She turned the half dozen children around her. "I'll cut, you each take a bundle and put it into the bag that Sandy's holding, cut end down and leafy end up. Understand?"

They nodded but not very convincingly.

"Good!" She got down on her knees in the drying soil and pulled her belt knife once more. She collected a handful of mint stalks, used the knife to slice them off just above ground level and passed the handful to the nearest child. She grabbed the next handful and repeated the process. She collected like types together, collecting several handfuls of common green peppermint before moving on to collect a large bundle of gray-leaved catmint. The more she cut, the more she identified, and the more she came to admire Mother Alderton's work in getting all these mints in one place.

They worked for almost a whole hour before the children became bored with the process. On the plus side, they'd nearly filled the gleaner's bag with various mints from common green mint to a pungent peppermint and a musky, gray-leaved catmint. There was even some lavender mint–not the woody lavender ground cover but a mint that carried some of the same oils and aromas that the woody lavender had. She called a halt to the gathering, thanked the children lavishly for their aid, and dismissed them with a wave before clambering ponderously to her feet. Her knees didn't want to unbend and she groaned quietly as the circulation took a more vertical path. She hefted the gleaner's bag onto her shoulder. The bag weighed more than she expected and she realized that it was probably a good thing that they'd stopped. She needed to bind and hang the freshly cut stems for drying and that much plant matter would take a bit of time to sort and bind properly.

She hobbled across the short distance to her back door–hips and knees letting her know that next time she should have the shorter members of her gathering crew kneel on the ground. A few items of small clothes had not blown away earlier so she collected those and took the whole lot into the hut. As she lowered herself gingerly down the steps, she was surprised to realize she felt renewed. Breathing the fresh scents of earth and plant, feeling the sun on her back and the breeze in her face had given her new spirit, new strength after two terrifying days. The boyos were still lurking in the undergrowth and there was still the curious relationship with the ravens, but she felt like these were, somehow, more manageable.

She smiled to herself. Being with the children for the afternoon didn't hurt either. They were so young, so earnest. Riley reminded her a bit of her own Robert as a small boy, all sturdy leg and nut brown summertime skin. She sighed half in regret, but half in contentment as well.

Inside the hut, she stoked up the fire and cleared the table so she had room to work. With front and back doors open the day's light provided all the illumination she needed and, indeed, it felt good to get out of the direct sun. The heat of the day still carried weight, even so close to the equinox.

Mother Alderton had left a ball of string on her shelves and Tanyth used the rough twine to bind the stalks of mint together, twining the stem and string in a way that left them collected together neatly without being crushed. As her fingers worked the string and stalks, her mind gnawed at the problem of the riders, and as terrifying as the dream episodes had been, she found herself wondering if she could use them to find the men and see what they were doing; to see if they were still out there somewhere, ready to make trouble. She used her broom to lift the bundles up to iron nails driven into the rafters where only a few days before she and Amber had pulled down the old and musty crop of dried materials. It didn't seem possible to her that so much had happened in so short a time.

With the last of the cuttings bound and hung, the hut took on the pungent aroma of fresh mint. Tanyth found it quite relaxing and a pleasant change from the neutral–and slightly dusty–aromas of ash and grass that had permeated the hut. She drew a deep breath and thought again of the raven.

She closed the doors, casting the interior into near darkness except for a cheery flame in the hearth. She crossed to the cot and folded up her small clothes, stowing them in her pack once more and feeling satisfied that she'd have fresh clothes on the morrow. With the bedroll cleared, she stretched out and deliberately closed her eyes thinking of the ravens and the boyos and willing herself to see what the men were up to. In moments she fell asleep.

After what seemed like only a few moments she awoke again. The light had shifted to late afternoon and her fire had burned down to a few embers. She felt quite rested but slightly disappointed that she'd not been able to contact the ravens and that she didn't know what the men might be up to, or even if they were still there.

She rose sighing and used the poker to pull the roasted chestnuts out of the hot ash before poking up the coals and adding a couple of fresh sticks. Her woodbox was getting a bit empty and filling her tea kettle almost emptied the water bucket. She wondered if she could impose on young Riley to refill one or the other for her.

"You're gettin' lazy in your dotage, old woman." She told herself good naturedly, but she had to admit, that having somebody take care of these two particular chores made life much more pleasant.

CHAPTER 15
A WARNING

While the tea kettle warmed, Tanyth took her bucket to the well. As she stepped out the front door, she saw Frank sitting on the ground in front of his hut across the way. He was whittling on a stick, and judging from the pile of slivers around him, he'd been at it quite awhile. He smiled when he saw her and gave a jaunty salute with the tip of the blade.

She waved back and continued on to the well. By the time she'd gotten there, Frank and Riley had fallen in beside her, man on one side, boy on the other. She was amused and a bit taken aback by the attention.

"Afternoon, mum." Frank's weather-creased face carried a gentle smile around the eyes.

"Hello, Frank." She turned to the boy. "And hello, Riley. Recovered from our gathering?"

He looked up at her. "Yes'm. Actually t'was fun. Woulda been funner if we coulda cut some." He shrugged. "But 'twas fun learnin' about the different mints. Ma says I can have some mint tea tonight with dinner."

Frank's mouth twitched in a smile. "You mind what Mother Fairport tells ya, boy. She's a rare one."

Tanyth considered the ravens and wondered if Frank knew the half of it, but she nodded to him in acknowledgement of the compliment.

"What'cha doin' now?" Riley eyed the bucket in her hand.

"Fetching some water and I'll need to refill my woodbox, too." She looked down at him. "You don't know of a strong young man who might help a poor old woman out, do you,

Riley?"

Frank snorted in what sounded suspiciously like a suppressed laugh and she shot him a wounded look. "What?
You don't think I'm a poor old woman?"

He glanced at her out of the corner of his eye. "Mum?
You're the least poor old woman I've ever seen in my life."

His amused tone carried an undercurrent of admiration
that Tanyth found both unexpected and warming. "Do I need
to hobble more?" She teased him playfully. "Perhaps I need
to be bent over a bit?"

He turned to her with a grin. "Well, mum, if you think
it needful, but I'm not sure anybody over the age of twelve
would believe it." He leaned forward and eyed Riley as they
walked.

The boy saw him looking and, not quite following the
conversation, announced. "I'm gonna be 'leven this winter!"

The two adults were careful not to laugh.

At the pump, Tanyth put her bucket under the spigot
and Riley helped Frank work the long lever to fill it. In a
few moments the splashing water overflowed the rim with a
cheerful slosh. She reached for the bale but Frank's strong
hand was there before hers and he hefted the heavy bucket
easily.

"I'll get that for you, mum." He smiled and arched an
eyebrow. "Wouldn't want a poor old woman to hurt herself
luggin' water back from the well."

"Thank you, Frank. Most kind." She smiled and bent over
in a mock hobble, shuffling her feet through the grass.

Riley eyed them both with a skeptical look in his eye, but
offered no commentary.

Frank laughed and started out for her hut at a brisk pace,
the bucket swinging easily at the end of his arm.

She straightened and picked up her stride to catch up with
him.

Riley's short legs meant he practically had to run to keep
up.

At the hut, she swung the door open and Frank took the
bucket in and placed it near the hearth and slipped the cover
on it.

"Thank you, kind sir. It's most appreciated."

He smiled and headed for the door again. "You're welcome, mum. Any time."

She followed him out onto the grass and looked at the shadows beginning to reach across the village. The peeled sticks marking the corners of the future inn's location showed up whitely in the gathering dusk.

"Will you dig another well, do you think?" She asked it idly, the question popping out of her mouth without thought.

He looked where she was looking and caught the meaning at once. His expression turned thoughtful and she could see him measuring the distance from the pump to where the inn would go. "That's a good question, mum." He considered the location of the inn and then turned back to look at the well. He snorted. "Much work as diggin' a second well would be, and getting' another pump working, might be easier to just take down those two houses and put the inn over the well."

She turned to look at the area in question and then at the markings on the ground. He was right. There were only two huts near enough to matter, Sadie's and Megan's. "Where would Sadie and Megan go? You'd have to build new huts for them."

Frank shook his head. "There's four or five standing empty now, mum. When we built 'em, we built enough for 20 families. We're down to less than 12 now and some of the single boys have moved into individual houses. They really should be doublin' or even triplin' up just to save the fuel in winter. Takes a lot less wood to heat one house than it does three."

"Would they mind movin', d'ya think?

"Could ask, but I suspect it don't matter to them." He nodded his head to indicate the various houses. "Case you haven't noticed, they're all the same. Only difference is where they sit. There's a couple of nice private spots on the far side of the village, might suit Sadie and Thomas better anyway."

They stood there long enough that Riley got side tracked and ran off on some important boy business.

As he scampered off, Frank spoke softly. "You haven't seen anybody else hanging about, have you, mum?"

She shook her head and glanced at him. "Have you?"

He shook his head and gave her a sideways look. "We should tell Thomas and William about it."

She nodded her agreement. "Right now, I want my tea. The water should be hot." She looked at him shyly. "Can I offer you a cup?"

He smiled and didn't look at her. "Actually, mum, that sounds real good, but I've got some things need seein' to so maybe another time?"

She felt a pang of let down but nodded. "Of course. Kettle's always on." The old formulas of housekeeping were coming back to her. None of the teachers she'd had over the past twenty winters stood much on ceremony, but the rituals of hospitality were well ingrained.

With a nod of his head, he strode off in the direction of the barn.

She watched him go for a moment before turning back to her hut. The water was probably hot and she was ready for a cup. She would also have to talk with William and Thomas soon, but still had no clear idea what the riders wanted. She splashed a little hot water into her teapot to christen it but paused as she reached for her rapidly dwindling cache of black tea. She had no way to get more and decided to husband what she had for the moment. She rummaged in her pack and found a small parcel of dried, crushed rose hips and smiled. "This will do." She crumbled a couple of the hips into her pot and pushed it a bit closer to the fire to steep. It would take a little longer to steep than the black, but the taste was one she enjoyed. She remembered the large rugosa in the forest and made a mental note to harvest as many of the rose hips as she could.

The crunch of wheel on gravel announced William's return about the time she was finishing her tea but she didn't hurry out. He'd need to deal with Bester and she suspected that Frank would meet him in the barn and fill him in on the details. She wasn't sure what she could say about the raven episode. The less she needed to talk about it, the happier she'd be. She filled in the time by sorting out the chestnuts, groundnuts, and apples from where she'd dumped her gleaner's bag earlier in the day. She left them in neat piles on the hearthstone and remembered that she needed some baskets to store things in. She reckoned that William had had time to care for the ox and get the highlights from Frank, so she grabbed her staff and hat and headed up to the barn. With luck, she'd be able to duck in and duck out again.

She opened the door and stepped out just as Frank with William and Thomas in tow, rounded the corner from the barn. Frank pushed a barrow of firewood in front of him and the other two waved as she stepped into view. She waved back and waited.

As they approached, Frank walked the barrow right up to the door and the three men proceeded to fill her woodbox from the barrow in next to no time at all. Thomas even hung a pair of dressed gamecocks on a hook beside her door to season. He smiled shyly and nodded his head. "Sadie thought you might like these, mum."

"Thank you, Thomas, and thank Sadie for thinking of me." She turned to include them all in her gaze. "And thank all of you for the wood delivery. I was going to need some soon."

William nodded. "Any time you get low, mum, you let one of us know. We'll see to it that you have wood."

Frank grinned at her and winked conspiratorially but said nothing.

William went on. "Frank here tells me you saw one of those boyos in the wood this morning?"

She nodded. "Yes, I did. I thought I saw somebody in the edge of the wood so I went up to the barn and fetched Frank. He went with me while we looked it over."

He nodded. "Do you mind going with us while we look the place over for ourselves before it gets any darker?"

"Not at all." She started out across the village, making a bee line directly toward the large oak.

The three men fell in behind her and they walked in silence. When they got to the edge of the woods, Tanyth stopped and pointed with the head of her staff. "He was in there just after dawn and watching the village."

Thomas gave her a long, sideways glance before he slipped almost noiselessly through the low brush and into the woods beyond. William turned to look back at the village, surveying the scope of the view.

Frank spoke into the growing silence. "I figger they musta sent one fella up to the quarry to see what we were doing up there, left another here to keep an eye on the home fires."

William nodded. "Good assumption. Even if they didn't, we're probably better off thinkin' they did." He finished his survey of the village and shook his head. "The question is what do they want?"

Frank shrugged. "That's the question, i'n't it?" He nodded to Tanyth. "If Mother Fairport hadn't seen it, we wouldn'ta known. As it is, we know but we don't know what to do about it 'cause we don't know what they want."

From the darkness under the trees, Thomas's voice seemed eerily unattached to any body. "We're about to find out I think. There's riders coming up the Pike."

They stood silent for a moment and then heard what Thomas's ears had already picked out—hoof beats on the hardpan surface of the road. Not moving fast, but more than one set.

Four familiar shapes rode into view and wheeled into the track to the village. With a grunt, William led the way across the sward to meet them before they got too close.

The sun wasn't quite down, and spears of light worked across the village, through the trees and between the huts. The leader of the small band, the dapper fellow, reined in his horse so that one of the transient bands of light illuminated him dramatically. Tanyth almost snickered when he turned his body and practically posed in the beam of setting sun.

William took a few more steps and halted a few feet from the riders. He snorted and spit on the ground. "Hello, Andy. Haven't seen you in a while."

The leader flinched, losing his composure for a moment and peering out of the brilliant light into the dimmer evening all around him. "Who's that?"

William stepped into the next band of brightness, casting himself in clear evening sunlight. "You don't recognize me, Andy? I'm hurt." William's voice was anything but hurt.

The leader screwed up his face in a frown, trying to remember. He started to shake his head, but then he frowned. "Pound me, but if it isn't William Mapleton. Sakes alive." The leader's face was transformed by a smile of false camaraderie. "I had no idea this was where you were livin' now, William." He looked around at his men. "Did you boys know?"

They grinned without much humor and shook their heads, making a big show of it.

Andy turned back to William and flashed his coattails back in a flurry of red satin lining. The pommel of his sword gleamed as he leaned forward on the bow of his saddle. "This is a right pretty little place you got here, William." He smiled with his teeth. "Be a right shame should anything happen to it."

"Don't even think it, Birchwood." William fairly spat the name.

"Why, William!" The man sat back on his horse. "Is that any way to be? I come here to offer you and yours a perfectly legal business arrangement. There's no need to be like that."

"You came in here yesterday and rousted out my wife and my friends. You've had your boyos spyin' on us today." He spat again. "I know your perfectly legal business arrangement and I want no part of it."

Andy shook his head with a sigh and several tsk, tsks. "You really should control that temper, William. You got that from your father, I know, and it really doesn't become you." He lowered his voice and leaned forward to whisper. "And it really would be tragic if something were to happen to this lovely little hideaway in the wood, now wouldn't it?"

"Nothing's going to happen, Birchwood." William stood his ground calmly, but Tanyth could see his left fist clench and the muscles in his back tense from where she stood behind him.

"Now, how can you say that, William. Why, just any kind of troublemaker could ride down the Pike and decide that this delightful little hamlet would make a wonderful place to live. Now what would you say to that?"

"Anybody's welcome to live here, so long as they do their share, tend their business, and respect the neighbors, Birchwood."

Birchwood made a show of being aghast. "You can't mean that, William! Surely, you'd not let murdering scum live next to your lovely wife and your two gorgeous children."

"I didn't say your kind was welcome, Birchwood. I said folks as was willing to do their share, tend their business, and respect the neighbors. I know you and your boyos, there, and you're not that kind."

"William, you wound me. I'm cut to the quick. You do me such disservice, and here I am just trying to help you hold on to what's yours." He sighed. "But I can see I've come at a bad time, end of the day and all. You must be tired after the day you've had cutting wood miles away in the forest." He gathered his reins in one immaculately gloved hand. "I'll just let you think about it for a bit. The boys and I will come back in a couple of days and you can tell me how much you think it's worth to not have trouble with strangers." He turned his horse and nodded to his men. The troop of them rode down the lane and turned south onto the Pike.

William stood still until the sound of their horses faded into the distance. Then he turned to the group arrayed behind him. "We'll need to keep watch."

CHAPTER 16
ON GUARD

Frank volunteered for the first watch. "I don't have much to do tomorrow." He looked at Thomas. "Wake you at midnight?"

Thomas shook his head. "I'll be up with you. We'll need to do this in pairs."

William nodded his agreement. "Wake me at midnight. I'll get one of Jakey's boys to sit up with me."

Frank agreed with a nod of his head. "They're just wrapping up now at the quarry. Should be able to finish loading with one less hand, but what about the days?"

William pursed his lips. "We'll need to keep a closer eye on the kids. Be just like him to grab one of them." He sighed. "I thought we were shut of him, once and for all."

"Who is he?" Tanyth looked from face to face.

"His name is Andrew Birchwood. Dandy Andy, they call him. Six or seven winters back. He and his boyos were running a protection racket on the docks. They were the muscle along with a half dozen others." His mind was turning over. Tanyth could almost see him pulling the knowledge out from another place and time. "They had a tidy little racket going, beating up women and children when the menfolk were at work unless they paid protection to 'em."

"Dandy Andy?" Frank asked. "That boyo was Dandy Andy?"

William nodded. "When Father got wind of it, he and several of the ship fitters paid a visit to Dandy Andy and convinced him to take his operation elsewhere."

Frank frowned. "I remember hearing something about that. Why didn't they call the King's Own?"

"Wasn't against the law."

Frank looked at the younger man. "How could that be?"

"Father went to the magistrate and was told that if they arrested Dandy Andy and his crew, they'd have to arrest all the insurers who were underwriting the voyages."

Frank spat. "Magistrates."

William shrugged. "Could see the point. A bit."

"Only point would be if the insurers were sinking the ships on purpose if anybody didn't buy insurance."

William looked at him coldly, but made no comment.

Frank saw the look and his mouth made a soundless, "Oh."

William continued. "Afterwards Andy and the boys left town. Rumor was they went down to Easton and tried their little insurance scheme down there."

Thomas shrugged. "Well, they're still sellin' insurance."

Tanyth caught William's eye. "You think they'll try something here." It wasn't a question.

William nodded slowly.

Frank scrubbed the back of his neck with a hand. "Why don't we just..." he paused and looked at Tanyth out of the corner of his eye. "...deal with him."

William looked at the older man. "Pay him?" William barked a laugh. "He'll want more than we can give and if he guesses too low at first, keep upping the bill until it is."

Frank shook his head. "No. Why don't we just remove the problem."

William sighed and looked at the ground. "We may have to, but I hate the idea of just killing him out of hand."

Thomas grinned in the gathering gloom. "Threatenin' us like that isn't exactly bein' neighborly." He paused. "You thinkin' he's gonna find redemption over night?"

William shook his head. "No. I think he's gonna cause just as much havoc as he can." He shrugged. "But if we don't catch him in the act, then we're no better than they are."

Frank grunted his agreement. "But we'd be alive. Can't say as he'd give us the same chances."

William nodded. "I know. But he's not done anything

yet. Maybe he won't."

Thomas snorted. "You don't believe that."

He shook his head. "No, I don't but I'm not going to ambush him on the road either."

Frank scuffed at the grass. "You probably won't have to. He'll come to us."

William's expression turned wolfish. "If he does, that's a different matter."

The gathering dusk closed around them and William turned to Tanyth. "You're welcome to bed down at our hearth, mum. Staying on your own might make for an uneasy night."

Tanyth thought about it, but dodged an answer. "Let's get some dinner in us. And everybody will need to know what's going on."

Frank nodded his agreement. "Jakey's quarry boys should bunk up together, too. We don't want to leave Birchwood any easy targets."

William nodded to Thomas. "Let's go tell Amber and Sadie. Then we can split up and go around the village and let people know."

Tanyth snorted. "I got a better idea." She shot a look at Frank that had a bit of mischief in it. "Is it ready?"

He caught her meaning and nodded. "Yes, mum. It is."

"No time like the present. Let's see how it works."

She marched off into the dusk with Frank right beside her. Thomas and William glanced at each other and scrambled to keep up. They headed for the back of Megan and Harry's hut and Tanyth spoke up loudly as she rounded the corner. "We need to ring the bell, Megan. Don't be startled."

Frank looked at her. "That was considerate."

She shrugged. "How would you like it if somebody started banging on your house without warning?"

He chuckled. "Not very much."

The iron hoop hung nicely from the eaves on the back of the hut and the poker stuck out of the ground right under it. Before Tanyth could pull it out of the ground, Megan and Harry came out the back door of the house, spilling warm firelight into the dusk.

"What's going on?" Harry asked.

"Alarm bell," Tanyth said. "We need to see how well it works and there's news everybody should have."

She pulled the poker out of the ground and handed it to Frank with an impish grin. "Your turn."

He took it and she stepped well back while Thomas, William, and the others looked on curiously. He drew back his arm. "You might wanna cover your ears," he said.

Tanyth took him at his word and did so but the others were slow to respond.

He struck, not once but again and again. After about five or six good whacks, people started running out of the dusk. The horrendous clangor echoed in the quiet of the evening. Frank grinned like a madman.

The town was soon assembled and gathered around the back door. William stepped into the open so everybody could at least see his shape in the dim light.

"Sorry about the noise, but we did need to test the alarm. If there's trouble here, ring it. Grab the poker there and pound until somebody comes to help."

Jakey had a hank of bread in his hand and a napkin tucked into his shirt. "Do we have a reason for this, William?" He waved the bread in a circular motion indicating the gathering and the bell. He didn't sound particularly pleased.

"Yes." That one word silenced the still muttering crowd. "The riders who were here yesterday just paid us another little visit. They've actually been visiting all along. They may be still visiting for all we know."

That brought anxious looks around at the darkened wood.

"They're tryin' to strong arm us into a protection scheme. In return for not beating us up, they'll take money."

Jakey snorted. "How much money?"

William shrugged. "We don't know yet, but it'll be more than we can afford and we'll have to keep paying them every time they come calling."

There was some grumbling from the group but nobody else had a comment so William continued. "We'll need people who are living alone in the houses to double up—at least for now. They're bullies and cowards so they'll only pick on the easiest and least likely to hit back." He paused. "That means we have to be doubly careful with the children and keep a closer eye on them for a while."

An anxious sounding woman's voice came out of the dusk. "How long, William?"

He shrugged. "Honestly, I don't know, but sooner or later they'll get bored and move on to an easier target if we're just careful and make it too difficult for them to hurt us."

Tanyth had her doubts and from the look on Frank's face, she thought he might have a few, too, but neither of them spoke.

William raised his voice one last time. "We'll be standing watches at night. We'll need pairs who're willing to stay up and keep an eye open. We've got one more day before the lorry wagon is loaded up and heading for Kleesport. Frank'll be taking the watch tonight and I'm hoping I can count on the quarry men to help out once the quarry gets shut down for the winter."

"Well, we usually put a little aside for spring, William. You know that." Jakey objected again.

"I know, Jakey, and pr'aps we can later, but right now the village is being threatened. If there's no village, the quarry won't mean much."

"Aye, I'll give ya that." Jakey grumbled his agreement even as he gnawed another bite off the bread.

"Thanks, everyone. We should be all right. Just keep an eye open and don't get separated."

The crowd dispersed after that. Megan and Harry shooed their small brood into the hut but stood outside until the last of the villagers had wandered back to their homes. Harry spoke softly. "You really think this is gonna turn out well, William?"

William shrugged. "I don't know, Harry. We've run 'em off once when they didn't expect any problem, but we weren't prepared for it either. With our heads up and points out, it'll be harder for them to pull anything."

The concern on Harry's face was evident even in the scant light from the fire inside his hut. "Well, count me in on the guard detail. We'll have the last of the barrels loaded tomorrow around midday, I'd guess. Then we'll all be available, so long as Jakey doesn't get too pushy."

William clapped the man on the shoulder. "Thanks, Harry."

Harry and Megan went down the stairs and, with a little wave, closed the door.

Amber and William headed for their house. Amber paused and turned to Tanyth. "You're coming to stay with us, mum. No question."

Tanyth nodded. "Of course, Amber. I'll just go get my bed roll."

Frank spoke up and forestalled William's objection. "I'll go with her so she's not alone in the dark."

William nodded, his face just a pale blur in the darkness. "Thank you. And you come back with her and have some dinner, too, eh? Amber's got a stew on the fire that's big enough to feed the village."

The two of them wandered off leaving Frank and Tanyth to make their way to fetch Tanyth's meager belongings.

"Seems like living on the road has an advantage, eh?" She looked up at him. "Packing is easy and I can carry everything on my back."

His chuckle rumbled in his chest but he offered no comment, just kept scanning the darkness.

"They won't try anything yet." Tanyth's voice was confident in the darkness.

"How do you figure that, mum?"

"Too soon. We're alert and warned. They'll wait until things quiet down."

His voice sounded amused. "You have a lot of experience with this kind of thing, mum?"

Her reply carried no amusement whatsoever. "Yes."

Thomas's voice came out of the darkness behind them. "She's right, Frank. Just before dawn, the hunter's time. Moon will be down, sun won't be up. We'll all be asleep."

As if on cue the silvery, nearly full Harvest moon peaked over the trees on the other side of the Pike. It's glow had been lighting the sky since sundown, but the tall spruces and pines on the far side of the road kept it from shining directly on the village.

Thomas stepped up to her other side and nodded to Frank,

who nodded back.

"Mum?" Thomas's voice was quiet and deferential. "Can I ask you somthin'?"

She glanced at him before nodding. "Of course, Thomas. What is it?"

"How did you see that man?" He paused. "The one in the woods this morning?"

Her heart skipped once. She wasn't ready to share that story in its entirety yet, but she also didn't want to lie. "I wasn't sure I had. That's why I asked Frank to come with me to look."

He nodded. "But what did you see that made you think there was somebody there, mum?"

"I don't know exactly." She was telling the truth, but she knew she was not being exactly forthright either.

He accepted her response, but she could tell he didn't believe her entirely.

"Well, mum? If you ever think you see something like that again? Make sure you get one of us? Or all of us?" His eyes bored into hers, shining in the silvery light of the moon.

She nodded. "Of course, Thomas."

"Thank you, mum." He sounded relieved and she couldn't imagine why. She certainly didn't feel relieved.

At her door, they paused and by some unspoken agreement, the two men took up station on either side of it. "We'll wait for you here, mum. Give you a chance to pack your things in private." Frank seemed almost embarrassed.

"Thank you, Frank. I won't be a moment." She slipped into the hut. In a matter of moments had rolled up her bedding, tossed a few loose items into the top of the pack, and then collected her small collection of cooking gear. She didn't think she'd need it, but she didn't want to leave anything behind, just in case. She stopped inside the door and took one last look around the dim interior to see if she had missed anything. Outside she heard the two men talking.

"She didn't see anything, Frank. She couldn't have."

Frank's response was a rumbling question.

"Whoever was there was laying behind the roots of the trees and looking through the weeds. Across the village, into the darkness of the woods, picking out a face in the bushes?" Thomas's voice was low and urgent. "I don't know what magic she used, but I'm glad she's on our side."

She froze. Magic? Preposterous! Her breath stopped in her lungs while her heart seemed to beat twice as fast. No. Impossible.

Frank's rumble in return was unintelligible in detail but clearly unconvinced in tone.

"I don't either, but I'm tellin' you—"

She coughed and scuffed her feet as if just coming up to the door and exited the small house. "Thank you, both. That was very considerate."

Frank smiled. "Our pleasure, mum."

She closed and secured the door, conscious of Thomas's intense gaze. She didn't sigh, but she wanted to. The whole idea was absurd. Was he watching to see if she'd cast a spell or something?

The man had been in the undergrowth. Tanyth had apparently seen him in a dream through the eyes of a raven. The thought made her momentarily dizzy as she recalled the dream vision being overlaid on the reality of the crushed seedling in the forest.

Frank's strong hand caught her arm to steady her. "You all right, mum?"

"Yes, thank you. A moment of dizziness." She let it rest and turned to smile up at him and then over at Thomas. "Shall we?"

They escorted her carefully, alert to any stumble. For all of her joking earlier in the day, she felt old, slightly frail, and swept along by some forces she understood too well–like Dandy Andy and his bully boys–and by others she wasn't even sure she could comprehend as the All-Mother's natural progression took her monthly habit from her and leave her an old woman in reality, not just name.

In the forest an owl called and the night winds began playing in the treetops, skittering leaf against leaf in the silver light of the moon.

CHAPTER 17
WINTER PLANS

In spite of the tension, the night passed uneventfully. Tanyth spread her bedroll against the wall farthest from the hearth and, after a hurried dinner, everyone took to their blankets. Even the children settled quickly, perhaps because the excitement of having a guest was overshadowed by parental solemnity in going to bed early themselves to allow William to get some needed sleep before going on watch at midnight.

The gray light of morning brought pale rain with it and the tension became layered in the smell of wet wool. The cold and damp did nothing to help the situation. The quarrymen headed up the track and Sadie and Amber got their heads together to move all the children into the Mapleton house for the morning, while the menfolk slept at the Hawthornes'.

The morning crept along as life in the village went on. Children and animals needed caring for. The work of the day was merely complicated by being confined. The additional tension of watching for danger from outside was overridden by managing restive children. More than once, Tanyth saw either Sadie or Amber looking out the front door at the soggy landscape and the peeled sticks marking the corners of their future inn. Tanyth had to admit that the tiny cottages had a certain disadvantage over a large common room with a roaring hearth. As small as they were, cozy was soon replaced by cramped and Tanyth longed for the quiet solitude of the road–even in the rain.

Still, she had to admit as she sat on her rolled up bedroll and sipped her tea, there was much to be thankful for. There had been no dreams of ravens to trouble her, and there had been no attack. Of course, each of these carried an element of anxiety as well, but she refused to dwell on those.

At mid-morning, while Sadie and Amber were working on bread, Frank and Thomas came in from the barn, their clothing damp and redolent of animal. They dried themselves in front of the hearth and Amber plied them with hot tea. The conversation soon turned to the coming trip to Kleesport.

"Have you given any thought to who you're going to take with you this trip, Frank?" Amber was frowning in concentration as she kneaded down a large ball of bread dough.

He seemed surprised by the question. "Take with me? Why would I take anybody with me?"

Sadie looked at him with a certain air of disbelief. "Well, Dandy Andy and his boyos aren't exactly going to miss the fact that a large, slow moving lorry wagon loaded with clay is leavin' now, are they?"

Frank shrugged. "I thought of that, but why would they bother it? If they interrupt the clay, they can't get paid."

"What if they steal it and sell it themselves? Along with the horses, and the wagon?"

Frank blanched and Thomas gave him a short glance out of the corner of his eye. "Didn't think of that one?"

Frank shook his head. "No, I was thinkin' they'd want us to get the money and bring it back to give to them." He looked chagrined. "Never occurred to me they'd cut out the middleman."

Amber tsked at him. "Well, think of it, foolish man. We can't afford to lose you."

"Me or the clay?"

She rolled her bread dough into a ball and covered it with a bit of toweling to rise again before turning to him with a serious look on her face. "You. The clay, even the horses and wagon, we can replace." She shook a finger at him. "You, you old coot, are not replaceable."

He smiled and looked into his mug in embarrassment.

Thomas stirred and spoke up. "Jakey can send a couple of boys with you. Andy's not going to bother a group of men." He glanced around the hut full of women and children. "It's not his style."

Sadie looked at her husband curiously. "Do you know him?"

He shook his head. "No, but I know the type."

Tanyth spoke up from her corner. "I agree. They'll not risk getting hurt themselves when they can hit at things that won't hit back."

Two of the smaller children started a spat over a doll and the resultant noise and commotion drowned out further conversation on the subject but Tanyth saw that Frank's attention had turned inward. When the two children had been mollified with slices of buttered bread, the talk returned to the pending trip.

Amber turned to Frank. "Speaking of your trip, when are you leaving? I don't have my list finished yet."

Frank looked up. "I was hoping to leave in the morning tomorrow. A lot will depend on who will go with me." He paused. "If anybody."

Amber grinned at him. "Somebody is going with you, Frank. If only to run back to tell us how much trouble you're in!"

He held up his hands in resignation. "All right, all right. Somebody is goin' with me, but I'm still hoping to get this settled this afternoon so I can get on the road in the mornin'."

Amber nodded and looked at Sadie. "Can we get the list ready by then?"

Sadie shrugged. "Well, nobody's gonna be goin' anywhere today, between the weather and the boogie men. If we got going on it, we could probably get it done by dinner time."

Amber turned to Tanyth. "We send a list to town with Frank. He gets what we need beyond the staples and brings them back to us."

Frank grinned. "It's somethin' of a challenge, findin' the stuff, but it livens things up when I go shoppin' for fabric with the ladies."

Tanyth admired his good humor over what must, at times, be a very trying experience for him.

His face turned serious after the general laughter died down. "This is the last run I'll be makin' a-fore spring so

I'll be needin' to get enough to see us through the winter."

"Lucky it's a big wagon!" Thomas grinned at the older man.

Frank laughed. "Too right. This time we'll be haulin' back almost as much as we're haulin' in."

Tanyth looked startled. "Really?"

Frank shook his head. "No, not really, mum. I'm exaggeratin' a bit."

Amber looked up from her mending. "Not by much he's not. We'll need extra grain for the animals and nearly a ton weight of flour."

"Flour, beans, tea. Anything we don't grow here, or make, I'll need to bring it back." Frank looked at Tanyth. "If you've got needs, mum?"

She looked uncertain. "Well, if I'm going to spend the winter here, I'll need some supplies, but I don't know if I have enough to pay for them all at once."

Amber and Sadie looked up. "Are you, mum? Are you going to spend the winter with us?"

Even Frank and Thomas looked at her, hope in their eyes..

"Well, I'd feel funny leavin' you all just now with the trouble and all." She looked at the tea in her mug. "But I was plannin' on gettin' my winter supplies and such when I got to Kleesport."

Amber and Sadie shared a glance and nodded. "You'll need some warmer clothes, mum?"

"Yes, and some oatmeal? Rough milled oats for my morning meal. And tea. I'm beginning to run a bit low and I can't be moochin' off the neighbors all the time." Her voice carried a note of uncertainty. "I don't like livin' on charity."

Amber said, "Mum? You don't ever think that here." She gathered the gazes of Frank, Thomas, and Sadie before looking back at Tanyth, warmly welcoming but soberly serious. "We know what you've done for us already. You've paid your way for this winter, so don't you be worryin' about moochin' off the neighbors."

Tanyth was touched in a way that she hadn't felt in many a winter. She'd always paid her way in hard coin and sometimes harder labor. She wasn't a young woman herself, but the teachers she'd studied under were older still. Many of them lived alone and were happy for a bit of company and an extra pair of relatively younger hands to help out in the cold and dark of winter. Most of them lived simply but Tanyth earned coin by selling her herbs and poultices, and was in the habit of contributing to the general larder wherever she stayed for extended periods. For the first time in a very long time, she was being welcomed as a member of the family.

She blinked back the moisture that threatened her composure and sipped her tea while she caught her breath. "Thank you."

Frank spoke up after clearing his throat. "You just put whatever you need on the list, mum. Tea, oatmeal, fabric, thread, needles. Anything you need, I'll see to it that you'll have it when I get back from Kleesport."

Two different children started squabbling and pushing and Amber clapped her hands sharply to get their attention. "You little critters behave or I'll make you go fight outside."

After the requisite round of "But, ma..." and "He was..." everybody settled down again. Frank and Thomas pulled on their outer clothes and headed for the door.

"We'll just take a swing around, see if there's anything happening out there," Thomas said, pecking his wife on the cheek.

She nodded and pecked him back. "You watch yourself, Thomas Hawthorne." She said it softly and there was a hint of real worry in it.

He smiled and nodded before following Frank out the door.

The morning spun to a finish after a fashion and even the children adapted to the enforced curtailment of activity. Lunch was bread and cheese toasted on sticks. Playing with the fire gave even the youngest a chance to cook her own lunch and occupied them for nearly an hour.

With full bellies, warmed by the fire, and just slightly bored from being cooped up all day, the children curled up in piles in the corners and fell asleep. Even Tanyth felt the pull of slumber as she sat on her bedroll and partook very sparingly of the general activity in the hut. She sat back out of the purposeful way of the two younger women who worked together to bake bread and keep the stew from burning on. The feeling of warmth and comfort conspired to find her nodding and napping, leaning back against the wall of the hut with nothing particular to do. Every so often she'd wake to find Amber or Sadie smiling in her direction. After the third time, she stood up.

Amber and Sadie both looked at her sudden movement. "Is everything all right, mum?"

"Yes, I'm fine, but if I sit there any longer I'm going to be napping with the children. How can I help?"

The two younger women looked at each other. "What's wrong with napping with the children?" Amber's clear smile made Tanyth smile back.

"Not a thing, but there's work to do, and I'm not some grandmother to tuck in a corner and nap the day away. What can I do?"

Amber looked about the hearth. "Well, the bread's baking and dinner is cooking. I've finished the mending and there's no sense washing clothes today." She looked pointedly at the door.

Sadie sat up straight. "We should be working on that list for Frank. He'll not want to wait for that, and I did say we'd have it for him tonight." She looked at Tanyth. "Can you write, mum? You could help us with makin' the list."

She blinked at them. "Why, yes, of course. That sounds very good. Just show me what to do."

Sadie looked at Amber. "I left it at the house. I'll just pop over and pick it up."

Amber looked shocked. "You'll do no such thing without somebody to go with you!"

"It's just next door, Amber. I'll be but a minute."

Amber was adamant so Tanyth grabbed her hat and a cloak. "I'll go with her. It'll be fine."

The two women stepped out of the back door and into a damp mist–too light to be rain, too wet to be fog–and crossed the few steps to Sadie's house. Inside Sadie found the rolled up list and a small pot of ink and a pen with a copper nib. She held up the pen for Tanyth to see. "We used to use charcoal but three winters back, Frank sweated all over the list and the charcoal ran. He had to guess what it said." She laughed. "He brought us back proper pens and Mother Alderton made us some ink."

"How'd he do on the guessing?"

"Well, just say that we ate a lot of gingerbread that winter and nobody got a new gingham dress."

Tanyth laughed. "Well, gingham dresses aren't exactly warm in winter."

Sadie grinned. "True enough, and the gingerbread sure tasted good."

They scampered back to the Mapleton's without incident and settled in to working up the supply list for Frank.

After an hour of careful thought, and even more careful calculations, they finished the list and Tanyth gained new respect for the resourceful pair.

CHAPTER 18
EQUINOX

Frank brought the loaded lorry wagon down from the quarry in late afternoon and parked it behind the village in preparation for an early departure. He was excused from guard duty and Jakey teamed up with Thomas for the early shift, leaving William and one of the more senior quarrymen for the later one. The grim business of deciding which of the younger quarrymen would go with Frank and which would stay with the village boiled down to a series of arm wrestling matches, three winners earning the privilege of a ride to town and back along with a certain amount of good-natured teasing about the trouble they'd be getting into while there. Hopeful expectation filled the air, driven in part by the realization that a full day had passed without the expected attack. Everybody but Thomas, William, and Tanyth believed that the bullying had been nothing but boast.

Afternoon faded to evening and the village quickened in preparations for the celebration of the equinox, a soft drizzle petering out as sunset approached. Frank and Tanyth, as the eldest members of the village, were designated to honor the All-Mother and All-Father by presenting the harvest gifts at moonrise. Frank knew the ceremony, having fulfilled the role in three of the four prior years. Tanyth felt honored–if a bit overwhelmed–to be taking Mother Alderton's role in the Harvest Celebration to mark the midpoint of autumn.

As the day drew to a close, Tanyth took Amber aside. "Is there something that Mother Alderton did that's special to

159

the village?"

Amber shook her head. "Just a simple offering in thanks for the harvest. She wasn't much on ceremony."

Tanyth nodded and thought about her prayer to the All-Mother while they waited in the gathering dark for the silver disk to rise above the trees. While she waited, she remembered previous Harvest Moon celebrations. Her teachers were frequently called on to thank the All-Mother and the seamed, smiling, and tanned faces from her past slipped through her mind.

At sunset, the scudding clouds broke open enough to reveal darkening sky and the whole village turned out to honor the full moon at equinox. At the first hint of silver through the trees, Frank turned to the north and sprinkled a bit of apple cider onto the ground. "Thank you to the Guardian of the Earth." He turned and spilled a few more drops onto the ground while facing the moon rising in the east. "Thank you to the Guardian of the Air." He turned to the south and repeated his delicate spilling. "Thank you to the Guardian of the Fire." He turned to the west where the setting sun had already dipped below the horizon but where the clouds that had covered them all day continued to obscure the sky. He spilled a few more drops from his cup. "Thank you to the Guardian of the Water." He closed his circle and poured out the final drops of cider and they spattered wetly on the soggy soil. "Thank you to the All-Father for the bounteous harvest and the cycle of another year." He stepped back to give Tanyth room.

The moon continued its inexorable climb. As she stepped up, the full sheen appeared above the trees and cast her in an almost blue light as she faced the north and shook her sheaf of wheat to release a few of the grains. "Thank you to the Guardian of the North, Bones of the World, for the soil in which we grow." Even as she turned she could feel the earth beneath her boot soles–gritty and moist, tired after a season of growing, but fecund yet and filled with potential. She shook her sheaf again as a gentle gust tossed the grains upon the ground. "Thank you to the Guardian of the East, Breath of the World, for the air that nourishes us–plant and animal alike." Turning south she repeated the shake. "Thank you to the Guardian of the South, Soul of the World for the passion of life that renews us." She felt the heat in her belly rising as she turned to the west, clouds breaking open to show the ruddy final glow of the sun sinking below the horizon, unseen behind tree and hill. "Thank you to the Guardian of the West, Blood of the world, for the water that let's us flourish and grow." She turned back to the north and shook the sheaf one last time, the final grains raining onto the damp soil. "Thank you, All-Mother, for the gifts of your body and the fruit of your fields which nurture and keep us all the year round." They stood there for a moment. Tanyth facing north with the villagers arrayed in a half circle behind her. Something quivered in the air and slowly subsided as the moon swam ever upwards and bathed the village in its argent light.

Tanyth turned to see them all staring at her. She looked uneasily from face to face starting with Frank's slack-jawed expression and then scanning across the small crowd of adults and children. Their eyes were all dark and round. Some looked awed. Some looked frightened. All looked at her.

She glanced up at Frank at her side and her voice was low. "Did I do something wrong?"

Frank shook his head dumbly, his eyes wide.

Tanyth looked back across the small crowd and they seemed to be blinking and moving about, if a bit dazedly. Almost as if they were waking up.

Amber moved first. She stepped forward and curtsied. William stepped up and bowed. One by one each of the inhabitants of the village stepped forward and bowed or curtsied while Frank and Tanyth stood for the All-Father and All-Mother. Tanyth smiled and nodded, acknowledging each one down to the smallest child. When they were done, everyone sauntered off in the silvery light to find their evening meals. William, Amber, and the two children waited for Frank and Tanyth at the edge of the track to escort them to the house for dinner.

Tanyth turned to Frank once more as the last of the villagers finished their obeisance and wandered off. She held out her arm as a prompt and he took the cue and held his up under hers in proper form to escort her from the field.

She leaned in and murmured to him. "That was unusual. I've never seen a Harvest Moon Celebration quite like that."

He turned his face toward her. "Me, either, mum."

She caught his look. "What? That wasn't the way it's been done here before? I thought Mother Alderton did the ceremony."

He all but laughed. "Mother Alderton wasn't much on ceremony, mum." He blew out a breath. "I've never seen–or felt–anything like that."

She cast him a look out of the corner of her eye, but they were approaching Amber and William who turned to lead them onward and she let it drop.

Amber and Sadie had prepared a feast with a roasted joint of venison, along with squash and potatoes fresh from their gardens. The crusty yeast bread added an almost sweet counterpoint to the savory smells coming off the hearth as they stepped back into the warm hut after being outside in the damp and chilly darkness.

At the threshold, Amber and William lost their dazed expressions and the party was soon joined by Thomas and Sadie and their children. In a matter of moments, Amber and Sadie had distributed cups of sweet cider and the feast began in earnest.

Frank and Tanyth sat in the places of honor near the hearth and Tanyth enjoyed being the All-Mother surrogate much more than she had expected. The children were all on their best behavior and the meal was wonderful with just the right amounts of savory and sweet, meat and bread to balance. For dessert there was pie and fruit and soft cheese.

As the evening wore on, Tanyth began to flag. The combination of hot food, full belly, and jocularity among friends moved her from stuffed to stupor in relatively short order. She found herself blinking and stretching her face to try to stay awake as sleep plucked the children away to dreamland. Even Amber and Sadie began to blink and yawn. The party broke up with Frank rising suddenly from his chair and announcing that he needed to find his bedroll in order to be fresh for the morrow.

The movement sparked action and in moments people were moving about, snuffing candles, banking fires, and making trips to the privy. Sadie caught Amber's eye and nodded at the pile of sleeping children. Amber just smiled. "Let'em be. We can sort 'em out in the morning."

Tanyth rose and stretched but still stumbled gratefully into her bedroll, stretching out on the firm floor, pulling the covers tightly around her, and drifting gently off into darkness even as Frank, William, and Amber finalized plans for morning.

The raven peered through the trees at the dark shapes just inside the forest's verge. Open ground beyond the forest's edge was painted in stark silver and the shapes moved in silhouette. They smelled to her, a sharp smell. Not the calling smell of meat but something else. Something man made. It came faintly on the breeze. Not pine pitch. A smell she knew from the forest but sharp like pines. Four of them now. Two held shiny glass and the smell came from the bottles.

The night around them was still. Even the raven huddled against the tree trunk heard only the soft murmur of night wind in tree tops. The day's soft rain had brought up the smells of rich loam and forest floor. The end of the rain had brought these man-shapes and she just wanted to sleep.

One man spoke and another man struck steel. A spark flicked onto a torch, the pale yellow light almost drowned by the brilliant silver beyond the wood. The two with bottles ran forward with the torch man in the rear. They broke from cover and ran to the nearest house, approaching without stealth or grace, stumbling on the rough ground. They stopped a few feet from the building and the bottles spun end over end as they threw them–flashing in the moonlight, arcs of pale liquid pinwheeling outward, until they hit the roof. The heavy glass didn't break, but thunked loudly on the damp wood and rolled down the steep incline, falling to soft, damp earth at the foot of the wall. The man with the torch threw it up onto the roof with a sidearm toss and together the three of them turned and bolted back to the woods, ducking into the trees and past the one man waiting.

The torch found the liquid on the roof and a ribbon of fire traced across the dark incline as the torch followed the bottles and fell to earth, rolling off the steepness and dropping into the wet grass to smolder and almost gutter out before finding the puddle of sharp smelling liquid and igniting in a quiet whump.

Tanyth woke with the word on her lips. "Fire!"

Amber was just settling down to her own bed and looked over at Tanyth struggling out of her bed roll and grabbing for her staff. "What is it, mum?"

"Fire! They've tried to set one of the huts on fire. Get help."

She raced for the front door and threw it open as she scrambled up out of the house, her bare feet aware of the cold, wet ground under her, but drawing strength with every step as she ran. The disorientation of the dream soon aligned with the flickering light behind one of the houses and she pelted across the yard to where she knew she'd find the two bottles of lamp oil in the weeds.

She skidded around the corner even as she heard Amber banging on a door and yelling for William and Thomas and Frank. The village seemed to spring into life all at once as men came out to see what was happening, pulling suspenders over shoulders even as they ran.

Tanyth slipped on the grass but managed to maintain her balance and shouted. "Here! Fire! Over here!"

The running men converged on her even as she ran at the fire, scattering the burning brands with the heel of her staff and even stomping out sparks with her bare, wet feet. By the time William and Thomas came around the corner only one small patch of lamp oil burned on the ground beside the torch that had ignited it.

Tanyth leaned on her staff and panted slightly to catch her breath. She pivoted to where she knew the men had come from. She could see their tracks in the moonlit grass where their rapid passage had shaken the water from the blades. Thomas turned and drew, but held since there were no targets, just as Frank pelted around the corner.

William and Frank stomped out the remaining fire with their heavier boots and the crisis was past.

The men all looked at Tanyth. Frank spoke. "Are you all right, mum?"

She glowered at the tree line for another moment but turned to look at them. "Yes. Fine." She took another deep breath. "It just scared me and I was afraid they'd come back and throw more lamp oil on it when they discovered it just rolled off."

Thomas glanced at Frank with a kind of "I told you so" look and Frank looked at Tanyth.

William, for his part, picked up the two heavy bottles and smelled each. "Lamp oil, right enough."

Thomas turned to Tanyth. "Thank you, mum."

She was too tired and too shaken to respond with more than a nod.

Frank offered his arm as if she were the All-Mother again and she took it, leaning on it heavily and let him lead her back to the cottage and her bed.

CHAPTER 19
SHARED SECRET

"That was just a warning." William looked around at the circle of faces, pale in the morning's light.

"A warning?" Jakey frowned and pointed to the singed ground. "If one of those bottles had actually broken up there, we'd have lost this house!"

William nodded. "I think that was their plan, but it didn't break." He turned to Jakey with a calm look. "And who lives in this house?"

Jakey spluttered a little but had to admit the truth in the end. "Nobody."

William shrugged. "It was a warning. Wasn't as effective as they'd have liked perhaps, but a warning."

Jakey grumbled but subsided.

"That's why we have to send your boys off with Frank, Jakey. You knew that before."

Jakey nodded. "But that was before they was attacking the town. Sending them off with Frank means we've got three fewer people here to defend us if we need 'em."

William sighed. "And not sending them means we leave Frank, the horses, the wagon, and the cargo open to attack. You like that thought better?" He glared at Jakey. "Here we've got more than enough folk to protect the village even with Ethan, Richard, and Harry going along to cover Frank."

Thomas spoke up for the first time since the confrontation over sending off the quarrymen began. "We're dealin' with cowards and bullies here, Jakey. They're not gonna try for equal numbers in a movin' wagon when they can hang around here and pick off the easy targets."

Jakey nodded and started to say something but Thomas cut him off.

"And if we don't give Frank cover, they'll hit him as the easy target and take away much more than we can afford to lose."

Jakey saw the logic but he was just bullheaded enough to need to fight about it.

Frank put an end to it. "Sooner gone, sooner back." He turned to his traveling companions and jerked his head toward the back of the wagon. "Mount up, boys, and let's get this thing moving. Daylight's burnin' and they're probably watchin' from the woods." He spat on the ground. "Let's give 'em something to look at besides us palaverin' the day away."

The three quarry men had already stowed their traveling gear in the wagon and they scrambled up onto the bed before their obstreperous boss could interfere with the departure any longer. Frank pulled the wagon's brake and flicked the reins with a clucking sound. "Hee up there!"

The horses leaned into the traces and the wagon moved off across the still damp ground toward the packed surface of the Pike, rumbling slightly. In a few minutes, the wagon had made it to the road and turned north. Several of the villagers watched them go, and Megan raised a hand to wave farewell to her husband, Harry, who waved back from the tailgate of the lorry-wagon as it moved slowly out of sight.

Jakey made a disgusted noise, gathered his remaining three helpers, and started trudging up the track toward the quarry. The villagers dispersed to their daily chores. William stood beside the path and frowned at his feet while Thomas crouched on his haunches nearby.

Amber and Sadie looked to William. Amber asked the question everybody was thinking. "Now what?"

Thomas grinned and William shrugged. "Now we wait."

"How long? We can't keep these kids bottled up forever and you and Thomas will need to get on with your work, too."

William sighed and ran a hand through his hair. "I know." He looked at Thomas who shrugged in return. "They've given us a warning. They'll give us another and then they'll be back." He took a deep breath and let it out. "I think, as long as we're vigilant, they can't really cause us much harm. They're not going to try a straight on attack, it wouldn't be useful to damage us so we can't pay."

"We're not going to pay anyway." Thomas spoke quietly but his voice carried to where Tanyth stood beside Amber's back door.

William sighed. "Yeah, and I'm not so sure what will happen when they realize that."

"They must know you're your father's son, Will. You think they've forgotten?"

William grimaced and shook his head. "No. I don't."

Thomas glanced at the women standing nearby and didn't say any more.

"Tell ya what? Let's give the kids a good run here for an hour or so and then I'll take them up to the barn with me and we'll get a jump on cuttin' and stackin' firewood."

Amber nodded and Sadie opened the door to let the children out of the house. They ran and screamed and hooped like wild things across the back of the village. Megan joined the group and her three went haring after the rest while the adults alternately grinned and glanced nervously at the woods. Tanyth smiled at the sight of the youthful enthusiasm and even Thomas seemed amused.

William looked around. "Is everyone accounted for? Where are Bethany, Rebecca and Charlotte?"

Thomas jerked his head toward Jakey's house. "They're holed up with Charlotte."

William ticked off some list silently in his head as he counted on his fingers and then nodded. "That's all of us." His voice sounded tired.

Amber and Sadie took Megan into the house and they all appeared shortly with mugs of tea. The adults sipped the hot brew and thought their own thoughts while the joyful shouts and laughter of children echoed down the vale. Tanyth felt their awkwardness. The easy camaraderie the women had shared before was not gone, but had become stilted. They looked at her in quick glances and flickering looks. She wasn't sure what it meant but it made her uneasy and she looked from one face to the next trying to get a hint.

She was startled to see that William watched her and not the children. "What is it?" The words were out of her mouth before she'd even thought them.

William looked to Amber who looked back at him with that look that wives give husbands when they need to stop shilly shallying and get on with it.

"Mum? Can we ask how you knew?"

The question caught Tanyth a bit sideways. As soon as he said it, she realized she should have expected it.

Impatient with the way he was handling it, Amber elbowed her husband out of the way and continued. "Mum? You jumped from your bedroll yellin' about fire and raced out into the night. You scared the stuffin' out of me." She smiled but there was a look of concern–even fear–in her eyes.

Tanyth sighed and closed her eyes, uncertain as to how much to say. She opened them with a sigh and turned to them. "I had a dream." She said it softly, but the morning breezes hadn't yet stirred the world and her voice carried to them even over the sounds of the children.

Sadie looked at Megan and shrugged but Amber pressed on. "A dream, mum? You dreamed that there was a fire? And you ran out into the night yellin'?" Her voice was gentle but her eyes were pleading.

Tanyth looked at the concern in all their eyes. "Yes. Sounds odd, but it wasn't the first time." She paused and sipped her tea to gain time to think. "I've had them before. At first I didn't believe them. Now, I do." Her voice dropped even more and she realized that she had spoken the truth. She did believe them. The raven visions had proven too reliable, too real, to be taken as anything but visions, gifts from the All-Mother.

A raven cawed in the forest. Tanyth's head snapped to look in the direction but the others seemed not to have heard it.

William followed her gaze. "What is it, mum? Another vision?"

"No." She shook her head. "They only seem to come when I'm sleeping."

"Then how do you know they're real, mum?" Amber looked more concerned than curious.

Tanyth felt a flash of irritation but damped it down. She sounded like a confused old woman, even to herself. She took a deep breath and let it out. She looked at them all looking back at her. They looked so concerned, so caring. She said a silent prayer to the All-Mother and felt the comforting warmth rise in her. She decided to tell them.

"At first, I didn't. The first vision was after the riders came and we drove them off. I went to my hut and sat down at the table." She smiled apologetically. "I was so tired. Standing up to them took a lot out of me."

Thomas nodded and his eyes said he remembered very well.

Amber's voice was soft and low. "Go on, mum. Then what?"

Tanyth sipped her tea and recalled the scene. "I fell asleep and had a dream. It was like I was lookin' through the eyes of a raven flying above the road. I saw the four riders heading south. They stopped and had some kind of talk, but rode on. I woke up then and thought it was an odd dream. It was so real. I could feel the wind." She shrugged almost apologetically. "That one was the first and I thought it was just a dream." She looked around to gauge her audience before continuing. "The next day, I was fixing a cup of tea and laid down on my bed roll. Just to rest while the water heated. I fell asleep and had another dream, but this time I dreamed that one of the men was watching us from the woods. I was looking at him through the eyes of a raven in a tree behind him. He saw the bird and threw a twig so I–it–flew off and I woke up. I was afraid that he'd still be there so I went up to the barn and got Frank to come with me and we found the spot in the woods where the man had been." She looked at Thomas. "You saw the place, too."

Thomas nodded slowly. "I wondered how you could have seen anybody in that wood, mum. Wasn't like you'd just be able to see through the tree."

She nodded. "I'm sorry I didn't say more but it sounds crazy, even to me."

"And then last night?" William prodded her to go on.

"Last night, I fell asleep after the feast. I dreamed I was back in the woods, watching them where they waited. All four of them. They had bottles but I didn't know what they were doing besides watching. When they threw the bottles up onto the roof, they spread lamp oil around but didn't break up there. Two men threw bottles and one threw a lighted torch. Then I woke up and just acted without thinking." She shrugged. "The rest you know."

"How did you know last night's dream was real, mum?" Amber was more curious now.

"It was a raven vision again." Tanyth shrugged helplessly. "The raven was sitting in a tree further in the woods and could see them outlined against the moonlight in the field."

The small group looked around at each other and then back at her.

William cleared his throat. "You'll tell us if you have another raven vision, mum?"

She gaped at him. "You believe me?"

They looked at each other again, looking confused this time, before William responded. "Well, of course, mum. Why wouldn't we?"

Tanyth found herself at a loss. "Because it's crazy? I'm dreaming that I'm a raven and acting like it's real? That doesn't sound a little bit odd to you?" Her voice rose in pitch as worry and fear came bubbling out.

Amber smiled. "Well, of course, it sounds odd, mum." She looked around and shrugged. "But the truth is you did see the man in the woods, or at least where he'd been." She looked at Thomas who answered with a wry smile and a nod of his head. She looked back at Tanyth. "And you certainly saved that house from the fire last night. That was certainly real and you had no other way to know it, did you?"

Tanyth shook her head, unable to speak.

Amber gave a little nod of her own. "So? There's lots of stuff we don't understand in this world, mum." She paused for a moment before continuing. "After the blessing you gave last night at Harvest Moon, I'm thinkin' you're touched by the All-Mother, mum, pardon my sayin' so."

Tanyth held back a snort. Those touched by the All-Mother were generally regarded as crazy, so Amber wasn't really making her feel any better, but she found it a great relief that her story wasn't met with scorn and derision. The relief was nearly palpable as she realized that the weight of uncertainty was greatly lessened by her sharing of the stories. She closed her eyes and bowed her head saying another silent prayer of thanks to the All-Mother. She sighed in relief and sipped her tea, which was growing cold. In the forest, a raven called hoarsely. All eyes flicked to that direction and not just Tanyth's. When they caught themselves, everyone gave a small, uneasy laugh which broke the knot of tension and allowed the group to break up.

William called to the children. He and Thomas escorted them up to the barn to play while the women returned to Amber's house to begin the cycle of food preparation anew. Tanyth was given a place by the hearth, a fresh mug of hot tea, and some small tasks to keep her hands busy. She feared that she'd feel odd in their company after sharing her secret. She delighted in being wrong.

CHAPTER 20
WAITING

Within two days, the village was back to near normal. Tanyth moved in with Megan and her children while Harry was on the road with Frank. After some initial awkwardness, the two women soon found they liked each other's company and fell into an easy comfort when together, even as Amber and Sadie treated Tanyth with a respectful reserve. In the meantime the quarrymen finished closing the quarry for the season and set up one of the spare houses as a kind of barracks where they could rotate the guard duties more equitably and still have a place to sleep without inconveniencing one of the households. If Jakey was a bit prickly about the lack of work that had been done, he took up a shift as guard readily enough and Tanyth thought he'd grown somewhat less concerned for the quarry as he was drawn into plans for building the inn.

As time went on, there was no repeat of the attack, nor had Andrew Birchwood and his bully boys returned to demand their tribute. Some of the villagers talked openly about their hope that it was over. Thomas was not one of them, nor was Tanyth. William was firmly convinced that the worst had not yet come.

Tanyth and Megan heard the men walk by their house and knock on Wiliam's door just before sundown on the second day after Harvest Moon. Megan and Tanyth followed in their wake to see what new thing had happened. They found three of the younger quarrymen outside Amber and William's back door talking earnestly to William who stood on the floor just inside. Karl Bolten, a squared off youngster with heavy

175

arms, seemed to be the leader of the group. Tanyth looked around but didn't see Jakey anywhere and wondered what that meant.

"It's only been two days, Karl." William was shaking his head. "They'll be back and when they do, it won't be to sprinkle a little lamp oil around."

Karl looked at his friends who shook their heads. "But how long are we going to have to stay up guardin', William? If I'd wanted to be a soldier, I'd have joined the King's Own."

"How long to you want to keep wakin' up on the green side of the sod, Karl?" William's voice was quiet and reasonable.

Karl looked startled at that.

William continued in his quietly reasonable voice. "As soon as we let down our guard, people will start getting' hurt. Some might be killed. Birchwood and his boys have killed before." He shrugged. "Out here? There's precious little to keep them from killin' again, except they're cowards and won't face a fair fight."

Karl recovered a bit of his composure. "Well, how long then, William? A week? A month? All winter? What?"

William shrugged. "Dunno, Karl. Until they get bored and wander on to the next town, I'd guess."

"Well, why don't we hunt 'em down and deal with them first?" Matthew Olivet spoke from behind Karl.

William shifted his gaze to Matthew. "You mean hunt them down and kill them?" His voice was flat.

Matthew clenched his hands into fists a couple of times as he considered the words. "Well, why not, if they're going to start killin' us?"

"They haven't yet, though, have they?" William asked.

"They mighta. You jes' said so." The burly quarryman was losing his assurance.

William stared at him for a long moment. "Are we killers then, Matthew?" His eyes turned harder than Tanyth had ever seen them before. "Are we the kind of people who'll hunt men because we're afraid of them? Too weak to hold what's ours by right?"

Matthew was shaken but not ready to back down. "But you just got done sayin' they're gonna come back and start

getting' serious about hurtin' people, William. You just said!"
He looked for support from his cronies. "Didn't he just say
that?"

They nodded and muttered assent but Tanyth thought it
wasn't particularly enthusiastic agreement.

William crossed his arms. "And they very well might. I
fully expect that they will."

Matthew grinned feeling vindication, but William wasn't
done.

"And they might not. I could be wrong. They might have
a change of heart and a sudden infusion of the All-Mother's
love and decide to become wanderin' monks."

Karl sniggered and Matthew looked confused. "What are
you sayin', man? Those boyos are no more gonna find religion
than I am." He realized that Tanyth was standing behind his
left shoulder and turned with a gruff and slightly embarrassed
smile. "No offense, mum."

Tanyth smiled and nodded an acknowledgment, but didn't
speak.

"I don't think so either, Matt." William softened his stance
a bit. "And if they show up here to do us hurt, they'll find
that Mama Mapleton raised no cowards." He looked from face
to face. "But if you boys can't see the difference between self-
defense and murder, we need to have a bit of a think about
that."

The word "murder" set them back.

William pressed his advantage. "They haven't even made
any demands yet. Just vague threats. If we keep our heads
up and our backs covered, they may decide we're too tough a
nut to dig the meat out of and go their way."

That logic touched something in Tanyth. Would they suc-
ceed in driving the thugs off only to have the next village down
the Pike have somebody hurt, or even killed? The thought
made her queasy, but she understood William's point.

In the face of their crumbling resistance, William offered
a token. "We'll keep watch for three more days. If nothin'
else happens, then we'll talk about it again and we can get
back to normal."

That seemed to mollify them. They looked at each other

and nodded before nodding to William and tramping off between the huts.

Thomas stepped out of the shadows and into the light of the doorway. He nodded to Tanyth and then crouched down so he could talk directly to William where he stood on the lower floor of the hut. "You believe that, Will? They'll leave us alone?"

He shook his head. "We keep up the guard for three more days. They'll strike. It's been two days now and Dandy Andy was never the most patient of beings." His eyes turned hard again. "If he can't strike us, he'll lose the confidence of his men. He can't allow that to happen."

Thomas grunted his agreement. "So what do we do?"

William's face lost its hardness and he shook his head in frustration. "We wait until they move and we pray to the All-Mother that we see it coming and can protect ourselves against it."

"And then what?" Thomas pressed.

Tanyth thought that William aged ten winters on that one question. "Then we do whatever we have to do," he said.

Thomas must have seen it, too, because he glanced up to where Tanyth and Megan observed from the edge of the light before looking back at his friend. "It's not gonna be pretty."

"Yes. I know." William looked to Tanyth. "You haven't had any more visions, mum?"

Tanyth shook her head. "No, but when I do, I'll let you know."

"Thank you, mum." William nodded respectfully. "It's all I can ask."

Thomas stood up from his easy crouch and sighed. "Well I best go find Karl. He's got guard duty with me 'til midnight."

"And I better get some sleep." William smiled. "I've got to relieve you." With a nod, he closed the door again.

Thomas turned to Tanyth and Megan. "Can I walk you ladies home?" His smile was a slash of white in the dimness of the not-quite-risen moon.

Megan giggled. "If you like."

Tanyth laughed. "All fifteen paces of it, and we'll be grateful for your company, kind sir."

Still he walked with them, keeping an eye roving across the shadows and alert to the sounds of the wind in the treetops and the night birds in the forest. He stood outside until they'd closed the door and latched it behind them. From inside the door, the two women didn't hear him leave, but Tanyth knew without a doubt that he'd gone.

Megan turned to her with eyes wide. "What do you think William meant by 'we'll do what it takes,' mum?"

Tanyth sighed. "Well, my dear, I think he meant we'll do whatever we need to do to protect the people of the village."

"Yes, mum, but that sounded ominous." She shuddered.

Tanyth shrugged. "Well, maybe it won't come to much. Bullies tend to back down when confronted."

Megan looked unconvinced but nodded a half-hearted agreement.

They retired to their usual places beside the hearth. The day was winding down and Tanyth felt it in her bones. Standing outside as the day chilled to night had left her thinking that a hot cup of chamomile tea would go nicely before she crawled into her bedroll. She started to stoke up the fire, but Megan stopped her.

"You just let me do that, mum." Megan pressed her back into her seat by the fire. "I'll make us a nice cup and then we can get some sleep."

Tanyth let the younger woman fuss over her a bit and soon they were seated side by side and sipping their tea. The companionable silence was broken only by the occasional snapping of the fire and the odd snort or moan from the pile of children sleeping in the corner.

"What do you think will become of us, mum?" Megan's voice was low and she stared into the fire with a dreamy expression.

Tanyth sipped and felt the warmth of the liquid sink down her throat. "That's not for us to know, I think." Her voice was equally low, barely a murmur. She, too, was raptly gazing into the play of flame above the log. "All we can do is the best we can, try to live a good life, and deal with each day that the All-Mother gives us."

Megan sighed. "I know, mum, but with these thugs out

in the dark somewhere and Harry out on the road and even the quarrymen gettin' restless..." She paused and sipped from her mug. "Seems hard to believe we'll be able to get an inn built in all this."

Tanyth gave a little sideways shrug. "Well, my dear, all we can really do is try. If things don't go exactly as planned, well, I think that's why the All-Mother gives us tomorrow." She turned to the younger woman and smiled gently. "Speaking of tomorrow, we should probably get some sleep. Tomorrow will be here soon."

Megan glanced at her out of the corner of her eye and smiled in return. "True enough, mum." She nodded at the sleeping children. "This bunch will be up looking for their breakfast before dawn."

They drained their tea mugs and rinsed them in a bit of clean water before setting them on the hearth board to wait for morning. Tanyth slipped into her bedroll after removing only her boots while Megan banked the fire and prepared herself for sleep. In moments the two were snug in their beds, the fading light of the banked fire giving the room a sunset glow as they drifted out onto the sea of slumber.

Chapter 21
Taken

Tanyth slept soundly, untroubled by ravens or odd dreams. If she dreamed at all, she didn't remember as she slowly swam up from the warm depths and surfaced in the gray light of morning. She stretched in her bedroll and glanced around the cottage. The children were still sleeping, although they'd shifted position in the night and small hands and heads protruded at odd angles from beneath their blankets.

Megan's bed was empty but her boots were gone. Tanyth felt the call of the privy herself, but stretched and stirred the fire before slipping on her boots. The bed of coals quickly ignited dry kindling and Tanyth had a small but cheery blaze going before she yielded to the inevitable. She grabbed a tunic from her pack and slipped it on for extra warmth before bracing herself for the morning chill. She slipped the latch on the door and scooted out, closing the door quickly behind her to keep as much of the warm air contained as possible.

She dashed for the privy, her boots leaving a scuffed trail in the dew sodden grass. She got there and tended to her morning business before the reality hit her. Megan wasn't there. Tanyth's world tilted slightly as she realized the fact. Megan wasn't in her bed, and wasn't in the privy. A cold chill that had nothing to do with the weather leached down her spine. She hurriedly refastened her clothing and bolted out the door. The children were in the house alone, asleep, and undefended.

She ran headlong into the chest and arms of a burly man who lifted her in a bear hug, squeezing her tightly so she couldn't get enough breath to shout. His breath stank as he grunted from the effort of holding her tightly and lifting. He leered at her. She recognized the man she'd knocked down, one of Birchwood's men, and she feared that the others were nearby. He started shuffling around the side of the privy and Tanyth knew she had only moments before one of his compatriots would come to help him–or she'd black out from not being able to suck in breath.

Her arms were pinned but her head and legs were free. She arched her back as if trying to pull away from his stinking breath. He chortled softly at the feeling of the squirming woman before she flexed her back in the other direction and drove her forehead into his nose. More than one overly lustful bravo had thought a small woman on her own made for an easy target. They never counted on her having her own ideas about that, nor the wiry strength and determination needed to see those ideas through. He released her and grabbed at his spurting nose and the pain centered right between his piggy little eyes. She fell to the wet ground but slipped on the grass, falling heavily on her backside. The position presented her with an ideal target. She let herself fall all the way onto her back and then brought both feet up and drove the heels of her boots into his crotch.

He was a burly man, and she was not a large woman, but bands of muscle wrapped her legs, developed while walking back and forth across the countryside for two decades. Her kick lifted him off his feet and dropped him on his back, unable to even whimper. She heard shuffling in the brush behind the privy and rolled out into the open, getting her feet under her and drawing in a lung full of air.

She bellowed "NO!" with all the power in her diaphragm. There was supposed to be a guard out there somewhere. William and one of the quarrymen were watching the grounds, but tucked away at the back of the village, Megan's house and privy were out of the main lines of sight. The bravo on the ground managed to curl himself into a ball around his crushed dainties but could only whimper while his nose bubbled blood as he writhed.

She scrambled to her feet and headed for the iron hoop

to sound the alarm, but William and Karl pelted around the edge of the hut, skidding on the dew slicked grass moments before Thomas tore out of his house, shirtless against the cold, but bow strung and drawn.

Tanyth pointed to where the sound had come from. "They got Megan. I heard them in the woods there."

William and Karl dashed into the undergrowth. Thomas covered the man on the ground and looked at Tanyth. "Are you hurt, mum?"

She shook her head, sucking air into her bruised lungs.

They heard the sound of William and Karl crashing through the woods but it was obvious that they found nothing. After a few minutes of thrashing about, they came back to find Thomas with a blade poised at the fallen man's eye–holding his attention while Tanyth bound his hands behind him with his own belt. The man's eyes were wide with pain and fear. He lay curled around his damaged groin and the small, high pitched grunting noises seemed out of place coming from a man his size.

Karl looked at the bravo and then at Tanyth as she put the finishing touches on his lashing.

"What did you do to him, mum?" Karl blurted the question, fear tinging his voice.

She stood up and dusted off her hands. She looked down at the bound man for a moment. "I think I might have broken his nose and then I kicked his worthless balls up into his chest somewhere." Her crude words sounded oddly flat and out of place in the clear morning air, but she was in no mood for the niceties of sparing tender male sentimentalities. "I think they've got Megan."

William focused on that. "What makes you think so, mum? A vision?"

She shook her head. "When I woke up, she wasn't in her bed. I thought she'd probably just gone to the privy, but I had time to stoke up the fire and get it going before I came out myself. She wasn't in there and when I came out, I ran into this thing." She kicked him none to gently in the kidney. "He tried to take me into the bushes but I got loose. I heard the others back there but I couldn't see them." She looked around at the staring men. "I figger he caught her the same way he caught me and they took her off with them when they ran."

William nodded to Thomas who sheathed his knife and slipped almost silently around the privy and into the woods behind. William crouched down to the wheezing, moaning man on the ground and turned his head to one side to get a good look at his face. His eyes narrowed as he thought. "Josh, right? Josh the Cosh?"

The man managed a small, if erratic nod, but seemed unable to focus too well.

William stood up. "Well, Josh. I'm guessin' it'll be a long time before you go swingin' that nightstick of yours again." He turned to Karl. "Would you go collect Jakey? Tell him what's happened and get the rest of the boys? When Thomas picks up their trail, we'll be going after Megan."

Karl nodded and hurried off toward Jakey's house.

William turned to Tanyth. "You sure you're all right, mum?"

She looked up at him. "Little bruised about the ribs but I'm fine, William. Thank you." She looked around at the women and children who'd come out to see what all the commotion was. "We should get him under cover and clear this path, though."

"You concerned for his health after what he tried to do, mum?" William had a look of incredulity on his face.

"In a way. I don't want anybody to hurt him until we have Megan back. We may need to convince him to tell us where they're camped." Tanyth looked down at the man on the ground. "When he can talk again."

William glanced at him and then around at the angry faces that were beginning to press a bit closer. "I take your meaning, mum."

Jakey came running over with his wife in tow. He'd had time to put on boots and clothes, but he'd obviously left the house in a hurry. He was still buttoning his shirt when he arrived. He took in the scene. "What cha got here, William?"

"This here is Josh Willowston. They called him Josh the Cosh back in Kleesport. He's one of the boyos that was riding with Andy Birchwood."

Jakey leaned over to examined the man closely. "He seems a mite worse for wear. What'd ya do to him?"

William shook his head. "Nothing. Mother Fairport here took him down and tied him up."

Jakey's eyes bulged a bit and he turned to regard the small woman still standing over the mewling man. "You, mum?"

"Yup." She nodded. "Hard for a man to stand with crushed knackers. Takes the fight out of 'em quite nicely."

Jakey winced a bit. "You hurt, mum?"

She gave a half shrug. "I'll be better when we get Megan back."

Jakey nodded. "Karl said they'd gotten her." He turned to William. "What's the plan?"

William jerked his head toward the woods. "Thomas is looking for their trail now. When he finds it, we'll go in and get her back."

Jakey nodded. "Lemme round up the crew–what's left of it–and we'll go with you."

William nodded.

Tanyth narrowed her eyes. "What should we do with this one?" She nudged him with her boot again.

William reached down and grabbed him by the collar. "Jakey, gimme a hand here, will ya? We need to get him over to the barracks house so we can watch him."

Jakey looked down at the hapless Josh once more. "He's not really gonna walk any where soon, you think?"

William shook his head. "Nope."

Jakey nodded and grabbed on beside William. Together they dragged him off, around the corner and down between the rows of houses.

When the men had gone, Amber and Sadie rushed to Tanyth's side. "You sure you're not hurt, mum?" Amber asked.

Tanyth took a deep breath. "I've been worse, but I'll feel a whole lot better when we get Megan back and these thugs leave us alone." Sadie joined them and Tanyth looked back at Megan's house. "We'll need to take care of the kids until we know."

Amber and Sadie nodded solemnly. Amber patted Tanyth's arm."We'll get all the kids together at my house today. Don't worry, mum. We'll take care of them."

Tanyth nodded and felt the strength in her legs waning rapidly. She turned and went back into Megan's house with the younger women in tow. She sat heavily down on her bedroll as Amber and Sadie bundled up the three, wide-eyed children.

On their way out, the small blonde girl–Tanyth remembered her name was Sandy–stopped and turned to Tanyth. "You'll watch over us all, won't you, mum?"

Tanyth smiled and swallowed back a lump. "I'll try, sweetling. I'll certainly try."

The little girl smiled beatifically. "Thank you, mum. That's all we can ask." She rejoined her sibs and they all trooped out, following Sadie.

Amber paused at the door uncertainly. "Will you be all right, mum? I shouldn't leave you alone..." Her voice trailed off.

Tanyth shook her head. "I'll be fine, my dear. I just need to sit quietly here for a moment. Put the kettle on. I'll be along for a cup of tea in a moment."

Amber hesitated but did as she was bid, and left the house, closing the door behind her.

Tanyth pulled her knees up to her chest and placed her forehead on them and prayed to the All-Mother for guidance and protection.

CHAPTER 22
A FEINT AND A FIRE

No matter how hard Tanyth tried, the edge of sleep was as elusive as a wave on the shore, slipping close and lapping her feet but always receding again. For the first time since she'd seen through the raven's eyes, she found herself desperately desiring a vision instead of fearing it.

She heard the men mustering behind the house and pulled herself up wearily and went to see what was happening. Amber had the same idea and the two women converged on the gathering just as Thomas slipped back out of the woods, his face grim.

William nodded to him. "Trail?"

Thomas held up a scrap of fabric. "Caught on a limb. Trail's there but it's rough. They're headed south and not very far ahead yet. We ready to move?" He looked to William.

William looked at his assembled party of quarrymen. Jakey nodded and the others looked grimly eager to be off. William turned to Amber. "We tied Josh to a cot in the barracks house. He should be okay 'til we get back." He spared a glance for Tanyth. "You really did a job on him, mum."

"Yes." She smiled in a way that had nothing to do with humor. "More'n one thought a little woman like me was easy pluckin' in the last twenty winters."

His breath huffed out in a single laugh at that but he turned back to his wife. "They'll be running and we'll be behind them, so you should be safe enough here, but keep everybody in the house and together until we get back."

She nodded and reached up to give him a quick peck on

the cheek. "Be careful."

He just nodded, his mind already on the trail ahead. He turned to Thomas. "Go!"

The men slipped into the undergrowth and in moments there was no sound at all except for the wind in the treetops and the morning birds chirping in the brush.

Amber turned to Tanyth. "I'll get Charlotte and Bethany. Why don't you go get warm in front of the fire, mum."

Tanyth smiled. "I will. Let me just pick up my things a bit and get some fresh clothes..." She looked down at her clothing–slept in and muddy from her scramble on the ground.

Amber grinned. "You've had a full morning, mum."

"Yes, and I haven't even had my tea. No wonder I'm grumpy." Her tone was vaguely self-mocking. "It's not good to accost me on the way back from the privy before I've had my tea."

Amber's giggle sparkled in the light of the rising sun. "No, mum. I can see that."

The reality of their grim situation reasserted itself and the two went their separate ways, Tanyth to collect her bed roll and pack and Amber to check on the remaining women and children.

In the house, Tanyth pulled the kettle back from the fire and banked what little fire was left. With all the excitement, it had almost burned itself out already. In just a few moments, she'd stashed her extra clothing in her pack, fetched her belt knife from the bedroll, and rolled the bed roll into a loose ball. She didn't bother to attach it to the pack, but just looped the pack over one arm, clapped her hat on her head, took staff in hand and grabbed the bedroll under the other arm for the short walk across the grass.

When she entered the hut, Sadie had the children all sitting in a circle playing a game that involved hand clapping in a complicated progression of patterns that seemed to make them all fall into gales of giggle whenever one of them missed and they had to start over.

Tanyth propped her pack in the corner and plunked the bedroll in front of it for a seat. As she started to settle on it, Sadie hurried over and before she knew it, Tanyth found herself sitting at the place of honor on the hearthstone and holding an earthenware mug of hot tea.

"You just rest there, mum. We'll have something hot for breakfast soon's Amber gets back."

On cue, Amber scurried into the house alone. "Bethany, Rebecca, and Charlotte have barricaded themselves in with their kids up there."

Sadie nodded. "Probably just as well." She nodded at the alarming large pile of children on the floor. "Gonna get noisy enough in here before the morning's out with just this lot." Her smile was warm even if her tone sounded resigned.

The lot in question dissolved in to shrieking laughter as their clapping pattern was broken once more and they started over again.

The two younger women bustled around the fire, heating water and warming a pot of stew for breakfast. They smeared soft cheese on slices of bread and broke into the circle of clapping children to hand out skewers of bread that they could warm for themselves over the coals at the edge of the hearth.

Their initial tasks completed, the women stepped back and let the kids get closer to the coals. There was the usual jockeying for position and the requisite number of burned and dropped pieces of bread, but all in all, the morning progressed in good order.

Tanyth watched the operation, faintly amused by the process.

"It's slow, mum, but it keeps 'em occupied for a bit." Amber said with a fond smile.

Tanyth returned the smile, including Sadie in her gaze. "You two are going to be wonderful innkeepers."

Sadie shook her head. "Not me, mum. That's all Amber's headache. I don't want anything to do with it."

Amber laughed a bit. "I'm gonna make you a bread oven the likes of which you've only dreamed of! You see if I don't."

The way Sadie's eyes lit up for a moment before she caught the handle on her enthusiasm made Tanyth think that Amber knew her friend very well indeed.

They sat quietly and sipped their tea while the gaggle of children finished toasting–and sometimes burning–their bread and cheese.

After a few minutes, Sadie turned to Tanyth. "D'you really think we'll have an inn here, mum? Really?"

Tanyth shrugged. "Why wouldn't you?"

"Well, there's not that many travelers on the Pike, mum. I got my doubts as to whether or not we could make a go of it."

Tanyth gave a little half shrug. "You won't really know until you try, will you?"

Sadie shrugged back. "I guess so, mum. Just seems like a lotta work for something that might not pan out in the end."

Tanyth looked back and forth between the two younger women. "What's the worst that can happen? The town gets a big building where you can all gather. If guests come to stay, then good. If not, then you still have the building for days when it's raining or snowing."

The two looked at each other and nodded. Amber's mouth turned up a little at the corners. "It would be nice to have someplace bigger than this little house to gather in." She eyed the crowded corners and small floor space. The only place that was really clear was where Tanyth realized the root cellar must be.

They laughed at Amber's half-wistful tone.

Tanyth nodded at the children. "As this lot gets older, and bigger, you're going to need something to keep them busy. Who knows? In a few winters you'll have all the staff you need right here."

Amber and Sadie looked a bit startled at that notion, but the idea soon settled into them and they nodded in agreement.

The children finished burning breakfast and returned to their places on the floor. The game of clapping and laughing began once more. They made a lot of noise but it was happy noise and the adults settled down to bowls of stew and hanks of bread and another round of tea before the day's work began.

The game reached the breaking point quickly, but instead of dissolving into peals of laughter, two of the children began squabbling. Tanyth didn't even have a chance to figure out which two before Sadie shouted. "Stop! If you can't play nice, you'll have to do chores."

Sandy piped up. "But he was–"

Sadie raised a hand, palm out. "Tut!"

The children silenced immediately.

"No tales! No tattle! If you can't get along..." She let the unstated threat hang in the air and let the children imagine something worse than she could reasonably threaten.

She started to say something else but in the silence another sound reached them, a low rumbling.

Sadie turned to Amber. "Thunder? This time of year?"

Tanyth was already moving. "Horses." She grabbed her staff and headed for the front door before anybody else could move. She burst through the door even as the three riders carrying burning torches galloped up the path from the Pike. One was headed right for her but she raised her staff and shouted in the horse's face "Oye! Hyah!" And the horse shied away.

The rider held on and glared at her as the horse wheeled. He got the animal under control and spurred it toward Sadie's house instead. Tanyth recognized Andrew Birchwood with a shock. He galloped up to the front, kicked the door open from where he sat and tossed a burning torch through the opening.

Behind her Tanyth heard Sadie gasp and glanced to see her start to run towards her home. Amber stopped her as Birchwood drew steel and wheeled his horse back in their direction. "Where is he?" he barked, his face clouded in red anger.

Tanyth laughed in his face. "You shoulda asked that before you started torchin' houses!"

Birchwood reined up, disconcerted for a moment, and Tanyth swung her staff at his sword hand. The horse wheeled and she missed, but it put the man even more off balance.

A shout echoed across the village. "Here!"

Birchwood spared a glance for the women and then charged to where his men helped Josh the Cosh up out of the house. The crippled man was still not able to stand upright on his own but the two on the ground hefted him over the saddle of a riderless horse like a sack of grain. One tossed the reins to Birchwood who sheathed his sword and caught up the leather. He trotted his horse back the way they'd come while the other two double mounted the remaining horse and followed–victorious grins plastered across their faces.

As they rode away, Tanyth bolted towards Sadie's house and skidded through the door into the fire. The torch had landed right in the middle of one of the woven grass mats and the fire had a good hold. The high peak was filling with smoke, but the ground level was still relatively clear. Sadie and Amber ran in behind her and Sadie started to grab a woolen blanket from the cot but Amber shouted. "No! Help me."

Between them they lifted the burning mat and dragged it out onto the grass before anything else caught fire. The billowing smoke from around the village told them they weren't going to be as lucky with the rest of the houses.

Charlotte and Bethany came running around the corner and the five women headed back toward Megan and Harry's house but the torch there had done its work and the flames were licking out of the open door. Tanyth ran up to the open front door and slammed it shut to try to slow the fire's spread. They ran past to the next house but it was unoccupied and the torch had fallen on bare earth and posed no risk.

"Buckets." Tanyth was panting now and the others stared numbly at her. "We might be able to save something! Buckets. Water!"

They scattered and Tanyth headed for the pump. "Riley! Riley! Come to me, boy! Riley!"

The stout lad lanced out of the backdoor of Amber's house as fast as his solid little legs could carry him and Tanyth pointed at the pump. "Keep the water going, lad. Just keep pumping!"

Amber was the first back with two buckets and Sadie was right on her heels. Tanyth helped Riley get the pump going and then she grabbed a bucket herself and they started running back and forth from the pump to Megan's back door, tossing bucket after bucket into the heart of the fire and splashing water around as quickly as they could. Charlotte and Bethany returned and added their muscles and buckets. The cold water did the trick and they began to beat the fire back slowly at first and then suddenly it was over.

Tanyth looked around at her soot smeared brigade, taking stock. "Is anybody hurt?"

Amber pointed to Tanyth where a burn welted up the skin of her lower arm. "Just you, mum, I think."

Tanyth looked at the burn and felt its sting but it was superficial. "I'll be fine. Where are the children."

Riley's voice piped up from outside. "Here, mum."

Riley had them all lined up in order of age outside by the pump. "They helped me pump!"

Tanyth smiled at the pride in his voice. "Good job, everyone."

The exhausted women practically crawled out of the fire ravaged hut, coughing a bit from the smoke and stinking of burned wool. They collapsed on the grass, muscles trembling from the exertion and gulping clean morning air. The wide eyed children gathered around and settled between and among them–some cuddling, some demanding reassurance, and others offering.

Young Riley stood at the open door and peered down into the blackened ruin. After a period of careful consideration, he turned to the assembled party and with a jerk of his thumb at the open door. "Boy, Ms. Megan is gonna be mad when she sees that mess."

The women all dissolved in to gales of laughter and their relief echoed through the forest and sailed on the last wisps of gray smoke up into the blue, morning sky.

CHAPTER 23
RECOVERY

Tanyth was the first to recover and leaped to her feet when Thomas and the quarrymen came crashing through the forest. The men skidded to a stop and surveyed the women and children–eyeing the burnt-out house and trying to see everything at once.

Thomas spoke first. "Is everybody all right?"

Tanyth nodded. "We're all fine. Singed a little here and there, but they got Josh and this house is probably not going to be habitable." She jerked her head in the direction of the burned house. "Where's Megan?"

"William and the boys are bringing her along. When we saw the smoke, he sent us ahead."

"How is she?" Amber looked at the children.

Little Sandy stepped forward. "Yes, Mr. Hawthorne. Is my mum all right?"

Thomas went down on one knee to look her in the eye. "Yes, Sandy, she's fine. Just a little shaken up and she can't move as fast through the woods as we can."

She flung her arms around his neck. "Thank you, Mr. Hawthorne."

When she stepped back, Thomas grinned and crossed to the burned house. He surveyed it from the door but didn't step in. "William and Megan aren't too far behind us." He looked around at the group sprawled out on the ground again. "I'll be interested to hear how this all happened when they get here."

The men drew water from the pump and each took long

drinks but conversation lagged as everybody just breathed and tried to cope. In a few minutes, William and Megan came out of the woods, winded and looking around frantically. Megan was scratched and looked a bit the worse for wear. William's eyes scanned the crowd looking for Amber and relief washed across his face when his eyes picked her out of the group on the ground.

Megan gave a cry and ran to her three kids, throwing herself onto the ground to hug them all into her arms. She burst into tears then and held them, rocking them all awkwardly in her embrace. The children tried to comfort the woman as she held them and slowly got herself under control.

Sandy finally managed to pull back a little bit. "You're fine now, Ma. We're here and you're here and Da, he'll be back soon, and we can make a new house."

"A new house, poppet?" Megan scrubbed the tears off her face with her fingers and looked intently at the soot streaked face in front of her. What she was seeing registered and she looked at her house, taking in the smoke streaks above the door and the wisps that still wafted upwards from the trapped smoke in the peak of the roof. Something in her face sagged for a moment, but she recovered almost instantly and looked from child to child to child. "Is anybody hurt? You're all all right, aren't you?"

"We're fine, mum. Mother Fairport chased them off and then put the fire out. We helped pump!" Sandy beamed.

William looked through the door at the damaged house and turned to address them. "So, now we know. They got Josh, I take it?"

Tanyth grunted before answering. "Yeah, they threw him over a horse and rode off down the Pike, after setting fire to the house. They threw three torches, but this is the only one that caught. Thomas and Sadie need a new floor mat, though."

William nodded and exchanged glances with Thomas. "I was afraid of somethin' like this when we found Megan in the woods."

Thomas nodded his agreement. "The horses were stashed there for a fast getaway, but they had to change their plans when Josh got caught." He nodded respectfully to Tanyth. "Thank you for that, mum."

Tanyth nodded and looked back at William. "Now what do you think they'll do?"

William's face hardened. "If they're smart, they'll keep riding. If they come back here, they won't be getting as civil a welcome as they got before."

Tanyth nodded her head. "Are they smart?"

William shook his head. "I'm afraid they think they're smart enough to get away with it." He sighed and looked at the sun. "Let's get this cleaned up and see if we can help Megan and the kids get settled in another house." He smiled sympathetically. "Is there one you'd fancy, Meg? I'm afraid this one won't be livable for awhile."

Thomas snorted. "If ever."

Tanyth caught William's eyes with a nod to the burned house. "If you took that house down altogether and built the inn up here near the pump, it would make getting water to the inn a lot easier. You wouldn't have to lug water down to it or dig another well. Frank and I were talkin' about it the night before he left." She looked at Sadie and Thomas. "You'd have to move, too, but then both these houses could come down and the inn could go here." She held out her arms to indicate the space. "Frank seemed to think it was a good place because it got the inn back off the road a bit."

Thomas was following the description but Sadie got caught up in the idea of moving. "Then we'd be further from the water."

William nodded at her. "True, but the inn would use the most, so having the inn handy to the water makes sense."

Amber nodded in agreement. "Yeah. That makes a lot of sense. I think we'd have to move too. I don't think I'd like to have my house that close to the inn."

William smiled. "Actually, my heart, I think you and I will be living in the inn by the time it's done. Somebody will need to."

Jakey spoke up for the first time since breaking out of the woods. "Havin' it back here would make it easier to protect the water supply and would also be closer to the barn."

They all looked at him.

He seemed a little startled by the attention for a change, but continued with a shrug. "Most folks will be coming with horses. They'll want the animals cared for as well." He smiled. "A silver for a place in the common room and three pennies for the horse in the barn. Four if they want grain."

William huffed a quick laugh but Thomas nodded. "I think that's what they charge at Mossport."

"Maybe we should make it more, then." Jakey grinned.

William raised his hands to break into the discussion. "Hang on. We've got too much plannin' with too little doin'. First things first." He turned to Megan and the children. "Which house do you want? There's several empty."

Megan looked a bit lost. "I don't know, Will. I never considered movin' before."

Tanyth smiled and held out her hand. "Well, why don't you and the kids move in with me for a bit in Mother Alderton's house. When Harry gets back, you can decide together what you want to do."

Megan took the hand and Tanyth pulled the younger woman up off the ground. "Thank you, mum. I'd feel much safer with you."

Tanyth snorted. "I didn't do ya much good this mornin', dearie."

Megan smiled with a shake of her head. "No, you saved my life this morning, mum. They'd have killed me or worse if you hadn't stopped Josh. The bossman there had a lot so say about it while we were runnin' through the woods."

Tanyth raised her eyebrows. "Really, hon? What happened?"

Megan shuddered a little but dug in. "They grabbed me just as I came out of the privy. Caught me by surprise, and that big one crushed me to his chest. I couldn't breathe to yell."

Tanyth nodded in sympathy. "He did that to me, too."

"I was back there in the bushes by the time you came out and they had me trussed up like a solstice goose, 'cept for my legs." She stopped for a moment and swallowed before continuing. "Anyway, one guy–they called him Mort–he was just inside the tree line–waiting. I didn't see what you did, mum, but it upset them something terrible." She smiled in satisfaction. "That's when we turned and headed into the woods. I tried to hold them back, but the big one, Mort, just picked me up and threw me over his shoulder like a sack of potatoes and we headed further and further into the forest."

Thomas nodded. "That's why I couldn't find your tracks among the others."

She shrugged. "A few hundred yards into the wood, their bossman ripped a bit of dress of my hem and hung it on a bush. That's when we really started moving fast. When we got to where they left the horses, Mort started to put me on a horse, but the boss made him tie me to a tree. I didn't understand why they went to all the trouble to kidnap me and then leave me out in the wilds."

William raised his hands to indicated the smoldering wreckage of her house. "You were supposed to keep us busy so we didn't have a chance to interfere with their rescue." He nodded his head in consideration. "They probably planned to hold you hostage, but had to change their plans a bit when Josh got caught. They drew us off, so they could come and get him back."

Megan nodded at the burned house. "It seems to have worked." She walked over to it and stared in at it a little sadly. "Do you think we can save much?"

Tanyth came to stand beside her while the rest of the women gathered round. "We fought hard enough. I think you'll be able to salvage most of it. You'll smell like smoke for a time, but only a few things got burned."

William headed up towards the barn. "I'll get the barrow. Meg? Start handing stuff out and we'll help you carry what you can to Mother Fairport's house."

Tanyth spoke up, then. "Do you have any spare floor mats? We never got around to laying fresh ones down when I moved in. Might be good to do that before we start dragging goods around."

Amber nodded. "Good thinking." She fell in with William. "There's some in the workroom. I'll load a few on the barrow and we'll bring them over to you."

Tanyth nodded and helped Megan down the fire-damaged steps into the soggy mass that had been her home. Megan wrinkled her nose and waved a hand in front of her face. "Ugh. This stinks." She crossed the house and opened the front door. The morning breeze swept through and cleared the air a bit more, while Megan stood with hands on hips and surveyed the damage.

As she looked she seemed to take strength. "Right. Well, Sandy? You watch your brothers and stay close to the house."

"I will, Mama."

"Thank you, sweetling. That'll help me most."

Riley came up to the door and stuck his head in. "What can I do to help, Ms. Megan?"

She smiled up at the boy. "Just keep an eye on all the children, Riley. We don't want anybody wanderin' off."

"Yes, mum!" He grinned and started herding the other children like a sheep dog.

Megan grinned and shrugged up to where the other women were looking into the house. "That might have been a mistake."

They laughed and Sadie waded down to give Megan a hand while the rest went around to the front door so they'd have the shortest walk to the new house.

Tanyth tapped Matthew and nodded to the burly quarryman. "If you've a mind to help? We could move my goods out of the way to make room for the new mats..."

"Oh, aye, mum." He smiled and followed in her wake as she crossed the yard. She stopped and picked up her staff where she'd dropped it in the grass. If she leaned on it rather more heavily than normal, Matthew didn't seem to notice.

Tanyth had trouble thinking of the young man as much more than a boy, but he was certainly strong enough and more than willing in his assistance. In her small hut, she took the oil lamp and other small things off the table and placed them up on the mantle board to get them out of harm's way. Matthew helped her move the table and chairs onto the hearthstone to free the floor space. They opened the back door and slid the rope-bound cot out onto the grass behind the house just as Amber and William showed up with the barrow full of floor mats.

With Matthew and William to help wrestle the awkward bundles out of the barrow and onto the floor, the job was done in a matter of minutes. They moved the table and chairs back off the hearthstone, but left it closer to the hearth than it had been. She left the oil lamp up on the mantle. "No sense tempting fate." She muttered it to herself but Matthew grunted in agreement.

Amber sent William up to Megan's to pick up a load and she stood in the middle of the house. Tanyth smiled gently at the younger woman's almost proprietary survey. Amber looked shyly at Tanyth. "You know, mum? This would be a good time to bless the house. It's empty as it's gonna be and changing spirits, so to speak." Her voice petered out.

Tanyth pursed her lips and considered it. "That's a good idea." She looked through the herbs she'd harvested and set to dry, but none of them were suitable. She remembered a bundle in the cast offs and crossed to the pile of dry and dusty materials that she hadn't yet had a chance to dispose of. She rummaged through it and pulled up a bundle of sage, brittle on the ends and edges, but still solid enough in the middle to be useful. She smiled as she held it up. "Aha!"

Matthew's eyes grew round and even Amber looked a bit surprised. Tanyth frowned slightly at them. "What? Is there something the matter?"

Matthew and Amber shared a glance. "No, mum." They said it almost in unison.

"Why are you looking like that then?"

Matthew glanced at Amber before speaking. "You're not going to do magic are you, mum? Should I leave?"

Tanyth smiled. "Not magic, no. You can leave if it makes you uncomfortable but don't feel like you need to."

Amber frowned. "What are you going to do with that? And what is it, mum?"

"Isn't this what Mother Alderton used to bless a house?"

Amber shrugged. "I don't know, mum. It might be. She never explained."

Tanyth nodded. "Well, this is sage." She turned to the hearth and laid a fire but didn't light it immediately. She took the bundle of very dry sage and placed it on the hearthstone before pulling the steel and flint out of her pocket. She struck three sparks into the end of the bundle and blew on them until they caught. The dusty herbs gave off a pungent smudge. Tanyth chuckled a bit to herself. "Just what I need. More smoke."

Amber was standing close enough to hear her mutter and she choked back a laugh.

Tanyth grinned at her and picked up the smoldering herbs. She took it to the north side of the hut to the middle of the wall where the back door was open onto the narrow bit of cleared land before the forest. She held up the bundle in front of her face and a wisp of smoke curled up to the rafters. "Guardian of the North, Bones of the Earth, protect this place from evil." She walked the perimeter of the room to the east and stopped in front of the fireplace which made up most of the narrower east wall. "Guardian of the East, Breath of the Earth, protect this place from evil." She continued around to stand in front of the front door, facing south and looking out onto the narrow track that led up to the village. "Guardian of the South, Spirit of the Earth, protect this place from evil." She went to the plain west wall and held the bundle once more. Guardian of the West, Blood of the Earth, protect this place from evil." She walked back around to where she began and made a swirl of smoke in the air as if tying a knot. "By my will and with this smoke, I bind this place once and beg the protection of the guardians." She walked around the circuit again, stopping at each cardinal point and making a similar swirl of smoke until she returned to the north. "By my will and with this smoke, I bind this place twice and beg the protection of the All-Father upon this house." She walked once more around pausing again and leaving a trail of pungent herbal smoke in her wake. "By my will and with this smoke, I bind this place thrice and beg the blessings of the All-Mother upon all who live within." She took the bundle of sage to the hearth and blew on it until it flared from glowing smolder into bright fire. "With earth and air and fire and water, I beg the blessings of the All-Mother upon this hearth and all that shelter here." She tossed the burning sage into the prepared shavings. The fire caught and spread into the dried kindling. Tanyth finished the ritual by dipping her hand in the water bucket and flicking a few drops of water onto the hearthstone, where they showed dark against the dry rock. "So mote it be."

She stood for a moment and admired her handiwork, before drying her hands off on the seat of her pants and turning back to Amber and Matthew. They stood transfixed, staring at her. Matthew's mouth did not exactly hang open, but he looked at once dazed and totally focused.

"What is it? You two look like you've seen a haunt or something."

Amber blinked back from wherever her mind had taken her. "That was wonderful, mum! I've never seen a blessing like that before."

Tanyth shrugged. "What did Mother Alderton do?"

Amber shrugged. "She just stood at the threshold and said, 'Bless this house and all who live here.'"

Tanyth smiled. "Well, that seems to have worked for her." She looked about the house. "I learned this from Mother Willowton, I think it was. She used to really get into blessing houses. She'd use salt and fire and water." Tanyth chuckled at the memory. "It could take her half a day sometimes to get through all the prayers when she did it for somebody else. I stayed with her one whole winter and when it came time to do her own house, she always cleansed it with burning sage." Tanyth shrugged. "I think she just liked to put on a show for her customers."

Amber and Matthew laughed, taken off guard by her frank appraisal of the mystical.

She smiled, satisfied, and felt more at home in the small hut already. She saw William bringing the first load of goods down from Megan's house and they all jumped to help him. Some of the goods–like blankets and clothing–were left to air out a bit, while other items came right in. Tanyth arranged the furnishings the way she remembered Megan's house, hoping to make the younger woman feel more at home. She knew it wasn't going to be an easy time until Harry returned, but she vowed to herself to make it as easy as she knew how.

CHAPTER 24
NEW DEMANDS

By the time the sun reached the treetops on its way toward night, Megan, Tanyth and the children were all safely settled in the new house. The whole village had a finer understanding of why a careful watch was necessary, but still no better idea about how to deal with the issue. Birchwood could come at them from any direction at any time, and they could only watch and wait for his next move.

It came sooner than they expected.

Just as the sun disappeared behind the treetops, but before true sunset, a voice rang out. "Mapleton! William Mapleton! Come out!"

The voice cut across the village from the direction of the Pike and doors popped open at the call, yellow firelight showing silhouettes of heads and shoulders. Thomas popped around the corner of a house and drew an arrow but held his fire as he saw who and what was riding up the path.

William boiled out of his house and ran toward the approaching riders but halted twenty paces back. Tanyth watched from the safety of the house with Megan by her side. The children sensed something amiss and stayed quiet. Little Sandy crawled up the step to peek her head just over the threshold.

Andrew Birchwood sat nonchalantly astride his horse. In front of him in the saddle sat a very pale and frightened looking Riley Mapleton. "Well, good evening, William." Birchwood pitched his voice to play to the audience. "I trust you'll stand your ground there and keep your archer in check?" He smiled. It wasn't a good look for him.

"Riley? Are you hurt?" William ignored Birchwood for the moment.

"I'm fine, Papa. I'm sorry, but–"

Birchwood patted the boy on the shoulder with his left hand. "That's enough, Riley. You'll be quite silent now, won't you? That's a good lad." Birchwood flourished the dagger he held in his right and turned back to the father. "Now that I have your attention, there's the small matter of–how do we phrase this?" He made a show of thinking. "Oh, yes. Insurance. That's the term."

William's face clouded and his fist clenched as he held himself helplessly in check. "Extortion, I think is the term you're struggling with, Birchwood."

"Oh, come now, William. Extortion is such a nasty word." He shrugged. "I'm just a businessman, trying to turn a profit. You're an honest man trying to protect what's yours. I can respect that, William. I can." His voice was oily and ingratiating. He patted Riley on the shoulder once more. "Young Riley, here, for example. It would be tragic should anything happen to him, now wouldn't it."

William took a deep breath. "What do you want, Birchwood? State your claim."

"Oh, I'm not a greedy man, William. I think a nice little operation like this should be able to afford, say, five hundred golds. Insurance, you understand, to make sure that nothing unfortunate happens?"

"Five hundred golds?!" William practically choked. "And you seriously believe we have five hundred golds here!"

Birchwood made a small tsk sound with his lips. "Oh, don't play coy, William. Of course you have it. I've seen the wagon carrying your cargo into town. I've seen your storehouse and I've seen your silver mine."

Tanyth saw the look on William's face go blank for a moment before what Birchwood had said fully registered. "My silver mine?" He paused, staring at the man. "Are you mad? You think we have a silver mine?"

Birchwood shook his head. "Come, come, William. I said, don't play coy. Lives are at stake here. Young lives." His left hand rested heavily on the boy's shoulder.

"It's a clay quarry, Birchwood. Clay. Like you make bricks from."

Birchwood shook his head. "I've been there. I've seen it, William." His voice wasn't so pleasant now. "Your men up there, diligently scraping it all up. Putting in barrels. You can't tell me that you're all out here grubbing up clay–the same clay you can get from any river bank within ten miles of the city?" He shook his head. "No, William. I'm not that gullible."

William sat heavily on the grass, his knees up and leaning back on his hands. "You've got to be joking, Birchwood. Surely, you can't be that foolish." His voice was low but it carried the tone of disbelief clearing through the evening air.

Birchwood's brow furrowed. "Don't play that game with me, Mr. Mapleton! Why would anybody come way out here to dig clay! You're a rich man's son. All these people here have connections in the city. You expect me to believe that you all came out here to live life close to nature and dig up clay?" He took a deep breath and his countenance returned to the more genial one he rode in with. "Please, William. How can you expect me to believe that?"

William closed his eyes and dropped his head back to stare at the darkening sky. "Because, my fine foppish fool, we're all the youngest sons and castoffs of the rich and powerful back in the city." He raised his head and leveled his gaze at the man. "Yes, Mapleton is my father, but I've four brother's who are closer to money than I and you know that to be true as well! You lived in Kleesport long enough to learn that much and as much as you preyed on our people, it must have taught you a thing or two about my father and my family!"

For the first time, Birchwood looked uncertain.

"And we didn't come out here to dig clay. We came out here to start a new town. A town where we might have some of the opportunities that we're denied in the city. A place we can call ours and not something cast off or passed down by our parents." His eyes bored into Birchwood. "The clay is how we raise the cash we need to buy the goods we can't produce yet. It's clay. Just clay. It's a particularly fine clay and someday we'll have a kiln here perhaps and start some manufacturing with that clay, but by the beard of the All-Father, Birchwood, what we take out of the ground up there is clay."

"Do you swear on the life of your eldest son, fool?" Birchwood fairly spit the rejoinder. The two men behind him were looking less certain for the first time since they road into town.

"I can only tell you the truth, Birchwood. It's clay." He paused. "There's another small problem with your plan. We don't keep any cash out here."

Birchwood frowned. "What do you mean, you don't keep any cash?"

William sat up and held out his hands to either side. "Do you see any shops? Pubs? Taverns? Any place where having cash would be of any use out here?" He uncoiled from the ground and stood there in front of the horse. "Do you think, perhaps, we're buyin' and sellin' biscuits from each other? That I'm sellin' the firewood I chop to the highest bidder maybe?"

"Oh, come, come, William. A jest is a jest but I've your son here. Are you sure you want to play these games?" Birchwood's men kept looking back and forth between themselves but Birchwood wasn't paying attention to them. His attention was focused on the man in front of him.

"Birchwood, I swear to you on the life of my son. We send the wagon in loaded. We sell the clay—and it's just clay—to the works in Kleesport. We have accountants and factors in town who keep our money, manage our accounts, and pay our bills for us. When the wagon comes back, he'll have no money—just the goods we'll need to get through the winter. I could pay you in hundred weights of flour, but I doubt if there's more than ten silvers cash money here in the village if you were to shake out all the purses and put the money in a pile." He looked at Birchwood and held out his hands to either side in a gesture of helplessness. "We have no money. We have no need for it out here."

Birchwood shook his head. "Well, I must say, William. This is a most amusing tale you spin, but I don't think you realize the gravity. If you have no money, then bad things will happen to you. And to yours. Like this delightful lad here."

He clapped the boy on the shoulder one more time. "The fires you had today are only a sample." His voice was cold. "I suggest you find some money and find it quickly before somebody you care for gets hurt."

"You can't get blood out of a stone, Birchwood."

"I know that, William." His genial tone faded. "I get blood out of the people who do not pay. It would behoove you to remember that little fact." He paused. "I'll give you a few days to think about it, but I'll be back, and the next time, you should try to find a better story to tell. One with a little more jingle in it."

He made a hand signal and his riders turned and rode back to the Pike. Birchwood himself backed his horse slowly away, keeping the boy between Thomas's arrow and himself.

"My boy, Birchwood! What about my boy?"

Birchwood only smiled and continued to back his mount. Thomas started to follow but Birchwood held the knife to Riley's neck. "You might consider standing where you are, archer. Arrows make me nervous, and when I get nervous, I get twitchy." He made a little jump with his face and arm when he said the word twitchy, and the knife at Riley's throat twitched, too, but didn't draw blood.

Thomas subsided and released the draw on his bow, pointing the arrow to the ground.

Birchwood smiled and backed his horse to the Pike. When he was out of bow shot, he unceremoniously dumped the boy onto the ground and heeled his horse into a gallop, heading south down the Pike with his two bravos.

Riley scrambled to his feet before his father could reach him, picked up a rock, and threw it after the riders. Boyish rage and frustration were writ large on his face and his aim true, but his power too slight and the stone fell to earth only a few feet away.

William reached the boy at a run and scooped him up in his arms before turning to race back to the safety of the house. Tanyth could see they were both crying and clinging to each other as William passed, heading for home and meeting Amber coming down.

Tanyth closed the door on the reunion, and turned to a

wide eyed Megan. "What does it mean, mum?"

Tanyth shook her head. "Our Mr. Birchwood just got a fast introduction to life in our little village of Ravenwood."

"Yes, but what will he do?"

Tanyth shook her head. "I'm not sure. William had a good idea to keep all your money in town where it can be kept safe and used where it'll do the most good." She shook her head. "But I don't know if Andrew Birchwood believes him."

They crossed to the hearth and Megan ran a spoon around in the soup hanging over the fire. "Why wouldn't he believe William, mum? William's never lied to him."

Tanyth took her seat beside the fire as the three children crept closer to hear the adults talking about adult things, eyes shining bright in the failing light of evening. "Well, I suspect it's common for people to claim they have no money. Villages along the Pike like this generally don't have much in the way of cash income. Just like here, they barter and share. That makes it difficult for people like Birchwood to force them to pay for protection."

Megan nodded. "Can't give what you don't have."

"Exactly, my dear. So, I suspect that Mr. Birchwood has heard it before and he doesn't believe it here in particular because he knows William's father is rich."

"Did he really think that the clay quarry is a silver mine?"

Tanyth shrugged. "Apparently. He just can't imagine that a rich man's son, like William, would be out here in the woods digging up clay." She paused. "I'm not sure I do, and I've been here to see."

"It's clay." Megan made the announcement very clearly. "It's good clay, but it's clay."

"Do you know a lot about clay?"

Megan grinned and giggled a little. "Yes, mum. My da owns the Kleesport Brickworks and my uncle owns Kleesport Pottery. I was throwing pots before I was ten winters old." She held up her mug. "This is pottery from Uncle Ezra's factory." She smiled. "He sells it to us cheap."

Tanyth blinked in disbelief. "So this really is good clay?"

Megan nodded soberly. "It surely is, mum." She looked

down for a moment and then leaned in to speak quietly. "Pound for pound, it's worth more than silver ore. At least the ore they get around here." She grinned at the older woman. "It has trace minerals that give it a nice color and texture."

Tanyth giggled a little in return. "It's just clay, but it's worth more than silver?"

Megan nodded. "Oh, yes, mum, but only to people who know what it is and what to do with it."

Tanyth shook her head in disbelief. "No wonder William keeps all the money in town. You couldn't afford a militia big enough to guard it out here."

Megan smiled happily. "It's why the whole village is set up the way it is. We don't have any money here, but we're slowly getting rich in town. And like William said. There's no place to spend it out here."

Tanyth grimaced. "But that still doesn't answer the question of what to do about Birchwood and his bully boys." She glanced at Megan. "I don't suppose we can turn them in to the King's Own?"

"If we could get their attention, maybe, mum."

Tanyth sighed. "Yes. I can see where that might be a problem."

Megan turned to the kids. "That's enough entertainment for one night, my wee cabbages. Shall we have some soup and go to bed?"

They lined up politely, got soup and bread and settled down to eat with a minimum of muss and fuss. Tanyth marveled at how well Megan was bearing up under the ordeal of being kidnapped, dragged through the forest, burned out of her home, and then moving her household–what parts of it survived the fire–all in the same day. With dinner over and the children tucked into snug beds beside the hearth, Megan sat by the fire with mending on her lap while the children nodded off in the warm, dimness of the snug cottage. As the last of the little ones drifted off, Tanyth realized that Megan was sitting very still and hadn't moved needle or thread for several minutes. She glanced over and saw the tears glistening on the young woman's face in the flickering light of the fire.

"Oh, my poor dear."

Megan shook once in a muffled sob.

Tanyth crossed to her and cradled her in her arms. "There, there, my dear. There, there." She held and rocked her as if she were a child herself, letting her sob silently against her and making sure the children didn't see by keeping her body between mother and children. She held her and stroked her hair until the sobs passed, finally, leaving Megan weak, shaken, and limp in Tanyth's lap. Tanyth helped the younger woman into her bed and tucked her in before banking the fire and settling on her own bedroll for the night.

CHAPTER 25
LAST STRAW

Tanyth sat on her bedroll, gazing into the golden depths of the banked coals and pondering. The day had been filled with terror. She knew they'd gotten off easily. Birchwood would not stop until he was forced to. Of that, she was certain. She'd seen enough of his type over the course of her life. By rights, it should be a matter of having the King's Own deal with him, but petty banditry–particularly in the edges of the kingdom–was practically a way of life. By the time the King's Own could deal with it, the village could be destroyed.

"Mother, what do we do?" The words were a whispered prayer but the only answer was the sound of night winds sighing across the top of the chimney. The sound drew a sigh from Tanyth as she settled into her blankets.

Her rest was fitful, each sound in the night, each shift in the wind half woke her. The dreams, as much as she could remember, were nonsensical–images of bears tearing open logs to eat the larvae within, one long disturbing passage of a tree falling in the forest and rotting away–eaten by bugs, filled with fungus–and others she would never remember at all until just before dawn she dreamed of a single drop of blood. It fell through a crystalline blue sky, a sphere of crimson shimmering in the light, falling, falling, falling, until it splattered into a darkened star burst on a hearthstone. The wet redness faded to black as the stone drank in the moisture, leaving only the star shaped stain on the rock.

A single sharp raven's caw brought her awake–eyes searching the dimness as the images of her dreams faded in the gray light of morning. The soft sound of sleeping children blended with the sound of the wind in the chimney. Her belt knife dug into her side where her habit placed it in her bedroll each night. She dressed in her bulky trousers and strapped on the knife. It took but a few minutes to stoke up the fire and fill the kettle from the covered bucket. By the time she was done, Megan stirred in her bedroll and blinked slowly up from slumber.

Tanyth smiled and nodded to the younger woman who smiled and gave a small wave in return. Her eyes closed again, and Tanyth watched her drowse off again in the space of three breaths.

She huffed a quiet laugh and went to the door, opening it a crack to peep out. The sun still hid below the tree tops to the east, but lit the sky with a clear, pale light. The gravel path that served the village as road stood whitely against the dark, wet grasses. A skirl of cold, morning air sneaked in through the crack and washed over her face, drying the night's moisture from her skin. She filled her lungs with the cool freshness of a new day.

She slipped out and walked to the main path, looking for the guard and spotting William and Karl walking between the houses. They saw her and waved. The cool morning air reminded her that she needed to use the privy and she walked quickly.

She dealt with the privy in short order and met William and Karl on the way back to the house. "Good morning, mum." William looked haggard and even Karl looked a bit worse for wear.

"Good morning, William. Good morning, Karl. How are you doing this morning?"

Karl smiled wanly. "Morning, mum. I'm ready for my bed, truth be told."

William shrugged. "I'm doing well, mum. How are things in your house? Did the kids settle in?"

She shrugged in return. "Kids are fine, I think. Megan may take a little longer to recover."

William grimaced. "I was afraid of that. Any problems over night?"

Tanyth remembered the sobbing, shuddering woman that she'd rocked the night before. "No. No problems. She just needs time."

Karl spat on the grass. "We need to deal with this guy. We can't go on like this."

"Now, Karl, we've been talking about this all night long." William tried to put a halt on the conversation.

Karl shook his head. "Don't you, 'Now, Karl,' me, William Mapleton. You know as well as I do that we just are not set up for this. Towns have walls and guards to guard them. We're a collection of huts, spread out and open." He paused for breath before continuing. "You saw that last night. If he can grab Riley..."

William nodded, defeated. "It mighta been any of them. Riley was in the wrong place at the wrong time, and by himself." William sighed and looked at Tanyth. "They were playing hide and seek before bed. He went to hide and before we knew he was gone. Birchwood brought him back." He shuddered and closed his eyes. "Anything could have happened."

"He's right, you know." Tanyth's voice was soft and low and she nodded to Karl.

William nodded without looking up. "I know, but what can we do about it?" His voice sounded ragged and harsh in the quiet morning. He paused and took a deep breath. He looked up and indicated the village around him with a sweep of his head. "We can't build a wall around this. It's too spread out. We don't have the manpower or the money to hire a full-time guard."

Tanyth and Karl followed his gaze around the village.

Tanyth nodded slowly. "I was in the southlands a few winters ago. Land there is flat and open and mostly grassy. Hot as blazes in the summer. Winter blows through for a month or so, but it's bitter cold."

She thought back to her winter with Mother Ashborne. "The King's Own was spread thin down that way, too, and it's right on the border with Barramoor. Every so often the towns got raided."

William looked incensed. "We have treaties with Barramoor. That's not supposed to happen!"

"Indeed we do and it's not supposed to but..." Tanyth shrugged.

Karl finished her thought. "The King's Own is spread too thin."

Tanyth nodded sadly. "The point is that they had to deal with it, and I think we'll need to deal with it, too. Not just Birchwood, but the next band of buggers as well."

William objected. "I thought that's what the Inn was about."

"It is." Tanyth agreed and pointed to Karl with her thumb. "But he's got the right of it, too. We need to deal with Birchwood and we're too vulnerable to him because we're all spread out."

"How do they deal with that in the southlands, mum?" Karl's eyes searched her face.

"They fort up."

William nodded and shrugged all at once. "Sure, but we don't have a fort!" The frustration was showing in his voice. "When we build the inn we can make it defensible but we don't have the inn yet and we can't build it so long as we have to keep looking over our shoulders for Birchwood and his bravos."

"Yes, the Inn will help but you've got a fort now." Tanyth's voice carried conviction and cut through his objections. "The barn."

Both men stopped and stared at her. "The barn?" William's voice almost cracked from surprise but Karl's face took on a thoughtful expression.

She pressed on. "The barn. It's big enough. It's where most of the village's supplies are. It's where the animals are–or at least most of them. The workroom even has a hearth for cooking." She paused to consider. "The only thing it doesn't have is a well."

The two men looked at each other. Karl turned to her. "What good will being in the barn do us, mum? They can still burn us out, one house at a time."

Tanyth shrugged. "Yes, they can, but houses can be rebuilt." She looked pointedly at William. "Children can't be. If we can keep Birchwood from killing anybody–or stealing the supplies we need for the winter–then there's nothing he can really do except be a boil on our backsides. Sooner or later he'll realize that and move on."

William frowned in thought and pinched his lips together between thumb and forefinger. Karl looked around the village as if measuring it with his eyes.

After a few moments, both men were nodding.

Karl spoke first. "With everybody in one space, guarding would be a lot easier and we'd have a smaller perimeter to watch."

William agreed. "We'd be packed in cheek by jowl for awhile but splitting the work of feeding everybody and watching the kids..." He shrugged. "More eyes mean less opportunities for Birchwood."

William sighed and turned to look at the barn back in the trees. "Well, we stayed there the first winter."

Karl looked shocked. "Why would we have to spend the winter there? Birchwood will be gone soon enough once he realizes he can't get at us and we're not going pay."

William glanced at Tanyth who sighed before she spoke. "Because he'll probably be so angry that he'll torch the houses out of spite."

Karl got very still and turned to look at the village with a slow sweep of his head before looking back at Tanyth and then at William. He sighed. "Well, if we muck out the stalls good and lay down fresh straw, we can put bedrolls there until Frank and the boys get back."

William nodded his agreement. "And when they get back we'll have more hands to help with rebuilding."

The three stood and looked at each other for a few more moments and the sun tipped up over the trees across the Pike. William nodded to Karl. "Help me get Bester in harness and we'll use the ox cart to move everybody up to the barn."

Karl nodded.

William turned to Tanyth. "You just moved in, so I hate to have you move again, but..." His voice petered out.

"We've not had much time to get settled yet." Tanyth finished for him.

He shrugged apologetically and she grinned. "I'll go see if

Megan and the kids are up."

They watched to make sure she arrived safely before turning toward the barn. She slipped into the house and four pair of eyes turned to look at her. "Good morning, everybody. I'm glad to see you all up. We're going to do something different today!"

Sandy perked up at that. "Really, mum? What's that? Something fun?"

Tanyth shrugged. "Well, I don't know if 'fun' is the word I'd use, but we'll all sleep better at night, I think."

Megan caught something in her voice. "What are we going to do today, mum?"

"Move."

Megan's eyebrows shot up. "Move? We just moved in. We have to move out?"

Tanyth crossed to the hearth and helped herself to a cup of tea before settling in the circle of children, Megan watching from the hearth. "Yes, well. We have this problem with the bad men." She addressed her comments to the kids but she was talking to Megan. Sandy sat enraptured by the older woman sitting on the hearthstone with her. "They might have hurt Riley yesterday and we were all trying to be so careful and everything."

Sandy's voice chirped in the morning stillness. "Yes, mum, but they didn't. They gave him back."

Tanyth nodded and patted the child comfortingly. "Yes, they did, and we are all very glad." She spared a glance for Megan who knew exactly what she was getting at. "But it taught us a very valuable lesson and we should pay attention to lessons like that."

Sandy nodded sagely. "Lessons are good. What lesson did we learn, mum?"

She smiled at the earnest young girl. "We learned that no matter how hard we try to watch, we're spread out too much to be able to see everything we need to in order to stay safe."

Sandy nodded and Tanyth looked around at the other small faces with a smile.

"So. We learned that we need to get people closer together so we can look out for each other better."

Sandy sat up. "Well, that makes sense, mum." A frown crossed her face. "But where?"

"We're going to move in with Bester."

The smallest boy's eyes went suddenly round. "In his stall?" He appeared to be totally aghast. "He'll poop on us!"

Tanyth laughed and even Megen giggled a bit. "No, lovie. Just in the barn. Bester will keep his stall." She looked up at Megan. "Although we may be spreading bedrolls in the horses' stalls for awhile."

The other boy, not to be outdone, tried his best to catch up. "In the poop?"

Megan barked a laugh. "Boys! That's enough with the poop. We'll clean the stalls and they'll be very nice and comfy." She sighed in exasperation before looking back at Tanyth with a shrug. "Boys." It was all the explanation she offered.

Tanyth smiled back with a shrug. "I have one myself."

Megan looked startled. "You have a boy, mum?"

She nodded. "He left home many, many winters ago and joined the King's Own." She glanced at the small round faces looking up at her and paused. "So are we ready for something new today?"

Sandy snorted. "Moving is what we did yesterday."

Tanyth nodded her agreement. "Well, yes, it was but today you get to move into the barn."

The little one's eyes got round as a new thought occurred to him. "Will we get to poop in the straw like Bester?"

"Anthony!" Megan all but shrieked in her embarrassment. "This is not appropriate for breakfast conversation!"

"But, Ma-ah. We're movin' to the barn!"

"Anthony! Hush, now!" Megan tried to look stern but her voice cracked from the strain and she had to hide her face in her hands to stifle the laughter as the whole group dissolved into the giggles.

When the fit of jocularity had run its course, they started picking up the remains of breakfast and started packing things away. As they finished tidying up and began looking around for what to do next, Tanyth heard the crunch of wheels on gravel and William's low voice talking to the ox. She crossed to the front door, flung it open, and waved to Karl and William as they backed the oxcart up to the door.

William stuck his head into the opening. "Good morning, everyone. You're the first on a long list! Are you ready?"

The kids danced around in excitement and started a sing song chant of "poopin' in the straw, poopin' in the straw."

Megan let out a shriek. "Anthony!" The children collapsed into giggling puddles and Karl joined William at the door to see what the commotion was about.

William looked at Tanyth. "Fun morning so far?"

She nodded with a rueful grin. "So far. It should be more fun later."

Karl looked on skeptically.

Behind her she heard a small boy's voice asking very quietly, "Well, will we?"

CHAPTER 26
SHADOWS IN THE DARK

The sun worked up over the trees and into the morning sky while Bester stood patiently each time the men filled the cart. He ambled to the barn, and waited again while ready hands unloaded each household's goods in turn. Tanyth and Megan moved into the barn first. The large box stalls felt cramped compared to a full household, but were more than large enough for bedrolls. The stalls themselves needed little cleaning. Frank kept his team in exceptional condition and William had already prepared the stalls for Frank's return at the next full moon. A few extra forks full of straw and the bedrolls laid flat and smooth around the sides of the stall, leaving the middle of the stall clear. Nobody needed to step over, or on, anybody else getting into or out of their bedrolls.

The single quarrymen–Karl, Kurt, and Matthew–helped get everybody settled. Karl and Matthew took Anthony out behind the workroom and worked to dig a new privy just outside the back door and by mid-afternoon, they'd set up a respectable privy, complete with house, seat, and at Anthony's insistence, a lining of straw.

William looked it over and nodded his approval. "Nice job, Anthony." He winked at the quarrymen and they went back to moving the village to safety.

Thomas and Jakey spent the day walking the perimeter of the village, watching the woods, and keeping an eye on things. During the early stages of the move, the children gathered in the barn and parents counted them twice before they placed a much chastened Riley in charge of keeping track of them all.

The children played in the large box stall across from Bester's and every adult in the barn made sure they all stayed in it.

Riley soon organized a game involving much posturing and fighting of bandits. It shocked Tanyth to find that at least two of the little girls had picked up sticks and held them like walking staffs. Amber saw her notice and pursed her lips in amusement. "You've had quite an effect on our lives, mum." She lowered her eyes. "We're very grateful."

Tanyth made a gruff sounding growl but hugged the younger woman briefly before clearing the way for Bester and the cart backing with the next load of household goods.

At midday, Amber, Tanyth, and Sadie fired up the hearth in the workroom and pulled a large pot out of stores. They set to work making a kettle-full of soup with items from the storeroom. As more families joined the group, more hands turned to the process of keeping the company fed and happy. They even built long tables down the middle of the spacious workroom by spanning saw horses with planks. Sawed logs topped with more planks formed benches down either side.

Things got a little tight as more households came into the barn. It became clear that the barn didn't contain enough stalls for every household to have one. The three single quarrymen moved their bedrolls up to the hayloft which left just enough room for the married couples to each have their own. Bethany, whose husband, Ethan, was on the road with Frank, moved her bedroll in with Tanyth, Megan, and the children.

Sadie and Charlotte spent the afternoon making bread, and the aromas wafted through the barn and mingled with the scent of straw and animal in a way that touched something in Tanyth's heart. An oversized kettle of boiling water kept tea brewing all through the day. The soup simmered and added a savory undercurrent to the aromas of yeasty bread and musky tea. As each household moved in, the atmosphere became less grim and more festive. The workroom at the back of the barn, with its hearth and long table, became the central gathering spot and hub of activity.

As the sun slipped behind the tops of the trees to the west, Tanyth stood in the open barn doors with Thomas and watched William and Bester make the last trip from the village. With the final household moved, William put Bester in his stall and gave him an extra scoop of grain and fresh water as a reward for a tedious job well done. Thomas swung the big barn doors closed and dropped a bar into place to keep them closed before telling off the three first-shift guards. With a grin and a final pat on Bester's flank, William led the way to the workroom with Thomas and Tanyth trailing behind.

Amber waved Tanyth to a place of honor near the hearth as they entered. If the night was chilly outside, the full population of the village, along with a roaring fire in the large hearth served to raise the temperature in the room to something approaching summertime levels. She saw William's eyes rove around the room, counting noses and making sure everybody was there except for the three men he knew were on lookout duty.

Tanyth saw his shoulders relax a bit as he realized that the day was finally over. She smiled and toasted him with her mug of tea. "Excellent job getting everybody moved, William."

He nodded his head in acknowledgement. "Thank you, mum. Bester did all the hard work, but everybody here deserves congratulations on a job well done." As he and Tanyth had begun speaking, the room quieted down until everybody could hear him clearly. He raised his mug of tea in the general direction of the room. "So congratulations everybody!"

The gathered throng met his announcement with much laughter and pounding of the table.

Tanyth thought he looked tired as he settled back into his chair and watched Amber at the hearth, but that thought was interrupted as Amber turned to her, ladle in hand. "Mum? If you'd care to bless the house, I'll get this soup served to a bunch of hungry people."

Tanyth snorted a little laugh. "I don't know when I've done more blessin' in all my life." She turned to William and played to the room. "I just got the last house blessed and you made me move. You're not gonna make me move again in the mornin' are ya?"

They all laughed and even William smiled at the jab. "No, mum. Not unless you're able to bless that rascal Birchwood into leavin' us alone!" His voice jested but his eyes seem to plead with her. She saw and shared his pain. In all likelihood the barn would be the last building standing by morning. It threatened to be a long winter.

The room grew still as Tanyth settled her mug on the mantle board and stood up from her chair. She lifted her head to remember where the cardinal directions lay and stepped to the center of the hearthstone where everyone could see her and where she had room to move about a bit. The large room seemed almost crowded with so many villagers in it. She thought, briefly about Frank and the boys out on the road and sent them a silent prayer of support even as she closed her eyes and gathered herself to make an offering to the All-Mother in the name of the village.

She turned to face the north and raised her arms in supplication. "I call upon the Guardian of the North, Bones of the Earth, to give us the strength we need to face the challenge that lies before us." A quarter turn to her right raised her seamed face to the east. "I call upon the Guardian of the East, Breath of the Earth, to fill our lungs with breath to sing the praises of the All-Mother and the All-Father in this, our time of adversity." Another quarter turn to face south. "I call upon the Guardian of the South, Spirit of the Earth, to give us the will and the passion to see our trials through to the end." Another turn faced her to the west. "I call upon the Guardian of the West, Blood of the Earth, to give us the flexibility of water, to flow where we can and to nourish as we flow." She turned once more to face the north and close her circle. "I beg the blessings and protections of the Guardians on this place and the people gathered in it. I ask in the name of the All-Father and the All-Mother. So mote it be."

She lowered her arms and stepped off the hearthstone to resume her seat without looking up. The room was silent except for the crackling of the fire and the wind through the eaves of the barn. No one spoke. No foot stirred or stool scraped. Tanyth felt their eyes on her but also felt very weak in the knees. The heat of the room and the tension of the day conspired against her and she was glad she to be seated. She reached for her mug and wet her lips with a sip of tea before looking down the long table. Slowly she came back to herself, and even in the heat of the fire behind her began to recover from whatever had caused the odd dizziness. All the faces were looking back at her silently. "What?" she asked. "Was I supposed to juggle eggs or somethin'?"

The unseen string in the room snapped and life resumed with laughter.

Amber, Sadie, and Charlotte started dishing up the food, with slabs of fresh bread in baskets passed down the length of the table followed by bowls of the rich stew until everybody had bread and bowl. Bethany and Megan had pots of tea and jugs of fresh water for drink and in a matter of a few minutes everyone was served and seated. The noise in the room consisted of spoons on bowls and appreciative murmurs for several minutes. Some of the more adventurous–and hungry–came back to the hearth for another bowl full.

William sat on one side of the table and Tanyth sat at the other while Amber sat next to her husband and Sadie sat beside Tanyth. From there the villagers stretched down the long boards until the level dropped to the children at the end where a good deal of happy chatter and giggling boiled up. In spite of the last few days, the children saw living in the barn as a grand lark and an opportunity to play. Tanyth smiled to herself. To them, it probably was.

William hunched over his bowl and ate methodically, almost mechanically. Tanyth watched Amber watch him with concern on her face. After his jovial manner earlier, the change seemed starkly apparent. As the meal wore on, conversations started quietly up and down the table. Sadie asked, "Do you think they saw?"

William glanced up at her and nodded. "Almost certainly. We may not have seen them, but it wouldn't have taken much of a scout to have watched us movin'."

Sadie nodded her understanding. "So, now we wait?"

William sighed and nodded again. "Unfortunately, yes, but we're in a better position to wait him out now." He looked at his wife beside him as she took his arm and patted it encouragingly. He gave her a small smile in return. "I don't think we'll have all that long to wait, really." He turned back to Sadie. "I suspect he'll be back tonight. Tomorrow at the latest."

"Then what?" Sadie looked concerned.

William shrugged. "Then we see."

The dinner hour eased along and the company found comfort in being together. As the bellies filled and bowls emptied, Amber put a large pot of water on to heat for washing up. She stood back and directed the cleanup.

Sadie grinned at her. "Practicing up for when the inn is built?"

They laughed together. "Unless you'd like to take over for me?" Amber's reply was delivered with a flick of a towel and broad grin.

Sadie dodged the towel and threw a grin of her own. "Not me! I've got my own cares to worry about. Don't need that!" They laughed some more and soon the pile of dirty crockery was transformed into a stack of gleaming dishes on the mantle board, ready for morning's breakfast. Many hands made the work go smoothly.

With cleanup done, they extinguished the extra lanterns and bundled already drowsing children off to bedrolls in the chilling barn. They giggled and shivered for a bit while they found their spots. As they piled together like puppies in a basket, the warmth of their small bodies under wool and straw soon lulled them to sleep.

William left one lamp lit, but turned the wick low, and most of the adults took to their bedrolls as well. Tanyth and Bethany followed Megan and the children out so they were able to close the gate on their stall. Women and children alike piled their bedrolls close. The sweet smelling straw and the musky animal scents swirled in Tanyth's nose and she remembered the strange dream of the single drop of blood as she fell off the edge of awareness, down into the well of sleep.

The raven sat hunched in the top of a fir. Heavy boughs protected her from the bite of the wind and she watched the shadows slipping through the moonlight on the field below. They moved through the open ground, the light of the moon behind them casting long, snaking shapes of black ahead of them. Four men. One walked oddly. One strode as if he owned the land and all he surveyed. She didn't like being awake in the cold dark but these men disturbed her slumber. She croaked hoarsely and the night wind swept the soft sound away into the silvered dark. The men slipped between the houses and flickered in and out of sight as they moved through the shadows. She shifted her weight on the limb and huddled in the boughs, watching as they came to the end of the houses and considered the two tracks, one to the barn and one to the digging in the ground. They stood in the shadows of the last house–the burned one, its smoky stench still riding the winds–and huddled against the breeze, protected from view. She watched patiently, waiting for them to move. Perhaps there'd be food. Bright metal flashed as they drew steel. They slipped from shadow to shadow and disappeared into the woods heading for the barn. She opened her mouth but only managed a soft croak that was swept away on the night's wind.

Chapter 27
Barn Dance

"No!" Tanyth gasped the word, a raw rasp in her throat. The gleam of steel in the moonlight still dazzled her eyes. She got her breath and sat up. "They're comin'." She said it louder and joggled Amber and Bethany. "They're comin'!"

She crawled up out of the bed roll and slipped into her boots, ignoring the sharp straws that stuck to her socks as she did so. "They're comin'!" She repeated it louder and grabbed up her staff. She slammed out through the gate in her stall and ran down the line banging on the wooden rails. "They're comin'. Wake up. They're comin'!"

She ran to the front of the barn and made sure the heavy bar was still in place across the large doors. She opened the smaller person-sized door to peek out and around the corner to where the guard should be. "Hey! They're coming. Watch for them. In the woods! They're coming!"

There was no response, no movement. "Hey!" She whispered hoarsely. "They're comin'!" Her eyes scanned the moon silvered darkness but the guard who was supposed to be there didn't respond. She got a cold knot in the pit of her belly. "Oh, Mother. Please, no." She whispered the prayer and looked up to the tall spruce at the back of the village. She couldn't see the raven, but she was certain that it was still there.

She pulled back into the barn and closed the door behind her. She turned and bumped into Jakey still pulling up his braces and looking a bit straw tossed. "What is it, mum?" He kept his voice low.

"They're comin'. Four men. Drawn steel. The sentry isn't answerin'."

His eyes went to the door and then back to her. "What should I do, mum?"

Her eyes scanned the barn and saw the three-tined hay fork. She pointed. "That. Guard the door. Watch for whoever's supposed to be guardin' the front. Get 'em back inside if you can."

He nodded, finally awake and focused on what she was saying.

She ran back through the stalls rattling her staff on the rails as she ran. "They're comin'. Wake up. They're comin'." She kept saying it over and over as a kind of prayer. Not wanting to stop to see if people were moving. She felt like she was shouting in the quiet of the barn but her footfalls pounded in her ears as she ran to the back.

Amber and the kids were awake and moving in the stall. She turned haunted eyes to Tanyth who tried to smile reassuringly. "Stay here. Keep an eye open."

She turned at a sound behind her to find Thomas already dressed, his boots on and stepping into his bow to string it. He caught her eye and nodded. "How many?"

"Four. Josh is with them but he's still limpin'." She nodded her head toward the front. "Jakey's at the door, but the outside guard didn't answer my call."

Thomas jerked his head in a short nod. "I'll check the back sentry. You check the workroom door. William should be there keeping an eye on the backside of the barn."

They both ran to the workroom as more people woke. They ran past Charlotte climbing the ladder to the hayloft to wake the quarry boys and she smiled fiercely in the darkness as they sped past. All around the barn, Tanyth could hear the sound of people waking and moving purposefully.

She turned the corner toward the workroom while Thomas sprinted for the back door of the barn, bow pumping and quiver slapping against his backside. She burst into the dimness of the workroom and skidded to a halt. The banked hearth fire provided only a dim orange glow. The dark shadows disoriented her for a moment, but her mind laid the memory of the room over the shadows and shapes that she could see.

"William?"

There was no answer.

She started down the near side, in the narrow alley between bench and barn wall. "William!" Her voice sounded loud in her ears, but he didn't respond. She hurried her steps but found nobody. "Better than finding his body, I suppose." Her grumbling to herself made her huff a laugh and refocused her on the task.

She sidled over to the door which led out to the privy behind the barn just as the latch released with a soft wooden clack. She froze and the door began swinging inward. She held her breath and drew back her staff ready to thrust the iron shod foot into the most available soft spot she could find.

The door swung open. She saw a shape outlined by the light of the last quarter moon. The person edged the door open, but looked back over his shoulder as he entered. The moon light showed him clearly as he stepped over the threshold.

"William!" Tanyth hissed the word.

He jumped as if stung and slammed back into the door frame, banging the door loudly against the wall as he pushed it all the way open. His moon-dazzled eyes couldn't see in the dim light of the workroom and she could see him squinting and trying to make out who was inside the door. "Mother Fairport?"

"Get in here! Close the door."

He grinned at her and pressed a hand to his chest. "Mother have mercy, you scared the–"

He never finished the thought as a sword from outside the door glittered in the moonlight and thrust cruelly through his shoulder, pinning him to the door.

He stared at the metal and followed its length back to the man who held it just around the corner and outside of Tanyth's view. "Hello, Andy. Just couldn't stay away, could you?" William's voice was smooth and calm, then his eyes rolled up and he slumped, his weight carrying the sword downward pulling it out of the door–pulling it out of the hand that held it.

Tanyth froze, not daring to breathe and waiting for the next person to come through the door. She ached to see to William, but dared not move from her place of concealment. The cold night air was rushing into the room and she could feel warmth fading even as she feared that William's life had just been snuffed in front of her eyes.

"Mort. Get in there!" Birchwood's voice was a hissing whipcrack.

Tanyth saw a shadow approaching the door and drew back her staff to strike.

Silvery steel edged through the door and then the burly shape of the man behind it. His head was lowered and casting side to side to try to make out what was inside. Tanyth held her pose, waiting for her moment and watching the man's movement. She could see him spot the banked hearth as his head cleared the cast light of the moon and the orange light glittered on the moisture on his eyes. He stepped awkwardly over the sprawled body on the threshold. As he teetered to regain his balance, Tanyth struck.

The iron bound foot of her staff speared the soft bone of his temple just as he tried to turn his head in her direction. The blow caught him fairly and bone broke under the iron as Tanyth released her pent fury on her attacker. She pulled it back just as a leather clad arm made a grab for the staff, dodging out of the way as the dead man fell at her feet and Andrew Birchwood stepped through the door, his dagger in his left hand hand, pommel up and blade down.

He stood in the doorway and faced her. "You killed my man." His voice was flat and angry. "You will pay for that, you know."

Tanyth shifted her weight but Birchwood's eyes didn't move to follow her. She realized that he couldn't see her and in that instant she struck again, driving the foot of her staff at his stomach with all of her strength. He was fast and managed to dodge her blow, stepping into the room and out of the dazzling moonlight. He made a grab for the staff with his free hand but she had more strength and better leverage. She wrenched it out of his grasp.

He sidled further into the building, his back against the outer wall and his eyes searching the darkness where he believed her to be. She sidled right along with him, her staff held in both hands across her body, waiting for the opening she knew had to come.

He paused to kick the planks of the table into her path and they clattered on the floor. She felt with her boot and kept her balance across the unevenness, getting slightly ahead of him and returning the favor by kicking the next set into his path. She had the advantage for the moment. Her eyes were used to the dark and she could make out his shape in the faint light of the fire. His eyes were adapting fast and she knew there would only be a few more moments before she'd be visible to him. They continued along their respective walls until they made it almost to the hearth. In a quick movement he reached with his free hand and pulled up a billet of wood and threw it at her. She dodged it easily, knocking it down with her staff even in the dimness, but while she was doing that, he tossed a handful of tinder into the fire and it caught quickly flaring up into a bright flame and giving him his first clear look at his adversary.

"You? The witch woman?" He sneered and almost lowered his guard.

She didn't answer, saving her breath and her focus.

He stepped up onto the hearthstone, being careful to stay on his side of the fire and she saw his eyes flicker to the open door of the store room. A small smile of satisfaction curled his lips. "Through there are they?" He nodded. "Good. It was nice of you to gather everybody in one place for me. It makes it so much easier. What with William dead and that dear boy in the front. Too bad about him, but he was so protective." He tsked.

Tanyth remained silent.

"Aww. Scared, little mother?" He shook his head sympathetically. "Killing men is a serious business and you've just killed one. How's that make you feel now? A little sick? A little queasy?"

She sidled over to stand between him and the door, but didn't say a word.

"You think you can stand in my way, little mother?" His look was almost incredulous. "One small woman with a stick."

Tanyth smiled. It was not a pretty smile. It did not make her weather-worn face light up. The bones of the earth were her teeth. Her breath was the wind. The fires of the earth were alight in her eyes and her blood pumped with the strength of the sea.

Birchwood saw the smile and his eyes narrowed. "Sorry, little mother. You should have stepped aside." He stepped onto the hearthstone and his free hand swept the crockery from the mantle board in a rain of mugs and bowls. He followed the glassware leading with this blade and expecting the small woman to be flinching from the flying bowls. He was unprepared for the apparition that stepped into him through the hail of pottery or the staff that shattered his right arm. Unfortunately for Tanyth, he held the dagger in his left and his anger drove him through the pain. He slashed upwards just as Tanyth stepped in, sweeping the knobbed head of her staff into his temple on her back stroke even as his blade hooked up to score her from navel to chin inside her guard, the razor edge slicing cleanly through clothing and skin alike.

They stood for a lifetime frozen in the follow-through of their respective strikes. She saw the light fade in Birchwood's eyes even as her own sight focused on the point of the blade just inches from her face. A single drop of her blood drooled in the fuller and dripped off the tip, a single perfect sphere of crimson shimmering in the guttering light of the burning tinder. Her eyes couldn't follow it, but in her mind she saw it falling, falling, falling to splatter in a perfect starburst on the warm hearthstone.

CHAPTER 28
MORNING LIGHT

Long fingers of morning groped across the grass below her. The clash and clangor in the night had passed as suddenly as it had come. She smoothed her feathers with her bill, worked a bit of oil into them, and side-stepped into the growing light of the morning sun. Her black plumage warmed in the direct gaze of the All-Mother and she basked for a time and preened, straightening and oiling her feathers to make them sleek and smooth against the winds and weathers.

Hunger moved her, finally, and strong wings snapped to catch the morning air–once, twice, thrice–before gliding to a favorite snag thrust up from the edge of a pond in the forest. Cattails browned on the edge of the pond, completing the cycle she'd seen before, but her sharp golden eyes watched the edges of the water, between the reeds, watching for food, looking for–there. She pounced, sharp talons snatching the wriggling thing, strong bill crunching it. It would hold her for a time and her strong legs thrust her into the air even as her wings pulled her upwards. She glided between the trees and back into the shadows of the forest. A few strokes and a gentle bank brought her to a comfortable perch, protected from the wind and open to the rising sun. She settled there, listening, occasionally preening a rough spot on wing or back, letting the sun warm and lull her and, for a time, there was no time at all.

The All-Mother completed her circuit of the sky. Darkness came for a time only to be banished by the All-Father's silvery face. And even before he finished his survey, All-Mother re-

turned. The raven fed herself on berries and juicy bugs. Winter was coming and, with it, the hungry time. She scoured her wood from hilltop to vale, from pond to break, dark wood to field. She listened and warned with her voice.

The men in the clearing were interesting and she took her perch above them, golden eyes watching. There was movement in the field again. Children ran. Women dug root crops and cut corn. She crooned. No more sweet corn for her, but perhaps some fruit would be left behind. She remembered sweet fruit from the ground and gave a soft croak of anticipation for the women to be done so she could search.

There was carrion down there, too. She smelled the meat on the breeze, but was unable to find it until movement drew her attention and she saw them putting the bodies in holes. They were wrapped in cloth but her talons gripped the branch beneath her and she knew cloth would not slow her long. So much meat would be good. She lifted her head and called loudly in anticipation and warning. The big male in the next valley might hear and she liked that idea. She called again and listened, but there was no answer.

The men below were done putting the meat in the holes. She danced in frustration as she watched them filling the holes, shoveling the musky earth down, covering the meat, hiding it. In moments it was done and the meat was gone. She crooned her frustration and looked about for her next meal. She was hungry and winter was coming. With a last loud cry, she launched herself onto the air and soared back into the forest. She needed water and headed for the pond. Perhaps there'd be another bit of food as well.

Her eyes were gummy but they opened a bit. Her lips were parched and her tongue felt stuck to her mouth. A shape moved and she focused on it. Megan smiled down at her. "Good afternoon, mum." Her voice was soft and low.

Tanyth managed to croak but her mouth was too dry to work right.

Megan brought a moistened cloth and stroked her face with it, wiping it across her mouth, wetting her lips. She pulled the cloth away but returned with a spoon and ladled a few drops of water onto the side of her mouth and Tanyth's tongue managed to find it and the cool liquid slipped down her throat, loosening and soothing as it went. They repeated the process several times before Tanyth was able to say, "Thank you."

A line of fire stitched her up the middle and she let herself escape it by falling back into slumber. She'd been wounded and she needed to heal. Sleep was the great healer and she embraced it willingly.

The cool water flashed in the failing light of the All-Mother. She left the sky empty longer now, taking to her nest and leaving the sky for All-Father. Her heavy bill crunched several times and a small fish slipped down easily as she swallowed. She needed to find more food and a perch for the night. It would be colder now and she needed her strength.

She took wing and sailed over the place where men worked the gray soil. No man walked the land so she circled to see if there were any bright things she might take, or perhaps some food left. Small animals visited the place sometimes and they were tasty and warm. Her bright golden eyes raked the ground but nothing moved and nothing shined, she flicked a wing and continued onward.

The men had carved a path through the trees and she followed it taking pleasure in swooping along and between. She was silent except for a faint whisper in her wings as she sailed rapidly. She checked her speed as the opening appeared and turned with a flare of wing and tail to alight on a branch where she would watch. The meat was buried and even the scent of it was gone from the air. The young were running and making a terrible racket but the large people were tearing at the burned house. It didn't stink as much any more.

The man with the bow came up the track and she watched him carefully. Men were seldom a threat but those with bows needed care. They sometimes took sport with her kind and she'd had to dodge more than one arrow in her life. The breeze carried a scent of offal and she perked up at the aroma. If he'd killed, there might be food. She took wing and soared.

Tanyth woke again. Stronger now and still in pain. She laughed. It was more a panting sound than a laugh but she laughed even though it hurt.

Sadie leaned over her and smiled to see her awake. "Hello, mum. Welcome back."

Tanyth tried to smile in return and it must have worked because Sadie's smile widened.

Sadie offered a cup of water and helped Tanyth lift her head to drink it. The line of fire up her belly didn't hurt as badly and she was feeling considerably more clear headed. The liquid moistened her throat and tongue and she was able to speak more than a simple croak. "William?"

Sadie nodded her head. "He'll heal. He won't be chopping any wood for awhile, but he'll recover." Her face clouded. "They killed Kurt."

Tanyth nodded. "Birchwood said that. I didn't believe him."

Sadie made a sideways shrug. "He was telling the truth."

"There's been no more trouble, then?"

Sadie shook her head. "Thomas killed one of them behind the barn. The other one threw down his sword and ran away."

Tanyth nodded. "I should have been quicker."

Sadie patted her on the shoulder. "There, there, mum. If it hadn't been for you and your warning, we'd have all been dead."

Tanyth took small comfort although she knew it was true. "Everyone else?"

Sadie smiled. "All fine, mum. And we have a nice soup for you here. Would you like some?"

Tanyth noticed that she was still in the workroom, although the saw horses and boards had been removed. She lay in a rope-bound cot on a sweet grass tick. A pot burbled gently over the fire and a kettle steamed nearby. Her stomach growled loudly enough that Sadie heard it.

"That sounded like a yes to me, mum." She grinned and patted the older woman's arm once more.

"Why am I still here?" Tanyth's voice was weak but still audible in the quiet room.

Sadie ladled a dipper of broth into an earthenware mug and then broke a hank of bread off a loaf that rested on a cutting board nearby. She brought the food over and set it on a sawed off log that stood on end as a table. "Because this was the easiest place to care for you. You were bleeding a lot and laying in the broken crockery when we found you, mum. We weren't sure what happened."

"Birchwood is dead, though, isn't he?"

"Yes, mum. He's dead." Sadie walked around the end of the cot above Tanyth's head and grabbed the frame. "Just a second, mum. Hold on."

Tanyth had a moment of disorientation until she realized that Sadie was lifting the cot with her on it. Wood scraped on wood and then the end of the cot lowered a bit, leaving her laying on a slight incline.

Sadie came back to the side of the cot and settled on another sawed off log. "There. That'll save you havin' to lift your head so far, mum."

"What'd you do?" Tanyth was unable to turn far enough to see.

"Put a log under the head to hold it up while you eat."

"You lifted the cot and me together?"

Sadie shrugged. "Well, of course, mum. Won't have done much good if I'd lifted you and not the cot and I certainly couldn't lift the cot without lifting you in it, now could I?"

Tanyth grinned and laughed softly. "I just meant you were strong."

Sadie raised an eyebrow and a spoon at the same time. "Strong? Me, mum? I'm not that strong and you're not that heavy! I think Riley weighs more than you." She levered the spoon and the rich broth rolled over Tanyth's tongue.

Tanyth smiled and swallowed gratefully. "You know, I could probably hold a cup and a spoon." She lifted her arms and showed Sadie.

"Can you lift your head so you don't spill the soup off the spoon before it gets into your mouth, mum?" She smiled skeptically, but seemed willing to try.

"If we can get me propped up enough to hold the mug and drink it, I won't need a spoon."

Sadie nodded at the wisdom of that. "But you nursed me, mum. Seemed only right that I should nurse you."

Tanyth blushed a bit at the earnestness of the young woman's response. "I appreciate it. Really, but the sooner I start doin' things for myself, the sooner I'll be up and about."

They spent a few more painful moments with Sadie trying to push pads of blankets under Tanyth's shoulders and to lift her up without her having to use her stomach muscles. In the end, Tanyth was propped up, partly by a wad of woolens, and partly through the expedient of getting a taller log to hold up the head of the cot. She started to slide down a bit, but her heels caught on the inside of the frame and she found she could brace her knees without undue strain.

All through the exercise, Tanyth tried to get a feel for how badly she was damaged but she seemed to be wrapped in strips of bandage from her collar bone to her hips. The line of fire was less precise the longer she tried to concentrate on it and even peeking under the covers only showed her in some kind of shift that she didn't recognize.

"Sadie?" Tanyth was hesitant about asking.

"Yes, mum?" The younger woman settled beside her and handed her the mug of broth.

Tanyth took the mug and looked pointedly down at herself. "How bad is it?"

Sadie looked up and down at the older woman. "Well, mum. You did need a few stitches across your chest, but the cut up your belly wasn't particularly deep. More a scratch. The wrappings you wore around your chest? They were cut clean through and the knife went pretty deep there, but we got you stitched up and wrapped pretty fast." She looked up at Tanyth's face, nodding at the mug of soup. "You'll want to drink that while it's still warm, mum."

Tanyth blinked a couple of times, having difficulty understanding what she'd heard. She brought the cup to her lips and carefully sipped it, working her head forward a bit to get her mouth on the lip of the cup to avoid pouring the soup down her front. The warmth and the moisture felt wonderful and she sipped again. "Stitched me up?"

"My Thomas was in the King's Own for a time. He was in a lot of battles and helped with the wounded." She lowered her eyes. "He was the one that actually stitched you, mum. I hope you don't mind."

Tanyth laid a tentative hand on her breastbone. It was

tender to the touch, sure enough, but the padding of the bandages gave her some protection. "Why would I mind, dear?" She was already feeling better and took another small sip of the broth.

Sadie didn't look up. "Well, we chaperoned him, mum, but he had to take some liberties with your clothing and all." Her eyes flickered to her chest.

Tanyth felt a brief flush of embarrassment that Thomas had seen what gravity and time had done to her body before realizing that she wasn't thinking too clearly. "I think I owe him a debt of gratitude, Sadie. I'm grateful that he was able to use his knowledge and skills to sew my old carcass back together." She smiled warmly. "How's his hemming? Did he run a straight seam?"

Her comment caught Sadie off guard and she looked up in horror before she realized that Tanyth was joking. "Yes, mum. We made sure he kept his stitches nice and even for you. Never know who you'll get to show them off for."

Tanyth huffed a small laugh and took another sip of soup. She looked over to where Sadie had left the hank of bread on the table. "Was that for me as well?"

Sadie grinned and handed Tanyth the bread which she dipped into the rich broth and let dissolve in her mouth. In less time that she'd have thought possible the mug was empty and she held it up to let the last savory drops run into her mouth. She handed the empty mug back. "That was very good, Sadie. Might I have a little more?"

"Are you sure you should, mum?"

Tanyth shrugged, but instantly regretted it. "Nothin' was damaged inside. Just a cut. Why not?"

"Mum, you lost a lot of blood." Sadie took the cup and crossed to the fire. "But if you want some, I'll give you a little but then you have to go back to sleep."

Tanyth heard Sadie's solicitous words as little more than a gentle noise in the background as she slid back down the slope to sleep.

CHAPTER 29
HEALING TIME

Within a couple of days, Tanyth was ready to get out of bed. "Megan, come help me a moment, please?"

Megan put down her mending and stepped over to the cot. "How can I help, mum?"

Tanyth struggled to a sitting position and swung her legs over the side of the cot. "Give me your hands, please? I need to stand up."

"Mum? I don't think that's wise."

Tanyth smiled. "I'm not sure either, but if I lay here much longer I'm not going to be able to get up again so please help me." She gave an apologetic shrug. "Besides, I need to use the privy."

Megan looked horrified. "Mum, you can't be walking all that way."

Tanyth gave a small laugh. "Well, then I'm gonna wet myself trying, my dear, so if you'd give me a hand? We'll see how far I get before I go, shall we?"

Megan held out her hands and Tanyth used them to pull herself upright. She swayed a bit as the blood that had been in her head rushed to her feet. For a moment or two she wasn't too sure she'd made the right decision after all. She gripped Megan's shoulder and held on until the dizziness passed. Her legs were weak, but they held her and she took a tentative step. Her hips groaned at her but soon were moving smoothly and she had Megan turn around and walk toward the back door and the privy beyond. If the steps were slow and some-times halting, they were steps and she grew more certain as

243

she walked along.

Megan made it to the back door and pulled a warm shawl down from a peg beside the door. "Here, mum. Don't get chilled."

Tanyth allowed the woman to fuss over her a bit and drape the shawl around her. The longer she stood the less certain she was that she'd make it all the way to the privy and back.

Megan must have seen the uncertainty in her eyes. "Are you sure you want to do this, mum? We've got the pot here for you."

Tanyth's mouth twisted into a sideways grin. "No, I'm not sure, but I'd much rather try this than use that pot again."

Megan grinned and turned so Tanyth could grab her shoulder once more. They shuffled out into the daylight.

The sudden sun stabbed Tanyth's eyes and she nearly stumbled, but she half closed them and lowered her head against the midday glare. Her feet scuffled her forward over the cold grass and damp soil.

"Oh, mum. We should have put some shoes on you!" Megan was horrified when she realized that Tanyth walked barefoot.

Tanyth patted Megan's shoulder lightly. "Hush, child, we're almost there and it feels quite pleasant." The icy fingers of grass stroked her feet and the soft soil beneath cushioned her steps, and each step she took seemed to be stronger, as if pulling strength from the very ground upon which she walked. She whispered a small prayer of thanks to the All-Mother and kept moving.

Eventually, they came to the door of the privy. Megan swung it open and led Tanyth inside. It took some maneuvering, but after two days of using the pot with the requisite attendances, Tanyth's sense of modesty had been shredded. Megan saw her charge safely enthroned and stepped out, discreetly closing the door behind her.

In a moment, Tanyth called Megan back and they retraced their steps back into the workroom. At the cot, Tanyth balked at laying back down.

"Mum? You need to lay down and sleep." Megan's voice was firm.

"Megan? I need to sit up and get something to eat. Is there any rabbit in that stew?" She nodded at the pot over the fire.

Megan nodded. "Yes, mum, there is."

"Good. Help me get a seat where I can lean back on the hearth and I'll eat something solid and then, I promise, I'll be a good girl and go back to bed." She smiled. She knew she was being impatient but also knew the danger of lying down for too long.

With the ground rules established, Tanyth and Megan had a pleasant meal of rabbit stew and more fresh bread and even a nice cup of tea. Tanyth began to feel much more human, even as the exertion took its toll on her. With the meal over, Megan helped her stand once more and, as she had promised, went back to bed.

"Oh, that's lovely, my dear. Thank you." Tanyth was already feeling the tug of sleep but struggled against it to speak. "When I wake, do you think we could have some hot water for washin' up? We should really change the dressin's, too."

"Of course, mum. We were talking about it among ourselves and thought we probably should have done it yesterday." She looked chagrined.

Tanyth smiled and reached out to pat her arm. "When I wake. That'll be soon enough, I think." Almost against her will, her eyes closed and sleep claimed her once more.

The raven watched the men tear down the house. They'd been working at it for two passages of the All-Mother through the sky. Some of the wood they saved. Some of it they stacked in a big pile. The logs were taken apart and laid out side by side. She eyed their activities and soaked up the warmth of the sun, but her belly was empty. She needed food. She took wing and soared over the men's heads unnoticed and out over the open space of the long path. She remembered a fruit tree and flew to it. The ground was littered with fallen fruit, some already soft and some crawling with stinging insects. The insects gave a lovely tang to the fruit, and their stings had no effect on the horny plates of her bill. She gorged herself and had to hop twice to get enough spring to get off the ground.

Once aloft, she sailed between the trunks and flapped heavily upwards, looking for a perch high in the fir where she could watch the men and drowse in the warm sun.

As the afternoon wore down toward night, Tanyth fought her way back to consciousness. The meal had helped and the exercise had, too, but the new levels of awareness were making her impatient. As she blinked herself awake, she saw that Megan had been joined by Sadie and the pair of them smiled happily to see her stirring.

"Are you ready to see what's under the bandages, mum?" Sadie was smiling gently.

"I am, indeed." Tanyth was afraid of what she'd find but determined to see it through.

The two women had a large tub set up beside the hearth and a substantial collection of kettles heating on the fire. They helped her rise and walked her out to the privy and back before beginning. She was already stronger and the round trip took much less time and effort. The workroom felt almost stifling after being out in the cool, fall air.

They took her to the tub and had her stand in it while they peeled her clothing away. They got her down to bandages and small clothes in almost no time and then had her sit on the edge of the tub while they used sewing sheers to clip carefully up her spine. The cold steel of the sheers gave her shivers as the narrow blade slid under the wrappings and against her skin. With each layer of wrapping released, they carefully peeled it back and dropped it into a pile on the floor beside the tub. The first few layers revealed nothing to Tanyth's eager gaze but as the subsequent layers were removed, the extent of her injury became more evident. By the time the were up to her navel, the bandage was stuck securely to her and they used a clean cloth soaked in hot water to moisten and loosen it before pulling it gently away.

It took almost half an hour to get the bandages off her. They gave her a warm shawl to put over her shoulders and hot water in the tub for her feet while they cleaned the long wound up her torso. As Sadie had said, the lower part of the cut, the most vulnerable and softest part of her body was sliced, but it was quite shallow. As the blade drove up the length of her body, it had bit more cruelly. Seeing the scabbing cut in her belly was shocking enough, but when the bandages pulled free of her chest, the neat row of x-shaped stitches in the flesh between her breasts was almost incomprehensible. Age, gravity, and a reduction in her body fat over the years had left her breasts sagging flat against the ribcage with only the slightest sway and the incongruousness of the stitches running up between them left her slightly disoriented.

The younger women seemed more shocked by the sight of her flattened, bare breasts than by the stitching in her skin. She smiled. "This is what happens if you live long enough." She waved a hand at them. "There are worse things." She paused and put a tentative finger to one of the stitches and eyed the redness along the edges of the wound. She looked up into the staring eyes of the two younger women. "Well? What do you see? Infected?"

Megan squinted her eyes a little and moved in for a closer look. Her nose was almost against the flesh and she sniffed delicately. "It doesn't smell bad, mum, but it's a bit redder than I'd like to see."

Sadie eyed her companion with an odd look, but then turned her attention to the cut. She reached out a tentative finger to touch the older woman's flesh, but stopped. "May I, mum?"

Tanyth nodded. "Of course, my dear. Tell me what you think and then I'll tell you what I think."

The two examined the cut and the stitching with critical eyes and a few tentative touches. They stepped back and shared a look.

Tanyth prompted them. "Well? I'm getting chilly here wavin' my dugs in the breeze. What do you think?" She had an amused grin on her face. "We might wanna figure it out before any of the children wander in and we scare them silly."

The two giggled a little, but Sadie's serious expression didn't go away. "That's not looking as good as I'd have hoped, mum."

Megan sighed and nodded her agreement. "It's awful red and puffy lookin', mum."

Tanyth nodded. "I agree. I don't think it's infected yet,

but I'm not likin' the way it's lookin' and not just because it's me." She smiled and looked down at herself. "What do we do about it?"

Megan shook her head. "I'd try a poultice of feverfew if there were any around here."

Sadie nodded. "Yep, if we were at home, I'd have the healer round. Witch hazel liniment maybe."

Tanyth nodded, impressed at Megan's practical approach and Sadie's practical knowledge. "Well, I haven't seen any feverfew yet, but there are some big patches of comfrey along the edge of the woods on the south side of the village. Do you know comfrey? Upright plant with fairly large leaves? Kinda spearhead-shaped?"

Megan nodded. "I know it. How much do we need?"

Tanyth gave a little shrug. "Probably two or three plants. Depends on the size. Break them off close to the ground. Bring them back here and I'll show you what to do with them." She looked at Sadie. "The big pine trees out behind the barn here?" She nodded with her head. "The ones with the long green needles?"

Sadie nodded. "Yes, mum? What about them?"

Tanyth nodded at one of the empty pots they'd heated water in. "Take that out and strip enough pine needle to half fill that pot."

Sadie reached for the pot and Megan was headed for the door when Tanyth stopped them. "If you'd be so good as to get me a shirt or something? I'd just as soon not sit here half naked while I wait?"

They grinned. "Yes, mum." Megan helped her put on a shift and then wrapped her in a blanket while she paddled her feet in the warm water of the tub.

"We'll hurry, mum." Sadie grinned as they scampered off in different directions.

Sadie returned first. She had the shorter distance to go and knew exactly what she was doing. She was back within minutes with a pot of the redolent needles. "Here we go, mum. What do we do with them?"

"Pour enough hot water on them to just float them and set the kettle over the fire to simmer."

Sadie followed her directions and set the pot to simmer. "I love the smell, mum, but will this help infections?"

Tanyth nodded. "The pine is a good all-around cleaner. Any kind of cut or scrape? Wash it with a little pine needle tea."

In a few minutes Megan came trotting back with three largish comfrey plants. There were even some seed pods that had not yet dropped. "How're these, mum?"

Tanyth smiled. "Perfect. Strip the leaves off the stems and put them in another pot. We'll make a poultice out of those and a bit of the pine needle tea." She looked down at herself. "Before we do that, can I have a bit of soap and hot water? May as well clean up a bit before we get serious."

The women eagerly helped her strip down and bathed her in hot water with some of their own soap. It was scented with lavender and Tanyth nodded approvingly. "The lavender will help healing, too."

They finished rinsing her off with more hot water, then dried her in a soft blanket before helping her into fresh small clothes and one of her own comfy pairs of trousers.

"You're going to have to wrap the poultice and I'll need to be laying down." Tanyth crossed to the cot but didn't lie down.

The two women nodded and Sadie produced a length of cotton to use for a winding. "We were going to tear this into bandages, but this should work, shouldn't it mum?"

Tanyth nodded approvingly. "Very good. Lay it down, and I'll lay on it, and then you can pile on the foliage." She grinned.

When the cotton was settled, they helped Tanyth lie down on it and she had them start with the kettle of pine needles. "One of you pour a bit of the liquid into the comfrey, and then squish it up with your hands. The other one, get a cloth and wash the cut with the pine needle tea."

They did as she asked. Megan poured a small amount of the pine liquid into the kettle with her leaves and proceeded to make as consistent a paste out of them as she could. The smell of pine saturated the air and even the musky comfrey scent didn't come near it in redolence.

Sadie took a clean cloth and gently patted the incision with the hot pine tea. The ends of the stitches occasionally caught in the cloth and tugged, but Tanyth was able to ignore the small twinges.

"Good. Now cover the cut with the mushed up comfrey. Make sure it's moist."

Megan made a line of warm leaf matter down the center of Tanyth's body and the three of them giggled at the sight.

Sadie started to pull the cloth over her. "Now wrap you up, mum?"

Tanyth thought for a moment. "Scoop some of the pine needles out and lay them down across the wound, too."

They built a layer of pine on top of the layer of comfrey and by the time they were done, the liquid was cooling and Tanyth was grateful for the warmth of the cotton being wrapped about her. They were careful to smooth the cloth over her body and then pulled the free end around her two more times. They helped her pull on a shift and smoothed it down over her to hold the loose end in place.

"There!" Tanyth looked down at herself. "Now if you have a bit of bread and some cheese? Perhaps a cup of chamomile tea? I think I'm about done for one day."

The two looked at each other, at the shambles they'd made of the hearth, and then at Tanyth and grinned. Megan started gathering up the pots and herbal material while Sadie put the kettle on.

As they were cleaning up, Tanyth offered a bit of advice. "Put the left over pine and comfrey into one pot and just add enough water to cover it. Then you can leave it on the side of the hearth to stay warm and we can use it for washing up."

Megan nodded and did as Tanyth suggested.

Sadie brought a whole loaf of fresh bread and sliced two or three chunks of cheese off a wheel for her. "I'm surprised you didn't want more rabbit, mum." She grinned.

Tanyth considered it. "No, I had rabbit for lunch. The bread is delicious and the cheese tastes good." She smiled. "At this rate, I should be back in my own hut in another day or two, don't you think?" She looked at Megan. "You've gone back there, haven't you?"

Megan shook her head. "We moved into one of the empty huts, mum. Yours is ready for you to move back in."

Tanyth found herself saddened that she'd not be living with Megan and her children, but Harry would be back soon, and the threat that had driven them together was gone. She also found the thought of being back on her own again almost hurtfully appealing. She was just not used to living so closely with so many people. As enjoyable as she'd found being around the young folk, she found herself longing for a bit of quiet.

She finished the cheese and chased it with a bit of bread and some healthy swallows of soothing chamomile tea. She gave a little wave to the two women at the hearth and settled herself into her bed. Her own private night fell, drawing the curtain of darkness across her eyes.

CHAPTER 30
RECUPERATION

Tanyth's days and nights fell into an easy, if sometimes uncomfortable, pattern. The mass of the barn blocked bright morning light so the gray light of early morning lasted almost to mid-day. She spent her time in the drowsy company of one or the other of the village's women. Each afternoon involved new poultices, and fresh dressings. Each new dawn saw her stronger and by the third day with comfrey and pine needle poultices the redness was leeched out and the stitching itched.

"You're going to have to take these out, Sadie." Tanyth was looking down at herself during their afternoon session.

Sadie nodded. "I think so, too, mum."

Sadie and Megan dragged in the tub and spent much of the afternoon heating water. Between them, they'd dragged the barrow down to the pump and filled several buckets to get enough for bathing. A couple of large kettles provided the hot water. It was a race to see if they get enough water hot before the tub turned cold. Finally, they set about snipping and pulling the threads out of Tanyth's skin.

It was a soggy, somewhat chilly, and ultimately painful experience for Tanyth. The snips and small tugs added up over time and working on the delicate flesh between her breasts didn't aid in her ability to put the pain aside. As they came out, one by one, she was glad she'd been unconscious when they'd gone in. The thought brought back the memory once more and her eyes went to the hearth.

The crockery had not been replaced on the mantel board. There were just the few pieces there for her use and not the piles of bowls and trenchers and mugs that the village had used. Her eyes traced downward to the hearthstone itself. Something about it caught her attention and she couldn't quite figure out what it was.

Sadie looked up at her. "That's the last one, mum." She saw Tanyth looking at the hearth. "Is there somethin' wrong, mum?"

Tanyth looked down at the small wellings of blood on her body and used the washcloth to daub at them with the sweet smelling lavender water. "No, my dear. Thank you."

Sadie looked over her shoulder and then back at Tanyth. "You had the oddest expression, mum. Are you sure?"

Tanyth frowned and looked back at the hearth. "There's something different about the hearth. Is the hearthstone a different color?"

Megan and Sadie shared a glance before Sadie nodded. "Perhaps a bit, mum."

Megan gave a little shrug. "You did lose a lot of blood before we found you, mum." She gave a sideways glance at the hearth.

Tanyth felt a bit light headed for a moment as the realization caught up with her. "How long was I laying there?"

Megan shook her head. "We don't know, mum. We heard the crash and then the horrible silence. We didn't dare leave the children unguarded and Jakey couldn't leave the front door. It might have been as much as a quarter hour before we heard William shout."

Sadie bobbed her head in agreement. "After that it went pretty fast. Thomas came in from the outside and he and Jakey dragged the bodies out. We got you out of the broken dishes and Thomas stitched you up and then worked on William after."

Megan glanced at the hearthstone. "There was a lot of blood, all of it yours. It kinda got spread around." She turned back to Tanyth with an apologetic look.

Tanyth shivered and Sadie thought it was because the water had cooled. The two youngsters helped her up and dried her off. She shooed them away and dressed herself with her own comfortable clothes from the pack. She'd need more, but she smiled to think of spending the winter in the snug little house.

By the time she finished dressing herself, she was weak and shaky again. The bath and stitch removal had taken a bit of the starch out of her, not that she'd had all that much to begin with. Seeing the entire hearthstone stained with her blood shocked her on a fundamental level.

Megan and Sadie took advantage of the hot water and tub to have baths of their own, unselfconsciously stripping down and taking turns pouring hot water over each other. Tanyth grinned at them and envied their youthful vigor for a moment.

She stepped gingerly onto the hearth and poked up the teapot a bit with some fresh water and a few more leaves. While she waited for it to steep, her eyes traced the contours of the stone and replayed the battle in her head. She found it morbid but couldn't stop thinking about it. In the middle of the stone, right in front of the fire place, a darker spot stood out in the faintly stained rock. She didn't need to look closely to see it had the shape of a perfectly formed star.

The knowledge washed through her and left her gasping in uncertainty. She'd dreamed it. As surely as the mark was on the stone, she remembered the dream and the sphere of blood. The raven dreams were real as well. Or as real as such dreams might be.

But if that was real, what could it mean? People didn't dream the future. Her world twisted suddenly. She realized that she'd crossed the threshold to somewhere else with the acceptance of the raven's vision.

She lowered herself onto the stump near the fire and closed her eyes to focus on stilling the spinning in her mind. Wherever she now lived, Tanyth knew that these young women were part of it. The whole village was part of it. The notion that perhaps it had always been so, and she was only now aware of it, began to bubble into the back of her mind. She didn't know if she found the thought comforting or frightening.

In the corner the splashing stopped and Sadie spoke to her. "Are you all right, mum?"

The voice brought her back and she opened her eyes and smiled at the concerned look in the younger woman's fresh face. Tanyth took a deep breath and let it out. "Yes, my dear, thank you. Just a moment of weakness but it's passed now."

Megan smiled. "Maybe you should lay back down, mum? It's been a busy morning." She seemed a bit chagrined to have been enjoying the bath time instead of tending to her business.

Tanyth nodded. "Perhaps in a bit. I'd like to sit here by the fire and have a cup of tea just now, though." She reached up and pulled a heavy mug from the mantle board and tipped the pot to fill it. The two young women exchanged glances and finished dressing before joining her at the hearth with mugs of their own.

When the tea was gone, Tanyth looked at them with a slight frown. "Tomorrow, I'm goin' to move back to my house."

They glanced at each other before Sadie asked. "Are you sure you're ready to be on your own, mum?"

"Yes, my dear, I am. I'll be closer to people down in the village and you two won't have to take time from your families."

They shared another doubtful glance.

"If I need help, I can ask easier when there's people around rather than tyin' up your time by draggin' you away." She smiled. "What I need most right now is to be up and movin'. Winter will be here soon and I want to harvest some of the ground nuts and rose hips that I found."

Sadie relented. "If you're sure, mum, we'll help you get settled again."

"Thank you, both of you–all of you, really–for taking such good care of me, but you've got families to tend to." She looked at Megan. "Your Harry will be back soon, as well."

"Yes'm. Another couple of weeks." She arched an eyebrow and gave the older woman a coy look. "Frank will be back, too."

It took Tanyth a moment to realize what she was getting at, but when she caught on she barked a laugh. "Oh, yes, I'm sure Frank has nothing better to do." Still, the thought gave her a strange flutter, and she felt her cheeks flush.

Sadie shrugged. "He's a good lookin' man for somebody that old, mum." She realized what she'd said and groaned. "Sorry, mum, I just meant somebody his age."

Tanyth chuckled and patted the younger woman's arm. "I know what you meant, my dear, and I'm older than Frank by more than a few winters. Us old folks may look alike to you, but believe me, we know how old we are." She smiled to reassure them.

Sadie was contrite. "I meant no disrepect, mum."

"You offered none, Sadie. It's fine." She paused and admitted. "He does fill a shirt nicely."

They giggled a bit and Megan replied, "Trousers, too."

Sadie looked at her aghast. "Why Megan Tannen! What have you been lookin' at!"

Megan gave an unapologetic shrug. "I'm married, ya git, not dead. I can still look." She cast another coy look in Tanyth's direction. "And he is a nice lookin' man–for any age."

Sadie snickered. "Wonder if Mother Alderton noticed? She always used to say 'Snow on the roof don't mean there's no fire on the hearth.'"

Megan smiled at the memory. "She always had something to say, but I think she was looking to rob cradles that one."

Sadie looked shocked. "What are you sayin'? Robbed cradles."

Megan guffawed. "Don't tell me you never noticed which quarryman it was that always filled her woodbox."

Sadie sat up and looked at her friend. "No! He didn't?" The delicious shock was too much for her to hold in and she covered her face with her hands and laughed.

Megan shrugged. "Well, nobody left to ask now, but as often as he was over there, I always figured he was fillin' more than her woodbox."

They giggled for a bit but it soon subsided. Sadie offered a final comment in the tones of a prayer. "May the All-Mother and All-Father find them place in the Summerlands together, if that's so." She looked up at Tanyth. "Kurt. Bless him."

They sat there for a moment, thinking private thoughts and finally, Tanyth rose. "I think I will lay down now."

"It's getting on dinner time, mum? Would you like something to eat?"

Tanyth looked outside and saw the dusk pooling in the corners of the barn. "Not just now. If you'd leave me a loaf of bread and a bit of cheese? I'll toast some over the hearth in a bit. Right now, I think I should lay down."

They helped her onto her cot and she let them fuss over her, tucking her in and making much of her progress. She smiled and settled into the delicious comfort of the woolen blankets. The two women dumped the tub and set the pots and kettles in order before giving her a small wave and heading back to their own houses.

Tanyth lay on the soft edge of slumber for some time, the soft coals in the hearth appearing to glow more brightly as day faded to night. She drifted on wings of whimsy, considering the raven dreams, and the way Frank's shoulders filled out his shirt. "Old fool." She muttered to herself. It was the last thing she heard as she fell over the edge into sleep.

CHAPTER 31
ANOTHER MOVING DAY

"Good morning, mum. Ready to move?" William stood at the back door of the workroom with a smile on his face and his arm in a sling.

Tanyth turned from banking the fire in the hearth and smiled. "William, it's so good to see you." She eyed his shoulder. "You know, I thought he'd killed you."

William grinned. "So did I." He paused with a mischievous twinkle in his eye. "Then I woke up with a corpse on me and big hunk of steel in my shoulder and I was sure of it. But how are you, mum? Sadie said you want to move back to your house this morning? Had enough livin' in the barn then?"

Tanyth laughed softly. "Yes. I didn't really expect to be here quite so long, but now that the problem has been dealt with..." She shrugged. "I'm ready to move back to my house."

He smiled and gazed into her eyes. "Thank you, mum. You saved us all, you know."

"Oh, go on. I nearly got you killed and that poor boy Kurt? I didn't do much to save him."

He gave a half shrug in acknowledgement. "Well, maybe not all." He smiled again. "But without your warnin' and without your actions here..." His voice trailed off. "Well, I'd hate to think of what might have happened."

"Then don't. Stop being silly and give me a hand with my pack."

He grinned. "Oh, we'll do more than that!" He stepped back from the door and a veritable parade of people came into the room led by Jakey.

In less than a quarter hour, the men had rolled up the bedding, and grabbed the cot, Tanyth's pack, and even a few of the storage baskets and two water buckets. It all went onto the barrow that waited just outside the door. Jakey himself took the handles and started trundling it down the track.

Tanyth watched with an amused expression on her face until William offered her his good arm. "Shall we go, mum?"

She smiled up at him. "Thank you, William. I was a little afraid you were going to put me in the barrow, too."

"The thought had occurred to me, mum. But I was a bit leery about the struggle you'd probably put up." He grinned. "I'm not sure I could win it."

She smiled, clapped her hat on her head, and took up her staff before accepting his arm. They started a gentle amble in the wake of the men with the barrow.

William lowered his voice and turned to her as they walked. "Can I ask you something, mum?"

She glanced up at him briefly but nodded and looked back at her feet to make sure she didn't stumble. "Ask away."

"Are you a witch, mum?"

Tanyth's bark of laughter echoed down the trail and Karl, who was tailing the procession, looked back with a quizzical expression for a moment.

William laughed softly himself. "I didn't really think you'd find it that funny, mum."

She patted his arm. "It just took me by surprise, William. Of all the things you might have wanted to ask, that wasn't one that I expected."

They walked along in silence for a few steps while Tanyth thought about her answer. "I don't know." She glanced up at him. "What's a witch?"

He screwed his mouth into a grimace and nodded. "Fair point." After a couple more steps he tried again. "Do you do magic? How did you know? Was it another raven dream?" The questions came out in a tumble.

She sighed. "I don't know. I don't think that magic exists, but if it doesn't then none of this makes sense." She looked up at him again. "In my dreams, I can see through the raven's eye. I see like I'm her and I see what she sees. Sometimes it's confusing." Tanyth paused, not sure how much to say. "She likes to eat hornets. She sees things differently, but she sees enough of what's happening to give me the warnings that we needed."

"Hornets, mum?"

She shrugged. "One dream, while I was healing, she was hungry and ate some dropped apples from under a tree in the forest. They were covered with hornets after the sweet and she ate them, too."

William looked at her in awe. "That's amazing, mum."

Tanyth nodded. "I'm not sure I believe it myself, but if it's not happening, then how did I know? Did I really know or was it just a dream? But if it t'was just a dream then what about the fire and Birchwood and all?"

William took a deep breath and blew it out. "Yeah. That's a riddle, for sure, mum." They walked along a bit before the next question bubbled out of him. "It's always the same raven?"

She nodded. "She defends her turf, and we're in it. She finds us interesting to watch."

He blinked. "Interesting to watch?"

She shrugged. "You tore the houses down and lined up the logs?"

He seemed startled. "Yes, mum. Did the raven show you that?"

Tanyth pointed to the spike of a tall fir tree. "She likes to sit up there and look." She paused. "She sees a lot."

William nodded, eying the tree. "Is she up there now?"

Tanyth shrugged. "I don't know. I can only see through her eyes when I'm asleep, I think. She could be up there, hidden in the branches." She shrugged again. "Or she could be out looking for food."

"Is that the only magic you can do?" William seemed genuinely curious. "If you don't mind my askin', mum?"

She smiled and patted his arm again. "I don't mind, William, but I'm afraid my answers will seem a bit like the ravings of a madwoman." She snorted. "Which, in a certain sense, they are."

"Mum? I'd sooner believe Amber is mad than you." He

looked at her seriously. "And she's as sane as the day is long."

"Well, I don't know if it's magic or a gift from the All-Mother or what, but that's about the extent of my powers, if that's what you wanna call 'em." She decided not to tell him about the dream of foretelling. She didn't know if that were real or just some odd brain trick brought on by the shock of the fight.

"Really, mum?" His tone said he believed her, but there was another question on his mind. "Then how'd you kill Mort and Andrew? You didn't cast a spell on them?"

She shook her. "No. Nothing magic." She sighed. "I was terrified. I bashed their heads in with my staff."

William stopped in his tracks. "You did what?"

Tanyth looked a bit chagrined. "I bashed their heads in. The first one as he stepped through the door. He never saw me. Birchwood, he was a bit more difficult." She sighed.

"Mum? You faced down a man with a sword? And killed him with your staff?" William was astonished.

"What did you think happened?" Her forehead furrowed.

It was William's turn to look chagrined. "I thought you'd spelled them to death." He shrugged and eyed her staff. "I thought it was just a walking stick."

She looked at her staff. "It's good solid oak shod with cold iron, William. I've been usin' it to fend off unwanted attention for twenty winters or more." She grinned. "Most boyos don't think an old lady with a stick is much of a challenge."

He grinned back. "You have to admit, mum. It is a bit odd."

She snorted. "Women been using brooms as weapons for long as there's been brooms. This one just lacks the brush on the end. Besides, Birchwood didn't have a sword. Just his dagger." She paused. "And he came within an inch of killin' me with it."

He regarded her evenly for a few moments. "Does it bother you, mum?"

"What? That I killed them?"

He nodded.

She thought about it. "No. Not in the way you think." She paused. "I'm sorry it was necessary. I don't regret doing

---

it when the need arose. They could have left us alone at any time. They didn't." She shrugged. "It was necessary. I did it."

He thought about that for several long moments before offering his arm once more and they continued along the trail.

She glanced up at him. "Do you think me cold, William?"

He considered her out of the side of his eye before shaking his head. "No, mum. Not cold." He shook his head. "But if Birchwood had known, he'd have gotten on his horse and kept riding until he was far away from here."

She snorted. "If he had, he'd likely still be alive." She looked up at him and tugged on his arm to get his attention. "But some other village would be threatened because he was too stupid and too arrogant to make an honest living."

William blew out a slow breath. "You've the right of it there, mum. You most certainly do."

They strolled in silence for the rest of the short walk, and in a few more minutes William helped her down the steps into her hut.

Jakey and the boys had laid a fire for her, and it was catching nicely as she entered. The cot and tick were set up, and her pack hung from a peg by the door. The woodbox and water bucket were both full and the spare baskets stood in the corner opposite the root cellar. There was even a set of crockery on the mantle board.

She stood her staff beside the door and hung her hat on the peg. "This was very considerate. Thank them for me?"

William nodded. "I'll leave you to get settled, mum. Amber asked me to invite you to dinner tonight, so don't worry about fixin' a meal."

She nodded. "That would be wonderful, thank you."

He nodded and knuckled his forehead. "My pleasure, mum. If you need anything, just yell."

He left the door open for the light and returned to the construction site.

She crossed to the hearth and noted that the water bubbled already and that some thoughtful person had left her a box of tea and a loaf of fresh bread. She smiled to herself and rinsed the teapot with hot water before beginning to brew. She sighed in satisfaction as she lowered herself onto an honest chair with a solid back instead of a stool. She looked around with a critical eye and had to admit, it felt like home.

While the tea steeped, she settled back to think about what she needed to accomplish before the snow came and what she could collect and store to work on over the dark months of deep winter. She sat and thought and planned as patches of sunlight traced their slow paths across the floor.

After what felt like a short time she realized that the mug in her hand held cold tea and that she could barely keep her eyes open. The unaccustomed exercise and stress of moving pressed her to close the doors and curl up on her cot with a blanket pulled over her. "Old woman needs her nap of a morning?" She asked herself the question but didn't get a chance to answer before slumber stole her away.

The activity in the yard below gave her something to look at, but she needed food. She took wing to soar deeper into the forest. The dropped apples were still there and delicious. She gorged on them but wished for meat–a rabbit perhaps or a squirrel. The cold wriggly things from the pond would do almost as well. She jumped into the air and winged to the pond but the hunting was not good and she only found one small frog. She hopped up to a broken limb and preened a bit in the warm sun. She felt winter approaching and knew she needed to hunt.

Tanyth awoke just before noon and took advantage of the fresh bread and a small block of cheese to make a light lunch for herself. Preparing the simple meal was a delicious change of pace from the round of rich broths and soups that had been made for her while convalescing. The routine activity let her think about what William had called her magic. Soaring with the raven during her nap showed her nothing of note, other than the raven felt the coming of winter and was driven to find as much food as she could. Tanyth considered that and wondered if she could help the raven, even as the raven had helped her. She made a mental note to ask Thomas for a plump squirrel the next time she saw him.

CHAPTER 32
GIFTS

Frank turned the lorry wagon off the Pike and back into the village just as the sun slipped down behind the trees, three days before the full Axe Moon. Everyone turned out to greet the returning party with much laughter and celebration. The somber note of Kurt's loss was overshadowed by the news that Birchwood and his gang were no more. Tanyth stood at her front door and watched the reunions but stayed back out of the melee.

After a few minutes of dooryard greetings, William climbed up beside Frank and they took the wagon up toward the barn. Most of the village followed along in the wake while Tanyth went back into her house and poked up the fire a bit. The evening was cold and she still needed some warmer clothing. She was wearing three layers of shirt already and sidled up to the fire to avoid having to put on her coat as well.

"You could have more than a small smudge of a fire." She muttered to herself but didn't take action. She knew every stick she burned would be one that William or one of the others would have to replace. She had organized Riley and some of the older children into a kind of work party to help her harvest some of the forest's bounty. They'd done very well dragging back several gleaner's bags full of apples. They saw harvesting the groundnuts as riotous adventure–if a bit muddier than she'd expected. She kicked herself over that one. She should have realized that at least half of the children would fall into the pond at some point or other–either accidentally or on purpose. She sighed but laughed softly at the memory. "Cute li'l buggers, they are."

The tea water came up to a boil and she was just thinking about what she wanted to brew when she heard footsteps approaching the house. She went to the door and opened it as Frank raised his hand to knock. His face split in a smile that seemed to glow in the dark against his weathered face. "Good evenin', mum. I hope I didn't disturb you, but I thought you might like this." He held out a cotton bag. "The rest of the things you wanted are up at the store room, but I thought you might like your oatmeal tonight."

She found her own face had taken on a smile to match his but she wasn't sure if she were happier to see him or the oatmeal. "That was very thoughtful of you, Frank." She took the bag from him. "Would you like to come in and sit? Have a cup of tea? I was just about to brew a pot."

He nodded. "Thank you, mum. I'd love a cup." He grinned. "But maybe I'll stand. I've been sittin' a lot the last few days."

She chuckled sympathetically and stepped back so he could come in. He closed the door and followed her to the fire. He stepped up close to the flame and warmed himself while she christened the pot and then set about brewing some rose hips.

She realized that he wasn't saying much, just staring into the fire and absorbing the warmth.

"How was the trip?"

He shrugged. "Long. The first week or so, we were afraid that they might come after us. Being out in the open, movin' slow, and with the horses. We took turns guardin'. It worked out good. The boys stayed up all night and then put down their bedrolls in the wagon for most of the day. First few days were the worst and then they got used to sleepin' while we were movin'."

She made a sympathetic noise. "How was it traveling with a crew?"

He shot her a sideways glance and snorted. "Not as bad as I thought. They're a funny bunch." He turned and presented his backside to the flames. "We were half mad with worry the whole time." His voice barely rose above the crackling fire.

She offered him a mug of hot tea and then took her chair.

"Oh, we were worried about you as well at first, but then Birchwood paid us so much attention, we were pretty sure you were safe."

Frank gave a small sideways shrug. "Yeah, well, he wouldn't want to interfere with the money, mum. It would not be in his best interest to keep us from market–especially since he'd expect us to bring back money."

She sipped her tea and nodded.

"All the way back we expected him to come jumpin' out of the trees after us." His voice turned serious. "We were all so worried about what he might be doin' here. It was hard to stop at night to give the horses enough rest." He sipped at his mug and gave her a sideways glance. "How are you, mum? William said you'd been hurt?"

She glanced down at her chest. "I'll be fine. It's still not fully healed but as long as I go easy, it's fine." She smiled up at him. "No lastin' damage."

He nodded over his cup but didn't smile. "He also said you killed two of them?"

"Sometimes you have to put an animal down." Tanyth frowned into her mug. "Not somethin' anybody likes doin' but sometimes it has to be done."

He nodded. "Yeah."

The conversation lapsed for a bit but the silence was more comfortable than awkward.

Frank broke the silence first. "I see they've moved the inn up to the pump."

"Yup. The fire gave them a bit of incentive and the houses up there are made of nicely seasoned logs. William thinks they'll make nice planks."

"So he said. I need to help him set up the saw pit."

She glanced at him curiously. "Saw pit?"

"It takes a lot of sawing to turn a log into a pile of planks. We do it in a pit with a man on the top and another on the bottom."

She visualized it. "Doesn't the man on the bottom get all covered with sawdust?"

He grinned and nodded. "That he does, mum."

"Do you think you can get it built by spring?"

He considered it as he sipped. "I do. If we can get the logs ripped into boards in the next few weeks, then we should be able to get up a frame and a roof before the snow flies."

"Will you need to fell more trees?"

He shook his head. "I thought so originally, but there's a lot of logs in the two houses there, and we've got three more empty ones that we could use if we need more seasoned wood." He shrugged. "I'm takin' up one whole house myself, and I could move in with the quarry men. That would free another."

"Would you do that?"

He looked at her. "Dunno. Before this trip, I'd have said no. I like my quiet." He shrugged and turned back to his tea. "Now? It was kinda nice having the boys around. During the summer I'm on my own for days at a time. During the winter?" He sighed. "It does get lonely at times."

She made a small noise in agreement and sipped her tea.

After a few minutes he asked her, "What about the visions, mum?"

She glanced up. "Visions?"

He kept his gaze on the glowing embers in the hearth. "The visions. William says you have visions and that they saved us."

She grunted and sighed. "I'm not so sure they saved us, but yeah. I get them now and again when I sleep." She looked up at him. "William thinks it's magic."

"Is it? Magic, I mean?"

"I dunno. Might be. But if it is, it's nothing I have any control over. It just happens or not." She lowered her face into her mug again. "Mostly not."

"If it's not magic, then what would you call it, mum?" His voice was warm and curious.

"I don't know." She looked up at him. "I've been askin' myself that for the last two weeks. I don't have any answers."

They lapsed into an easy silence again.

"I thought I was goin' mad." She said it softly.

"Why's that, mum?"

She gave a nervous laugh. "Well you hear about ranting old women. They live in the woods and go a little off in the head? I've met a few of them. Heard about a lot more."

He nodded. "Yes, mum. It's a pretty common tale, no doubt."

She sipped her tea before speaking. "I thought I was turning into one of them."

He considered her words. "I can see why, mum." He paused and glanced at her to try to gauge her mood. "But what if they're not ranting old women?"

He caught her by surprise and her head snapped up. "What do you mean?"

He looked away with a shrug. "What if they're not ranting? Not crazy? What if they're just sayin' what they know and it sounds crazy?"

The thought was startling and she relaxed into her chair to think about it.

"I mean, think of it, mum. You live alone in a cottage in the woods, maybe. Don't see many people. When you have a vision like this and start talkin' about it to people who maybe don't know you very well?"

She frowned in thought. "The people who talk to you don't understand it, because maybe you don't understand it either."

Frank turned to her, leaning a shoulder against the mantle board. "So they think maybe you're a little 'round the bend and things go downhill from there."

She glanced up at him. "But you're suggesting that maybe they're having the same kinds of visions as I am?"

He shrugged one shoulder. "Well, it fits. You thought you were going mad yourself, but you were able to find out that the visions were real–even helpful. I can see a lot of people gettin' spooked by the idea and not bein' able to check the reality. Maybe the vision wasn't from a raven's eye, but something different. Something they couldn't check easily."

She nodded slowly as she considered it. "Why old women?" She sipped her tea and asked it almost of herself.

"Well, there aren't that many old men who live alone. We die off too quick."

She looked at him. He was only half joking and he had some valid points. "Well, I prefer to think that old men are rare and valuable because only the good ones survive that long."

"I'm working on that myself," he said with a grin.

"You're doing good so far." The words jumped out of her mouth before she could bite down and stop them. They both blushed.

"Thank you, mum." He sipped his tea, embarrassed, and tried to get the conversation back on track. "But what if there's something in a woman that makes her open to this magic–this thing–whatever you want to call it–that gives you special powers?"

"That seems unfair."

He blinked, confused. "Unfair, mum?"

"Somthing only women can do? Like a special power? The world doesn't work like that."

He snorted a short laugh. "Mum? You realize that's ridiculous?"

"What?"

"Women already have special powers. They already do things men can't. What's one more thing?"

She snorted back. "Really? Special powers?"

He stared at her. "Mum? You may not have noticed but women have this power to create new life? There's no man in the world can carry a baby to term." He shrugged. "If that's not a special power, I don't know what is."

"Well, of course, women give birth, Frank." She sighed in exasperation. "That's not something special. And it's not somethin' we do on our own, either. It's just part of bein' a woman."

He stared at her and lifted one shoulder in defense. "Well, maybe these vision things are, too. Just part of bein' a woman."

She stood up to face him, unable to sit any longer. "Then why don't all women have it? Why am I suddenly getting these things now that I'm facin' the change?"

His face smoothed and he smiled as he looked into her face. "Maybe they do. Maybe it's a gift from the All-Mother. Maybe you don't lose anything at all, just trade it for some-thin' else."

His voice felt soft in her ears and she realized that she was standing very close to him. He smelled musky from too many days on the road, and she didn't mind. She almost lost what he was saying because of the blood rushing in her ears. When it sank in, she stepped back a pace to think. Her eyes went wide. "Is that even possible?"

"I don't know, mum. I'm just tryin' to find a pattern here and that seems like a pretty clear pattern to me."

"I can't be the first." Her objections sounded a bit shrill even to her own ears.

"You're not. If you were then the 'crazy old woman who lives in the woods' wouldn't be so familiar." He grimaced.

She sat heavily, her knees weak. "Or what if the visions drove them mad?" She looked up at him, stricken. "I don't want to go mad."

He squatted down to be able to look her in the eye. "You're never going to go mad, mum. Ever."

She met his warm, smiling gaze. "You sound fairly certain."

"I am."

She thought of all the Mothers she'd worked with over the years. Almost all of them were older than she was, even now. Some of them had seemed more than a little crazy at times. She had to admit to herself that she probably appeared a bit crazy at times herself. Almost all of them had alluded to magic, or showed knowledge of a subject they had no real way of knowing. Yet they did.

The thought was startling. Almost as startling as the nearness of Frank's sparkling brown eyes.

She cleared her throat and he looked away, then stood up and stepped back again.

"How do I find out more?" She spoke the question aloud as much for her own benefit as actually asking Frank.

"Find more women and compare notes?"

She paused, brow furrowed in thought. "They call Gertie Pinecrest the last of the witch women. I was on my way to visit her when I got held up here."

He nodded with pursed lips. "That sounds like a good place to start, mum."

"But that has to wait until Spring now. It's going to be a long winter."

"We'll find plenty to pass the time. And you're not around people who think you're crazy. Even if you're having visions, it doesn't matter to us."

Her breath came a little faster as she looked up at him lounging easily by the hearth, the ruddy light of the fire painting him in a rosy light. Right at that moment she could think of a couple of things they could do to pass the time, but the thoughts so startled her that she retreated into her mug and drained it to the dregs. When she surfaced, he was placing his own empty mug on the mantle board.

"Well, I need to go check on the team, mum. Make sure things got stowed properly. I promised them an extra helping of grain when we got here." He smiled a very charmingly boyish smile. "Thanks for the tea."

"You're most welcome, and thank you for the talk."

"My pleasure, mum." He headed for the door. "My very great pleasure."

She walked him to the door and held it open while he climbed out onto the grassy path. He nodded his farewell and headed for the barn in the near dark of evening. She watched him go until his form faded into the shadows before closing the door and latching it.

Odd thoughts of having her woodbox filled made her giggle.

CHAPTER 33
PREPARATIONS

With Frank and the rest of the quarrymen back from town, the pace in the village picked up. Tanyth watched with a certain fascination as the men dug out the pit they'd first used to saw the planks that built the barn and houses. It lay just off the path to the barn and ran the length of a small gully in the woods that appeared unremarkable.

While Jakey supervised the quarrymen on the shovel detail, William and Frank put Bester in harness and used the ox to drag the salvaged logs up to the barn. It took all day to dig out the pit and, by that time, Bester and William had fetched all the logs and stacked them for cutting. Most of the timbers were over ten feet long and were already flattened on two sides from where they'd been used for the houses.

William saw her looking at the logs and grinned. "Seems like a big pile, doesn't it, mum?"

"That it does, William. That's just two houses worth?"

"Aye, mum. Just the two. Although we're thinkin' we may take two more. With the lay of the land and where we think the foundation should go, Amber and I are thinkin' we should give up our house and move into one of the empty houses across from you. I think Ethan and Bethany may move into one, as well."

She shook her head in wonder. "You know, William, when I suggested you build an inn, I had no idea how much was involved."

He laughed. "Neither did I, mum, but the nice thing about havin' this group? Somebody knows somethin' about anythin' we want. Jakey came from a hard stone quarry, Ethan knows building, Harry is a good hand with the stock even though he spends most of his time in the clay. I know how to build boats and do designs but they make sure I don't make any mistakes when I bring my boats ashore and turn them into roofs and walls."

"You did well to pick this group then."

He looked around at his crew. "They picked me, actually, mum. When they heard what I proposed, they all found me out and wanted to join. Most of them stuck with us, even though we lost a few. I think we'll see more join us as the inn gets going."

Jakey called down to the crew in the pit and they crawled out of the hole and headed to the storage room to put away their tools. He walked over to William and nodded to Tanyth.

"There's the hole, Will. We just need to get the bracin' in place to hold the logs and we're ready to rip some lumber."

"Easier the second time, huh?" He grinned at the burly quarryman.

"Oh, aye. That it is."

"What do you think about foundation stones?"

Jakey grimaced and ran a hand over his mouth. "We need some, but I don't know of any good rock around here to take. There's some good granite up behind where we're digging out the clay, but we don't have the tools or knowledge to get it out and down where we need it."

William nodded. "That's what I thought, too." He turned and looked down the path to where the inn would go. "What ya think about foundation then?"

Jakey followed his gaze and sucked air through his teeth. "That's gonna be a heavy building. We get away with puttin' the logs on the ground for the houses. They'll rot out sure enough but they're small enough we can replace the whole house if we need to." He shook his head. "I've been thinkin' 'bout that foundation ever since you said you wanted to do it and I don't have any real good answers."

William grunted. "I was afraid of that. What's Ethan say?"

Jakey shrugged. "He's got some ideas." He raised his voice

and called Ethan over.

As the younger man approached, Jakey jerked his head to where the inn would be. "Whatcha think about foundation?"

Ethan grimaced. "Full stone would be the best in this ground. Logs will rot too fast and with that much weight on 'em, I doubt the building'd stay plumb past the first good freeze."

Jakey and William nodded. William looked him in the eye. "We don't have stones enough to do a full foundation and we don't have the tools or help here to cut stone. What do we do?"

Ethan squinted his eyes as if to see better. "We got coins enough to buy some?"

Jakey and William shared a glance. "Perhaps a few. Why?"

"Arletton cuts blue stone for the trade. If we got nine stone posts with footers, we could sink the footers down below frost line, use the posts to keep the building off the ground, and then build from there."

Both men nodded. He made good sense. William looked in toward the barn. "Can the lorry wagon handle that much load?

Jakey shrugged but Ethan nodded an affirmative. "It should. I don't think stone weighs as much as clay. Six horses should be able to haul it easy on the open road."

William looked at Ethan. "Right then, you know what we need. In the mornin' I want you to head up to Arletton and arrange for them to cut it for us. Can you do that?"

Ethan shrugged. "Sure. I think so."

"Good. Tell 'em we need it by Hunter's Moon and we'll send Frank to pick it up in the lorry, but they'll have to load it for him."

Ethan nodded. "That shouldn't be a problem."

Jakey stuck his chin up to get their attention. "Do we need stones for the hearth or ovens?"

William shook his head. "I had Frank order oven brick from Megan's father while he was in town. It should be here in a couple of weeks. They're sending a shipment down to Easton and they'll drop it off on the way by."

Jakey grinned and whistled in appreciation. "Well, my

goodness. Ain't we gettin' fancy now. Oven brick and ever'thin'."

Ethan snickered. "Well, from what I heard, we get an inn out here and Harry's gonna be seein' more of his in-laws than he might like."

Jakey's smile got broader. "What? They can't come live like common folk?"

Ethan shrugged. "Somethin' about grandkids and not wantin' to sleep on the ground."

William laughed at that. "How do they think they're gonna get here? Fly?"

Ethan grinned good naturedly. "Dunno. But Harry was spittin' all the way back so apparently it's not just noise."

When the chuckling died down, William refocused the discussion. "So, we sink the posts on the corners, the middles and one in the center? Run footers and build from there?"

Ethan looked back at the empty lot, and Tanyth could practically see him measuring with his eyes. "Yeah. Should be 'bout right. You gonna put a chimney up the middle?"

"'Bout two thirds back. We got stone and mortar enough for that and I got a hearthstone all picked out for it." William turned to Jakey. "You still think you can make two fire places and the oven into one chimney?"

Jakey pursed his lips and nodded. "Oh, ya. Easier to do that than make two chimneys. Bigger base to work on. It'll be heavy, but we can put that on the ground, give it it's own foundation of packed rock and gravel. The All-Father knows we got enough rock and gravel."

They chuckled and William dusted his hands together. "Guess that's it for now." He turned to the younger man. "See me in the morning before you leave, Ethan, and I'll give you some coin for down payment."

He nodded and headed off down the path toward his house.

Jakey knuckled his forehead, nodded politely to Tanyth, and followed Ethan.

William turned back to her. "You still think it's a good idea, mum?"

She laughed. "I better. You've already bought the brick."

He grinned. "We can always use the brick." He stopped grinning and looked her in the eye. "Seriously, mum. Do you think we should?"

She leaned on her staff and raised her head, drawing a full breath of the musky fall air in through her nose. The sun sank behind the trees and the village fairly vibrated with life. She blew the air out through her mouth. "Yes." She turned to him. "But why is my opinion so important, William?" She jerked her chin in the direction of the houses. "This is your village. These are your people. Why does what I think matter so much?"

He smiled. "Mum? You have the benefit of age and wisdom and you've traveled from one end of this land to the other." Tanyth started to snicker and waved her hand dismissively but William pressed on, his voice low, steady, and earnestly serious. "You killed to protect us and you bled from the battle. You're a gift from the All-Mother. Your opinion matters because if you believe in us, we can believe in us." He smiled down at her. "And if we believe we can, we will."

His words sent a rush of embarrassment through her but everything he said was true, except possibly about her wisdom. She was caught speechless and just looked into his very serious and very young face.

"So, do you believe in us, mum?"

She smiled, then, and nodded. "Yes, William. I do."

He nodded back. "Thank you, mum. And now if you'll excuse me, I need to make sure that Frank's got the saw ready for us and then go grab some dinner."

The evening closed in fast with the shorter days of autumn. He headed for the storage room, leaving her standing there for a few more moments admiring the view.

The thickening dusk masked the colors but here and there a brilliant yellow still reflected enough light to stand out of the dusk. She listened to the wind through the treetops and her eyes searched the tall fir to see if she could spy the raven looking down. She couldn't and she wondered if the episodes had been nothing but her imagination after all.

She sighed and was surprised to feel disappointment. She would have liked to feel like she were special, magical. "Somethin' other than an old fool," she muttered to the setting sun before starting off down the path to find a cup of tea.

She worked herself into a high dudgeon as she strode along, ignoring the twinges from the cut down her belly and striking the earth with her staff harder than she needed to. She knew she was being pouty but she didn't care and vented her frustration on the night by stomping along like a five-year-old told she couldn't have a sweet before dinner. The image delighted her and she screwed up her face the way she remembered her own Robert used to and pretended she was a pouting child for no other reason than her own amusement. The silliness of it washed over her and she laughed aloud at herself. Her stride loosened and she stopped stabbing the ground with her staff on every step. By the time she got to her house, she was in pretty good spirits, thinking about which tea she'd like to have and what she'd like for dinner.

She got almost to her door before she realized that Thomas had been there and left a fine fat hare hanging on the peg at the edge of the roof. The shape swung gently in the soft night air. She looked up at it and smiled. He was such a thoughtful man. A familiar soft croaking sound drew her eyes upward even further and she looked into the golden eyes of the raven perched politely on the ridgepole of her roof.

"Well, there you are." She looked at the rabbit and then back to the raven. "Come for dinner have you?"

The raven croaked again.

"Well, give me a minute, and I'll find you a piece or two."

CHAPTER 34
ROOM AND BOARDS

Tanyth woke with the sunrise and crawled out of her bed roll. It promised to be a busy day and she didn't want to miss a minute of it. It felt good to be up and about. She stirred up the fire, and added a couple of small sticks before pushing the tea kettle closer to the heat. Her porridge was cool but she slopped a little warm water on the top and gave it a stir, too. It would warm and the apple she'd cored and put in the night before gave it a lovely smell.

She pulled warm clothes out of the bed roll and slipped baggy pants on over her naked–and now chilly–legs. A pair of warm socks covered naked toes and her worn boots slipped easily onto her feet. She stamped them down and grabbed a wrap before bolting for the privy. "Shouldn't have waited so long." It was a good natured grumble and almost made her giggle. Only the thought that giggling might have damp consequences kept her from doing it.

Taking the return trip a bit more sedately, she noticed that frost had touched the grass in some of the sheltered areas. She knew it wouldn't be long before every morning would be a frosty one. She marveled that this would be the first winter in her life that she wouldn't be stuck in a cottage with somebody else. For the past twenty winters, she'd lived with her teachers. Each of them asking only her help during the coldest months and, in return, feeding her and letting her stay warm by their fires. She'd whiled away long dark hours in discussions over this or that preparation, how to best get the goodness from some herb or other, and the most useful ways of combining beeswax and oils to make salves and balms. This winter, she was the "old woman" and it amused her to think that others valued her as more than just an extra pair of hands or a strong back. She wondered if she should give up her plan of finding Mother Pinecrest and stay in the village for a while.

In the forest, the raven cawed loudly.

"Perhaps not," she muttered to herself.

By the time she got back to her hut, the water was boiling, the oatmeal was warm, and the sun peeked over the tree line across the way. She made short work of her breakfast and cleaned up the pots before refilling the tea kettle, banking the fire, and dressing for a walk up to the saw pit. She'd never seen planks being cut and she found the idea interesting. It seemed almost incomprehensible that the men would be able to saw the length of those logs, not just once, but several times, in order to turn them into boards. She knew, in her mind, that they would but in her heart the labor seemed prodigious.

When she got up there, hat on her head and staff in her hand, the crews had already assembled. Jakey, William, and Frank would be on top of the logs, pulling the saw up and keeping the line straight. Harry, James, and Matthew would be in the pit, pulling the saw back down again. They'd work in pairs, only one pair at a time but trading off regularly to keep fresh.

The men treated the saw–a long band of toothed steel–with all the respect due a poisonous snake. The teeth could bite flesh as easily as wood and nobody wanted to get a bite taken out of them. Tanyth could relate to that.

Frank took the first turn on top and Harry clambered down into the pit. The log itself was held in a clever arrangement of cross bars and supports that could be moved to allow the saw's passage. Before he began, Frank took a ball of heavy cord and unrolled it along the length of the log. He rubbed it with a block of chalk and, with Jakey's help, snapped it along the length of the log leaving a clean white line about an inch in from the side.

Frank lifted the saw off its supports and lowered the end

down into the pit very carefully. "You ready, Harry?"

Tanyth watched the bending steel straighten and line up as Harry took the handle on his end and Frank kept the tension on top.

"Ready, Frank." Harry's voice sounded muffled.

"Easy does it then." Frank placed the saw on the mark where it crossed the end of the log and slowly pulled the handle upward. When he got to the end of his stroke, he paused before Harry started pulling from the other end. Frank kept just enough tension on the handle to keep the steel level and straight. They moved cautiously at first, getting a feel for the saw and the wood and the rhythm of the movement. Within ten strokes, they moved rapidly up and down, the saw ringing almost musically as it rasped through the wood. They sawed steadily for nearly a quarter hour before Frank and Harry traded off to Jakey and Matthew. The sawing continued. Tanyth watched for maybe half an hour more as the pairs traded off after each short shift.

Amber, Sadie, and Megan came up the path and smiled at Tanyth watching the sawing.

Amber smiled brightly and nodded at the men. "Good morning, mum. Pretty amazing isn't it?"

Tanyth shook her head in amazement. "I've never seen anything like it."

Sadie took her by the arm and continued up the path to the barn. "Well, come on, mum. They'll be there for days cuttin' logs. We got work to do." She grinned and leaned in close to whisper. "Besides if you're standin' there watchin', Frank'll be so busy showin' off he may hurt himself."

Amber overheard and her laughter trilled through the woods even over the sound of the whipsaw.

Megan walked up beside them and tutted Sadie. "You stop being rude."

"How do you know I was bein' rude? You didn't hear what I said."

She sniffed. "Amber only laughs like that when you are and Mother Fairport is blushin'."

Sadie and Amber both laughed at that and continued on their way through the barn to the storage area in the back.

Amber took charge as they entered the workroom. "We need the worktable set up, a fire laid, and a kettle put on for tea." With surprising efficiency, Tanyth found herself lighting the fire while Megan ran a bucket to the pump and Amber and Sadie wrestled some of the horses and planks into place to form a work surface.

In addition to the food supplies, Frank also brought back bolts of winter weight fabrics and skeins of yarn for knitting, along with spools of heavy thread and three cards of needles. So while the men worked in the saw pit, the women moved into the workroom and set to work outfitting the village in winter clothing. The adults only needed to have their winter gear checked and patched, but each child in the village needed to be outfitted anew for the coming season. In most cases that meant passing the heavy clothes from older child to younger, but need outnumbered the available hand-me-downs and everybody needed something. Tanyth needed something warmer for outer wear and some warmer shifts and leggings. The houses were snug, and the winter snows served to insulate them even more, but the temperatures were frigid and, even inside with the fire going, they were never as warm as a summer day.

Amber, Sadie, and Megan–having spent so much time helping Tanyth with her recovery–took to having her join their sewing circle with a ready familiarity. When Charlotte and Bethany joined them in the workroom, they treated her with a shy reserve at first, even seeming to be shocked by the lack of propriety shown by the others. Over time, as they became more comfortable, the six women relaxed in each other's company and got on with the tasks of stitch and hem.

The days took on a rhythm that was as much driven by the rasp-rasp-rasp of the saw as the passage of the sun through the sky. It became common for the men coming off the saw to walk into the workroom for tea, or just water, and to chat for a few moments before returning to their labors. Even lunch was done in shifts with the work not stopping for food but with the men grabbing bites between their turns at the handles.

The days grew steadily shorter. Hard frosts pinched off the

softer plants. The leaves all turned to festive colors and then fell to the ground, leaving bare branches stark against the sky. Dark green pine, spruce, and hemlock stood out in patches among the drab grays and browns. Migrating birds filled the sky with wings as the Axe Moon gave way to Hunter's.

On the new moon that marked the end of the month of the Axe, the work of sawing boards came to an end. William calculated the impressive stack of planks would be enough for their immediate needs. There were still posts and beams that needed shaping but that would be done with the logs that William had felled earlier in the fall. In the meantime, one more task remained before they could begin construction on the inn proper.

The village was up early in the cold, breath puffing in the chill light of predawn. Frank, Jakey, and William took the empty lorry wagon and headed south to the town of Hendrix Crossing. While they were gone, most of the villagers went up to the hay loft in the barn and began moving the old hay out of the way. Some of it went to chink cracks. Some was tied in bundles and the bundles laid out along the foundations of the more exposed houses. More was spread as mulch over those root crops that were still in the ground. In the end, they cleared the hay loft and opened a large door in the top of the barn to let the cold air blow through to air the place out.

Tanyth watched the preparation with some trepidation, even as she tended the fire in the workroom with Megan. "What if there's not enough?"

Megan shrugged. "It's a chance for everyone, isn't it, mum? But the people down in Hendrix have never let us down yet. It was a good year for hay. Not too wet, not too dry. We pay good gold for the feed for our beasts and they have the best fields around."

"The idea of buying feed just seems odd." She sighed. "What do they feed their animals?"

Megan grinned. "The same as we do. They just have more fields, we have more woods. That first year we traded wood for hay, but when we stopped cutting the trees, we offered them cash instead. They took it, gladly. Good coin is hard to come by out here, and not everything can be bartered for."

Tanyth blinked at Megan. "I thought William said you had no coin out here. You kept all the money in Kleesport?"

"He did. Frank brought it back with him from town. Just enough to pay the hay factor in Hendrix." She shrugged. "And maybe a few extra. It's how we've done it these last few winters and it seems to work out."

"I suppose you do what works."

She nodded and took a pot of tea and some mugs out to the workers.

Three days later the lorry wagon was back, piled high with hay held down and protected from the weather by a broad swatch of canvas. It took almost half a day to unload the hay and get it all up into the barn's loft, even with everybody helping.

Amber invited Tanyth to dinner that night–a festive meal with Frank, Thomas, Sadie, William and all the children. Thomas had taken several fat geese earlier in the week and most of them were being spit roasted in various of the houses in the village. Amber and Sadie had spent the day cooking together and had built a feast of roasted vegetables, bread, and spitted goose.

As they settled in for their meal, Amber turned to Frank. "Are you ready to go again?"

He shook his head with a chuckle. "No, but I guess I better be, eh?" He sighed and worked his shoulders. "At least driving six horses isn't as hard as pulling a saw."

William groaned sympathetically. "That's true, and tomorrow I've got to get the foundation holes dug before the ground freezes."

Thomas looked up from a trencher of goose. "You took a chance waitin' this long, didn't ya?"

William shook his head. "Not really. It doesn't usually freeze until Hunter's Moon." He shrugged. "And besides we needed to get the boards cut so we'll be able to tack the whole thing in place."

"True." Thomas turned to Frank. "You think the placement is right now?"

"Of the inn?" Frank asked.

Thomas bobbed his head once.

"Yeah, I do. Buildin' it up around the pump, we won't be draggin' buckets of water to the inn. Maybe we can put in a horse trough."

William snapped his fingers. "I knew there was something I was forgetting."

They all looked at him.

"We need to put an extension on the barn so that we can stable more horses."

Sadie looked down the table at William. "Why not just put some stalls in the workroom?"

Amber looked shocked. "Where will we work?"

Sadie grinned. "At the inn. I have a feeling we'll be spending a lot of time there and it'll be a lot bigger than the workroom is now."

Amber seemed startled by the idea but frowned in concentration as she considered it. "Of course."

William smiled at Sadie. "That's a good idea. I should have thought of that."

Amber patted his arm. "That's fine, dear. We keep you around for your looks and your strong back, not your keen mind." She gathered Sadie and Tanyth in with her eyes. "We'll do the heavy thinkin'. You boys just do the heavy liftin'."

They all laughed and William raised his mug in toast. "To my friends with good looks and strong backs, and the lovely women who let us stay around."

Everybody laughed and clinked mugs.

They filled up on the rich meat and hot bread. Eventually the little ones crawled off to their corner to huddle in a pile under the covers, leaving the adults to graze among the leftovers. As the conversation started flagging, Tanyth turned to William. "Did the sawing help or hurt your shoulder?"

He grinned and put a hand to his wounded shoulder. "The first day it hurt a lot. The second day, the rest of me hurt so much I didn't notice. By the fourth day, I was getting' used to it again." He jerked his head at Frank. "There's the man who was sore."

Frank hung his head. "I got a bit overextended, but I worked through it."

Tanyth shook her head. "I should have thought. Mother Alderton left some liniments that would have helped sore muscles."

Sadie giggled. "You shoulda said somethin', Frank. I bet Mother Fairport woulda been happy to rub your sore shoulders for you." She winked at Tanyth and Amber laughed.

Tanyth blushed and she thought Frank did, too, but she was too embarrassed to look.

Thomas changed the subject. "How we fixed for firewood, William? You haven't had a chance to cut any for a while."

"We've enough for the time bein', I think. When we get the inn going so we can leave Ethan overseein' the build, I'll be able to go out again. There's still a month's supply in the barn and I think all the huts have full woodboxes."

Sadie mumbled something about Mother Fairport's woodbox needing fillin' that didn't carry all the way to the head of the table but had Amber choking on her tea and left Thomas and William looking confused. Frank, for his part, just sighed and muttered. "Kids."

Tanyth braved a glance in his direction and thought she saw a small smile on his face, but he kept it hidden behind his teacup until the general jocularity petered out.

As the laughter faded, the party broke up and Tanyth returned to her hut while Frank headed for the barn to check on the horses. Thomas and Sadie were walking arm in arm toward their house and Sadie was talking earnestly to Thomas. She couldn't hear the conversation, only the tone. About half way home, she heard Thomas bark a single laugh before it was loudly shushed and she groaned. "Now everybody is gonna know about my woodbox."

She sighed and let herself into the house, latching the door closed against the cold. She debated stirring the fire up, but decided to leave it banked until the morning, and changed quickly into a night shift before crawling into her bed roll. It was desperately cold and she shivered for a few moments before her body heat began to drive out the chill. She rolled over onto her belt knife and gasped at the feel of the hard metal pressing into her side. She reached down and slipped it to a more comfortable position. She felt a little silly keeping up her habit of the road, but she shrugged it off and within a few minutes her body heat created a pocket of warmth between the heavy layers of covers on top and the sweet grass ticking and woolen cot liner beneath her. She forgot about the knife and drifted off to sleep.

At day break she heard the wagon leaving the village on the next run to get hay.

CHAPTER 35
FIRST SNOW

The first snow of the season fell on the morning of the Hunter's Moon. Tanyth heard the difference when she woke. There was something in the air, a quiet that didn't match the other mornings. The gray sky with drifting flakes kept the sun from brightening the day and her hut was unnaturally dark.

She shivered as she crawled out of her bed roll and her left knee shot a twinge up her leg. Cold always made it worse and changes in the weather added sand to the ointment. She'd taken to sleeping in her socks and slipped from bed to boot without touching the floor. Her night shift–a warm flannel gown that Amber and Sadie had made for her–fell around her ankles as she stood. It helped keep the warmth close to her body, but she still slipped on a shawl before poking up the fire and adding a few sticks of wood.

When she opened the door to head for the privy, a clump of snow clung to the wood long enough to get dragged into the cottage before falling off on the step with a plump splat that sent snow flakes everywhere. Looking out, she could see that it wasn't that much snow, but it was still coming down. She thought at once of Frank. He was due back later in the day with the blue stone footings for the inn, but he'd be waking in a camp and having to deal with snow. She didn't envy him.

She hung by her hearth, waiting for the sound of horses. She kept worrying about his being out there on the road in the snow alone. It bothered her beyond reason. She tried several times to distract herself by working on some tinctures of rosemary that she planned for Solstice gifts but couldn't focus on the process. She gave it up after a time, afraid that she'd make a mistake and burn the oils she was trying to extract.

By midmorning she was certain that something had happened and that she needed to do something. Her agitation made her skin feel hot and she stepped back from the fire in confusion. The room had suddenly gotten much hotter. Hot as summer. Except the room was still the same. The small fire wasn't throwing that much heat. Her eyes widened as she realized that she was having a hot flash–her own body was causing the heat. She'd been with Mother Gilroy some ten winters back and helped the poor woman through what she called her winter of heat.

She calmed herself. Or tried to. She breathed deliberately in, held it for a moment, and then blew it out. The room wasn't quite cold enough to see her breath, but it felt good on the fevered skin of her face and hands. She loosened her collar and flapped her shift a bit to pump some air around under her clothing. Then she thought of Frank, again. Possibly lying dead beside the road, crushed by a shifting stone in the lorry, or pinned under it, unable to get free slowly freezing to death out there in the snow.

"All-Mother, help me." It was less prayer than disgusted grumble. She knew her mind was going full bore but she wasn't thinking clearly at all.

She crossed to her bed, kicked off her boots, and crawled back into the bedroll. The flash was subsiding. The room was cold, and she needed to get a handle on her emotions before she did something stupid like haring down the Pike in search of a man who'd undoubtedly be driving along, huddled in his driving cloak and sipping a hot mug of tea while singing a bawdy song.

The idea of Frank singing a bawdy song made her giggle, but the warmth of her bedroll reached into her and soothed her jangled spirit. She took a deep breath of the cool air, then snuggled down into the woolen blankets and was surprised to find sleep waiting for her, ready to pounce. "All-Mother, help me." More sigh than prayer, she wasn't sure she'd actually said it before the wave of darkness washed over.

The snow floated down outside the tent of boughs. She crooned a bit as she roused and noted that the storm had not yet blown itself out. She puffed up her feathers but was unable to get really warm. Winter was a hard season. With a loud caw, she launched herself off the limb and into the falling snow.

She snapped at a few of the flakes as she soared through them, banking sharply and winging across the village. The ground was blurry in the dim light and soft blanket of new fallen snow but she watched carefully for the small animals that might give up their lives to keep hers going. At the gap in the trees, she turned and followed man's wide path. The exercise warmed cold muscles, but the snow obscured her vision and she found herself sailing only a few feet above the road, down in the gap between the trees and scanning for food. Looking for . . . something.

She heard it before she saw it. The jingle sound and a muffled rumble of hoof and wheel gave her warning enough to swoop sideways and avoid the wagon that loomed out of the curtain of snow. She cawed in alarm and circled once eying the man propped up on the seat and the horses plodding along through the snow. The man turned to look at her, the snow coating the brim of his hat and dusting across his shoulders. She dodged away through the trees. The attention of men was something to be avoided.

With a shock she realized that she'd left her own territory and turned herself toward home. It wouldn't do to be caught here. She knew the pair who raised their young in this patch and they guarded it fiercely. The call she'd made might have alerted them so she kept silent and concentrated on moving quickly through the forest until she'd returned to her own turf.

She celebrated her return by cawing loudly three times to warn off anybody who may have thought she'd left and then she remembered the house where there were sometimes fat rabbits. She cawed once more and picked up her pace. Perhaps there'd be another rabbit today.

Tanyth felt exuberant as she broke through the surface of sleep. She crawled groggily out of her nest. It would be awhile yet, but she felt much better knowing he was safe and on his way back. She scurried to the hearth and tossed a couple more sticks onto the fire. Today she would stay home and not visit Amber or Sadie as was her wont. Solstice was coming and she needed to think of what she could make for her friends. She fanned the coals with her wing and blew on it. Her lips wouldn't blow, there was no pucker, no give. Just the long horny bill and she realized she was still raven, or partly raven, or–

She awoke with a start and a banging in her chest. She held her hands up and looked at them. Fingers, yes. Fingers were good. She pursed her lips and blew before she dared to touch her face to see. She lifted the woolen blankets and looked down at her normal body–the cold air of the cabin washing the length of her, chilling her sweat. She pulled the blankets back down and held on to them tightly. The banging in her chest became a banging in her head and then it stopped. Her eyes flew open and her hand when to her chest to feel, but then the banging began again and she realized that it was somebody at her door.

"Mother Fairport! Mother Fairport! Are you all right?"

She opened her mouth to speak and the croak that came out scared her until she recognized her own dried throat and swallowed once to moisten it before calling again.

"I'm fine!"

She threw herself out of her bed and took one more inventory of extremities before slipping into her boots and hurrying to the door. She released the latch and swung it open to see Sadie standing there, bundled against the snow and carrying a basket over her arm.

"I'm fine. Really." She stood back. "Come in and warm yourself, my dear."

Sadie smiled brightly. Her cheeks were pinked by the wind and cold but she seemed energized by the snow. She came in and hurried over to stand by the side of the fire where the snow dropping off her boots and clothes would fall on the side of the hearthstone and soon evaporate.

Tanyth peeked out to see the snow fall tapering off. A ray of golden sun tried to break through the overcast. She closed the door securely, and turned to her visitor.

"When you didn't come over after breakfast, we thought you might be under the weather, mum." Sadie pulled down her muffler and extricated her arm from the basket."

Tanyth pulled a couple of sticks from the woodbox and poked up the fire. "I'm fine, Sadie. Really. I just didn't want to go out in the snow so I stayed close to the fire. I got drowsy and saw no good reason not to go back to bed."

Sadie didn't look convinced but she put the basket on the mantle board. "I brought you a couple loaves of fresh bread, mum, and there's some cheese in there, too." She looked around the small house and smiled. "You keep things so neat."

Tanyth snorted. "It's just me here and I don't have that much to spread around." She nodded with her head in the direction of Sadie's house. "You've got your two, Thomas, all your things, all their things, and then visitors and hangers on." She shook her head with a warm smile. "Your house is full of joy, Sadie. Joy isn't neat."

Sadie looked at the older woman for a moment before crossing to her and giving her a big hug and kiss on the cheek. "Thank you, mum." Her voice was a husky whisper. "You're welcome in my house any time, you know."

Tanyth smiled. "Thank you, child. I'll take you up on that, never fear. By spring you'll be sick of seein' me layin' about on your hearth."

Sadie pulled back to look her in the eye before hugging her even harder. "That will never happen, mum. Ever."

Sadie pulled back suddenly and started bundling up. "Well, I better get back to my little house full of joy before the children decide to experiment with how well blankets burn on the hearth. We'll be having dinner with Amber and William, if you'd like to join us, mum."

Tanyth nodded with a smile. "Thank you, my dear. Perhaps I'll pop over there this afternoon."

Sadie grinned as she finished wrapping up. "Frank should be back today."

Tanyth smiled. "Yes, and just in time."

"Mum?" Sadie looked up confused.

Tanyth waved a hand. "Snow falling. William wanted to get the roof up before the snow."

"Oh! This is nothing. I bet it'll be gone by tomorrow. This time of year we get a bit of snow one day and go back to fall the next. Makes a mess, but doesn't stay around. Hunter's Moon is like that, but once we hit the Solstice..." She shivered dramatically. "Then the snow will get serious." She shook her head. "No, with the foundation stones that Frank's bringing, they'll have a frame up within a week and a roof on by the new moon, you see if they don't."

Tanyth was surprised. "That fast?"

Sadie nodded with a grin. "They're men, but they can move when they want to and there hasn't been this much excitement here in ages." Her musical laugh bounced off the rafters and Tanyth held the door for her while she climbed out and back into the snow.

The sun had broken through and while there were still flakes in the air, they sparkled brightly as they tumbled to earth. Sadie held out her hands to her sides, palm up. "See, mum? Almost stopped and I bet it's half melted by nightfall."

"I hope so! I'm not quite ready for snow yet."

Sadie laughed again and gave a little wave as she headed back to her house, taking kicks at the snow as she walked just to see the sparkling drifts fall back to the ground.

Tanyth couldn't help but laugh softly to herself. The terror of her waking dream had dissipated and if her vision were true then Frank should be along within a couple of hours. Remembering her vision, she frowned and stuck her head closer to the door, looking out to see if the raven had, in fact, come back. She didn't see anything and had almost closed the door when she heard a faint thump on the roof followed by some scratching sounds. A small fall of snow cascaded down in front of the open door.

"Well, there you are." She said it out loud wondering if the raven would hear, or understand.

She closed the door and latched it, listening to the scrabbling sound on her roof. She looked around for a moment before pulling yesterday's bread heel from her breadbox and broke it into several pieces in the bottom of a flat basket. Her root cellar yielded one of the wild apples, and she scraped her left over oatmeal from the morning's pot onto the side.

She looked around but didn't have anything else that looked appropriate and was leery about putting out too much.

Conscious of the rest of the village, she opened her back door and pushed the snow back from her threshold with her broom, clearing the loose snow from a small area before sliding the basket out onto the ground. "Thank you, my dear. Here's a bit of breakfast for you in payment of your efforts. Sorry, I have no rabbit today."

She felt strange talking to the raven and wasn't even sure the bird could hear her, but the scrabbling sound of talons made a deliberate-sounding scratch and Tanyth saw the large bird sail out toward the tree line a few yards before turning and flying back toward the house. The raven landed on the snow a few feet from the back door and eyed her–or more probably the basket of food–but didn't approach any closer.

With a feeling of something like awe, something like fear, she swung the door closed and clicked the latch down.

CHAPTER 36
HOMECOMING

In the middle of the afternoon, Tanyth heard the jingle of harness and the heavy tread of draft horses. She grabbed her wrap and woolen cap and ventured out into the bright sunny afternoon with staff in hand. As Sadie had predicted, the storm had cleared and the sun blazed in the afternoon sky. The snow seemed to evaporate even as she watched.

Frank saw her come out of her house. He nodded with a tip of his hat and big smile as he passed. The whole village turned out to meet him. The children broke off their snowman building in the back to come running down to see what was on the wagon. When they saw it was just a few rocks, they lost interest and went back to playing. From her vantage, Tanyth could see they were already soaked through. She didn't envy whoever would be peeling the cold, clammy clothes from chilly bodies when the sun set.

William ran up to the building site to direct Frank and the team in the placement of the lorry wagon and after a bit of discussion, Jakey and the quarrymen hefted the heavy stones, one by one, off the bed of the wagon. Nine blocks were roughly cube shaped and about two feet on a side. Nine more were squared columns of rock some five feet long and nearly a foot across. They were all lashed to wooden handles that allowed six men to heave together to move them. As it was, six men could barely move the blocks and they didn't move the stones far, except to pull them down off the wagon and place them near the prepared holes.

Tanyth stood with the women at the back of Amber's

house and watched the proceedings anxiously. The treacherous footing could easily result in a broken limb or worse with the heavy stones. Jakey directed and crew soon placed the stones neatly around the site.

When the crew pulled the last stone from the lorry, William climbed up beside Frank and the two men rode the wagon toward the barn while Jakey and his crew finished fiddling with the blue stones.

Amber blew out a breath as it became clear that the excitement for the day was well over. "That coulda been ugly."

Sadie agreed with a nod. "But they really needed to get the weight off the wagon. If they'd left it sitting there the wheels would have been up to their hubs by morning."

"I know." Amber sighed. "Still makes me nervous, them messing about with stuff that can kill 'em."

Megan laughed. "They're just big excited kids. They can't wait to play with the toys."

Amber grinned. "Yes, well, I worry about the little kids, too."

"What'll they do now?" Tanyth watched the men looking at the stones and peering down the holes. The sun cast sparkles off the scuffed and muddy snow, but the crew remained at the site.

Amber pursed her lips and twitched her nose while she was thinking. "I think they'll wait at least until tomorrow, if not the day after."

Sadie made a humph sound. "Yeah. Probably so. I bet those holes are pretty wet on the bottom right now."

Amber grinned. "I was thinking of them trying to get traction on the grass, but you're probably right."

Megan shook her head. "I bet they try to put one in today so they can use the Hunter's Moon as the founding date."

Amber frowned. "Does that matter?" She looked at Tanyth. "Mum?"

Tanyth shrugged her shoulders. "Beats me. I've never been around when they started buildin' a building before." She thought about it. "Usually you plant on the new moon, but that's two weeks out and I can't imagine they'd wait that long."

The women all stood in the warming rays of the sun, sheltered by the house and listening to the kids shrieking as they played on the other side of the village. The men stood out in the middle of the scuffed up snow and continued to mill about looking down in the holes.

"What are they doing out there?" Sadie's exasperation was evident in her voice but she kept the volume down. "You'd think somebody out there would be looking for a cuppa tea or something, by now."

Amber shook her head. "They're waiting for something. Maybe William is coming back."

Tanyth saw movement through the trees and nudged Amber. "Yep. And he's got Bester. Looks like you were right, Megan."

"Looks like." She shook her head. "I was really just joking."

They shared a quiet laugh before Amber nudged Tanyth. "Well, mum. You'd best get out there. If they're gonna lay a stone, it would best if you blessed it."

Tanyth started to object. She really wasn't a holy woman to be blessing stones. She couldn't remember ever praying more in her life than she had since arriving in the village. As she opened her mouth to say something, she saw the raven fly up out of the forest and alight in the top of the tall spruce at the edge of the wood. She thought better of her objections and walked out onto the cleared area, leaning heavily on her staff.

As William and Bester approached, Jakey and the boys picked up a tripod arrangement from the ground, brushed off the snow and then stood it up to straddle the northeasternmost hole in the ground. By the time William had Bester in place, Jakey and the crew had positioned the stone over the hole and it sat there on its handles.

The men stepped back and nodded as Tanyth approached. She surveyed the ground as she went, making sure she knew where all the holes were so she didn't fall into one. William smiled and nodded a greeting.

She stopped and leaned on her staff, peering down to look in the hole. It wasn't as deep or as dark as she thought and she saw a bed of gravel in the bottom of it–wet-looking but unsullied by snow. She looked around at the men who were looking at her. "So? You're going to start laying stones now?"

Jakey nodded and spoke before William could. "Yes, mum. It'll be good if we can sit the footers on the sand while it's wet. It should help stabilize the stone and keep it from shifting." He shrugged. "We won't wanna fill in the hole until it's had a bit of a chance to dry, but this should make a good solid footer."

Ethan, the building expert was bobbing his head, and William stood at Bester's traces, getting ready to use the muscular animal to do what the men would have trouble doing on their own.

She looked at William who shrugged. "That's the plan, mum. Would you say a blessing on the space, please? I have a feeling we're going to need all the help we can get." He grinned boyishly.

She looked around at all the serious faces before sighing to herself. "Very well. Give me a moment."

The sun was warm, but it was on the way down and it had been a cold, cold day. She was tired and still scared by the raven dream. As she stepped to where the men had marked out where the chimney would be she had to stop and gather herself. She leaned heavily on her staff, holding it with both hands and leaning her head against the top. The iron foot was stabbing through the snow and into the yet unfrozen ground below. "Mother give me strength." It was more than a whisper, less than a grumble, and none of the men standing around seemed to notice.

She lifted her eyes to the northern sky and began. "We ask the Guardian of the North, Bones of the Earth, to bless and protect the foundation, to make our stones as solid as the mountains, unyielding in adversity and strong as the earth itself." Turning to the east, she spoke again. "We ask the Guardian of the East, Breath of the Earth, to bless and protect the walls, to fill them with life and spirit and to welcome all who enter our doors in good will." Turning to the south, she felt a tension growing in her that she couldn't name. "We ask the Guardian the South, Spirit of the Earth, to bless our hearth, to keep our fires warm and welcoming and our hearts open to all who sit before them." The tension mounted as she turned to the west. "We ask the Guardian of the West, Blood of the Earth to bless and protect our roof, to shed the rain and snow and to protect those who seek shelter beneath it." She closed the circle by turning to the north and she felt the tension tighten more. It was something behind her eyes and the blood pounded in her ears so loudly she couldn't hear the wind in the trees any longer. "We children of Earth beg your help, your protection, and your blessings in the name of the All-Mother and the name of the All-Father. So mote it be." With that she raised her staff and struck the stone that was resting beside the central hole. The iron shoe rang against the rock and a bell-like note echoed through the village. She grounded the staff again and didn't so much lean on it as hung from it to gather herself while the tension inside her leached away into the ground beneath her feet and radiated into the air around her.

It took her a few breaths to get her strength back and when she looked up, William was standing just feet away from her, concern on his face. "Are you all right, mum? You looked like you were about to fall over there for awhile."

She nodded without speaking and smiled faintly. "I'm fine, William. I'm just a bit tired and I think I'd like a cup of tea."

He smiled and offered her his arm. "Amber has a pot ready, I'm sure."

She took his arm and let him lead her off the building site. As she walked she noticed that the men were taking down the scaffolding. She nodded. "Did you change your mind?"

He shook his head. "No, mum. We just needed you to show us where to start."

By the time he'd gotten her to the sunny nook behind the house, Amber had brought out a chair for her and the men had re-built the scaffold over the central hole. They muscled the stone she'd hit into position. William walked Bester to the middle of the lot where they tied heavy woven ropes to the patient beast's yoke. William urged him forward a few feet and he lifted the stone gently off the ground. He held it while the men quickly removed the lashings and handles. As it spun slowly on the end of the rope, the slanting rays of the sun glinted off a silvery mark that her staff had left on the surface. When the way was clear, William backed Bester slowly and lowered the footer gently down the shaft of the hole. Jakey and Ethan stood at right angles to each other and shifted the stone slightly by leaning on the ropes as it was lowered until finally it rested where they wanted it in the sand at the bottom and the tension went out of the line. Jakey tugged a release cord. The men hauled the heavy lines up and got ready to do the next stone. In all, it had taken less than a quarter hour.

Tanyth felt somewhat refreshed from the mug of hot tea that Amber pressed into her not quite trembling hand. She glanced at the sun and then at the men getting ready to work on the second stone. "Well." She announced it suddenly and so loudly that the women around her jumped at the sound. She handed the mug back to Amber and then levered herself up from the chair. "This is all well and good, but I think I'd better go check the fire in my hearth."

Megan stepped up and offered an arm. "Would you like me to help you, mum?"

Tanyth smiled and waved her off. "No, no, my dear. I'm quite refreshed. I'm pretty sure I can walk that far, even in this slush."

Megan grinned as Tanyth stabbed the wet melting snow with her staff. "all right, mum." She paused and then looked up at her shyly. "Thank you, mum."

That took Tanyth by surprise. "Thank you for what?"

Megan waved her hand vaguely in the direction of the men working. "That."

Sadie stepped up and nodded with Amber close behind. "Yes, mum. Thank you."

Tanyth regarded them, each individually, looking into their fresh young faces, their clear young eyes. She smiled. "You're welcome." She headed carefully along the path. The footing was a bit slippery in places with melting snow turning normally stable ground into the consistency of soft cheese. She made it to her door without mishap and paused to look back at the construction.

Megan stood at the corner of the house. She waved. Tanyth returned the wave then opened the door to her hut. Before she went in, she looked up at the sky. "Thank you, All-Mother." It was less grumble than prayer and she made her way carefully into the house, ducking under the low lintel to keep from banging her head.

She shrugged off her wrap and stood her staff beside the door. Her hat went on the peg. She slipped off the wet, muddy boots before carrying them across the sweetgrass mats to the hearth. She looked them over carefully and brushed the worst of the dirt off with her hand before deciding that a more thorough cleaning would need a boot brush and saddle soap. She was pretty sure there was some in the tack room at the barn and she wondered if she could get Riley to run up and fetch them for her. She set the boots aside, pulled a couple of sticks out of the woodbox and poked up the fire. The sun would be down soon and she felt the need of a little comfort. The fire was a start and a nice pot of chamomile and mint would follow. There was plenty of bread and cheese and a bushel of apples waited in her root cellar. She contemplated that and wondered if Thomas would bring her a rabbit. "What would you do with a rabbit?" She smiled as she realized, she'd probably share it with the raven, and then stew the rest.

Thinking of the raven reminded her of her morning's activity and the terribly frightening dream. It chilled her and she stepped closer to the fire. There was something there. Something she didn't understand. Perhaps it was something to do with having the raven do her will. Looking for Frank was certainly not something the raven would do on her own, especially not straying into another's territory. The whole episode was troubling from the first blush of unreasoned worry to the final horror of the nightmare. She breathed deeply of the sweet, smoky air and then blew it out. She was so focused she didn't hear the footsteps approaching her door and was startled when the knock came.

"Mum? It's Thomas!" His voice was muffled by the door. "I have some grouse for you."

She padded across the mats in her stocking feet and opened

the door to a smiling Thomas. "Hello, Thomas. How's the hunting?"

He grinned. "Well it is Hunter's Moon, mum. Hunting is good." He reached into his game bag and pulled out a brace of grouse. "I thought you might like a change from rabbit, mum." He handed them to her.

"Thank you, Thomas, that's very considerate. I was just wondering what I'd do for dinner tonight."

He glanced over his shoulder at the sun. "Well, it's coming up on dinner time now, mum, and those might be better tomorrow after they've hung for a bit."

She weighed them in her hands and nodded. "You're right. And I'm not up to plucking them tonight."

He shrugged and frowned in concentration. "Do you have enough for dinner tonight, mum?"

"Oh, yes, of course, Thomas. Thank you. Sadie has been stopping by every few days with fresh bread and cheese. What with what I've gleaned and gathered, and your game, I'm very well fed these days."

"Well, if there's anything you'd like in particular, mum. Let me know." He held out his hands. "Here, mum. Let me hang these for you."

She handed the birds back and he tied them up on the peg. She wondered if they'd be safe from the raven there. "Thank you again, Thomas. You've all been taking very good care of me."

"We try, mum, now close that door!" He made a shutting motion with his hand. "You're letting the heat out."

She did and heard his boots crunching as he walked away. She padded quickly back to the fire. Standing there with the door open had let the evening air in and the warm air out. The fire burned cheerfully, though, so she filled the kettle and set it to heat. The grouse would be better on the morrow and she had a feast of bread, cheese, and fruit for the evening.

While the water came up to boil she crossed to the root cellar and pulled up a couple of apples. While she had her head down there, she looked around at the baskets tucked in the cool room under the floor. There were baskets of potatoes and carrots, onions and turnips. Several pounds of dried beans of different colors in bags rested on her pantry shelves along with flour, salt, and chilled crock of sourdough starter. Between them, the villagers had outfitted her handsomely to live on her own. She felt a bit guilty that she hadn't done more to teach them the herb lore she was supposed to be teaching them.

She sighed. "Old fool."

She shrugged and grabbed an onion along with an extra apple for her oatmeal and put it all on the floor. Her stocking feet were getting cold and damp on the dirty floor so she clambered quickly, if not too nimbly, back up and slammed the hatch. She gathered her produce and took it to the table, outlining in her mind how to proceed, concentrating on that and not on the raven–not on the dreams.

She pulled her belt knife and dealt with the onion, throwing it and measures of beans and water into one of her small pots, setting it back in the fire to simmer. She dealt just as quickly with one of the apples, peeling and coring it before chopping it up and putting it in another small pot with a measure of oats and more water. That left the cheese, bread, and apples for dinner. She placed a grate over the fire irons, raking some coals under it for heat and tossed another stick onto the fire.

As she moved about the hearth, she felt herself unwinding. The strangeness from the blessing, the visions from the raven, even the prophetic dreams and nightmares faded into the background as she found her center in the tending of the fire and in the preparation of simple foods. She felt the air moving in her lungs and the blood sliding through her body. It felt good.

The kettle bubbled over so she christened the pot and threw in a mix of rose hips, mint, and a touch of chamomile then poured the hot water onto the dried materials, smelling the aroma of summer wafting up from the open pot. She covered it and set it on a warming stone. She was about to address the issue of bread and cheese when she heard more footsteps.

"You're popular tonight, old woman." It was a good natured grumble and she wondered who might be visiting.

Crossing to the door, she swung it open as Frank stepped up to knock. He had a large bundle of firewood in his arms and an odd look on his face. "Good evening, mum." His smile erased the odd look. "Sorry to bother you, but Sadie said you needed some wood and that I should bring it over." He jerked his head in the direction of Sadie and Thomas's house. Tanyth looked and could see a blonde head silhouetted in the open door way by the rosy glow of a fire. One hand waved to her before the door closed.

"That was very considerate of her, and of you for doing it." Tanyth felt light headed. "Why don't you come in and have some dinner. I've just put the kettle on and I'm making some cheese sandwiches." She held the door for him and he tucked low, with his armload of wood and she closed the door firmly behind him.

He crossed to the hearth and stood there for a moment, confused, looking at the nearly full woodbox. "Mum? Where would you like me to put this wood?"

"Oh, just stack it behind the box for now." She smiled at him. "And, Frank...?"

He dropped the armload of split logs on the floor against the side of the chimney before looking up. "Yes, mum?"

"Do you think you could call me, Tanyth?" She smiled at him and gave a little shrug with one shoulder. "We're not kids and I'm not your mum."

Frank straightened and dusted the wood chips off his hands and the front of his coat while he gazed at her, his mouth just slightly open. He looked a little surprised, a little confused, and then his face relaxed and his whole body followed suit. He smiled and his eyes seemed to shine a bit in the firelight. "Yes. I think I can." He paused before saying it. "Tanyth."

She liked the way his tongue flirted over his teeth when he said her name. "Thank you. I'm getting a little tired of being 'mum.'" She shrugged. "Some tea? I was about to pour. Please, there's a peg by the door. Make yourself comfortable."

She watched him slide the heavy outer coat off and hang it on the peg beside hers but turned to tend the tea kettle before he caught her watching. "Thank you, Mother." It was less a grumble than a prayer.

CHAPTER 37
SOLSTICE

Solstice morning dawned crisp and clear and Tanyth woke just as the sun filled the sky with a clean, glowing light above the trees to the east. Winter Solstice marked the shortest day of the year, an inflection point at the middle of winter when domination of darkness over light would reverse and the sun would begin to reassert her place in the sky. The holiday mood had been building for days as the villagers looked forward to a day of rest and play and the beginning of a new year.

As she lay there in the pile of covers, the cold air in the hut tweaked at her nose and she giggled a little to herself. "Where's that man when you need him?" It was a good-natured grumble and she wasn't sure if she was wishing he were there to warm her with his body or if she just wanted him to go stoke the fire before she had to crawl out of the snug nest of covers. She giggled again as she made her decision. "Both."

Her longstanding habit of sleeping with her clothing in the bedroll to keep it warm for morning paid off as she fished around without getting up and found her trousers and tunic, slipping on the tunic without climbing out of bed and standing quickly to slip on her pants. She already wore her socks and she added a second pair–rather than her boots–to pad to the hearth and poke up the fire.

In a few moments she had the fire stoked, the kettle filled, and herself girded for the morning migration to the privy. The cold nipped at her as she scampered across to the small building and inside was even chillier. For a few moments she wondered if she'd waited too long but managed to get in, get the door closed, and her pants down before any serious accidents happened. On the way back, she stopped to admire the progress on the inn. As good as his word, William had frame, floor, and roof up. Sturdy posts and beams held up a sharply slanted, saltbox roof with the long slope toward the back. She could see the heavy chimney through the skeleton of the building with open maws where the ovens and hearthstones would go.

William was already up and walking about the place. He waved to her from where a pair of double doors would hang at the front of the building. "Good mornin', mum! What do you think?" He spread his hands to indicate the edifice.

"I'm impressed, William." Her voice echoed across the morning stillness. "Are you still plannin' on lighting a Solstice fire there tonight? There's no hearthstone."

He grinned. "Oh, I have the stone picked out. Bester and I will be movin' it today. We'll be ready by sunset." The sun began breaking through the tops of the trees and a ray speared him in the eyes so he laughed and had to raise a hand against the dazzling light. "Will you be joinin' us for the vigil, mum?"

"I wouldn't miss it."

"Good! I better go wake up Bester and get him moving." With a wave, he turned and headed toward the barn, weaving his way through the shell of the building.

She made it back to her house just as the water came to a boil. She set about having her breakfast, following her morning routine which included starting some bread dough each morning for baking later in the day.

The Solstice holiday properly started at sunset but there was much to do on the shortest day of the year. They'd light a fire at sunset and hold a vigil until dawn. The new year would start at sunrise and, by tradition, everybody would be one year older. It was a time of introspection as the old year came to a close and a time for new beginnings with the new year just begun. Tanyth thought the inn was beginning rather auspiciously with the first fire being the Solstice vigil, even if she wasn't terribly thrilled about being another year older. "Better than the alternative." It was a grumble but a good natured one.

As she finished kneading the bread dough for the first proof, she thought about the year, especially the past few weeks. She felt–in a certain sense–that she'd awakened from a long slumber. Since leaving Roger twenty-odd winters before, she'd been moving from place to place, teacher to teacher, and learning her craft. She'd thought herself, in many ways, fulfilled and if there were parts of her life lacking, the richness of new knowledge, new people, new places seemed a fair trade for the things she had missed.

She finished forming the dough into a ball and put it in a wooden bowl with a square of towel over it to protect it from drying out. She placed it near the hearth to be warm enough to rise, but not so near that she needed to worry about it cooking–or the bowl burning.

She pulled another stick out of the woodbox and added it to the fire and watched it start to smolder, then slowly catch and begin burning. She thought of the raven. She hadn't shared any visions since looking for Frank in the snow. She wasn't sure how or why or if it were just that she'd not been upset or desperate enough since then. The memory of the nightmare following was enough to make her heart beat a little faster and she looked at her hand, wiggling the fingers to make sure they were not feathers.

She grumbled as she realized what she was doing. "Mother have mercy." With the grumble she reminded herself of the oddnesses that had come with her various prayers since coming to the village and something inside her quailed. The last one, asking the blessing on the inn had left her weak and trembling. Still, that was the day that Frank had come to fill her woodbox and stayed for dinner, and breakfast. For a moment, she basked in the inner glow that he gave her, even when he wasn't there.

The log in the fireplace snapped and tossed a spark out onto the hearth. She brushed it back into the ashes with the toe of her boot and started thinking about the future. Tomorrow she'd be a year older. The winter would come and after that, the spring. Gertie Pinecrest would also be a year older and Tanyth had a pang of anxiety over the idea that the woman she hoped would be her last teacher might cross over before she could get there.

And what about Frank? His place was here with the village. The village needed him and he'd not be welcome at Mother Pinecrest's. Even if he would want to go with her, he could not. She looked around the cozy house and wondered if her plan to find Gertie Pinecrest was really meant to be. She toyed with the idea of giving up on it. It might be nice to stay with Frank, to help with the village.

She sighed and shook herself. "You've work to do, old woman. Move."

She'd found a supply of small tins with tight fitting lids in Mother Alderton's shelves. She found several on the shelves with liniments and unguents already in them–most with additions for various inflammations and abrasions. With the coldest part of winter coming, she decided to make pots of lip balm. The children would need it and she knew she'd need some herself.

Over the course of several days she'd distilled enough mint and lavender oil to use for her balms which only left mixing the oil and wax to the correct consistency and adding the oils before pouring into the tins. She floated a small pot in a large kettle of boiling water and put in a block of beeswax for the base. As it melted she added a measure of almond oil and mixed it until it took on a smooth consistency. With the pot of balm base made, she poured half of it into a crock and mixed in the lavender oil quickly before pouring the concoction into half of the small tins. She poured her supply of fresh mint oil into the other pot and repeated the process. As it cooled, the oil kept the wax from becoming hard again, and added a bit of flavor and scent. The ointment, when coated on the lips with a fingertip, kept the cold, dry air of winter from drying and cracking them. She smiled at her morning's handiwork and transferred the small tins to the mantle board to cool and set slowly while she punched down her bread and got the loaves ready to bake in the afternoon.

The morning raced by and she paused in her work to have

a bit of soup for lunch and to stir her pot of beans. Part of the evening's vigil would include a feast and she made a large pot of beans which she'd place to bake at sunset so they'd have a hot meal at midnight. She knew Sadie and Amber were planning breads as well, and Thomas would be spit roasting various game choices through the night. Everybody would bring something to contribute to the feast. While the new inn might be lacking walls, this would still be the first party in it and the whole town planned to turn out for the Solstice vigil.

By midafternoon, Tanyth looked around and found that she was ready for the evening. Her small loaves of bread had baked and she grimaced at how horrible they looked. Whenever she watched Sadie and Amber sling bread dough around and create the perfect, globular boules, it made her small, misshapen lumps seen somehow inadequate. It tasted good enough. Frank said he liked it and she found the sourdough starter that she used had a mildly piquant flavor, but they just looked wrong to her and she couldn't figure out how to fix it. She made a mental note to get Sadie to help her after the Solstice. Perhaps she'd be able to see the problem.

She pulled a largish stick from the woodbox and banked the fire around it before kicking off her boots and crawling into her bed. It would be a long night and prudence dictated a short nap would not be amiss. As the blankets warmed from her body, she slipped over the edge and into sleep.

She sat in the top of the spruce and watched the preparations below. She crooned softly to herself, her belly full of rabbit that the man had left unguarded. The roof below her covered much of the ground that had once been open but still left her able to see what occurred in the village. With the short days and long nights and the weather getting colder, she husbanded her strength and stayed close to the tree. There was often food for the taking around these people and she didn't need to spend a lot of time and effort to find it. She puffed up her feathers and closed her eyes against the afternoon sun.

Tanyth roused a bit, surprised at the raven dream. It was the first she'd had in weeks, but the day was not close to done and she had time to sleep. Feeling decadent, she rolled over and pulled the warm blankets up higher on her shoulders and wondered idly where Frank was before falling back into the delicious darkness of sleep.

The cawing awakened her and even through her half closed eyes, she knew the afternoon was waning fast. As she struggled through the grogginess she realized that the back door of her house stood open and Frank was lowering himself into the house, bent almost double to avoid the low lintel. She closed her eyes and stretched languorously, wondering if they had time before the festivities started.

"What a nice surprise." Her voice was low but the house was small and she was sure he would be able to hear the invitation in her tone.

He straightened and turned, rushing to her in one smooth movement. She blinked struggling against the nightmare that she could not wake up from even as the snarling face of Josh the Cosh peered down at her and his fist took her back into unconsciousness.

CHAPTER 38
FAMILIAR HURTS

Her face hurt. She'd known this hurt many times before but she thought she'd left it behind with her husband. She didn't need to touch her face to feel the bruising with her fingers. She knew it like an old friend. It was just as well. She couldn't seem to move her arms.

She blinked the one eye that would open. The other was either swollen shut or the lid was stuck together. She couldn't tell. Under her chin she saw the familiar woolen blanket from her bed. But she wasn't in her bed. She was propped against a wall, rolled in the blankets and wrapped with a long piece of rope around the outside. She smelled horse, and a pungent privy smell. A fire flickered somewhere just out of her sight and she tried to muster the strength to turn her head and look.

"Witch."

The word came from the darkness and she remembered the face, the snarl, the name. "Josh." Her words were blocked. Her mouth had trouble speaking around swollen lips and a wad of cloth. Her tongue rasped across the weave of the fabric.

"You. Ruined. Me." The words were low, harsh. Each one discrete. Each one freighted with meaning that she heard but didn't understand.

Her eyes flickered, her brain rattling in her her head from the beating and she slowly regained her senses. Each new awareness triggered another stab of pain. She grunted around the gag.

"You ruined me." He loomed out of the darkness to stand in front of her.

She could smell him then. He smelled bad. Not dirty. Bad. Not the smell of a man who hadn't bathed in weeks, although that reached her even through the blood clots in her nose. Vaguely rotten. The smell caught her throat, a smell that made her glad for the clots in her nose. She turned her head but he stepped closer.

"You ruined me. You killed my friends." He knelt awkwardly in front of her. "And now you're going to pay for that."

She knew she should be afraid, but her battered body knew the pain, knew it as something that might pass. Eventually. Knew the pain made her forget something important. She tried to find it.

He slugged her and she fell forward, feeling something dig into the side of her thigh as she fell.

"You ruined me. And now, I'm going to ruin you."

Her mind cleared enough to remember that he'd surprised her in her bedroll, and she realized that he had just rolled her in the covers and taken her. Her stomach and ribs felt very much like she'd been slung over somebody's shoulder and carried.

He grabbed her shoulder and slammed her back against the wall, rattling her head against the earth behind her.

The shift in weight dug the stick into her thigh again. A stray detached thought flashed through her rattled brain. Trussed like a Solstice goose, battered, being held prisoner by a man getting ready to kill her, and she focused on the fact that a stick chafed the outside of her thigh raw. The incongruity of it nearly made her laugh through the blood soaked gag.

She saw the blow coming, but couldn't dodge in time. It bounced her off the wall back down into the well of unconsciousness. As the darkness filled her again she said a prayer to the All-Mother for delivering her from the stick.

Shouting woke her and she shifted her weight on the limb. The men were making noises. Not noises. The same noise. Over and over. Different voices in different areas of the vil-

lage. The sun was down and the moon was up so the village was washed in silver light. She could see them moving about, calling.

They were clustered around the house with rabbits. Would there be a rabbit tonight? There was something wrong. Something she needed to do. Her belly was still full and the sky was cold but she pushed off from the limb and her dark wings caught the breeze as she soared toward the house with rabbits and over the ridgepole.

Meat. It wasn't there now, but it had been. Something reeking had been there but was gone. That smell, she needed to follow it, find it. There would be food there. There would be... something. The wind caught the scent and she lost it, but she was patient and flew on silent wing, quartering the sky and sailing over the wide path where men rode, back and forth until she called in frustration. It was gone.

A large pine on the edge of her territory offered shelter from the cold and she took roost near the trunk and let the thick needles and thicker wood protect her from the wind. She fluffed up her feathers and tucked down as best she could. There was meat here. Somewhere. In daylight maybe she could find it.

Tanyth woke. The raven was out there, somewhere, but where? She turned her head and the room spun but settled again. The dim light glowed from a fire that burned somewhere to her left. The cold, wet ground soaked through the blanket under her. She didn't see Josh in the dim, shadowed light. She tried to get her one good eye to focus but it was too difficult to make out anything in the dark. She gave up and let her eye close and her head sag forward. Sleep took her but the dreams and the pain kept waking her. Through it all, every shift in weight dug the stick into her leg.

Eventually the long night ended. "Figgers it's the longest night of the year." She grumbled but the gag in her mouth turned it into incomprehensible gargle. The movement and noise brought him out of the shadows.

"What's that, witch? You best not be casting more of your spells or you'll find out real fast." He still hid in the shadows but pale morning light filtered from above in small patches, overwhelming the ruddy glow from the coals. Or perhaps the fire had gone out. She couldn't tell.

He reached out with three filthy fingers and plucked the wad of cloth from her mouth, leaving her gasping for breath.

"Longest night of the year." Her voice croaked awkwardly from the stickiness in her mouth and the swelling in her lips. She didn't think she'd be able to drink even if he offered.

"Oh, if you think that night was long, witch, you just wait until tonight. Oh, yes. Just wait." He loomed out of the shadows then, his eyes glittering oddly, and he stuffed the wad back into her mouth, practically gagging her with it as he stuffed it deep. "You ruined me. And I'm going to ruin you. See if I don't." His eyes dodged back and forth looking at things she didn't see. As he crouched there in the shadows, the pale morning light showed her that he was totally mad. Enough of her wit returned to make her very afraid.

She heard a raven caw three times–a territorial warning–but she couldn't tell what direction, or even how far away. She hoped Thomas would be able to pick up the track.

A familiar pounding sound came from outside. It carried the jingle of harness with it and she recognized the sound of one of the King's Own messengers galloping along the Pike. The muffled sounds came from some distance, but that she heard it at all told her the road ran near her cave.

Somewhere close a horse wickered and Josh's head snapped at the sound. He half crawled, half walked around her, and disappeared. She felt rather than heard the stamp of a horse's hoof. She thought she heard a low voice but when she held her breath to listen it was gone.

Her shifting in the night had loosened the bindings a little and she shifted again, trying to get some circulation back in her hips. The stick dug into her leg again and she couldn't imagine what in the world he'd managed to bind up with her. She slithered her arms down from where they were crossed above her chest which released some of the pressure on her lungs and she was able to get a breath, even around the obstructions in her mouth and nose. She worked her hand down to her thigh to push the stick away.

She shifted her weight back and forth again to get some

more room in the tightly wound blanket. As she did her hand finally found the object that had been digging into her. Her fingers wrapped around the hilt of her belt knife.

He would be back soon. The gray light of dawn brightened and it looked for all the world like she lay in a very low ceilinged cave. There was something odd about it but she couldn't quite place it. It would come to her. She released the hilt of her knife, repositioning it so that it lay more comfortably along her leg and left her fingers resting on the cross guard. She just needed to rest and to think. The damp cold of the ground was beginning to leach away her body heat as it soaked the blankets under her. She closed her eye and offered a silent prayer. "Guardian of the North, Bone of the Earth, loan me your strength that I may survive." Exhaustion and cold conspired to push her back down into the darkness.

She crooned to the morning from her hiding place in the tall pine. The meat smell had not come back but she watched the man with the bow. He killed rabbits and grouse and sometimes left the entrails where she could find them. Maybe he'd find a rabbit. Maybe she could find the meat smell. She had seen him moving out of the house with rabbits. He came out the back door and watched the ground and entered the forest which interested her. He was on the trail of something. Perhaps it was the meat. The track turned and he went out into the wide path and stood there in the middle of the packed surface. He looked up and down the path and she sidled sideways along the limb to watch him around the tree. Perhaps there would be grouse.

No, she needed to find something. The woman with the food would feed her, but where was she?

The man in the path turned away from the village and walked quickly along, she watched his head turning back and forth, back and forth as he searched for something. She needed to find something, too. The sun was coming up and maybe the meat smell would come back.

She dropped off the limb and sailed quietly through the forest fetching up on limbs now and again to see if he'd kill a rabbit. The apple tree was here and she stopped to peck at some of the half frozen apples on the ground. Food, but not as good as meat. She could hear the man walking away along the path. She ate a few more apples but needed water.

Her strong legs pushed her into the air and three heavy beats of her wing gave her speed enough to glide between the tree trunks. She gained a bit of altitude and came to the large fallen tree that had the tasty rose hips. She scented man and she flared away. His horse flickered an ear as she passed over and stamped his heavy hoof. She fetched up on a branch and looked. A horse meant grain sometimes and grain was tasty.

She eyed the horse but didn't see the man. She smelled him and he smelled like meat but she couldn't see him. His scent rode the morning air but try as she might she couldn't see him. That made her uneasy. A man she couldn't see was not a good thing. She launched again and winged to the pond for water.

Tanyth woke with a start and knew where she was and why the cave looked odd. She was under the tree. She couldn't believe she was so close to the village and yet, unless they found her soon, it wouldn't matter. She could feel herself fading. Too much was broken and she was cold, even in her blanket, so cold. She wondered where Josh had gone and turned her head to find his mad eyes inches from hers.

"Are you awake now, witch? They'll never find you, you know? Oh, no." He chortled and drooled a little. He lifted his hand and she flinched but he laughed and bit into the apple he held in it.

He smiled at her and the effect should have terrified her but her fingers caressed the knife under her hand. He'd have to untie her if he planned to do much of anything besides beat her about the face. When he did, she'd be ready.

He saw the change in her face. He stared at her. "No, you're not going to die yet. No." His denial came out low and insistent. "Oh, no. Not after you ruined me. I have to ruin you before you can die. You'll be glad to die when I'm done with you, but not yet. No."

His eyes scanned her face and she smiled. She started to shiver but her muscles lacked the strength. In her mind she formed another prayer. "Guardian of the East, Breath of the Earth, loan me your quickness that I may survive until I

318

can once more breathe the gentle air of spring." The prayer gave her strength but his punch to the side of her head overwhelmed her, and she fell into unconsciousness once more.

She poked her bill into the thin ice and got her drink. She needed to help. She needed to do something. She launched. Up, up, she flew and arrowed between the trunks. There would be meat in the end and she would feast but first she needed to find the man with the hat, the man she'd seen before. She needed to find him, the man in the snow.

She broke into the village clearing and cawed her frustration. Nobody stirred. Not a man, not a child. She wheeled in the sky and looked down but nothing moved. She flew through the woods, fast between the trunks and over the brush. The horse stood there beside the tree and she smelled the meat and smoke. She smelled the man and the woman who fed her, too. She picked the faint scent out of the background smells as she skimmed along the length of the fallen tree. She smelled the people and she smelled the meat and she smelled the blood. Her call echoed through the forest and she banked sharply to fly back to the village to find the man with the hat.

The cold, hard ground beneath her battered face pulled Tanyth back to consciousness. The now sodden blankets leached more of her body heat away. "Guardian of the South, Fire of the Earth, warm me against the chill of winter. Fill my heart with fire." The prayer echoed through her brain even before she tried to open her eyes. He was still there. She could hear him, smell him.

"It's almost time, witch." He giggled. "What part do you want to lose? Eh? Shall I cut off your tits?" He spit on her. "You're too old already for men to look at you but you'll see. You'll know, won't you, witch?"

She looked at him, unable to muster enough strength to hate him, saving her energy against the cold, saving her strength. When he unwrapped her, she'd be ready.

He pulled back his fist and took aim at her bruised face and she flinched but he drove it into her gut, forcing the wind from her lungs and driving her back into unconsciousness as he laughed. "Surprised you with that one, didn't I?" She heard him even as she fell.

Her wings bit the cold air and she streaked upwards to clear the trees. She needed speed and speed meant open sky. She went up and then rolled at the treetops to drive for the buildings. As she came over the last line of trees, she saw a man walking to the big building with no walls but the wrong man. He didn't look up even as her caw split the morning sky. She flew beyond and over to the building with horses. Yes, she found grain sometimes but the man with the hat cared for the horses. Perhaps she could find him there.

Big doors blocked the way so she couldn't see in. She screamed her rage. The woman needed help. She banked hard and streaked back through the treetops to the village and saw only the man who wouldn't look up. Her lungs burned and her wings ached from the extended flight. She perched on the top of the house that sometimes had rabbits. The house had no rabbit, and the woman who fed her hid under a fallen tree and the meat hid there with her.

She cawed and cawed again. Her anger and her hunger drove her. Something else drove her, too, and she cawed some more. She paced up and down the ridge of the roof and heard a sound under her talons–sound from inside the house that sometimes had rabbits. The door opened and the man came out. The right man. The man she'd seen before in the snow. He wasn't wearing a hat but it was the man and she cawed.

He made the sound. The sound all the men made before, but he didn't shout it.

She launched for the woods, darting between the boles, heading for the tree with the rose hips. The tree where the horse stood. The tree with the meat under it. The tree where the woman who sometimes fed her lay dying.

The cold dirt against her face brought her back once more and she struggled to push herself upright. She didn't really want to sit up, but she was laying on her knife arm and she needed to free that arm before she lost feeling in it, before she lost any more strength. She lacked the strength to pull herself up without using her hand to push and so just rocked slightly.

She panted against the dirt. "Guardian of the West, Blood of the Earth, give me the strength of the river to wash over the pain."

He grabbed her shoulder and rolled her over, slamming her head against the packed earth of the floor. His dagger glittered in the faint light of morning and it flashed down at her but only cut the cords holding the blankets tight around her.

"I think it's time." He giggled and a line of spittle drooled off his lip. "Let's see what part you want to lose." He poised the tip of his dagger over her one clear eye. "Maybe I'll just take an eye to start." He grabbed her nose with his free hand and gave it a wrench, breaking the clots, and opening the passages to air again. "Maybe the nose? Eh? If I take your nose, how will you smell, old woman? Eh?" He paused, the cold steel glittering over her right nostril. "Just as bad as ever!" He chortled at his own, old, joke.

From outside the calling of a raven echoed through the wood and the man's head jerked around. He froze for a moment and the caw repeated, becoming more insistent. He cursed and released her nose. "Cursed bird!" He spat on the ground and turned back to Tanyth. "Don't go away, little mother. We've got business yet!" His boot lashed out, clipping her on the jaw and her head rang from the blow as she slipped away once more.

The man ran behind her. He wore no hat but he shouted something after her. She didn't stop but kept going. She shouted back to him her calls bouncing from the tree trunks as she flew. In moments she was back at the tree and fetched up on a limb. The meat was there. She could smell it now. She called again. The man's shouts were faint in the distance but getting louder. He made the sound again, the sound they'd all made.

She called several times and the horse rolled his eyes and swished his tail but he looked bad, too. Maybe the horse would be meat soon and she'd feast, but first the woman needed help, so she cawed.

The shouts got closer and the meat crawled out from a hole under the tree. He waved his arms at her. He made whooshing sounds at her and picked up a stick to throw at her. She dropped off the limb and dodged the stick and circled around. He picked up another stick and waved it at her. She cawed loudly and stooped. Her talons raked his face and he dropped his stick, clutching the bleeding wounds. The meat smell maddened her and his hot blood warmed her toes. She flapped around and came in again, cawing and striking with her wings, she slashed with her talons once more and his flailing arm swatted her roughly. She screamed and grabbed his face with both feet, holding on and pecking at his face, his head, his hair. His heavy hands struck at her but she bit his fingers and drew strips of flesh from his hands. His screams were as loud as hers but he pounded her and she had to let go. She released him and one last clumsy strike of his arm tossed her heavily against the bole of a tree, stunning her. She fell to the ground.

He loomed over her, moving quickly to reach for her even as she floundered in the snow to get her feet under her. If his hands found her, she'd die. Her wings flapped snow into his face as she tried to escape. She banged against the tree as he reached again and she cawed her defiance into his stinking face even as he bent to grab her.

He screamed back at her and fell heavily to his side, clutching at his leg even as a strong arm grabbed his shoulder and dragged him onto his back in the snow. The woman who fed her was there in the snow, her face a snarl. She heaved herself up from the ground with the arm that held him pinned even as she raised her knife high in the air and plunged it down into his shock filled eye, staking his head to the frozen ground with a peg of sharpened steel.

Tanyth's vision was oddly split, seeing half with her eyes and half with the eyes of the raven across from her. She panted and fell heavily across the stinking body but watched as the raven found her feet and launched herself up, over the fallen tree and flared her wings to take refuge in a small spruce. Their hearts pounded in their chests. Their bodies still rang from the blows.

She had some feathers that were damaged and she did what she could to preen them into shape. The meat-man's blood was in her talons and a strip of his flesh. She ate it, cleaning her talons of the gore, but wondered if there would be a rabbit later.

They watched Frank come thrashing through the trees and take in the scene with wild eyes and a shocked expression.

Tanyth looked up at him with her one good eye, her head turned at an awkward angle. "In the name of the All-Mother and the All-Father, would you please get me off this stinking corpse?" Her strength failed her one last time. She never felt the ground slap her in the face.

CHAPTER 39
RAVEN DREAMS

In her dream she woke. She knew it was a dream this time. Her fingers were feathers and her arms were wings. Her nose was long and she had to turn her head from left to right to see with one eye and then the other. It was an odd feeling but she laughed and it bubbled up out of her like a raven's croon. In her dream she sailed the blue, blue sky and saw the earth below, spooling out like a river flowing beneath her strong black wings. She called but her voice was silent. It didn't ring in the morning air. Just a dream, she knew, but still it was her dream and her voice should sound. She opened her mouth to call again.

"Hey!" Her voice woke her. It didn't ring out, but it was her voice. Faint and breathy, but her own and she opened her eyes and looked up at the rafters. "The house with rabbits."

Amber's face moved into her line of sight. "There, mum. You're safe now." The words echoed oddly but she was able to understand. She didn't feel safe.

"The house with rabbits." She looked at Amber's face. She looked terrible. Her eyes were puffy and her nose was red.

"Rabbits, mum?" Amber frowned curiously.

The darkness called Tanyth back and pain pulled her but she smiled and tried to speak clearly through the swollen lips. "The house with rabbits. Rabbits."

She saw Amber's expression change from curiosity to alarm. "The house with rabbits?" She bit her lower lip. "There are no rabbits here, mum."

Tanyth sighed and fought the darkness once more. "Get

some. Tell Thomas." She couldn't fight it any more and let the darkness call her back.

In her dream she stood in the bow of a ship and it was like flying. The wind blew through her hair and she had to leave her hat and staff below. The morning sun warmed the right side of her body even as the icy wind stuck daggers of cold through her clothing but she threw back her head and laughed. Above her the taut triangles of sail gleamed whitely against the deep azure sky of spring. She looked ahead once more–north–and saw the smudge of land on the horizon.

A voice behind her said, "Mum? You shouldn't be on deck in this cold, mum. Mum?"

She turned to face the sailor but opened her eyes to Sadie's concerned gaze. "Mum? You need some willow bark tea, mum." She held a mug up into view. "Do you think you can drink?"

Tanyth felt the knives of fever and rejoiced. "Yes."

With the help of Sadie's strong arms, she lifted enough to sip at the cup that Sadie held to her lips. It tasted awful. The bitterness puckered her tongue but it felt like the swelling in her mouth was going down. She drank as much as she could and then pulled her head back to breathe. "Tell Thomas. The house with rabbits." She leaned back into the mug and finished the bitter draught before Sadie laid her back down, pulling the warm covers up to her chin even as the fever's trembling started pulling her strength. She closed her eyes, and started the slow slide down.

Amber's voice came from the hearth. "Is she still talking about rabbits?"

Sadie's voice answered with a sigh. "Yes. Something about the house with rabbits and tell Thomas."

Tanyth heard Amber sigh before the darkness pulled her down once more and for once, her sleep was dreamless.

The smell of rabbit stew woke her. She blinked her eyes open to see late afternoon light. "Thank you, Mother." It was less prayer than a whisper but it got an instant response.

"She's awake again." It was Sadie's voice.

Tanyth turned to see Sadie rising from the table even as Megan poured hot water into the teapot.

"How are you doing, mum?" Sadie frowned in concern.

Tanyth smiled tentatively. "I seem to be alive. I'm counting that on the plus side."

She saw Sadie's face relax. "Oh, mum. Welcome back." Her voice was filled with relief and she beamed a smile at Megan. She picked up a mug and crossed to the cot. "Here's some water, mum. You must be thirsty."

She nodded gratefully and was even well enough to sit up mostly on her own. Sadie held the mug for her and she sipped at it, moistening lips and tongue, resting, then doing it again. At the touch of water her body almost betrayed her and tried to gulp it down, but she resisted and sipped. There'd be more.

"Thank you, Sadie." She smiled up at her. "Is that rabbit stew I smell?"

A worried frown creased Sadie's face. "Yes, mum. Rabbit."

"Good. Did you feed some to the raven?"

"The raven, mum?"

"The raven. She likes rabbits to eat. Dead ones, of course."

Sadie's face turned from concern to alarm and she looked to Megan who rushed over to the cot.

"You mustn't concern yourself with that, mum." Megan's voice was soft and soothing and her hands fluttered helplessly at the top of the blankets, pulling them up, tucking them in, patting them down. "You need to get well."

Tanyth looked from one concerned face to the other and frowned in concentration. "Listen to me, ladies. This is important. I am not mad–at least, I don't think so–and I am not ravin'." She took a breath to see them look at her with matching startled impressions. "Well, perhaps a bit." She paused to smile at them. "There is a raven that lives in the big spruce tree west of the village. That raven saved my life. She likes to eat rabbits. I owe her a few. If you would ask Thomas to take a winter hare and leave the carcass in the grass behind my house? Don't dress it. Just the dead rabbit?" She looked from one face to another. "Think of it as an offering to the All-Mother if that helps."

They shared a quick glance before Sadie turned back to her. "In the snow, mum?"

"Snow?"

"Leave it in the snow?"

"Is there snow? When did it snow?" Tanyth asked.

"Two days ago, mum. The day after the Solstice, the afternoon of the day we found you."

Tanyth grunted in surprise. "I thought you just found me this morning!"

The two younger women shook their heads. "No, mum, you've been layin' there sleepin' off and on for a couple days now." She paused uncertainly. "Every once in a while you'd wake up, tell us about rabbits, and then go back to sleep."

Tanyth barked a laugh but pain chopped it off. There was still too much left to heal to be laughing loudly. "And you thought I'd gone mad?"

The look they shared was painted with guilt and she laughed again, if more gently.

"I'm fine, my dears." She paused. "At least I think so." She looked back and forth between them. "Yes, on the snow is fine and only one rabbit for now. Think of it as an offering to the All-Mother. Just tell Thomas."

They shared a dubious glance but nodded to her.

"Where's Frank?"

Sadie cocked her head at Tanyth. "Frank's probably working on the Inn. He's stopped by every day to find out how you're doing but we don't let him in."

She frowned. "Why not?"

Sadie covered her mouth with both hands to stifle a laugh and Megan looked horrified. "Oh, gods, mum! That wouldn't be quite proper now would it? Man like that visiting a woman while she's bed-ridden?"

Sadie was shaking with suppressed laughter. She got it under control at Megan's sharp look. "Besides, mum. You'll wanna get cleaned up a bit before he comes to call. Brush your hair, wash your face." She grinned slyly. "You'll not want him to see you like that."

Tanyth snickered. "I don't think the condition of my hair will be anywhere near as shockin' as the bruises on my face, do you?"

Sadie gave a little shrug but nodded in acknowledgement.

"Probably true, mum. You do look a little worse for wear."

Tanyth smiled and gave a small nod of acknowledgement of her own. "I'm sure, but I'd like to thank him for dragging me out of that hole." She looked back and forth between them. "Next time he comes, please let him in?"

They both nodded, Megan somewhat reluctantly. "Well at least let us clean you up a bit, mum?"

"Oh, yes, that would be lovely! Please?"

For half an hour they fussed over her, washing her face and hands with hot water, lavender soap, and a soft cloth. They even took a brush to her hair. All the activity reminded Tanyth of the small tins on the mantle board and she had Sadie and Megan each take one.

"I'm a little late, but Happy Solstice and may the new year bring your hearts' desire."

They smiled and accepted the small gifts. "Happy new year, mum, and thank you."

All the activity caught up with her then. She closed her eyes for just a moment but inadvertently dropped off to sleep.

At the top of the tree, she basked in the final rays of winter sunshine. The golden sun warmed her feathers, even as the village below sank into the spreading shadows of the tree line. She'd need food soon and regretted not feeding on the meat before the men had dragged it off and buried it. She cawed in frustration. It didn't do any good for her hunger, but she let the others know she was still there. It was still her territory. The pair to the south answered her but it was more acknowledgement than challenge. With the snowy season just starting, they'd all need to conserve energy against the cold and the dark.

The man with the bow came out of the woods across the wide path and trudged up the snowy track toward the village. She leaned forward with interest. The day was drawing to a close but sometimes he left rabbits. Maybe he'd leave another. The door to the house with rabbits opened and she became more excited, but it wasn't the woman who fed her who came out. It was the woman who chased her from the corn. She sulked back onto the branch and crooned. She was hungry and would have to go find some rose hips or dig for the apples under the snow.

She watched as the woman and man talked. They looked up at her tree, which startled her and she froze in place. It wasn't good to be looked at, still it made her curious and she tilted her head left and right as the man reached into his bag and pulled out a rabbit. He handed the rabbit to the woman before continuing up the path, glancing up at the tree as he walked. The woman took the rabbit inside and she cawed her frustration.

No rabbit.

She launched from the tree and swooped down into the shadows of the village, heading for the bush with rose hips. They weren't rabbit, but they filled her. Movement at the back door of the house with rabbits caught her attention and the reddish light shined out onto the snow for a moment. It was long enough for her to see the woman step out and lay the rabbit on the snow before quickly stepping back inside and closing the door.

She flared upwards in a banking turn to grab a limb and look back. Nobody stirred. The shadows of evening crept across the wide path and into the trees on the other side. She cawed and stooped. The flesh warmed her as she feasted there in the snow.

Tanyth's strength returned quickly once she was warmed and fed. Within a few days she banished her nurses back to their own homes. Sadie left with a knowing smile and a cheeky wink. "Woodbox needs tendin', eh, mum?"

Tanyth gave her a shrug, a hug, and a sly grin of her own. "Takes a lot of wood to keep old bones warm in the winter, my dear."

Sadie giggled. "You be careful of splinters!"

Tanyth blushed a little but shoo'ed her out.

Around sunset, Frank showed up at her door with an armload of firewood, some venison chops and a jug of sweet cider. "Thought you might like somethin' other than rabbit for dinner."

"Don't stand on ceremony, man! Get in here." She smiled at him.

He dropped the firewood in the box and turned to her.

They stood for a few moments and she saw his eyes tracing the bruises. She knew several shockingly purple splotches still marked her face, but at least the swelling had subsided and she could see out of both eyes again, even if one had a pretty serious shiner.

Still, his examination made her self-conscious. "Mother, I must be a sight."

His eyes stopped their tracing and centered on her face. "You certainly are. One I'm glad to see."

She went to him and took the cider and meat from his hands, placing them on the table. "Then give me a hug. Gently." She nuzzled up to his chest and put her arms around him. "I'm still a little sore."

He did and they stood there for a time. Finally he spoke. "I was so scared. We had no idea where you'd gone, but..." He paused. "You know, if you wanted to skip the Solstice prayer you could have just said so."

She pulled back and looked up at him confused.

"You didn't have to go running off to the woods with another man." His eyes twinkled and his lips twitched with a barely controlled grin.

It caught her by such surprise that she barked laughter into his chest and smacked him playfully on the shoulder. "You beast."

He hugged her gently once more, and she snuggled into him, smelling him and savoring his warmth for a few moments before pushing him away. "Enough of that. I'm hungry."

She turned to the food. As the venison cooked, they pulled up their chairs side by side on the hearthstone and let the wind blow through the eaves while they were snug, warm, and together inside.

CHAPTER 40
NEW BEGINNINGS

By the new moon, they'd closed in the walls and with the extra shelter that afforded, they started keeping a fire burning in the hearth all the time to keep the chimney warmed. The extra heat permitted them to begin laying the firebrick for a real oven and by the end of the month of the Ice Moon, Sadie and Amber did much of their cooking at the inn.

Tanyth watched it all with a certain fascination, but her time was taken up with tasks of her own and the days took on an easy pattern. She started the morning with break-fast—occasionally shared with Frank, much to the amusement of Sadie and Amber who seemed inordinately pleased with themselves on the issue. After breakfast, she helped Sadie and Amber with the daily bread making. She was an expert at flat, unleavened breads—camp bread that could be mixed and cooked over a campfire, but Sadie and Amber were tal-ented bread makers and Tanyth admired their skill with flour and water, salt and yeast. They frequently worked together to set the dough for as many as a dozen loaves a day. The amount of flour they used was shocking to Tanyth when she first saw them working, but she soon realized that the two women provided much of the bread for the village. Watching Sadie and Amber wrestle with the dough made Tanyth realize why Sadie's lifting of her cot seemed so easy for her. Both of them had developed tight bands of muscle from years of mixing and kneading the bread.

At midmorning, while the bread rested in its first proof, they'd adjourn to Tanyth's hut to work on herbs. In spite of the difficulties in the fall, Tanyth had harvested considerable amounts of bark, leaf, plant, root, and berry. Over the course of winter's coldest weeks, she taught them how to make tinctures, teas, and tisanes to preserve and extract the various medicinal components. In the week leading up to the Cradle Moon, she taught them how to make balms and ointments, letting them practice with beeswax and oil to find the consistency they needed and showed them how to make the little tins of balm that she'd given for Solstice gifts.

In the afternoons, after feeding everyone, they'd return to bread making, setting a second proof of individual loaves while they tended to sewing, knitting, or mending. Children didn't stop growing in winter so there was always somebody who needed something and often Charlotte and Bethany would join them to ply needle and thread, hook and yarn, while the bread rose and baked.

Evenings gave more variety. Some nights Tanyth spent with Amber or Sadie, often both families at once. She even guested with Charlotte and Jakey a few times. The bluff and often blustery quarryman turned out to have wicked, dry wit when away from his crew and closeted in the privacy of his own hearth. Through it all, Frank stood by her, lending his gentle humor and strong arm when she needed it. Holding her quietly in the night when the nightmares came.

The cycle of the year ratcheted onward, and work on the inn progressed under the raven's golden eye. Two or three times a week, Thomas took an extra hare and dropped it at the foot of her tree behind the village. As the weather turned warmer and the trees began to quicken, the raven took to walking along the inn's roof and seeming to comment–sometimes loudly–on the progress of the work.

By Cradle Moon, the inn was done except for a sign to hang in front. New grasses pressed up through browned mats of old growth and snow remained only in the deepest shadows of the forest. On the night of the full moon, the village decided to throw a party. It was too early for a real equinox celebration but with the completion of major construction, and the re-opening of the quarry at hand, a party was inevitable.

As the afternoon's labor wore down, they congregated

around the fireplace in the common room at the inn and, for the first time, Tanyth entered through the main door. Squared off logs formed steps at the front of the building and a pair of barn-hinged doors hung in the extra wide opening at the front.

Jakey and Ethan had installed a spit in the main hearth in the common room and a trio of winter turkeys turned slowly over the coals by the time Tanyth arrived. William and Thomas tended the spit and she could hear Sadie, Amber, and Charlotte in the kitchen. The place smelled divine with the scents of roasting fowl and baking bread melding with woodsmoke and fresh cut wood.

"Mother Fairport! Come sit by the fire!" William patted the seat on one of the new chairs.

She nodded her thanks and joined the two men in front of the hearth. She felt like she'd no sooner gotten seated when her friends and neighbors started filling the room. Frank came out of the kitchen with a cross-legged contraption and set it next to the fire. Thomas's eyes lit up at the sight as Frank disappeared back into the kitchen. He soon returned with a heavy cask, a spigot already set in the head. He placed it gently on the cradle and proceeded to fill and distribute mugs of a sweet, honey mead–drawing each one carefully and handing them around the room to the adults. Thomas added some mead to the sauce he was brushing onto the turkeys and the drippings flaring in the fire took on a new and delicious aroma.

As the sun finally set and the moon rose over the trees, they opened the doors to toast the moon and the gleaming light seemed to shine straight in, adding a strand of silver to the gold of the hearth. Within an hour, they'd set the table and food started coming out of the kitchen. Amber, Sadie, Megan, and Bethany all brought out baskets of bread, huge bowls of baked beans, and even a large bowl of roasted groundnuts. There were smaller bowls of pickles and even several pots of apple sauce flavored with mint.

William and Jakey put on padded gloves, lifted the heavy spit off the brackets in the fireplace, and slid the three large birds onto separate platters on the table. With that, the feast stood ready and they all gathered round the table to revel in the food, the company, and the knowledge that the back of winter was broken. Tanyth sat apart a bit from the celebrations, although she certainly ate heartily.

Frank noticed and leaned in so he could speak to her softly. "Are you all right?"

She looked over at the concern in his face and patted his arm. "Yes, dear man. I'm fine. This is a marvelous accomplishment. I'm just feeling a bit tired." She smiled at him.

He frowned at her under lowered brows. "You're sure?"

She paused and looked at the faces around the table. "Yes. I'm sure. It's just..." She paused and turned back to look him in the eye. "It's just that my time here is coming to an end, I think."

She could see the cloud descend across his face and he sighed. "I wondered." He looked at where her hand rested on his forearm and he reached with his free hand to pat it. He looked back at her. "Can I get you anything? Cup of tea? More mead?"

She nodded. "Thank you. A cup of tea would be lovely."

He returned shortly with mugs and a teapot and the two of them sat together and enjoyed their own company while the party roared on around them.

Two hours into the feast, Jakey rose and rapped the table with the pommel of his knife. When everybody calmed down he picked up his mug and turned to the crowd.

"I got some things to say." He grinned at the returning catcalls and waited for them to die down. "First..." he turned to Tanyth at the end of the table. "Thank you, Mother Fairport, for a great idea. I think this will make a big difference." He waved his hand to indicate the building. The assembled company cheered and clapped and pounded the table. "Second. . . " He paused and looked around at the quarrymen. "You lot have work in the morning. We'll be openin' up the quarry again to get our first shipment of the season out. So, don't drink too much tonight and I'll see your worthless carcasses on the trail at sun-up." They all laughed. When they stopped laughing, he held his mug up in an honest toast. "Third, to Kurt. He was a good man. We'll miss him."

They all stood and raised whatever mug or cup they had. "To Kurt." They drank deeply and somberly regained their seats.

Charlotte turned to her husband and with a bit of a slur whispered loudly. "You sure know how to end a party, honey."

The assembly burst into laughter once more but in the space of half an hour, they'd cleared the tables and ferried the dishes to the sink in the kitchen for clean-up. In a half hour more, many hands had helped to clean, dry, and stack them in the kitchen, ready for the morning.

With the clean-up done, Tanyth tightened her wrap about her and warmed herself once more in front of the fire in the great room. William stood there, banking the hot coals and adding a few odd knots to the pile to keep the fire warm. He smiled at her as she came out of the kitchen and crossed to the fireplace. "Thank you, mum."

"For what, William?"

He smiled down at her. "For believing in us." He cast his eyes around the room. "We'd have been trying to make a kiln or some such if not for this." He took a deep breath of the wood-scented air and smiled at her once more. "This is a better choice."

She smiled and patted him on the arm. "You would have made it without me, I'm sure."

William shook his head. "I don't know, mum. Maybe we would and maybe we wouldn't, but the point is you made this happen as much as any of us."

She gave a small, embarrassed shrug and cast her eyes down. She saw the coloration then, for the first time. The hearthstone was a different color from the rest of the fireplace. She stared at it as her mind worked to make sense of what she was seeing. She cast her eyes back and forth across the stone and spotted a small, perfectly shaped star on the stone. "This is–" She couldn't finish.

William's eyes gleamed in the faint light from the coals. "Yes, mum. This is the hearthstone from the workroom. We all thought it deserved to be here."

"But it's stained." She knew it sounded inane, but couldn't stop herself.

"No, mum." William smiled back at her. "It's been blessed."

Tanyth stood in mute shock until Frank came out of the kitchen and offered his arm to her. "Shall we go?"

With one last wondering look at William and a glance at the small black stain on the stone, she nodded and looked up a Frank, taking his arm. "Yes, please."

The rest of the villagers went their separate ways while Frank walked Tanyth home by the light of the moon. The air was far from warm, but the smell of spring was on the breeze. The quickening life fairly thrummed the night air.

Frank glanced down at her. "Looks like the inn is a big success."

"Looks like. We'll see if people start staying here. It's a little early to say, but it certainly came out nice."

He looked away from her, ostensibly at their path. "So, you're planning on going north?"

"Yes. I need to find out about the raven visions, if I can. Right now Mother Pinecrest is the only clue I have." She rested her head on his shoulder as they walked.

"You're welcome to stay here, you know." He swallowed. "The village would welcome having you stay."

She looked up at him.

He looked back at her. "I'd like it if you stayed."

She sighed and looked down. "I can't stay, Frank. I need to find out what's happening to me."

He echoed her sigh. "Yeah. I figgered." They walked the last few feet in silence. He held the door open for her and handed her over the threshold.

She stopped at the foot of the stairs and turned back to him in surprise. "You're not staying?"

He leaned over and looked in. "Are you sure you want me to?"

She saw the hurt in his eyes, even as she read the understanding behind it. "Why wouldn't I?"

He looked down at the ground and shrugged. "Well, you'll be leavin' soon..." He cleared his throat. "I just thought maybe you'd wanna..." He paused and looked up at her. "Stop."

She reached up her hand for his and smiled gently. "We have some time left, Frank. We don't really ever know how much, do we?" She grinned mischievously. "'Cept folks our age don't have a lot of it to squander by letting it slip by unmarked."

He smiled, took her hand, and let her draw him into the house.

The Golden Age of the Solar Clipper

Quarter Share

Half Share

Full Share

Double Share

Captain's Share

Owner's Share

South Coast

Tanyth Fairport Adventures

Ravenwood

Zypherias Call

The Hermit Of Lammas Wood

Nathan Lowell

Awards

2011 Parsec Award Winner for Best Speculative Fiction
(Long Form) for *Owners Share*

2010 Parsec Award Winner for Best Speculative Fiction
(Long Form) for *Captains Share*

2009 Podiobooks Founders Choice Award for Captains Share

2009 Parsec Award Finalist for Best Speculative Fiction
(Long Form) for *Double Share*

2008 Podiobooks Founders Choice Award for *Double Share*

2008 Parsec Award Finalist for Best Speculative Fiction
(Long Form) for *Full Share*

2008 Parsec Award Finalist for Best Speculative Fiction
(Long Form) for *South Coast*

341

Contact

Website: nathanlowell.com
Twitter: twitter.com/nlowell
Email: nathan.lowell@gmail.com

About The Author

Nathan Lowell first entered the literary world by podcasting his novels. The Golden Age of the Solar Clipper grew from his life-long fascination with space opera and his own experiences shipboard in the United States Coast Guard. Unlike most works which focus on a larger-than-life hero, Nathan centers on the people behind the scenes—ordinary men and women trying to make a living in the depths of interstellar space. In his novels, there are no bug-eyed monsters, or galactic space battles, instead he paints a richly vivid and realistic world where the hero uses hard work and his own innate talents to improve his station and the lives of those of his community.

Dr. Nathan Lowell holds a Ph.D. in Educational Technology with specializations in Distance Education and Instructional Design. He also holds an M.A. in Educational Technology and a BS in Business Administration. He grew up on the south coast of Maine and is strongly rooted in the maritime heritage of the sea-farer. He served in the USCG from 1970 to 1975, seeing duty aboard a cutter on hurricane patrol in the North Atlantic and at a communications station in Kodiak, Alaska. He currently lives on the plains east of the Rocky Mountains with his wife and two daughters.